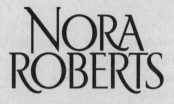

Dear Reader,

Sometimes you have to trust your instincts and let your heart run wild. In these classic romances from bestselling author Nora Roberts, we see the wonderful things that can happen when you open your heart to the right person—even if at first glance he seems like the wrong one.

In *Risky Business,* Liz Palmer likes the safe little world she's created for herself and isn't sure what to make of Jonas Sharpe, the handsome stranger who's barged into her life demanding answers. Cynical Jonas has come to Cozumel in search of his brother's killer, but things get complicated when the sizzling attraction between him and Liz heats up, especially since the beguiling beauty is turning out to be his strongest suspect.

In *Boundary Lines,* Jillian Baron returns home to the ranch after her grandfather falls ill. She's determined to make Utopia the best spread in Montana! But a long-standing family feud soon threatens to reignite when Jillian finds herself falling for the enemy, Aaron Murdock. She's confident she would never let her heart rule her head—would she?

We hope you enjoy these exhilarating tales of untamed hearts and undeniable romance!

The Editors
Silhouette Books

NORA ROBERTS

Hearts Untamed

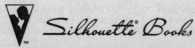

Published by Silhouette Books
America's Publisher of Contemporary Romance

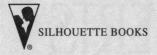

SILHOUETTE BOOKS

Hearts Untamed

ISBN-13: 978-0-373-28184-8

Recycling programs
for this product may
not exist in your area.

Copyright © 2014 by Harlequin Books S.A.

The publisher acknowledges the copyright holder
of the individual works as follows:

Risky Business
Copyright © 1986 by Nora Roberts

Boundary Lines
Copyright © 1985 by Nora Roberts

Visit Silhouette Books at www.Harlequin.com

Printed in U.S.A.

CONTENTS

RISKY BUSINESS

For Michael and Darlene,
good friends.

Chapter One

"Watch your step, please. Please, watch your step. Thank you." Liz took a ticket from a sunburned man with palm trees on his shirt, then waited patiently for a woman with two bulging straw baskets to dig out another one.

"I hope you haven't lost it, Mabel. I told you to let me hold it."

"I haven't lost it," the woman said testily before she pulled out the little piece of blue cardboard.

"Thank you. Please take your seats." It was several more minutes before everyone was settled and she could take her own. "Welcome aboard the *Fantasy*, ladies and gentlemen."

With her mind on a half dozen other things, Liz began her opening monologue. She gave an absentminded nod to the man on the dock who cast off the ropes before she started the engine. Her voice was pleasant and easy as she took another look at her watch. They were already fifteen minutes behind schedule. She gave one last scan of the beach, skimming by lounge chairs, over bodies already stretched and oiled slick, like offerings to the sun. She couldn't hold the tour any longer.

The boat swayed a bit as she backed it from the dock and took an eastern course. Though her thoughts were scattered, she made the turn from the coast expertly. She could have navigated the boat with her eyes closed. The air that ruffled around her face was soft and already warming, though the hour was early. Harmless and powder-puff white, clouds dotted the horizon. The water, churned by the engine, was as blue as the guidebooks promised. Even after ten years, Liz took none of it for granted—especially her livelihood. Part of that depended on an atmosphere that made muscles relax and problems disappear.

Behind her in the long, bullet-shaped craft were eighteen people seated on padded benches. They were already murmuring about the fish and formations they saw through the glass bottom. She doubted if any of them thought of the worries they'd left behind at home.

"We'll be passing Paraiso Reef North," Liz began in a low, flowing voice. "Diving depths range from thirty to fifty feet. Visibility is excellent, so you'll be able to see star and brain corals, sea fans and sponges, as well as schools of sergeant majors, groupers and parrot fish. The grouper isn't one of your prettier fish, but it's versatile. They're all born female and produce eggs before they change sex and become functioning males."

Liz set her course and kept the speed steady. She went on to describe the elegantly colored angelfish, the shy, silvery smallmouth grunts, and the intriguing and dangerous sea urchin. Her clients would find the information useful when she stopped for two hours of snorkeling at Palancar Reef.

She'd made the run before, too many times to count. It might have become routine, but it was never monotonous. She felt now, as she always did, the freedom of open water, blue sky and the hum of engine with her at the controls. The boat was hers, as were three others, and the little concrete block dive shop close to shore. She'd worked for all of it, sweating through months when the bills were steep and the cash flow slight. She'd made it. Ten years of struggle had been a small price to pay for having something of her own. Turning her back on her country, leaving behind the familiar, had been a small price to pay for peace of mind.

The tiny, rustic island of Cozumel in the Mexican Caribbean promoted peace of mind. It was her home now, the only one that mattered. She was accepted there, respected. No one on the island knew of the humiliation and pain she'd gone through before she'd fled to Mexico. Liz rarely thought of it, though she had a vivid reminder.

Faith. Just the thought of her daughter made her smile. Faith was small and bright and precious, and so far away. Just six weeks, Liz thought, and she'd be home from school for the summer.

Sending her to Houston to her grandparents had been for the best, Liz reminded herself whenever the ache of loneliness became acute. Faith's education was more important than a mother's needs. Liz had worked, gambled, struggled so that Faith could have everything she was entitled to, everything she would have had if her father...

Determined, Liz set her mind on other things. She'd promised herself a decade before that she would cut

Faith's father from her mind, just as he had cut her from his life. It had been a mistake, one made in naïveté and passion, one that had changed the course of her life forever. But she'd won something precious from it: Faith.

"Below, you see the wreck of a forty-passenger Convair airliner lying upside down." She slowed the boat so that her passengers could examine the wreck and the divers out for early explorations. Bubbles rose from air tanks like small silver disks. "The wreck's no tragedy," she continued. "It was sunk for a scene in a movie and provides divers with easy entertainment."

Her job was to do the same for her passengers, she reminded herself. It was simple enough when she had a mate on board. Alone, she had to captain the boat, keep up the light, informative banter, deal with snorkel equipment, serve lunch and count heads. It just hadn't been possible to wait any longer for Jerry.

She muttered to herself a bit as she increased speed. It wasn't so much that she minded the extra work, but she felt her paying customers were entitled to the best she could offer. She should have known better than to depend on him. She could have easily arranged for someone else to come along. As it was, she had two men on the dive boat and two more in the shop. Because her second dive boat was due to launch at noon, no one could be spared to mate the glass bottom on a day trip. And Jerry had come through before, she reminded herself. With him on board, the women passengers were so charmed that Liz didn't think they even noticed the watery world the boat passed over.

Who could blame them? she thought with a half smile. If she hadn't been immune to men in general, Jerry might have had her falling over her own feet. Most women had a difficult time resisting dark, cocky looks, a cleft chin and smoky gray eyes. Add to that a lean, muscular build and a glib tongue, and no female was safe.

But that hadn't been why Liz had agreed to rent him a room, or give him a part-time job. She'd needed the extra income, as well as the extra help, and she was shrewd enough to recognize an operator when she saw one. Previous experience had taught her that it made good business sense to have an operator on your side. She told herself he'd better have a good excuse for leaving her without a crew, then forgot him.

The ride, the sun, the breeze relaxed her. Liz continued to speak of the sea life below, twining facts she'd learned while studying marine biology in college with facts she'd learned firsthand in the waters of the Mexican Caribbean. Occasionally one of her passengers would ask a question or call out in excitement over something that skimmed beneath them. She answered, commented and instructed while keeping the flow light. Because three of her passengers were Mexican, she repeated all her information in Spanish. Because there were several children on board, she made certain the facts were fun.

If things had been different, she would have been a teacher. Liz had long since pushed that early dream from her mind, telling herself she was more suited to the business world. Her business world. She glanced over where the clouds floated lazily over the horizon. The sun danced white and sharp on the surface of blue water. Below, coral rose like castles or waved like fans. Yes, she'd chosen her world and had no regrets.

When a woman screamed behind her, Liz let off the throttle. Before she could turn, the scream was joined by another. Her first thought was that perhaps they'd seen

one of the sharks that occasionally visited the reefs. Set
to calm and soothe, Liz let the boat drift in the current.
A woman was weeping in her husband's arms, another
held her child's face protectively against her shoulder.
The rest were staring down through the clear glass. Liz
took off her sunglasses as she walked down the two steps
into the cabin.

"Please try to stay calm. I promise you, there's nothing down there that can hurt you in here."

A man with a Nikon around his neck and an orange
sun visor over a balding dome gave her a steady look.

"Miss, you'd better radio the police."

Liz looked down through the clear glass, through
the crystal blue water. Her heart rose to her throat. She
saw now why Jerry had stood her up. He was lying on
the white sandy bottom with an anchor chain wrapped
around his chest.

The moment the plane finished its taxi, Jonas gathered
his garment bag and waited impatiently for the door to be
opened. When it did, there was a whoosh of hot air and
the drone of engines. With a quick nod to the flight attendant he strode down the steep metal stairs. He didn't have
the time or the inclination to appreciate the palm trees,
the bursts of flowers or the dreamy blue sky. He walked
purposefully, eyes straight ahead and narrowed against
the sun. In his dark suit and trim tie he could have been
a businessman, one who'd come to Cozumel to work,
not to play. Whatever grief, whatever anger he felt were
carefully masked by a calm, unapproachable expression.

The terminal was small and noisy. Americans on vacation stood in groups laughing or wandered in confusion. Though he knew no Spanish, Jonas passed quickly

through customs then into a small, hot alcove where men waited at podiums to rent cars and Jeeps. Fifteen minutes after landing, Jonas was backing a compact out of a parking space and heading toward town with a map stuck in the sun visor. The heat baked right through the windshield.

Twenty-four hours before, Jonas had been sitting in his large, elegantly furnished, air-conditioned office. He'd just won a long, tough case that had taken all his skill and mountains of research. His client was a free man, acquitted of a felony charge that carried a minimum sentence of ten years. He'd accepted his fee, accepted the gratitude and avoided as much publicity as possible.

Jonas had been preparing to take his first vacation in eighteen months. He'd felt satisfied, vaguely tired and optimistic. Two weeks in Paris seemed like the perfect reward for so many months of ten-hour days. Paris, with its ageless sophistication and cool parks, its stunning museums and incomparable food was precisely what suited Jonas Sharpe.

When the call had come through from Mexico, it had taken him several moments to understand. When he'd answered that he did indeed have a brother Jeremiah, Jonas's predominant thought had been that Jerry had gotten himself into trouble again, and he was going to have to bail him out.

By the time he'd hung up the phone, Jonas couldn't think at all. Numb, he'd given his secretary instructions to cancel his Paris arrangements and to make new ones for a flight to Cozumel the next day. Then Jonas had picked up the phone to call his parents and tell them their son was dead.

He'd come to Mexico to identify the body and take his

brother home to bury. With a fresh wave of grief, Jonas experienced a sense of inevitability. Jerry had always lived on the edge of disaster. This time he'd stepped over. Since childhood Jerry had courted trouble—charmingly. He'd once joked that Jonas had taken to law so he could find the most efficient way to get his brother out of jams. Perhaps in a sense it had been true.

Jerry had been a dreamer. Jonas was a realist. Jerry had been unapologetically lazy, Jonas a workaholic. They were—had been—two sides of a coin. As Jonas drew up to the police station in San Miguel it was with the knowledge that part of himself had been erased.

The scene at port should have been painted. There were small fishing boats pulled up on the grass. Huge gray ships sat complacently at dock while tourists in flowered shirts or skimpy shorts strolled along the sea wall. Water lapped and scented the air.

Jonas got out of the car and walked to the police station to begin to wade through the morass of paperwork that accompanied a violent death.

Captain Moralas was a brisk, no-nonsense man who had been born on the island and was passionately dedicated to protecting it. He was approaching forty and awaiting the birth of his fifth child. He was proud of his position, his education and his family, though the order often varied. Basically, he was a quiet man who enjoyed classical music and a movie on Saturday nights.

Because San Miguel was a port, and ships brought sailors on leave, tourists on holiday, Moralas was no stranger to trouble or the darker side of human nature. He did, however, pride himself on the low percentage of violent crime on his island. The murder of the American bothered him in the way a pesky fly bothered a man sitting contentedly on his porch swing. A cop didn't have to work in a big city to recognize a professional hit. There was no room for organized crime on Cozumel.

But he was also a family man. He understood love, and he understood grief, just as he understood certain men were compelled to conceal both. In the cool, flat air of the morgue, he waited beside Jonas. The American stood a head taller, rigid and pale.

"This is your brother, Mr. Sharpe?" Though he didn't have to ask.

Jonas looked down at the other side of the coin. "Yes."

In silence, he backed away to give Jonas the time he needed.

It didn't seem possible. Jonas knew he could have stood for hours staring down at his brother's face and it would never seem possible. Jerry had always looked for the easy way, the biggest deal, and he hadn't always been an admirable man. But he'd always been so full of life. Slowly, Jonas laid his hand on his brother's. There was no life there now, and nothing he could do; no amount of maneuvering or pulling of strings would bring it back. Just as slowly he removed his hand. It didn't seem possible, but it was.

Moralas nodded to the attendant. "I'm sorry."

Jonas shook his head. Pain was like a dull-edged knife through the base of his skull. He coated it with ice. "Who killed my brother, Captain?"

"I don't know. We're investigating."

"You have leads?"

Moralas gestured and started down the corridor. "Your brother had been in Cozumel only three weeks, Mr. Sharpe. At the moment, we are interviewing everyone who had contact with him during that time." He opened

a door and stepped out into the air, breathing deeply of
the fresh air and the flowers. The man beside him didn't
seem to notice the change. "I promise you, we will do
everything possible to find your brother's killer."

The rage Jonas had controlled for so many hours
bubbled toward the surface. "I don't know you." With a
steady hand he drew out a cigarette, watching the captain
with narrowed eyes as he lit it. "You didn't know Jerry."

"This is my island." Moralas's gaze remained locked
with Jonas's. "If there's a murderer on it, I'll find him."

"A professional." Jonas blew out smoke that hung in
the air with no breeze to brush it away. "We both know
that, don't we?"

Moralas said nothing for a moment. He was still waiting to receive information on Jeremiah Sharpe. "Your
brother was shot, Mr. Sharpe, so we're investigating to
find out why, how and who. You could help me by giving me some information."

Jonas stared at the door a moment—the door that led
down the stairs, down the corridor and to his brother's
body. "I've got to walk," he murmured.

Moralas waited until they'd crossed the grass, then
the road. For a moment, they walked near the sea wall
in silence. "Why did your brother come to Cozumel?"

"I don't know." Jonas drew deeply on the cigarette
until it burned into the filter. "Jerry liked palm trees."

"His business? His work?"

With a half laugh Jonas ground the smoldering filter
underfoot. Sunlight danced in diamonds on the water.
"Jerry liked to call himself a freelancer. He was a drifter."
And he'd brought complications to Jonas's life as often
as he'd brought pleasure. Jonas stared hard at the water,
remembering shared lives, diverse opinions. "For Jerry,

it was always the next town and the next deal. The last I heard—two weeks ago—he was giving diving lessons to tourists."

"The Black Coral Dive Shop," Moralas confirmed. "Elizabeth Palmer hired him on a part-time basis."

"Palmer." Jonas's attention shifted away from the water. "That's the woman he was living with."

"Miss Palmer rented your brother a room," Moralas corrected, abruptly proper. "She was also among the group to discover your brother's body. She's given my department her complete cooperation."

Jonas's mouth thinned. How had Jerry described this Liz Palmer in their brief phone conversation weeks before? A sexy little number who made great tortillas. She sounded like another one of Jerry's tough ladies on the lookout for a good time and the main chance. "I'll need her address." At the captain's quiet look he only raised a brow. "I assume my brother's things are still there."

"They are. I have some of your brother's personal effects, those that he had on him, in my office. You're welcome to collect them and what remains at Miss Palmer's. We've already been through them."

Jonas felt the rage build again and smothered it. "When can I take my brother home?"

"I'll do my best to complete the paperwork today. I'll need you to make a statement. Of course, there are forms." He looked at Jonas's set profile and felt a new tug of pity. "Again, I'm sorry."

He only nodded. "Let's get it done."

Liz let herself into the house. While the door slammed behind her, she flicked switches, sending two ceiling fans whirling. The sound, for the moment, was company enough. The headache she'd lived with for over twenty-four hours was a dull, nagging thud just under her right temple. Going into the bathroom, she washed down two aspirin before turning on the shower.

She'd taken the glass bottom out again. Though it was off season, she'd had to turn a dozen people away. It wasn't every day a body was found off the coast, and the curious had come in force. Morbid, she thought, then stripped and stepped under the cold spray of the shower. How long would it take, she wondered, before she stopped seeing Jerry on the sand beneath the water?

True, she'd barely known him, but he'd been fun and interesting and good company. He'd slept in her daughter's bed and eaten in her kitchen. Closing her eyes, she let the water sluice over her, willing the headache away. She'd be better, she thought, when the police finished the investigation. It had been hard, very hard, when they'd come to her house and searched through Jerry's things. And the questions.

How much had she known about Jerry Sharpe? He'd been American, an operator, a womanizer. She'd been able to use all three to her benefit when he'd given diving lessons or acted as mate on one of her boats. She'd thought him harmless—sexy, attractive and basically lazy. He'd boasted of making it big, of wheeling a deal that would set him up in style. Liz had considered it so much hot air. As far as she was concerned, nothing set you up in style but years of hard work—or inherited wealth.

But Jerry's eyes had lit up when he'd talked of it, and his grin had been appealing. If she'd been a woman who allowed herself dreams, she would have believed him.

But dreams were for the young and foolish. With a little tug of regret, she realized Jerry Sharpe had been both.

Now he was gone, and what he had left was still scattered in her daughter's room. She'd have to box it up, Liz decided as she turned off the taps. It was something, at least. She'd box up Jerry's things and ask that Captain Moralas what to do about them. Certainly his family would want whatever he'd left behind. Jerry had spoken of a brother, whom he'd affectionately referred to as "the stuffed shirt." Jerry Sharpe had been anything but stuffy.

As she walked to the bedroom, Liz wrapped her hair in the towel. She remembered the way Jerry had tried to talk his way between her sheets a few days after he'd moved in. Smooth talk, smooth hands. Though he'd had her backed into the doorway, kissing her before she'd evaded it, Liz had easily brushed him off. He'd taken her refusal good-naturedly, she recalled, and they'd remained on comfortable terms. Liz pulled on an oversized shirt that skimmed her thighs.

The truth was, Jerry Sharpe had been a good-natured, comfortable man with big dreams. She wondered, not for the first time, if his dreams had had something to do with his death.

She couldn't go on thinking about it. The best thing to do was to pack what had belonged to Jerry back into his suitcase and take it to the police.

It made her feel gruesome. She discovered that after only five minutes. Privacy, for a time, had been all but her only possession. To invade someone else's made her uneasy. Liz folded a faded brown T-shirt that boasted the wearer had hiked the Grand Canyon and tried not to think at all. But she kept seeing him there, joking about sleeping with one of Faith's collection of dolls. He'd fixed

the window that had stuck and had cooked paella to celebrate his first paycheck.

Without warning, Liz felt the first tears flow. He'd
been so alive, so young, so full of that cocky sense of confidence. She'd hardly had time to consider him a friend,
but he'd slept in her daughter's bed and left clothes in
her closet.

She wished now she'd listened to him more, been
friendlier, more approachable. He'd asked her to have
drinks with him and she'd brushed him off because she'd
had paperwork to do. It seemed petty now, cold. If she'd
given him an hour of her life, she might have learned who
he was, where he'd come from, why he'd died.

When the knock at the door sounded, she pressed her
hands against her cheeks. Silly to cry, she told herself,
when tears never solved anything. Jerry Sharpe was gone,
and it had nothing to do with her.

She brushed away the tears as she walked to the door.
The headache was easing. Liz decided it would be best
if she called Moralas right away and arranged to have
the clothes picked up. She was telling herself she really
wasn't involved at all when she opened the door.

For a moment she could only stare. The T-shirt she
hadn't been aware of still holding slipped from her fingers. She took one stumbling step back as she felt a rushing sound fill her head. Because her vision dimmed, she
blinked to clear it. The man in the doorway stared back
at her accusingly.

"Jer-Jerry," she managed and nearly screamed when
he took a step forward.

"Elizabeth Palmer?"

She shook her head, numb and terrified. She had no
superstitions. She believed in action and reaction on a

purely practical level. When someone died, they couldn't come back. And yet she stood in her living room with the fans whirling and watched Jerry Sharpe step over her threshold. She heard him speak to her again.

"Are you Liz Palmer?"

"I saw you." She heard her own voice rise with nerves but couldn't take her eyes from his face. The cocky good looks, the cleft chin, the smoky eyes under thick dark brows. It was a face that appealed to a woman's need to risk, or to her dreams of risking. "Who are you?"

"Jonas Sharpe. Jerry was my brother. My twin brother."

When she discovered her knees were shaking, she sat down quickly. No, not Jerry, she told herself as her heartbeat leveled. The hair was just as dark, just as full, but it lacked Jerry's unkempt shagginess. The face was just as attractive, just as ruggedly hewn, but she'd never seen Jerry's eyes so hard, so cold. And this man wore a suit as though he'd been born in one. His stance was one of restrained passion and impatience. It took her a moment, only a moment, before anger struck.

"You did that on purpose." Because her palms were damp she rubbed them against her knees. "It was a hideous thing to do. You knew what I'd think when I opened the door."

"I needed a reaction."

She sat back and took a deep, steadying breath. "You're a bastard, Mr. Sharpe."

For the first time in hours, his mouth curved…only slightly. "May I sit down?"

She gestured to a chair. "What do you want?"

"I came to get Jerry's things. And to talk to you."

As he sat, Jonas took a long look around. His was not the polite, casual glance a stranger indulges himself in when he walks into someone else's home, but a sharp-eyed, intense study of what belonged to Liz Palmer. It was a small living area, hardly bigger than his office. While he preferred muted colors and clean lines, Liz chose bright, contrasting shades and odd knickknacks. Several Mayan masks hung on the walls, and rugs of different sizes and hues were scattered over the floor. The sunlight, fading now, came in slats through red window blinds. There was a big blue pottery vase on a woven mat on the table, but the butter-yellow flowers in it were losing their petals. The table itself didn't gleam with polish, but was covered with a thin layer of dust.

The shock that had had her stomach muscles jumping had eased. She said nothing as he looked around the room because she was looking at him. A mirror image of Jerry, she thought. And weren't mirror images something like negatives? She didn't think he'd be fun to have around. She had a frantic need to order him out, to pitch him out quickly and finally. Ridiculous, she told herself. He was just a man, and nothing to her. And he had lost his brother.

"I'm sorry, Mr. Sharpe. This is a very difficult time for you."

His gaze locked on hers so quickly that she tensed again. She'd barely been aware of his inch-by-inch study of her room, but she couldn't remain unmoved by his study of her.

She wasn't what he'd expected. Her face was all angles—wide cheekbones, a long narrow nose and a chin that came to a suggestion of a point. She wasn't beautiful, but stunning in an almost uncomfortable way. It might have been the eyes, a deep haunted brown, that rose a bit exotically at the outer edge. It might have been the mouth, full and vulnerable. The shirt overwhelmed her body with its yards of material, leaving only long, tanned legs bare. Her hands, resting on the arms of her chair, were small, narrow and ringless. Jonas had thought he knew his brother's taste as well as his own. Liz Palmer didn't suit Jerry's penchant for the loud and flamboyant, or his own for the discreet sophisticate.

Still, Jerry had lived with her. Jonas thought grimly that she was taking the murder of her lover very well. "And a difficult time for you."

His long study had left her shaken. It had gone beyond natural curiosity and made her feel like a specimen, filed and labeled for further research. She tried to remember that grief took different forms in different people. "Jerry was a nice man. It isn't easy to—"

"How did you meet him?"

Words of sympathy cut off, Liz straightened in her chair. She never extended friendliness where it wasn't likely to be accepted. If he wanted facts only, she'd give him facts. "He came by my shop a few weeks ago. He was interested in diving."

Jonas's brow lifted as in polite interest but his eyes remained cold. "In diving."

"I own a dive shop on the beach—rent equipment, boat rides, lessons, day trips. Jerry was looking for work. Since he knew what he was doing, I gave it to him. He crewed on the dive boat, gave some of the tourists lessons, that sort of thing."

Showing tourists how to use a regulator didn't fit with Jonas's last conversation with his brother. Jerry had talked about cooking up a big deal. Big money, big time. "He didn't buy in as your partner?"

Something came into her face—pride, disdain, amusement. Jonas couldn't be sure. "I don't take partners, Mr. Sharpe. Jerry worked for me, that's all."

"All?" The brow came up again. "He was living here."

She caught the meaning, had dealt with it from the police. Liz decided she'd answered all the questions she cared to and that she'd given Jonas Sharpe more than enough of her time. "Jerry's things are in here." Rising, she walked out of the room. Liz waited at the doorway to her daughter's room until Jonas joined her. "I was just beginning to pack his clothes. You'd probably prefer to do that yourself. Take as much time as you need."

When she started to turn away, Jonas took her arm. He wasn't looking at her, but into the room with the shelves of dolls, the pink walls and lacy curtains. And at his brother's clothes tossed negligently over the back of a painted white chair and onto a flowered spread. It hurt, Jonas discovered, all over again.

"Is this all?" It seemed so little.

"I haven't been through the drawers or the closet yet. The police have." Suddenly weary, she pulled the towel from her head. Dark blond hair, still damp, tumbled around her face and shoulders. Somehow her face seemed even more vulnerable. "I don't know anything about Jerry's personal life, his personal belongings. This is my daughter's room." She turned her head until their eyes met. "She's away at school. This is where Jerry slept." She left him alone.

Twenty minutes was all he needed. His brother had traveled light. Leaving the suitcase in the living room, Jonas walked through the house. It wasn't large. The next bedroom was dim in the early evening light, but he could see a splash of orange over a rattan bed and a desk cluttered with files and papers. It smelled lightly of spice and talcum powder. Turning away, he walked toward the back and found the kitchen. And Liz.

It was when he smelled the coffee that Jonas remembered he hadn't eaten since morning. Without turning around, Liz poured a second cup. She didn't need him to speak to know he was there. She doubted he was a man who ever had to announce his presence. "Cream?"

Jonas ran a hand through his hair. He felt as though he were walking through someone else's dream. "No, black."

When Liz turned to offer the cup, he saw the quick jolt. "I'm sorry," she murmured, taking up her own cup. "You look so much like him."

"Does that bother you?"

"It unnerves me."

He sipped the coffee, finding it cleared some of the mists of unreality. "You weren't in love with Jerry."

Liz sent him a look of mild surprise. She realized he'd thought she'd been his brother's lover, but she hadn't thought he'd have taken the next step. "I only knew him a few weeks." Then she laughed, remembering another time, another life. "No, I wasn't in love with him. We had a business relationship, but I liked him. He was cocky and well aware of his own charms. I had a lot of repeat female customers over the past couple of weeks. Jerry was quite an operator," she murmured, then looked up, horrified. "I'm sorry."

"No." Interested, Jonas stepped closer. She was a tall woman, so their eyes stayed level easily. She smelled of the talcum powder and wore no cosmetics. Not Jerry's type, he thought again. But there was something about the eyes. "That's what he was, only most people never caught on."

"I've known others." And her voice was flat. "Not so

harmless, not so kind. Your brother was a nice man, Mr. Sharpe. And I hope whoever... I hope they're found."

She watched the gray eyes ice over. The little tremor in her stomach reminded her that cold was often more dangerous than heat. "They will be. I may need to talk with you again."

It seemed a simple enough request, but she backed away from it. She didn't want to talk to him again, she didn't want to be involved in any way. "There's nothing else I can tell you."

"Jerry was living in your house, working for you."

"I don't know anything." Her voice rose as she spun away to stare out the window. She was tired of the questions, tired of people pointing her out on the beach as the woman who'd found the body. She was tired of having her life turned upside down by the death of a man she had hardly known. And she was nervous, she admitted, because Jonas Sharpe struck her as a man who could keep her life turned upside down as long as it suited him. "I've talked to the police again and again. He worked for me. I saw him a few hours out of the day. I don't know where he went at night, who he saw, what he did. It wasn't my business as long as he paid for the room and showed up to work." When she looked back, her face was set. "I'm sorry for your brother, I'm sorry for you. But it's not my business."

He saw the nerves as her hands unclenched but interpreted them in his own way. "We disagree, Mrs. Palmer."

"Miss Palmer," she said deliberately, and watched his slow, acknowledging nod. "I can't help you."

"You don't know that until we talk."

"All right. I won't help you."

He inclined his head and reached for his wallet. "Did Jerry owe you anything on the room?"

She felt the insult like a slap. Her eyes, usually soft, usually sad, blazed. "He owed me nothing, and neither do you. If you've finished your coffee…"

Jonas set the cup on the table. "I've finished. For now." He gave her a final study. Not Jerry's type, he thought again, or his. But she had to know something. If he had to use her to find out, he would. "Good night."

Liz stayed where she was until the sound of the front door closing echoed back at her. Then she shut her eyes. None of her business, she reminded herself. But she could still see Jerry under her boat. And now, she could see Jonas Sharpe with grief hard in his eyes.

Chapter Two

Liz considered working in the dive shop the next thing to taking a day off. Taking a day off, actually staying away from the shop and the boats, was a luxury she allowed herself rarely, and only when Faith was home on holiday. Today, she'd indulged herself by sending the boats out without her so that she could manage the shop alone. Be alone. By noon, all the serious divers had already rented their tanks so that business at the shop would be sporadic. It gave Liz a chance to spend a few hours checking equipment and listing inventory.

The shop was a basic cinder-block unit. Now and again, she toyed with the idea of having the outside painted, but could never justify the extra expense. There was a cubbyhole she wryly referred to as an office, where she'd crammed an old gray steel desk and one swivel chair. The rest of the room was crowded with equipment that lined the floor, was stacked on shelves or hung from hooks. Her desk had a dent in it the size of a man's foot, but her equipment was top grade and flawless.

Masks, flippers, tanks, snorkels could be rented individually or in any number of combinations. Liz had learned that the wider the choice, the easier it was to move items out and draw the customer back. The equipment was the backbone of her business. Prominent next to the wide square opening that was only closed at night with a heavy wooden shutter was a list, in English and Spanish, of her equipment, her services and the price.

When she'd started eight years before, Liz had stocked enough tanks and gear to outfit twelve divers. It had taken every penny she'd saved—every penny Marcus had given a young, dewy-eyed girl pregnant with his child. The girl had become a woman quickly, and that woman now had a business that could accommodate fifty divers from the skin out, dozens of snorkelers, underwater photographers, tourists who wanted an easy day on the water or gung-ho deep-sea fishermen.

The first boat she'd gambled on, a dive boat, had been christened *Faith,* for her daughter. She'd made a vow when she'd been eighteen, alone and frightened, that the child she carried would have the best. Ten years later, Liz could look around her shop and know she'd kept her promise.

More, the island she'd fled to for escape had become home. She was settled there, respected, depended on. She no longer looked over the expanses of white sand, blue water, longing for Houston or a pretty house with a flowing green lawn. She no longer looked back at the education she'd barely begun, or what she might have been. She'd stopped pining for a man who didn't want her or the child they'd made. She'd never go back. But Faith could. Faith could learn how to speak French, wear silk dresses and discuss wine and music. One day Faith would go back and mingle unknowingly with her cousins on their own level.

That was her dream, Liz thought as she carefully filled tanks. To see her daughter accepted as easily as she herself had been rejected. Not for revenge, Liz mused, but for justice.

"Howdy there, missy."

Crouched near the back wall, Liz turned and squinted against the sun. She saw a portly figure stuffed into a black-and-red wet suit, topped by a chubby face with a fat cigar stuck in the mouth.

"Mr. Ambuckle. I didn't know you were still on the island."

"Scooted over to Cancun for a few days. Diving's better here."

With a smile, she rose to go to her side of the opening. Ambuckle was a steady client who came to Cozumel two or three times a year and always rented plenty of tanks. "I could've told you that. See any of the ruins?"

"Wife dragged me to Tulum." He shrugged and grinned at her with popping blue eyes. "Rather be thirty feet down than climbing over rocks all day. Did get some snorkeling in. But a man doesn't fly all the way from Dallas just to paddle around. Thought I'd do some night diving."

Her smile came easily, adding something soft and approachable to eyes that were usually wary. "Fix you right up. How much longer are you staying?" she asked as she checked an underwater flash.

"Two more weeks. Man's got to get away from his desk."

"Absolutely." Liz had often been grateful so many people from Texas, Louisiana and Florida felt the need to get away.

"Heard you had some excitement while we were on the other side."

Liz supposed she should be used to the comment by now, but a shiver ran up her spine. The smile faded, leaving her face remote. "You mean the American who was murdered?"

"Put the wife in a spin. Almost couldn't talk her into coming back over. Did you know him?"

No, she thought, not as well as she should have. To keep her hands busy, she reached for a rental form and began to fill it out. "As a matter of fact, he worked here a little while."

"You don't say?" Ambuckle's small blue eyes sparkled a bit. But Liz supposed she should be used to that, as well.

"You might remember him. He crewed the dive boat the last time you and your wife went out."

"No kidding?" Ambuckle's brow creased as he chewed on the cigar. "Not that good-looking young man—Johnny, Jerry," he remembered. "Had the wife in stitches."

"Yes, that was him."

"Shame," Ambuckle murmured, but looked rather pleased to have known the victim. "Had a lot of zip."

"Yes, I thought so, too." Liz lugged the tanks through the door and set them on the stoop. "That should take care of it, Mr. Ambuckle."

"Add a camera on, missy. Want to get me a picture of one of those squids. Ugly things."

Amazed, Liz plucked one from the shelf and added

it to the list on a printed form. She checked her watch, noted down the time and turned the form for Ambuckle's signature. After signing, he handed her bills for the deposit. She appreciated the fact that Ambuckle always paid in cash, American. "Thanks. Glad to see you back, Mr. Ambuckle."

"Can't keep me away, missy." With a whoosh and a grunt, he hefted the tanks on his shoulders. Liz watched him cross to the walkway before she filed the receipt. Unlocking her cash box, she stored the money.

"Business is good."

She jolted at the voice and looking up again stared at Jonas Sharpe.

She'd never again mistake him for Jerry, though his eyes were almost hidden this time with tinted glasses, and he wore shorts and an open shirt in lieu of a suit. There was a long gold chain around his neck with a small coin dangling. She recalled Jerry had worn one. But something in the way Jonas stood, something in the set of his mouth made him look taller and tougher than the man she'd known.

Because she didn't believe in polite fencing, Liz finished relocking the cash box and began to check the straps and fasteners on a shelf of masks. No faulty equipment went out of her shop. "I didn't expect to see you again."

"You should have." Jonas watched her move down the shelf. She seemed stronger, less vulnerable than she had when he'd seen her a week ago. Her eyes were cool, her voice remote. It made it easier to do what he'd come for. "You have quite a reputation on the island."

She paused long enough to look over her shoulder. "Really?"

"I checked," he said easily. "You've lived here for ten

years. Built this place from the first brick and have one of the most successful businesses on the island."

She examined the mask in her hand meticulously. "Are you interested in renting some equipment, Mr. Sharpe? I can recommend the snorkeling right off this reef."

"Maybe. But I think I'd prefer to scuba."

"Fine. I can give you whatever you need." She set the mask down and chose another. "It isn't necessary to be certified to dive in Mexico; however, I'd recommend a few basic lessons before you go down. We offer two different courses—individual or group."

He smiled at her for the first time, a slow, appealing curving of lips that softened the toughness around his mouth. "I might take you up on that. Meantime, when do you close?"

"When I'm ready to." The smile made a difference, she realized, and she couldn't let it. In defense, she shifted her weight on one hip and sent him a look of mild insolence. "This is Cozumel, Mr. Sharpe. We don't run nine to five here. Unless you want to rent some equipment or sign up for a tour, you'll have to excuse me."

He reached in to close his hand over hers. "I didn't come back to tour. Have dinner with me tonight. We can talk."

She didn't attempt to free her hand but stared at him. Running a business had taught her to be scrupulously polite in any circumstances. "No, thank you."

"Drinks, then."

"No."

"Miss Palmer..." Normally, Jonas was known for his deadly, interminable patience. It was a weapon, he'd learned, in the courtroom and out of it. With Liz, he found it difficult to wield it. "I don't have a great deal to go on at this point, and the police haven't made any progress at all. I need your help."

This time Liz did pull away. She wouldn't be sucked in, that she promised herself, not by quiet words or intense eyes. She had her life to lead, a business to run and, most important, a daughter coming home in a matter of weeks. "I won't get involved. I'm sorry, even if I wanted to, there'd be nothing I could do to help."

"Then it won't hurt to talk to me."

"Mr. Sharpe." Liz wasn't known for her patience. "I have very little free time. Running this business isn't a whim or a lark, but a great deal of work. If I have a couple of hours to myself in the evening, I'm not going to spend them being grilled by you. Now—"

She started to brush him off again when a young boy came running up to the window. He was dressed in a bathing suit and slick with suntan lotion. With a twenty-dollar bill crumpled in his hand, he babbled a request for snorkeling equipment for himself and his brother. He spoke in quick, excited Spanish as Liz checked out the equipment, asking if she thought they'd see a shark.

She answered him in all seriousness as she exchanged money for equipment. "Sharks don't live in the reef, but they do visit now and again." She saw the light of adventure in his eyes. "You'll see parrot fish." She held her hands apart to show him how big. "And if you take some bread crumbs or crackers, the sergeant majors will follow you, lots of them, close enough to touch."

"Will they bite?"

She grinned. "Only the bread crumbs. Adios."

He dashed away, kicking up sand.

"You speak Spanish like a native," Jonas observed, and thought it might come in handy. He'd also noticed the pleasure that had come into her eyes when she'd talked with the boy. There'd been nothing remote then, nothing sad or haunted. Strange, he mused, he'd never noticed just how much a barometer of feeling the eyes could be.

"I live here," she said simply. "Now, Mr. Sharpe—"

"How many boats?"

"What?"

"How many do you have?"

She sucked in a deep breath and decided she could humor him for another five minutes. "I have four. The glass bottom, two dive boats and one for deep-sea fishing."

"Deep-sea fishing." That was the one, Jonas decided. A fishing boat would be private and isolated. "I haven't done any in five or six years. Tomorrow." He reached in his wallet. "How much?"

"It's fifty dollars a person a day, but I don't take the boat out for one man, Mr. Sharpe." She gave him an easy smile. "It doesn't make good business sense."

"What's your minimum?"

"Three. And I'm afraid I don't have anyone else lined up. So—"

He set four fifty-dollar bills on the counter. "The extra fifty's to make sure you're driving the boat." Liz looked down at the money. An extra two hundred would help buy the aqua bikes she'd been thinking about. Several of the other dive shops already had them and she kept a constant eye on competition. Aqua biking and wind surfing were becoming increasingly popular, and if she wanted to keep up… She looked back at Jonas Sharpe's dark, determined eyes and decided it wasn't worth it.

"My schedule for tomorrow's already set. I'm afraid I—"

"It doesn't make good business sense to turn down a

profit, Miss Palmer." When she only moved her shoulders, he smiled again, but this time it wasn't so pleasant. "I'd hate to mention at the hotel that I couldn't get satisfaction at The Black Coral. It's funny how word of mouth can help or damage a small business."

Liz picked up the money, one bill at a time. "What business are you in, Mr. Sharpe?"

"Law."

She made a sound that might have been a laugh as she pulled out a form. "I should've guessed. I knew someone studying law once." She thought of Marcus with his glib, calculating tongue. "He always got what he wanted, too. Sign here. We leave at eight," she said briskly. "The price includes a lunch on board. If you want beer or liquor, you bring your own. The sun's pretty intense on the water, so you'd better buy some sunscreen." She glanced beyond him. "One of my dive boats is coming back. You'll have to excuse me."

"Miss Palmer…" He wasn't sure what he wanted to say to her, or why he was uncomfortable having completed a successful maneuver. In the end, he pocketed his receipt. "If you change your mind about dinner—"

"I won't."

"I'm at the El Presidente."

"An excellent choice." She walked through the doorway and onto the dock to wait for her crew and clients.

By seven-fifteen, the sun was up and already burning off a low ground mist. What clouds there were, were thin and shaggy and good-natured.

"Damn!" Liz kicked the starter on her motorbike and turned in a little U toward the street. She'd been hoping for rain.

He was going to try to get her involved. Even now, Liz could imagine those dark, patient gray eyes staring into hers, hear the quietly insistent voice. Jonas Sharpe was the kind of man who took no for an answer but was dogged enough to wait however long it took for the yes. Under other circumstances, she'd have admired that. Being stubborn had helped her start and succeed in a business when so many people had shaken their heads and warned her against it. But she couldn't afford to admire Jonas Sharpe. Budgeting her feelings was every bit as important as budgeting her accounts.

She couldn't help him, Liz thought again, as the soft air began to play around her face. Everything she'd known about Jerry had been said at least twice. Of course she was sorry, and had grieved a bit herself for a man she'd hardly known, but murder was a police matter. Jonas Sharpe was out of his element.

She was in hers, Liz thought as her muscles began to relax with the ride. The street was bumpy, patched in a good many places. She knew when to weave and sway. There were houses along the street with deep green grass and trailing vines. Already clothes were waving out on lines. She could hear an early newscast buzzing through someone's open window and the sound of children finishing chores or breakfast before school. She turned a corner and kept her speed steady.

There were a few shops here, closed up tight. At the door of a market, Señor Pessado fumbled with his keys. Liz tooted her horn and exchanged waves. A cab passed her, speeding down the road to the airport to wait for the early arrivals. In a matter of moments, Liz caught the first scent of the sea. It was always fresh. As she took the last turn, she glanced idly in her rearview mirror. Odd, she thought—hadn't she seen that little blue car yesterday? But when she swung into the hotel's parking lot, it chugged past.

Liz's arrangement with the hotel had been of mutual benefit. Her shop bordered the hotel's beach and encouraged business on both sides. Still, whenever she went inside, as she did today to collect the lunch for the fishing trip, she always remembered the two years she'd spent scrubbing floors and making beds.

"*Buenos días,* Margarita."

The young woman with a bucket and mop started to smile. "*Buenos días,* Liz. *¿Cómo està?*"

"*Bien.* How's Ricardo?"

"Growing out of his pants." Margarita pushed the button of the service elevator as they spoke of her son. "Faith comes home soon. He'll be glad."

"So will I." They parted, but Liz remembered the months they'd worked together, changing linen, hauling towels, washing floors. Margarita had been a friend, like so many others she'd met on the island who'd shown kindness to a young woman who'd carried a child but had no wedding ring.

She could have lied. Even at eighteen Liz had been aware she could have bought a ten-dollar gold band and had an easy story of divorce or widowhood. She'd been too stubborn. The baby that had been growing inside her belonged to her. Only to her. She'd feel no shame and tell no lies.

By seven forty-five, she was crossing the beach to her shop, lugging a large cooler packed with two lunches and a smaller one filled with bait. She could already see a few tubes bobbing on the water's surface. The water would be warm and clear and uncrowded. She'd like to have had an hour for snorkeling herself.

"Liz!" The trim, small-statured man who walked toward her was shaking his head. There was a faint, pencil-thin mustache above his lip and a smile in his dark eyes. "You're too skinny to carry that thing."

She caught her breath and studied him up and down. He wore nothing but a skimpy pair of snug trunks. She knew he enjoyed the frank or surreptitious stares of women on the beach. "So're you, Luis. But don't let me stop you."

"So you take the fishing boat today?" He hefted the larger cooler and walked with her toward the shop. "I changed the schedule for you. Thirteen signed up for the glass bottom for the morning. We got both dive boats going out, so I told my cousin Miguel to help fill in today. Okay?"

"Terrific." Luis was young, fickle with women and fond of his tequila, but he could be counted on in a pinch. "I guess I'm going to have to hire someone on, at least part-time."

Luis looked at her, then at the ground. He'd worked closest with Jerry. "Miguel, he's not dependable. Here one day, gone the next. I got a nephew, a good boy. But he can't work until he's out of school."

"I'll keep that in mind," Liz said absently. "Let's just put this right on the boat. I want to check the gear."

On board, Liz went through a routine check on the tackle and line. As she looked over the big reels and massive rods, she wondered, with a little smirk, if the lawyer had ever done any big-game fishing. Probably wouldn't know a tuna if it jumped up and bit his toe, she decided.

The decks were clean, the equipment organized, as

she insisted. Luis had been with her the longest, but anyone who worked for Liz understood the hard and fast rule about giving the clients the efficiency they paid for.

The boat was small by serious sport fishing standards, but her clients rarely went away dissatisfied. She knew the waters all along the Yucatan Peninsula and the habits of the game that teemed below the surface. Her boat might not have sonar and fish finders and complicated equipment, but she determined to give Jonas Sharpe the ride of his life. She'd keep him so busy, strapped in a fighting chair, that he wouldn't have time to bother her. By the time they docked again, his arms would ache, his back would hurt and the only thing he'd be interested in would be a hot bath and bed. And if he wasn't a complete fool, she'd see to it that he had a trophy to take back to wherever he'd come from.

Just where was that? she wondered as she checked the gauges on the bridge. She'd never thought to ask Jerry. It hadn't seemed important. Yet now she found herself wondering where Jonas came from, what kind of life he led there. Was he the type who frequented elegant restaurants with an equally elegant woman on his arm? Did he watch foreign films and play bridge? Or did he prefer noisy clubs and hot jazz? She hadn't been able to find his slot as easily as she did with most people she met, so she wondered, perhaps too much. Not my business, she reminded herself and turned to call to Luis.

"I'll take care of everything here. Go ahead and open the shop. The glass bottom should be ready to leave in half an hour."

But he wasn't listening. Standing on the deck, he stared back at the narrow dock. She saw him raise a shaky hand to cross himself. *"Madre de Dios."*

"Luis?" She came down the short flight of stairs to join him. "What—"

Then she saw Jonas, a straw hat covering his head, sunglasses shading his eyes. He hadn't bothered to shave, so that the light growth of beard gave him a lazy, vagrant look accented by a faded T-shirt and brief black trunks. He didn't, she realized, look like a man who'd play bridge. Knowing what was going through Luis's mind, Liz shook his arm and spoke quickly.

"It's his brother, Luis. I told you they were twins."

"Back from the dead," Luis whispered.

"Don't be ridiculous." She shook off the shudder his words brought her. "His name is Jonas and he's nothing like Jerry at all, really. You'll see when you talk to him. You're prompt, Mr. Sharpe," she called out, hoping to jolt Luis out of his shock. "Need help coming aboard?"

"I can manage." Hefting a small cooler, Jonas stepped lightly on deck. "The *Expatriate*." He referred to the careful lettering on the side of the boat. "Is that what you are?"

"Apparently." It was something she was neither proud nor ashamed of. "This is Luis—he works for me. You gave him a jolt just now."

"Sorry." Jonas glanced at the slim man hovering by Liz's side. There was sweat beading on his lip. "You knew my brother?"

"We worked together," Luis answered in his slow, precise English. "With the divers. Jerry, he liked best to take out the dive boat. I'll cast off." Giving Jonas a wide berth, Luis jumped onto the dock.

"I seem to affect everyone the same way," Jonas observed. "How about you?" He turned dark, direct eyes to her. Though he no longer made her think of Jerry, he unnerved her just the same. "Still want to keep me at arm's length?"

"We pride ourselves in being friendly to all our clients. You've hired the *Expatriate* for the day, Mr. Sharpe. Make yourself comfortable." She gestured toward a deck chair before climbing the steps to the bridge and calling out to Luis. "Tell Miguel he gets paid only if he finishes out the day." With a final wave to Luis, she started the engine, then cruised sedately toward the open sea.

The wind was calm, barely stirring the water. Liz could see the dark patches that meant reefs and kept the speed easy. Once they were in deeper water, she'd open it up a bit. By midday the sun would be stunningly hot. She wanted Jonas strapped in his chair and fighting two hundred pounds of fish by then.

"You handle a wheel as smoothly as you do a customer."

A shadow of annoyance moved in her eyes, but she kept them straight ahead. "It's my business. You'd be more comfortable on the deck in a chair, Mr. Sharpe."

"Jonas. And I'm perfectly comfortable here." He gave her a casual study as he stood beside her. She wore a fielder's cap over her hair with white lettering promoting her shop. On her T-shirt, the same lettering was faded from the sun and frequent washings. He wondered, idly, what she wore under it. "How long have you had this boat?"

"Almost eight years. She's sound." Liz pushed the throttle forward. "The waters are warm, so you'll find tuna, marlin, swordfish. Once we're out you can start chumming."

"Chumming?"

She sent him a quick look. So she'd been right—he

didn't know a line from a pole. "Bait the water," she began. "I'll keep the speed slow and you bait the water, attract the fish."

"Seems like taking unfair advantage. Isn't fishing supposed to be luck and skill?"

"For some people it's a matter of whether they'll eat or not." She turned the wheel a fraction, scanning the water for unwary snorkelers. "For others, it's a matter of another trophy for the wall."

"I'm not interested in trophies."

She shifted to face him. No, he wouldn't be, she decided, not in trophies or in anything else without a purpose. "What are you interested in?"

"At the moment, you." He put his hand over hers and let off the throttle. "I'm in no hurry."

"You paid to fish." She flexed her hand under his.

"I paid for your time," he corrected.

He was close enough that she could see his eyes beyond the tinted lenses. They were steady, always steady, as if he knew he could afford to wait. The hand still over hers wasn't smooth as she'd expected, but hard and worked. No, he wouldn't play bridge, she thought again. Tennis, perhaps, or hand ball, or something else that took sweat and effort. For the first time in years she felt a quick thrill race through her—a thrill she'd been certain she was immune to. The wind tossed the hair back from her face as she studied him.

"Then you wasted your money."

Her hand moved under his again. Strong, he thought, though her looks were fragile. Stubborn. He could judge that by the way the slightly pointed chin stayed up. But there was a look in her eyes that said *I've been hurt, I won't be hurt again*. That alone was intriguing, but added

to it was a quietly simmering sexuality that left him wondering how it was his brother hadn't been her lover. Not,
Jonas was sure, for lack of trying.

"If I've wasted my money, it won't be the first time.
But somehow I don't think I have."

"There's nothing I can tell you." Her hand jerked and
pushed the throttle up again.

"Maybe not. Or maybe there's something you know
without realizing it. I've dealt in criminal law for over
ten years. You'd be surprised how important small bits
of information can be. Talk to me." His hand tightened
briefly on hers. "Please."

She thought she'd hardened her heart, but she could
feel herself weakening. Why was it she could haggle for
hours over the price of scuba gear and could never refuse
a softly spoken request? He was going to cause her nothing but trouble. Because she already knew it, she sighed.

"We'll talk." She cut the throttle so the boat would
drift. "While you fish." She managed to smile a bit as
she stepped away. "No chum."

With easy efficiency, Liz secured the butt of a rod
into the socket attached to a chair. "For now, you sit and
relax," she told him. "Sometimes a fish is hot enough
to take the hook without bait. If you get one, you strap
yourself in and work."

Jonas settled himself in the chair and tipped back his
hat. "And you?"

"I go back to the wheel and keep the speed steady so
we tire him out without losing him." She gathered her
hair in one hand and tossed it back. "There're better spots
than this, but I'm not wasting my gas when you don't care
whether you catch a fish or not."

His lips twitched as he leaned back in the chair. "Sensible. I thought you would be."

"Have to be."

"Why did you come to Cozumel?" Jonas ignored the rod in front of him and took out a cigarette.

"You've been here for a few days," she countered. "You shouldn't have to ask."

"Parts of your own country are beautiful. If you've been here ten years, you'd have been a child when you left the States."

"No, I wasn't a child." Something in the way she said it had him watching her again, looking for the secret she held just beyond her eyes. "I came because it seemed like the right thing to do. It was the right thing. When I was a girl, my parents would come here almost every year. They love to dive."

"You moved here with your parents?"

"No, I came alone." This time her voice was flat. "You didn't pay two hundred dollars to talk about me, Mr. Sharpe."

"It helps to have some background. You said you had a daughter. Where is she?"

"She goes to school in Houston—that's where my parents live."

Toss a child, and the responsibility, onto grandparents and live on a tropical island. It might leave a bad taste in his mouth, but it wasn't something that would surprise him. Jonas took a deep drag as he studied Liz's profile. It just didn't fit. "You miss her."

"Horribly," Liz murmured. "She'll be home in a few weeks, and we'll spend the summer together. September always comes too soon." Her gaze drifted off as she spoke, almost to herself. "It's for the best. My parents take wonderful care of her and she's getting an excellent education—taking piano lessons and ballet. They sent me pictures from a recital, and…" Her eyes filled with tears so quickly that she hadn't any warning. She shifted into the wind and fought them back, but he'd seen them. He sat smoking silently to give her time to recover.

"Ever get back to the States?"

"No." Liz swallowed and called herself a fool. It had been the pictures, she told herself, the pictures that had come in yesterday's mail of her little girl wearing a pink dress.

"Hiding from something?"

She whirled back, tears replaced with fury. Her body was arched like a bow ready to launch. Jonas held up a hand.

"Sorry. I have a habit of poking into secrets."

She forced herself to relax, to strap back passion as she'd taught herself so long ago. "It's a good way to lose your fingers, Mr. Sharpe."

He chuckled. "That's a possibility. I've always considered it worth the risk. They call you Liz, don't they?"

Her brow lifted under the fringe that blew around her brow. "My friends do."

"It suits you, except when you try to be aloof. Then it should be Elizabeth."

She sent him a smoldering look, certain he was trying to annoy her. "No one calls me Elizabeth."

He merely grinned at her. "Why weren't you sleeping with Jerry?"

"I beg your pardon?"

"Yes, definitely Elizabeth. You're a beautiful woman in an odd sort of way." He tossed out the compliment as casually as he tossed the cigarette into the water. "Jerry had a…fondness for beautiful women. I can't figure out why you weren't lovers."

For a moment, only a moment, it occurred to her that no one had called her beautiful in a very long time. She'd needed words like that once. Then she leaned back on the rail, planted her hands and aimed a killing look. She didn't need them now.

"I didn't choose to sleep with him. It might be difficult for you to accept, as you share the same face, but I didn't find Jerry irresistible."

"No?" As relaxed as she was tensed, Jonas reached into the cooler, offering her a beer. When she shook her head, he popped the top on one for himself. "What did you find him?"

"He was a drifter, and he happened to drift into my life. I gave him a job because he had a quick mind and a strong back. The truth was, I never expected him to last over a month. Men like him don't."

Though he hadn't moved a muscle, Jonas had come to attention. "Men like him?"

"Men who look for the quickest way to easy street. He worked because he liked to eat, but he was always looking for the big strike—one he wouldn't have to sweat for."

"So you did know him," Jonas murmured. "What was he looking for here?"

"I tell you I don't know! For all I know he was looking for a good time and a little sun." Frustration poured out of her as she tossed a hand in the air. "I let him have a room because he seemed harmless and I could use the money. I wasn't intimate with him on any level. The closest he came to talking about what he was up to was bragging about diving for big bucks."

"Diving? Where?"

Fighting for control, she dragged a hand through her hair. "I wish you'd leave me alone."

"You're a realistic woman, aren't you, Elizabeth?"

Her chin was set when she looked back at him. "Yes."

"Then you know I won't. Where was he going to dive?"

"I don't know. I barely listened to him when he got started on how rich he was going to be."

"What did he say?" This time Jonas's voice was quiet, persuading. "Just try to think back and remember what he told you."

"He said something about making a fortune diving, and I joked about sunken treasure. And he said…" She strained to remember the conversation. It had been late in the evening, and she'd been busy, preoccupied. "I was working at home," Liz remembered. "I always seem to handle the books better at night. He'd been out, partying I thought, because he was a little unsteady when he came in. He pulled me out of the chair. I remember I started to swear at him but he looked so damn happy, I let it go. Really, I hardly listened because I was picking up all the papers he'd scattered, but he was saying something about the big time and buying champagne to celebrate. I told him he'd better stick to beer on his salary. That's when he talked about deals coming through and diving for big bucks. Then I made some comment about sunken treasure.…"

"And what did he say?"

"Sometimes you make more putting stuff in than taking it out." With a line between her brows, she remembered how he'd laughed when she'd told him to go sleep it off. "He made a pass neither one of us took seriously, and then…I think he made a phone call. I went back to work."

"When was this?"

"A week, maybe one week after I took him on."

"That must have been when he called me." Jonas looked out to sea. And he hadn't paid much attention, either, he reminded himself. Jerry had talked about coming home in style. But then he had always been talking about coming home in style. And the call, as usual, had been collect.

"Did you ever see him with anyone? Talking, arguing?"

"I never saw him argue with anyone. He flirted with the women on the beach, made small talk with the clients and got along just fine with everyone he worked with. I assumed he spent most of his free time in San Miguel. I think he cruised a few bars with Luis and some of the others."

"What bars?"

"You'll have to ask them, though I'm sure the police already have." She took a deep breath. It was bringing it all back again, too close. "Mr. Sharpe, why don't you let the police handle this? You're running after shadows."

"He was my brother." And more, what he couldn't explain, his twin. Part of himself had been murdered. If he were ever to feel whole again, he had to know why. "Haven't you wondered why Jerry was murdered?"

"Of course." She looked down at her hands. They were empty and she felt helpless. "I thought he must've gotten into a fight, or maybe he bragged to the wrong person. He had a bad habit of tossing what money he had around."

"It wasn't robbery or a mugging, Elizabeth. It was professional. It was business."

Her heart began a slow, painful thud. "I don't understand."

"Jerry was murdered by a pro, and I'm going to find out why."

Because her throat was suddenly dry, she swallowed. "If you're right, then that's all the more reason to leave it to the police."

He drew out his cigarettes again, but stared ahead to where the sky met the water. "Police don't want revenge. I do." In his voice, she heard the calm patience and felt a shiver.

Staring, she shook her head. "Even if you found the person who did it, what could you do?"

He took a long pull from his beer. "As a lawyer, I suppose I'd be obliged to see they had their day in court. As a brother..." He trailed off and drank again. "We'll have to see."

"I don't think you're a very nice man, Mr. Sharpe."

"I'm not." He turned his head until his eyes locked on hers. "And I'm not harmless. Remember, if I make a pass, we'll both take it seriously."

She started to speak, then saw his line go taut. "You've got a fish, Mr. Sharpe," she said dryly. "You'd better strap in or he'll pull you overboard."

Turning on her heel, she went back to the bridge, leaving Jonas to fend for himself.

Chapter Three

It was sundown when Liz parked her bike under the lean-to beside her house. She was still laughing. However much trouble Jonas had caused her, however much he had annoyed her in three brief meetings, she had his two hundred dollars. And he had a thirty-pound marlin— whether he wanted it or not. *We deliver,* she thought as she jingled her keys.

Oh, it had been worth it, just to see his face when he'd found himself on the other end of the wire from a big, bad-tempered fish. Liz believed he'd have let it go if she hadn't taken the time for one last smirk. Stubborn, she thought again. Yes, any other time she'd have admired it, and him.

Though she'd been wrong about his not being able to handle a rod, he'd looked so utterly perplexed with the fish lying at his feet on the deck that she'd nearly felt sorry for him. But his luck, or the lack of it, had helped her make an easy exit once they'd docked. With all the people crowding around to get a look at his catch and congratulate him, Jonas hadn't been able to detain her.

Now she was ready for an early evening, she thought. And a rainy one if the clouds moving in from the east delivered. Liz let herself into the house, propping the door open to bring in the breeze that already tasted of rain. After the fans were whirling, she turned on the radio automatically. Hurricane season might be a few months off, but the quick tropical storms were unpredictable. She'd been through enough of them not to take them lightly.

In the bedroom she prepared to strip for the shower that would wash the day's sweat and salt from her skin. Because it was twilight, she was already reaching for the light switch when a stray thought stopped her. Hadn't she left the blinds up that morning? Liz stared at them, tugged snugly over the windowsill. Odd, she was sure she'd left them up, and why wasn't the cord wrapped around its little hook? She was fanatical about that kind of detail, she supposed because ropes on a boat were always secured.

She hesitated, even after light spilled into the room. Then she shrugged. She must have been more distracted that morning than she'd realized. Jonas Sharpe, she decided, was taking up too much of her time, and too many of her thoughts. A man like him was bound to do so, even under different circumstances. But she'd long since passed the point in her life where a man could dominate it. He only worried her because he was interfering in her time, and her time was a precious commodity. Now that he'd had his way, and his talk, there should be no more visits. She remembered, uncomfortably, the way he'd smiled at her. It would be best, she decided, if he went back to where he'd come from and she got on with her own routine.

To satisfy herself, Liz walked over to the first shade and secured the cord. From the other room, the radio announced an evening shower before music kicked in. Humming along with it, she decided to toss together a chicken salad before she logged the day's accounts.

As she straightened, the breath was knocked out of her by an arm closing tightly around her neck. The dying sun caught a flash of silver. Before she could react, she felt the quick prick of a knife blade at her throat.

"Where is it?"

The voice that hissed in her ear was Spanish. In reflex, she brought her hands to the arm around her neck. As her nails dug in, she felt hard flesh and a thin metal band. She gasped for air, but stopped struggling when the knife poked threateningly at her throat.

"What do you want?" In terror her mind skimmed forward. She had less than fifty dollars cash and no jewelry of value except a single strand of pearls left by her grandmother. "My purse is in on the table. You can take it."

The vicious yank on her hair had her gasping in pain. "Where did he put it?"

"Who? I don't know what you want."

"Sharpe. Deal's off, lady. If you want to live, you tell me where he put the money."

"I don't know." The knife point pricked the vulnerable skin at her throat. She felt something warm trickle down her skin. Hysteria bubbled up behind it. "I never saw any money. You can look—there's nothing here."

"I've already looked." He tightened his hold until her

vision grayed from lack of air. "Sharpe died fast. You won't be so lucky. Tell me where it is and nothing happens."

He was going to kill her. The thought ran in her head. She was going to die for something she knew nothing about. Money...he wanted money and she only had fifty dollars. Faith. As she felt herself on the verge of unconsciousness, she thought of her daughter. Who would take care of her? Liz bit down on her lip until the pain cleared her mind. She couldn't die.

"Please..." She let herself go limp in his arms. "I can't tell you anything. I can't breathe."

His hold loosened just slightly. Liz slumped against him and when he shifted, she brought her elbow back with all her strength. She didn't bother to turn around but ran blindly. A rug slid under her feet, but she stumbled ahead, too terrified to look back. She was already calling for help when she hit the front door.

Her closest neighbor was a hundred yards away. She vaulted the little fence that separated the yards and sprinted toward the house. She stumbled up the steps, sobbing. Even as the door opened, she heard the sound of a car squealing tires on the rough gravel road behind her.

"He tried to kill me," she managed, then fainted.

"There is no further information I can give you, Mr. Sharpe." Moralas sat in his neat office facing the waterfront. The file on his desk wasn't as thick as he would have liked. Nothing in his investigation had turned up a reason for Jerry Sharpe's murder. The man who sat across from him stared straight ahead. Moralas had a photo of the victim in the file, and a mirror image a few feet away. "I wonder, Mr. Sharpe, if your brother's death was a result of something that happened before his coming to Cozumel."

"Jerry wasn't running when he came here."

Moralas tidied his papers. "Still, we have asked for the cooperation of the New Orleans authorities. That was your brother's last known address."

"He never had an address," Jonas murmured. Or a conventional job, a steady woman. Jerry had been a comet, always refusing to burn itself out. "I've told you what Miss Palmer said. Jerry was cooking up a deal, and he was cooking it up in Cozumel."

"Yes, having to do with diving." Always patient, Moralas drew out a thin cigar. "Though we've already spoken with Miss Palmer, I appreciate your bringing me the information."

"But you don't know what the hell to do with it."

Moralas flicked on his lighter, smiling at Jonas over the flame. "You're blunt. I'll be blunt, as well. If there was a trail to follow to your brother's murder, it's cold. Every day it grows colder. There were no fingerprints, no murder weapon, no witnesses." He picked up the file, gesturing with it. "That doesn't mean I intend to toss this in a drawer and forget about it. If there is a murderer on my island, I intend to find him. At the moment, I believe the murderer is miles away, perhaps in your own country. Procedure now is to backtrack on your brother's activities until we find something. To be frank, Mr. Sharpe, you're not doing yourself or me any good by being here."

"I'm not leaving."

"That is, of course, your privilege—unless you interfere with police procedure." At the sound of the buzzer on his desk, Moralas tipped his ash and picked up the phone.

"Moralas." There was a pause. Jonas saw the captain's

thick, dark brows draw together. "Yes, put her on. Miss Palmer, this is Captain Moralas."

Jonas stopped in the act of lighting a cigarette and waited. Liz Palmer was the key, he thought again. He had only to find what lock she fit.

"When? Are you injured? No, please stay where you are, I'll come to you." Moralas was rising as he hung up the phone. "Miss Palmer has been attacked."

Jonas was at the door first. "I'm coming with you."

His muscles ached with tension as the police car raced out of town toward the shore. He asked no questions. In his mind, Jonas could see Liz as she'd been on the bridge hours before—tanned, slim, a bit defiant. He remembered the self-satisfied smirk she'd given him when he'd found himself in a tug-of-war with a thirty-pound fish. And how neatly she'd skipped out on him the moment they'd docked.

She'd been attacked. Why? Was it because she knew more than she'd been willing to tell him? He wondered if she were a liar, an opportunist or a coward. Then he wondered how badly she'd been hurt.

As they pulled down the narrow drive, Jonas glanced toward Liz's house. The door was open, the shades drawn. She lived there alone, he thought, vulnerable and unprotected. Then he turned his attention to the little stucco building next door. A woman in a cotton dress and apron came onto the porch. She carried a baseball bat.

"You are the police." She nodded, satisfied, when Moralas showed his identification. "I am Señora Alderez. She's inside. I thank the Virgin we were home when she came to us."

"Thank you."

Jonas stepped inside with Moralas and saw her. She

was sitting on a patched sofa, huddled forward with a glass of wine in both hands. Jonas saw the liquid shiver back and forth as her hands trembled. She looked up slowly when they came in, her gaze passing over Moralas to lock on Jonas. She stared, with no expression in those deep, dark eyes. Just as slowly, she looked back at her glass.

"Miss Palmer." With his voice very gentle, Moralas sat down beside her. "Can you tell me what happened?"

She took the smallest of drinks, pressed her lips together briefly, then began as though she were reciting. "I came home at sunset. I didn't close the front door or lock it. I went straight into the bedroom. The shades were down, and I thought I'd left them up that morning. The cord wasn't secured, so I went over and fixed it. That's when he grabbed me—from behind. He had his arm around my neck and a knife. He cut me a little." In reflex, she reached up to touch the inch-long scratch her neighbor had already cleaned and fussed over. "I didn't fight because he had the knife at my throat and I thought he would kill me. He was going to kill me." She brought her head up to look directly into Moralas's eyes. "I could hear it in his voice."

"What did he say to you, Miss Palmer?"

"He said, 'Where is it?' I didn't know what he wanted. I told him he could take my purse. He was choking me and he said, 'Where did he put it?' He said Sharpe." This time she looked at Jonas. When she lifted her head, he saw that bruises were already forming on her throat. "He said the deal was off and he wanted the money. If I didn't tell him where it was he'd kill me, and I wouldn't die quickly, the way Jerry had. He didn't believe me when I said I didn't know anything." She spoke directly to Jonas. As she stared at him he felt the guilt rise.

Patient, Moralas touched her arm to bring her attention back to him. "He let you go?"

"No, he was going to kill me." She said it dully, without fear, without passion. "I knew he would whether I told him anything or not, and my daughter—she needs me. I slumped as if I'd fainted, then I hit him. I think I hit him in the throat with my elbow. And I ran."

"Can you identify the man?"

"I never saw him. I never looked."

"His voice."

"He spoke Spanish. I think he was short because his voice was right in my ear. I don't know anything else. I don't know anything about money or Jerry or anything else." She looked back into her glass, abruptly terrified she would cry. "I want to go home."

"As soon as my men make certain it's safe. You'll have police protection, Miss Palmer. Rest here. I'll come back for you and take you home."

She didn't know if it had been minutes or hours since she'd fled through the front door. When Moralas took her back, it was dark with the moon just rising. An officer would remain outside in her driveway and all her doors and windows had been checked. Without a word, she went through the house into the kitchen.

"She was lucky." Moralas gave the living room another quick check. "Whoever attacked her was careless enough to be caught off guard."

"Did the neighbors see anything?" Jonas righted a table that had been overturned in flight. There was a conch shell on the floor that had cracked.

"A few people noticed a blue compact outside the

house late this afternoon. Señora Alderez saw it drive off when she opened the door to Miss Palmer, but she couldn't identify the make or the plates. We will, of course, keep Miss Palmer under surveillance while we try to track it down."

"It doesn't appear my brother's killer's left the island."

Moralas met Jonas's gaze blandly. "Apparently whatever deal your brother was working on cost him his life. I don't intend for it to cost Miss Palmer hers. I'll drive you back to town."

"No. I'm staying." Jonas examined the pale pink shell with the crack spreading down its length. He thought of the mark on Liz's throat. "My brother involved her." Carefully, he set the damaged shell down. "I can't leave her alone."

"As you wish." Moralas turned to go when Jonas stopped him.

"Captain, you don't still think the murderer's hundreds of miles away."

Moralas touched the gun that hung at his side. "No, Mr. Sharpe, I don't. *Buenas noches.*"

Jonas locked her door himself, then rechecked the windows before he went back to the kitchen. Liz was pouring her second cup of coffee. "That'll keep you up."

Liz drank half a cup, staring at him. She felt nothing at the moment, no anger, no fear. "I thought you'd gone."

"No." Without invitation, he found a mug and poured coffee for himself.

"Why are you here?"

He took a step closer, to run a fingertip gently down the mark on her throat. "Stupid question," he murmured.

She backed up, fighting to maintain the calm she'd

clung to. If she lost control, it wouldn't be in front of him, in front of anyone. "I want to be alone."

He saw her hands tremble before she locked them tighter on the cup. "You can't always have what you want. I'll bunk in your daughter's room."

"No!" After slamming the cup down, she folded her arms across her chest. "I don't want you here."

With studied calm, he set his mug next to hers. When he took her shoulders, his hands were firm, not gentle. When he spoke, his voice was brisk, not soothing. "I'm not leaving you alone. Not now, not until they find Jerry's killer. You're involved whether you like it or not. And so, damn it, am I."

Her breath came quickly, too quickly, though she fought to steady it. "I wasn't involved until you came back and started hounding me."

He'd already wrestled with his conscience over that. Neither one of them could know if it were true. At the moment, he told himself it didn't matter. "However you're involved, you are. Whoever killed Jerry thinks you know something. You'll have an easier time convincing me you don't than you will them. It's time you started thinking about cooperating with me."

"How do I know you didn't send him here to frighten me?"

His eyes stayed on hers, cool and unwavering. "You don't. I could tell you that I don't hire men to kill women, but you wouldn't have to believe it. I could tell you I'm sorry." For the first time, his tone gentled. He lifted a hand to brush the hair back from her face and his thumb slid lightly over her cheekbone. Like the conch shell, she seemed delicate, lovely and damaged. "And that I wish I could walk away, leave you alone, let both of us go back to the way things were a few weeks ago. But I can't. We can't. So we might as well help each other."

"I don't want your help."

"I know. Sit down. I'll fix you something to eat."

She tried to back away. "You can't stay here."

"I am staying here. Tomorrow, I'm moving my things from the hotel."

"I said—"

"I'll rent the room," he interrupted, turning away to rummage through the cupboards. "Your throat's probably raw. This chicken soup should be the best thing."

She snatched the can from his hand. "I can fix my own dinner, and you're not renting a room."

"I appreciate your generosity." He took the can back from her. "But I'd rather keep it on a business level. Twenty dollars a week seems fair. You'd better take it, Liz," he added before she could speak. "Because I'm staying, one way or the other. Sit down," he said again and looked for a pot.

She wanted to be angry. It would help keep everything else bottled up. She wanted to shout at him, to throw him bodily out of her house. Instead she sat because her knees were too weak to hold her any longer.

What had happened to her control? For ten years she'd been running her own life, making every decision by herself, for herself. For ten years, she hadn't asked advice, she hadn't asked for help. Now something had taken control and decisions out of her hands, something she knew nothing about. Her life was part of a game, and she didn't know any of the rules.

She looked down and saw the tear drop on the back of her hand. Quickly, she reached up and brushed others from her cheeks. But she couldn't stop them. One more decision had been taken from her.

"Can you eat some toast?" Jonas asked her as he dumped the contents of the soup in a pan. When she didn't answer, he turned to see her sitting stiff and pale at the table, tears running unheeded down her face. He swore and turned away again. There was nothing he could do for her, he told himself. Nothing he could offer. Then, saying nothing, he came to the table, pulled a chair up beside her and waited.

"I thought he'd kill me." Her voice broke as she pressed a hand to her face. "I felt the knife against my throat and thought I was going to die. I'm so scared. Oh God, I'm so scared."

He drew her against him and let her sob out the fear. He wasn't used to comforting women. Those he knew well were too chic to shed more than a delicate drop or two. But he held her close during a storm of weeping that shook her body and left her gasping.

Her skin was icy, as if to prove the fact that fear made the blood run cold. She couldn't summon the pride to draw herself away, to seek a private spot as she'd always done in a crisis. He didn't speak to tell her everything would be fine; he didn't murmur quiet words of comfort. He was simply there. When she was drained, he still held her. The rain began slowly, patting the glass of the windows and pinging on the roof. He still held her.

When she shifted away, he rose and went back to the stove. Without a word, he turned on the burner. Minutes later he set a bowl in front of her then went back to ladle some for himself. Too tired to be ashamed, Liz began to eat. There was no sound in the kitchen but the slow monotonous plop of rain on wood, tin and glass.

She hadn't realized she could be hungry, but the bowl was empty almost before she realized it. With a little sigh, she pushed it away. He was tipped back in his chair, smoking in silence.

"Thank you."

"Okay." Her eyes were swollen, accentuating the vulnerability that always haunted them. It tugged at him, making him uneasy. Her skin, with its ripe, warm honey glow was pale, making her seem delicate and defenseless. She was a woman, he realized, that a man had to keep an emotional distance from. Get too close and you'd be sucked right in. It wouldn't do to care about her too much when he needed to use her to help both of them. From this point on, he'd have to hold the controls.

"I suppose I was more upset than I realized."

"You're entitled."

She nodded, grateful he was making it easy for her to skim over what she considered an embarrassing display of weakness. "There's no reason for you to stay here."

"I'll stay anyway."

She curled her hand into a fist, then uncurled it slowly. It wasn't possible for her to admit she wanted him to, or that for the first time in years she was frightened of being alone. Since she had to cave in, it was better to think of the arrangement on a practical level.

"All right, the room's twenty a week, first week in advance."

He grinned as he reached for his wallet. "All business?"

"I can't afford anything else." After putting the twenty on the counter, she stacked the bowls. "You'll have to see to your own food. The twenty doesn't include meals."

He watched her take the bowls to the sink and wash them. "I'll manage."

"I'll give you a key in the morning." She took a towel and meticulously dried the bowls. "Do you think he'll be back?" She tried to make her voice casual, and failed.

"I don't know." He crossed to her to lay a hand on her shoulder. "You won't be alone if he does."

When she looked at him, her eyes were steady again. Something inside him unknotted. "Are you protecting me, Jonas, or just looking for your revenge?"

"I do one, maybe I'll get the other." He twined the ends of her hair around his finger, watching the dark gold spread over his skin. "You said yourself I'm not a nice man."

"What are you?" she whispered.

"Just a man." When his gaze lifted to hers, she didn't believe him. He wasn't just a man, but a man with patience, with power and with violence. "I've wondered the same about you. You've got secrets, Elizabeth."

She was breathless. In defense, she lifted her hand to his. "They've got nothing to do with you."

"Maybe they don't. Maybe you do."

It happened very slowly, so slowly she could have stopped it. Yet she seemed unable to move. His arms slipped around her, drawing her close with an arrogant sort of laziness that should have been his undoing. Instead, Liz watched, fascinated, as his mouth lowered to hers.

She'd just thought of him as a violent man, but his lips were soft, easy, persuading. It had been so long since she'd allowed herself to be persuaded. With barely any pressure, with only the slightest hint of power, he sapped the will she'd always relied on. Her mind raced with questions, then clouded over to a fine, smoky mist. She wasn't aware of how sweetly, how hesitantly her mouth answered his.

Whatever impulse had driven him to kiss her was lost in the reality of mouth against mouth. He'd expected her to resist, or to answer with fire and passion. To find her so soft, yielding, unsteady, had his own desire building in a way he'd never experienced. It was as though she'd never been kissed before, never been held close to explore what man and woman have for each other. Yet she had a daughter, he reminded himself. She'd had a child, she was young, beautiful. Other men had held her like this. Yet he felt like the first and had no choice but to treat her with care.

The more she gave, the more he wanted. He'd known needs before. The longer he held her, the longer he wanted to. He understood passions. But a part of himself he couldn't understand held back, demanded restraint. She wanted him—he could feel it. But even as his blood began to swim, his hands, as if under their own power, eased her away.

Needs, so long unstirred, churned in her. As she stared back at him, Liz felt them spring to life, with all their demands and risks. It wouldn't happen to her again. But even as she renewed the vow she felt the soft, fluttering longings waltz through her. It couldn't happen again. But the eyes that were wide and on his reflected confusion and hurt and hope. It was a combination that left Jonas shaken.

"You should get some sleep," he told her, and took care not to touch her again.

So that was all, Liz thought as the flicker of hope died. It was foolish to believe, even for a moment, anything could change. She brought her chin up and straightened her shoulders. Perhaps she'd lost control of many things, but she could still control her heart. "I'll give you a receipt for the rent and the key in the morning. I get up at six." She took the twenty-dollar bill she'd left on the counter and walked out.

Chapter Four

The jury was staring at him. Twelve still faces with blank eyes were lined behind the rail. Jonas stood before them in a small, harshly lit courtroom that echoed with his own voice. He carried stacks of law books, thick, dusty and heavy enough to make his arms ache. But he knew he couldn't put them down. Sweat rolled down his temples, down his back as he gave an impassioned closing plea for his client's acquittal. It was life and death, and his voice vibrated with both. The jury remained unmoved, disinterested. Though he struggled to hold them, the books began to slip from his grasp. He heard the verdict rebound, bouncing off the courtroom walls.

Guilty. Guilty. Guilty.

Defeated, empty-handed, he turned to the defendant. The man stood, lifting his head so that they stared, eye to eye, twin images. Himself? Jerry. Desperate, Jonas walked to the bench. In black robes, Liz sat above him, aloof with distance. But her eyes were sad as she slowly shook her head. "I can't help you."

Slowly, she began to fade. He reached up to grab her hand, but his fingers passed through hers. All he could see were her dark, sad eyes. Then she was gone, his brother was gone, and he was left facing a jury—twelve cold faces who smiled smugly back at him.

Jonas lay still, breathing quickly. He found himself staring back at the cluster of gaily dressed dolls on the shelf beside the bed. A flamenco dancer raised her castanets. A princess held a glass slipper. A spiffily dressed Barbie relaxed in a pink convertible, one hand raised in a wave.

Letting out a long breath, Jonas ran a hand over his face and sat up. It was like trying to sleep in the middle of a party, he decided. No wonder he'd had odd dreams. On the opposing wall was a collection of stuffed animals ranging from the dependable bear to something that looked like a blue dust rag with eyes.

Coffee, Jonas thought, closing his own. He needed coffee. Trying to ignore the dozens of smiling faces surrounding him, he dressed. He wasn't sure how or where to begin. The coin on his chain dangled before he pulled a shirt over his chest. Outside, birds were sending up a clatter. At home there would have been the sound of traffic as Philadelphia awoke for the day. He could see a bush close to the window where purple flowers seemed to crowd each other for room. There were no sturdy elms, no tidy evergreen hedges or chain-link fences. No law books would help him with what he had to do. There was nothing familiar, no precedents to follow. Each step he took would be taken blindly, but he had to take them. He smelled the coffee the moment he left the room.

Liz was in the kitchen dressed in a T-shirt and what appeared to be the bottoms of a skimpy bikini. Jonas wasn't a man who normally awoke with all batteries charged, but he didn't miss a pair of long, honey-toned legs. Liz finished buttering a piece of toast.

"Coffee's on the stove," she said without turning around. "There're some eggs in the refrigerator. I don't stock cereal when Faith's away."

"Eggs are fine," he mumbled, but headed for the coffee.

"Use what you want, as long as you replace it." She turned up the radio to listen to the weather forecast. "I leave in a half hour, so if you want a ride to your hotel, you'll have to be ready."

Jonas let the first hot taste of coffee seep into his system. "My car's in San Miguel."

Liz sat down at the table to go over that day's schedule. "I can drop you by the El Presidente or one of the other hotels on the beach. You'll have to take a cab from there."

Jonas took another sip of coffee and focused on her fully. She was still pale, he realized, so that the marks on her neck stood out in dark relief. The smudges under her eyes made him decide she'd slept no better than he had. He tossed off his first cup of coffee and poured another.

"Ever consider taking a day off?"

She looked at him for the first time. "No," she said simply and lowered her gaze to her list again.

So they were back to business, all business, and don't cross the line. "Don't you believe in giving yourself a break, Liz?"

"I've got work to do. You'd better fix those eggs if you

want to have time to eat them. The frying pan's in the cupboard next to the stove."

He studied her for another minute, then with a restless movement of his shoulders prepared to cook his breakfast. Liz waited until she was sure his back was to her before she looked up again.

She'd made a fool of herself the night before. She could almost accept the fact that she'd broken down in front of him because he'd taken it so matter-of-factly. But when she added the moments she'd stood in his arms, submissive, willing, hoping, she couldn't forgive herself. Or him.

He'd made her feel something she hadn't felt in a decade. Arousal. He'd made her want what she'd been convinced she didn't want from a man. Affection. She hadn't backed away or brushed him aside as she'd done with any other man who'd approached her. She hadn't even tried. He'd made her feel soft again, then he'd shrugged her away.

So it would be business, she told herself. Straight, impersonal business as long as he determined to stay. She'd put the rent money aside until she could manage the down payment on the aqua bikes. Jonas sat at the table with a plate of eggs that sent steam rising toward the ceiling.

"Your key." Liz slid it over to him. "And your receipt for the first week's rent."

Without looking at it, Jonas tucked the paper in his pocket. "Do you usually take in boarders?"

"No, but I need some new equipment." She rose to pour another cup of coffee and wash her plate. The radio announced the time before she switched it off. She was ten minutes ahead of schedule, but as long as she continued to get up early enough, they wouldn't have to eat together. "Do you usually rent a room in a stranger's house rather than a hotel suite?"

He tasted the eggs and found himself vaguely dissatisfied with his own cooking. "No, but we're not strangers anymore."

Liz watched him over the rim of her cup. He looked a little rough around the edges this morning, she decided. It added a bit too much sexuality to smooth good looks. She debated offering him a razor, then rejected the notion. Too personal. "Yes, we are."

He continued to eat his eggs so that she thought he'd taken her at her word. "I studied law at Notre Dame, apprenticed with Neiram and Barker in Boston, then opened my own practice five years ago in Philadelphia." He added some salt, hoping it would jazz up his cooking. "I specialize in criminal law. I'm not married, and live alone. In an apartment," he added. "On weekends I'm remodeling an old Victorian house I bought in Chadd's Ford."

She wanted to ask him about the house—was it big, did it have those wonderful high ceilings and rich wooden floors? Were the windows tall and mullioned? Was there a garden where roses climbed on trellises? Instead she turned to rinse out her cup. "That doesn't change the fact that we're strangers."

"Whether we know each other or not, we have the same problem."

The cup rattled in the sink as it slipped from her hand. Silently, Liz picked it up again, rinsed it off and set it in the drainer. She'd chipped it, but that was a small matter at the moment. "You've got ten minutes," she said, but he took her arm before she could skirt around him.

"We do have the same problem, Elizabeth." His voice was quiet, steady. She could have hated him for that alone.

"No, we don't. You're trying to avenge your brother's death. I'm just trying to make a living."

"Do you think everything would settle down quietly if I were back in Philadelphia?"

She tugged her arm uselessly. "Yes!" Because she knew she lied, her eyes heated.

"One of the first impressions I had of you was your intelligence. I don't know why you're hiding on your pretty little island, Liz, but you've got a brain, a good one. We both know that what happened to you last night would have happened with or without me."

"All right." She relaxed her arm. "What happened wasn't because of you, but because of Jerry. That hardly makes any difference to my position, does it?"

He stood up slowly, but didn't release her arm. "As long as someone thinks you knew what Jerry was into, you're the focus. As long as you're the focus, I'm standing right beside you, because directly or indirectly, you're going to lead me to Jerry's killer."

Liz waited a moment until she was sure she could speak calmly. "Is that all people are to you, Jonas? Tools? Means to an end?" She searched his face and found it set and remote. "Men like you never look beyond their own interests."

Angry without knowing why, he cupped her face in his hand. "You've never known a man like me."

"I think I have," she said softly. "You're not unique, Jonas. You were raised with money and expectations, you went to the best schools and associated with the best people. You had your goal set and if you had to step on or over a few people on the way to it, it wasn't personal.

That's the worst of it," she said on a long breath. "It's never personal." Lifting her chin, she pushed his hand from her face. "What do you want me to do?"

Never in his life had anyone made him feel so vile. With a few words she'd tried and condemned him. He remembered the dream, and the blank, staring eyes of the jury. He swore at her and turned to pace to the window. He couldn't back away now, no matter how she made him feel because he was right—whether he was here or in Philadelphia, she was still the key.

There was a hammock outside, bright blue and yellow strings stretched between two palms. He wondered if she ever gave herself enough time to use it. He found himself wishing he could take her hand, walk across the yard and lie with her on the hammock with nothing more important to worry about than swatting at flies.

"I need to talk to Luis," he began. "I want to know the places he went with Jerry, the people he may have seen Jerry talk to."

"I'll talk to Luis." When Jonas started to object, Liz shook her head. "You saw his reaction yesterday. He wouldn't be able to talk to you because you make him too nervous. I'll get you a list."

"All right." Jonas fished for his cigarettes and found with some annoyance that he'd left them in the bedroom. "I'll need you to go with me, starting tonight, to the places Luis gives you."

A feeling of stepping into quicksand came strongly. "Why?"

He wasn't sure of the answer. "Because I have to start somewhere."

"Why do you need me?"

And even less sure of this one. "I don't know how long it'll take, and I'm not leaving you alone."

She lifted a brow. "I have police protection."

"Not good enough. In any case, you know the language, the customs. I don't. I need you." He tucked his thumbs in his pockets. "It's as simple as that."

Liz walked over to turn off the coffee and move the pot to a back burner. "Nothing's simple," she corrected. "But I'll get your list, and I'll go along with you under one condition."

"Which is?"

She folded her hands. Jonas was already certain by her stance alone that she wasn't set to bargain but to lay down the rules. "That no matter what happens, what you find out or don't find out, you're out of this house and out of my life when my daughter comes home. I'll give you four weeks, Jonas—that's all."

"It'll have to be enough."

She nodded and started out of the room. "Wash your dishes. I'll meet you out front."

The police car still sat in the driveway when Jonas walked out the front door. A group of children stood on the verge of the road and discussed it in undertones. He heard Liz call one of them by name before she took out a handful of coins. Jonas didn't have to speak Spanish to recognize a business transaction. Moments later, coins in hand, the boy raced back to his friends.

"What was that about?"

Liz smiled after them. Faith would play with those same children throughout the summer. "I told them they were detectives. If they see anyone but you or the police around the house, they're to run right home and call Captain Moralas. It's the best way to keep them out of trouble."

Jonas watched the boy in charge pass out the coins. "How much did you give them?"

"Twenty pesos apiece."

He thought of the current rate of exchange and shook his head. "No kid in Philadelphia would give you the time of day for that."

"This is Cozumel," she said simply and wheeled out her bike.

Jonas looked at it, then at her. The bike would have sent a young teenager into ecstasies. "You drive this thing?"

Something in his tone made her want to smile. Instead, she kept her voice cool. "This thing is an excellent mode of transportation."

"A BMW's an excellent mode of transportation."

She laughed. He hadn't heard her laugh so easily since he'd met her. When she looked back at him, her eyes were warm and friendly. Jonas felt the ground shift dangerously under his feet. "Try to take your BMW on some of the back roads to the coast or into the interior." She swung a leg over the seat. "Hop on, Jonas, unless you want to hike back to the hotel."

Though he had his doubts, Jonas sat behind her. "Where do I put my feet?"

She glanced down and didn't bother to hide the grin. "Well, if I were you, I'd keep them off the ground." With this she started the engine then swung the bike around in the driveway. After adjusting for the added weight, Liz kept the speed steady. Jonas kept his hands lightly at her hips as the bike swayed around ruts and potholes.

"Are there roads worse than this?"

Liz sped over a bump. "What's wrong with this?"

"Just asking."

"If you want sophistication, try Cancun. It's only a few minutes by air."

"Ever get there?"

"Now and again. Last year Faith and I took the *Expatriate* over and spent a couple of days seeing the ruins. We have some shrines here. They're not well restored, but you shouldn't miss them. Still, I wanted her to see the pyramids and walled cities around Cancun."

"I don't know much about archaeology."

"You don't have to. All you need's an imagination."

She tooted the horn. Jonas saw an old, bent man straighten from the door of a shop and wave. "Señor Pessado," she said. "He gives Faith candy they both think I don't know about."

Jonas started to ask her about her daughter, then decided to wait for a better time. As long as she was being expansive, it was best to keep things less personal. "Do you know a lot of people on the island?"

"It's like a small town, I suppose. You don't necessarily have to know someone to recognize their face. I don't know a lot of people in San Miguel or on the east coast. I know a few people from the interior because we worked at the hotel."

"I didn't realize your shop was affiliated with the hotel."

"It's not." She paused at a stop sign. "I used to work in the hotel. As a maid." Liz gunned the engine and zipped across the intersection.

He looked at her hands, lean and delicate on the handlebars. He studied her slender shoulders, thought of the slight hips he was even now holding. It was difficult to imagine her lugging buckets and pails. "I'd have thought you more suited to the front desk or the concierge."

"I was lucky to find work at all, especially during the off season." She slowed the bike a bit as she started down the long drive to El Presidente. She'd indulge herself for a moment by enjoying the tall elegant palms that lined the road and the smell of blooming flowers. She was taking one of the dive boats out today, with five beginners who'd need instruction and constant supervision, but she wondered about the people inside the hotel who came to such a place to relax and to play.

"Is it still gorgeous inside?" she asked before she could stop herself.

Jonas glanced ahead to the large stately building. "Lots of glass," he told her. "Marble. The balcony of my room looks out over the water." She steered the bike to the curb. "Why don't you come in? See for yourself."

She was tempted. Liz had an affection for pretty things, elegant things. It was a weakness she couldn't allow herself. "I have to get to work."

Jonas stepped onto the curb, but put his hand over hers before she could drive away. "I'll meet you at the house. We'll go into town together."

She only nodded before turning the bike back toward the road. Jonas watched her until the sound of the motor died away. Just who was Elizabeth Palmer? he wondered. And why was it becoming more and more important that he find out?

By evening she was tired. Liz was used to working long hours, lugging equipment, diving, surfacing. But after a fairly easy day, she was tired. It should have made her feel secure to have had the young policeman identify himself to her and join her customers on the dive boat. It should have eased her mind that Captain Moralas was keeping his word about protection. It made her feel caged.

All during the drive home, she'd been aware of the police cruiser keeping a discreet distance. She'd wanted to run into her house, lock the door and fall into a dreamless, private sleep. But Jonas was waiting. She found him on the phone in her living room, a legal pad on his lap and a scowl on his face. Obviously a complication at his office had put him in a nasty mood. Ignoring him, Liz went to shower and change.

Because her wardrobe ran for the most part to beachwear, she didn't waste time studying her closet. Without enthusiasm, she pulled out a full cotton skirt in peacock blue and matched it with an oversized red shirt. More to prolong her time alone than for any other reason, she fiddled with her little cache of makeup. She was stalling, brushing out her braided hair, when Jonas knocked on her door. He didn't give her time to answer before he pushed it open.

"Did you get the list?"

Liz picked up a piece of notepaper. She could, of course, snap at him for coming in, but the end result wouldn't change. "I told you I would."

He took the paper from her to study it. He'd shaved, she noticed, and wore a casually chic jacket over bone-colored slacks. But the smoothness and gloss didn't mesh with the toughness around his mouth and in his eyes. "Do you know these places?"

"I've been to a couple of them. I don't really have a lot of time for bar-or club-hopping."

He glanced up and his curt answer slipped away. The shades behind her were up as she preferred them, but the light coming through the windows was pink with early evening. Though she'd buttoned the shirt high over her throat, her hair was brushed back, away from her face. She'd dawdled over the makeup, but her hand was always conservative. Her lashes were darkened, the lids lightly touched with shadow. She'd brushed some color over her cheeks but not her lips.

"You should be careful what you do to your eyes," Jonas murmured, absently running his thumb along the top curve of her cheek. "They're a problem."

She felt the quick, involuntary tug but stood still. "A problem?"

"My problem." Uneasy, he tucked the paper in his pocket and glanced around the room. "Are you ready?"

"I need my shoes."

He didn't leave her as she'd expected, instead wandering around her room. It was, as was the rest of the house, furnished simply but with jarring color. The spicy scent he'd noticed before came from a wide green bowl filled with potpourri. On the wall were two colored sketches, one of a sunset very much like the quietly brilliant one outside the window, and another of a storm-tossed beach. One was all serenity, the other all violence. He wondered how much of each were inside Elizabeth Palmer. Prominent next to the bed was a framed photograph of a young girl.

She was all smiles in a flowered blouse tucked at the shoulders. Her hair came to a curve at her jawline, black and shiny. A tooth was missing, adding charm to an oval, tanned face. If it hadn't been for the eyes, Jonas would never have connected the child with Liz. They were richly, deeply brown, slightly tilted. Still, they laughed out of the photo, open and trusting, holding none of the secrets of her mother's.

"This is your daughter."

"Yes." Liz slipped on the second shoe before taking the photo out of Jonas's hand and setting it down again.

"How old is she?"

"Ten. Can we get started? I don't want to be out late."

"Ten?" A bit stunned, Jonas stopped her with a look. He'd assumed Faith was half that age, a product of a relationship Liz had fallen into while on the island. "You can't have a ten-year-old child."

Liz glanced down at the picture of her daughter. "I do have a ten-year-old child."

"You'd have been a child yourself."

"No. No, I wasn't." She started to leave again, and again he stopped her.

"Was she born before you came here?"

Liz gave him a long, neutral look. "She was born six months after I moved to Cozumel. If you want my help, Jonas, we go now. Answering questions about Faith isn't part of our arrangement."

But he didn't let go of her hand. As it could become so unexpectedly, his voice was gentle. "He was a bastard, wasn't he?"

She met his eyes without wavering. Her lips curved, but not with humor. "Yes. Oh yes, he was."

Without knowing why he was compelled to, Jonas bent and just brushed her lips with his. "Your daughter's lovely, Elizabeth. She has your eyes."

She felt herself softening again, too much, too quickly. There was understanding in his voice without pity. Nothing could weaken her more. In defense she took a step back. "Thank you. Now we have to go. I have to be up early tomorrow."

* * *

The first club they hit was noisy and crowded with a high percentage of American clientele. In a corner booth, a man in a tight white T-shirt spun records on a turntable and announced each selection with a display of colored lights. They ordered a quick meal in addition to drinks while Jonas hoped someone would have a reaction to his face.

"Luis said they came in here a lot because Jerry liked hearing American music." Liz nibbled on hot nachos as she looked around. It wasn't the sort of place she normally chose to spend an evening. Tables were elbow to elbow, and the music was pitched to a scream. Still, the crowd seemed good-natured enough, shouting along with the music or just shouting to each other. At the table beside them a group of people experimented with a bottle of tequila and a bowl of lemon wedges. Since they were a group of young gringos, she assumed they'd be very sick in the morning.

It was definitely Jerry's milieu, Jonas decided. Loud, just this side of wild and crammed to the breaking point. "Did Luis say if he spoke with anyone in particular?"

"Women." Liz smiled a bit as she sampled a tortilla. "Luis was very impressed with Jerry's ability to…interest the ladies."

"Any particular lady?"

"Luis said there was one, but Jerry just called her baby."

"An old trick," Jonas said absently.

"Trick?"

"If you call them all baby, you don't mix up names and complicate the situation."

"I see." She sipped her wine and found it had a delicate taste.

"Could Luis describe her?"

"Only that she was a knockout—a Mexican knockout, if that helps. She had lots of hair and lots of hip. Luis's words," Liz added when Jonas gave her a mild look. "He also said there were a couple of men Jerry talked to a few times, but he always went over to them, so Luis didn't know what they spoke about. One was American, one was Mexican. Since Luis was more interested in the ladies, he didn't pay any attention. But he did say Jerry would cruise the bars until he met up with them, then he'd usually call it a night."

"Did he meet them here?"

"Luis said it never seemed to be in the same place twice."

"Okay, finish up. We'll cruise around ourselves."

By the fourth stop, Liz was fed up. She noticed that Jonas no more than toyed with a drink at each bar, but she was tired of the smell of liquor. Some places were quiet, and on the edge of seamy. Others were raucous and lit with flashing lights. Faces began to blur together. There were young people, not so young people. There were Americans out for exotic nightlife, natives celebrating a night on the town. Some courted on dance floors or over tabletops. She saw those who seemed to have nothing but time and money, and others who sat alone nursing a bottle and a black mood.

"This is the last one," Liz told him as Jonas found a table at a club with a crowded dance floor and recorded music.

Jonas glanced at his watch. It was barely eleven. Action rarely heated up before midnight. "All right," he said easily, and decided to distract her. "Let's dance."

Before she could refuse, he was pulling her into the crowd. "There's no room," she began, but his arms came around her.

"We'll make some." He had her close, his hand trailing up her back. "See?"

"I haven't danced in years," she muttered, and he laughed.

"There's no room anyway." Locked together, jostled by the crowd, they did no more than sway.

"What's the purpose in all this?" she demanded.

"I don't know until I find it. Meantime, don't you ever relax?" He rubbed his palm up her back again, finding the muscles taut.

"No."

"Let's try it this way." His gaze skimmed the crowd as he spoke. "What do you do when you're not working?"

"I think about working."

"Liz."

"All right, I read—books on marine life mostly."

"Busman's holiday?"

"It's what interests me."

Her body shifted intimately against his. Jonas forgot to keep his attention on the crowd and looked down at her. "*All* that interests you?"

He was too close. Liz tried to ease away and found his arms very solid. In spite of her determination to remain unmoved, her heart began to thud lightly in her head. "I don't have time for anything else."

She wore no perfume, he noted, but carried the scent of powder and spice. He wondered if her body would look as delicate as it felt against his. "It sounds as though you limit yourself."

"I have a business to run," she murmured. Would it be the same if he kissed her again? Sweet, overpowering. His lips were so close to hers, closer still when he ran his hand through her hair and drew her head back. She could almost taste him.

"Is making money so important?"

"It has to be," she managed, but could barely remember why. "I need to buy some aqua bikes."

Her eyes were soft, drowsy. They made him feel invulnerable. "Aqua bikes?"

"If I don't keep up with the competition…" He pressed a kiss to the corner of her mouth.

"The competition?" he prompted.

"I…the customers will go someplace else. So I…" The kiss teased the other corner.

"So?"

"I have to buy the bikes before the summer season."

"Of course. But that's weeks away. I could make love with you dozens of times before then. Dozens," he repeated as she stared at him. Then he closed his mouth over hers.

He felt her jolt—surprise, resistance, passion—he couldn't be sure. He only knew that holding her had led to wanting her and wanting to needing. By nature, he was a man who preferred his passion in private, quiet spots of his own choosing. Now he forgot the crowded club, loud music and flashing lights. They no longer swayed, but were hemmed into a corner of the dance floor, surrounded, pressed close. Oblivious.

She felt her head go light, heard the music fade. The heat from his body seeped into hers and flavored the kiss.

Hot, molten, searing. Though they stood perfectly still, Liz had visions of racing. The breath backed up in her lungs until she released it with a shuddering sigh. Her body, coiled like a spring, went lax on a wave of confused pleasure. She strained closer, reaching up to touch his face. Abruptly the music changed from moody to rowdy. Jonas shifted her away from flailing arms.

"Poor timing," he murmured.

She needed a minute. "Yes." But she meant it in a more general way. It wasn't a matter of time and place, but a matter of impossibility. She started to move away when Jonas's grip tightened on her. "What is it?" she began, but only had to look at his face.

Cautiously, she turned to see what he stared at. A woman in a skimpy red dress stared back at him. Liz recognized the shock in her eyes before the woman turned and fled, leaving her dance partner gaping.

"Come on." Without waiting for her, Jonas sprinted through the crowd. Dodging, weaving and shoving when she had to, Liz dashed after him.

The woman had barely gotten out to the street when Jonas caught up to her. "What are you running away from?" he demanded. His fingers dug into her arms as he held her back against a wall.

"Por favor, no comprendo," she murmured and shook like a leaf.

"Oh yes, I think you do." With his fingers bruising her arms, Jonas towered over her until she nearly squeaked in fear. "What do you know about my brother?"

"Jonas." Appalled, Liz stepped between them. "If this is the way you intend to behave, you'll do without my help." She turned away from him and touched the woman's shoulder. *"Lo siento mucho,"* she began, apologizing for Jonas. "He's lost his brother. His brother, Jerry Sharpe. Did you know him?"

She looked at Liz and whispered. "He has Jerry's face. But he's dead—I saw in the papers."

"This is Jerry's brother, Jonas. We'd like to talk to you."

As Liz had, the woman had already sensed the difference between Jonas and the man she'd known. She'd never have cowered away from Jerry for the simple reason that she'd known herself to be stronger and more clever. The man looming over her now was a different matter.

"I don't know anything."

"*Por favor.* Just a few minutes."

"Tell her I'll make it worth her while," Jonas added before she could refuse again. Without waiting for Liz to translate, he reached for his wallet and took out a bill. He saw fear change to speculation.

"A few minutes," she agreed, but pointed to an outdoor café. "There."

Jonas ordered two coffees and a glass of wine. "Ask her her name," he told Liz.

"I speak English." The woman took out a long, slim cigarette and tapped it on the tabletop. "I'm Erika. Jerry and I were friends." More relaxed, she smiled at Jonas. "You know, good friends."

"Yes, I know."

"He was very good-looking," she added, then caught her bottom lip between her teeth. "Lots of fun."

"How long did you know him?"

"A couple of weeks. I was sorry when I heard he was dead."

"Murdered," Jonas stated.

Erika took a deep drink of wine. "Do you think it was because of the money?"

Every muscle in his body tensed. Quickly, he shot Liz a warning look before she could speak. "I don't know— it looks that way. How much did he tell you about it?"

"Oh, just enough to intrigue me. You know." She smiled again and held out her cigarette for a light. "Jerry was very charming. And generous." She remembered the little gold bracelet he'd bought for her and the earrings with the pretty blue stones. "I thought he was very rich, but he said he would soon be much richer. I like charming men, but I especially like rich men. Jerry said when he had the money, we could take a trip." She blew out smoke again before giving a philosophical little shrug. "Then he was dead."

Jonas studied her as he drank coffee. She was, as Luis had said, a knockout. And she wasn't stupid. He was also certain her mind was focusing on one point, and one point alone. "Do you know when he was supposed to have the money?"

"Sure, I had to take off work if we were going away. He called me—it was Sunday. He was so excited. 'Erika,' he said, 'I hit the jackpot.' I was a little mad because he hadn't shown up Saturday night. He told me he'd done some quick business in Acapulco and how would I like to spend a few weeks in Monte Carlo?" She gave Jonas a lash-fluttering smile. "I decided to forgive him. I was packed," she added, blowing smoke past Jonas's shoulder. "We were supposed to leave Tuesday afternoon. I saw in the papers Monday night that he was dead. The papers said nothing about the money."

"Do you know who he had business with?"

"No. Sometimes he would talk to another American,

a skinny man with pale hair. Other times he would see a Mexican. I didn't like him—he had *mal ojo*."

"Evil eye," Liz interpreted. "Can you describe him?"

"Not pretty," she said offhandedly. "His face was pitted. His hair was long in the back, over his collar and he was very thin and short." She glanced at Jonas again with a sultry smile that heated the air. "I like tall men."

"Do you know his name?"

"No. But he dressed very nicely. Nice suits, good shoes. And he wore a silver band on his wrist, a thin one that crossed at the ends. It was very pretty. Do you think he knows about the money? Jerry said it was lots of money."

Jonas merely reached for his wallet. "I'd like to find out his name," he told her and set a fifty on the table. His hand closed over hers as she reached for it. "His name, and the name of the American. Don't hold out on me, Erika."

With a toss of her head, she palmed the fifty. "I'll find out the names. When I tell you, it's another fifty."

"When you tell me." He scrawled Liz's number on the back of a business card. "Call this number when you have something."

"Okay." She slipped the fifty into her purse as she stood up. "You know, you don't look as much like Jerry as I thought." With the click of high heels, she crossed the pavement and went back into the club.

"It's a beginning," Jonas murmured as he pushed his coffee aside. When he looked over, he saw Liz studying him. "Problem?"

"I don't like the way you work."

He dropped another bill on the table before he rose. "I don't have time to waste on amenities."

"What would you have done if I hadn't calmed her down? Dragged her off to the nearest alley and beaten it out of her?"

He drew out a cigarette, struggling with temper. "Let's go home, Liz."

"I wonder if you're any different from the men you're looking for." She pushed back from the table. "Just as a matter of interest, the man who broke into my house and attacked me wore a thin band at his wrist. I felt it when he held the knife to my throat."

She watched as his gaze lifted from the flame at the end of the cigarette and came to hers. "I think you two might recognize each other when the time comes."

Chapter Five

"Always check your gauges," Liz instructed, carefully indicating each one on her own equipment as she spoke. "Each one of these gauges is vital to your safety when you dive. That's true if it's your first dive or your fiftieth. It's very easy to become so fascinated not only by the fish and coral, but the sensation of diving itself, that you can forget you're dependent on your air tank. Always be certain you start your ascent while you have five or ten minutes of air left."

She'd covered everything, she decided, in the hour lesson. If she lectured any more, her students would be too impatient to listen. It was time to give them a taste of what they were paying for.

"We'll dive as a group. Some of you may want to explore on your own, but remember, always swim in pairs. As a final precaution, check the gear of the diver next to you."

Liz strapped on her own weight belt as her group of novices followed instructions. So many of them, she knew, looked on scuba diving as an adventure. That was fine, as long as they remembered safety. Whenever she instructed, she stressed the what ifs just as thoroughly as the how tos. Anyone who went down under her supervision would know what steps to take under any circumstances. Diving accidents were most often the result of carelessness. Liz was never careless with herself or with her students. Most of them were talking excitedly as they strapped on tanks.

"This group." Luis hefted his tank. "Very green."

"Yeah." Liz helped him with the straps. As she did with all her employees, Liz supplied Luis's gear. It was checked just as thoroughly as any paying customer's. "Keep an eye on the honeymoon couple, Luis. They're more interested in each other than their regulators."

"No problem." He assisted Liz with her tank, then stepped back while she cinched the straps. "You look tired, kid."

"No, I'm fine."

When she turned, he glanced at the marks on her neck. The story had already made the rounds. "You sure? You don't look so fine."

She lifted a brow as she hooked on her diving knife. "Sweet of you."

"Well, I mean it. You got me worried about you."

"No need to worry." As Liz pulled on her mask, she glanced over at the roly-poly fatherly type who was struggling with his flippers. He was her bodyguard for the day. "The police have everything under control," she said, and hoped it was true. She wasn't nearly as sure about Jonas.

He hadn't shocked her the night before. She'd sensed

that dangerously waiting violence in him from the first. But seeing his face as he'd grabbed Erika, hearing his voice, had left her with a cold, flat feeling in her stomach. She didn't know him well enough to be certain if he would choose to control the violence or let it free. More, how could she know he was capable of leashing it? Revenge, she thought, was never pretty. And that's what he wanted. Remembering the look in his eyes, Liz was very much afraid he'd get it.

The boat listed, bringing her back to the moment. She couldn't think about Jonas now, she told herself. She had a business to run and customers to satisfy.

"Miss Palmer." A young American with a thin chest and a winning smile maneuvered over to her. "Would you mind giving me a check?"

"Sure." In her brisk, efficient way, Liz began to check gauges and hoses.

"I'm a little nervous," he confessed. "I've never done this sort of thing before."

"It doesn't hurt to be a little nervous. You'll be more careful. Here, pull your mask down. Make sure it's comfortable but snug."

He obeyed, and his eyes looked wide and pale through the glass. "If you don't mind, I think I'll stick close to you down there."

She smiled at him. "That's what I'm here for. The depth here is thirty feet," she told the group in general. "Remember to make your adjustments for pressure and gravity as you descend. Please keep the group in sight at all times." With innate fluidity, she sat on the deck and rolled into the water. With Luis on deck, and Liz treading a few feet away, they waited until each student made his dive. With a final adjustment to her mask, Liz went under.

She'd always loved it. The sensation of weightlessness, the fantasy of being unimpeded, invulnerable. From near the surface, the sea floor was a spread of white. She loitered there a moment, enjoying the cathedral-like view. Then, with an easy kick, she moved down with her students.

The newlyweds were holding hands and having the time of their lives. Liz reminded herself to keep them in sight. The policeman assigned to her was plodding along like a sleepy sea turtle. He'd keep her in sight. Most of the others remained in a tight group, fascinated but cautious. The thin American gave her a wide-eyed look that was a combination of pleasure and nerves and stuck close by her side. To help him relax, Liz touched his shoulder and pointed up. In an easy motion, she turned on her back so that she faced the surface. Sunlight streaked thinly through the water. The hull of the dive boat was plainly visible. He nodded and followed her down.

Fish streamed by, some in waves, some on their own. Though the sand was white, the water clear, there was a montage of color. Brain coral rose up in sturdy mounds, the color of saffron. Sea fans, as delicate as lace, waved pink and purple in the current. She signaled to her companion and watched a school of coral sweepers, shivering with metallic tints, turn as a unit and skim through staghorn coral.

It was a world she understood as well as, perhaps better, than the one on the surface. Here, in the silence, Liz often found the peace of mind that eluded her from day to day. The scientific names of the fish and formations they passed were no strangers to her. Once she'd studied them diligently, with dreams of solving mysteries and bringing the beauty of the world of the sea to others. That had been another life. Now she coached tourists and gave them, for hourly rates, something memorable to take home after a vacation. It was enough.

Amused, she watched an angelfish busy itself by swallowing the bubbles rising toward the surface. To entertain her students, she poked at a small damselfish. The pugnacious male clung to his territory and nipped at her. To the right, she saw sand kick up and cloud the water. Signaling for caution, Liz pointed out the platelike ray that skimmed away, annoyed by the intrusion.

The new husband showed off a bit, turning slow somersaults for his wife. As divers gained confidence, they spread out a little farther. Only her bodyguard and the nervous American stayed within an arm span at all times. Throughout the thirty-minute dive, Liz circled the group, watching individual divers. By the time the lesson was over, she was satisfied that her customers had gotten their money's worth. This was verified when they surfaced.

"Great!" A British businessman on his first trip to Mexico clambered back onto the deck. His face was reddened by the sun but he didn't seem to mind. "When can we go down again?"

With a laugh, Liz helped other passengers on board. "You have to balance your down time with your surface time. But we'll go down again."

"What was that feathery-looking stuff?" someone else asked. "It grows like a bush."

"It's a gorgonian, from the Gorgons of mythology." She slipped off her tanks and flexed her muscles. "If you remember, the Gorgons had snakes for hair. The whip gorgonian has a resilient skeletal structure and undulates like a snake with the current."

More questions were tossed out, more answers supplied. Liz noticed the American who'd stayed with her, sitting by himself, smiling a little. Liz moved around gear then dropped down beside him.

"You did very well."

"Yeah?" He looked a little dazed as he shrugged his shoulders. "I liked it, but I gotta admit, I felt better knowing you were right there. You sure know what you're doing."

"I've been at it a long time."

He sat back, unzipping his wet suit to his waist. "I don't mean to be nosy, but I wondered about you. You're American, aren't you?"

It had been asked before. Liz combed her fingers through her wet hair. "That's right."

"From?"

"Houston."

"No kidding." His eyes lit up. "Hell, I went to school in Texas. Texas A and M."

"Really?" The little tug she felt rarely came and went. "So did I, briefly."

"Small world," he said, pleased with himself. "I like Texas. Got a few friends in Houston. I don't suppose you know the Dresscots?"

"No."

"Well, Houston isn't exactly small-town U.S.A." He stretched out long, skinny legs that were shades paler than his arms but starting to tan. "So you went to Texas A and M."

"That's right."

"What'd you study?"

She smiled and looked out to sea. "Marine biology."

"Guess that fits."

"And you?"

"Accounting." He flashed his grin again. "Pretty dry stuff. That's why I always take a long breather after tax time."

"Well, you chose a great place to take it. Ready to go down again?"

He took a long breath as if to steady himself. "Yeah. Hey, listen, how about a drink after we get back in?"

He was attractive in a mild sort of way, pleasant enough. She gave him an apologetic smile as she rose. "It sounds nice, but I'm tied up."

"I'll be around for a couple of weeks. Some other time?"

"Maybe. Let's check your gear."

By the time the dive boat chugged into shore, the afternoon was waning. Her customers, most of them pleased with themselves, wandered off to change for dinner or spread out on the beach. Only a few loitered near the boat, including her bodyguard and the accountant from America. It occurred to Liz that she might have been a bit brisk with him.

"I hope you enjoyed yourself, Mr...."

"Trydent. But it's Scott, and I did. I might just try it again."

Liz smiled at him as she helped Luis and another of her employees unload the boat. "That's what we're here for."

"You, ah, ever give private lessons?"

Liz caught the look. Perhaps she hadn't been brisk enough. "On occasion."

"Then maybe we could—"

"Hey, there, missy."

Liz shaded her eyes. "Mr. Ambuckle."

He stood on the little walkway, his legs bulging out of the short wet suit. What hair he had was sleeked wetly back. Beside him, his wife stood wearily in a bathing suit designed to slim down wide hips. "Just got back in!" he shouted. "Had a full day of it."

He seemed enormously pleased with himself. His wife looked at Liz and rolled her eyes. "Maybe I should take you out as crew, Mr. Ambuckle."

He laughed, slapping his side. "Guess I'd rather dive than anything." He glanced at his wife and patted her shoulder. "Almost anything. Gotta trade in these tanks, honey, and get me some fresh ones."

"Going out again?"

"Tonight. Can't talk the missus into it."

"I'm crawling into bed with a good book," she told Liz. "The only water I want to see is in the tub."

With a laugh, Liz jumped down to the walkway. "At the moment, I feel the same way. Oh, Mr. and Mrs. Ambuckle, this is Scott Trydent. He just took his first dive."

"Well now." Expansive, Ambuckle slapped him on the back. "How'd you like it?"

"Well, I—"

"Nothing like it, is there? You want try it at night, boy. Whole different ball game at night."

"I'm sure, but—"

"Gotta trade in these tanks." After slapping Scott's back again, Ambuckle hefted his tanks and waddled off toward the shop.

"Obsessed," Mrs. Ambuckle said, casting her eyes to the sky. "Don't let him get started on you, Mr. Trydent. You'll never get any peace."

"No, I won't. Nice meeting you, Mrs. Ambuckle." Obviously bemused, Scott watched her wander back toward the hotel. "Quite a pair."

"That they are." Liz lifted her own tanks. She stored them separately from her rental equipment. "Goodbye, Mr. Trydent."

"Scott," he said again. "About that drink—"

"Thanks anyway," Liz said pleasantly and left him standing on the walkway. "Everything in?" she asked Luis as she stepped into the shop.

"Checking it off now. One of the regulators is acting up."

"Set it aside for Jose to look at." As a matter of habit, she moved into the back to fill her tanks before storage. "All the boats are in, Luis. We shouldn't have too much more business now. You and the rest can go on as soon as everything's checked in. I'll close up."

"I don't mind staying."

"You closed up last night," she reminded him. "What do you want?" She tossed a grin over her shoulder. "Overtime? Go on home, Luis. You can't tell me you don't have a date."

He ran a fingertip over his mustache. "As a matter of fact…"

"A hot date?" Liz lifted a brow as air hissed into her tank.

"Is there any other kind?"

Chuckling, Liz straightened. She noticed Ambuckle trudging across the sand with his fresh tanks. Her other employees talked among themselves as the last of the gear was stored. "Well, go make yourself beautiful then. The only thing I have a date with is the account books."

"You work too much," Luis mumbled.

Surprised, Liz turned back to him. "Since when?"

"Since always. It gets worse every time you send Faith back to school. Better off if she was here."

That her voice cooled only slightly was a mark of her affection for Luis. "No, she's happy in Houston with my parents. If I thought she wasn't, she wouldn't be there."

"She's happy, sure. What about you?"

Her brows drew together as she picked her keys from a drawer. "Do I look unhappy?"

"No." Tentatively, he touched her shoulder. He'd known Liz for years, and understood there were boundaries she wouldn't let anyone cross. "But you don't look happy either. How come you don't give one of these rich American tourists a spin? That one on the boat—his eyes popped out every time he looked at you."

The exaggeration made her laugh, so she patted his cheek. "So you think a rich American tourist is the road to happiness?"

"Maybe a handsome Mexican."

"I'll think about it—after the summer season. Go home," she ordered.

"I'm going." Luis pulled a T-shirt over his chest. "You look out for that Jonas Sharpe," he added. "He's got a different kind of look in his eyes."

Liz waved him off. *"Hasta luego."*

When the shop was empty, Liz stood, jingling her keys and looking out onto the beach. People traveled in couples, she noted, from the comfortably married duo stretched out on lounge chairs, to the young man and woman curled together on a beach towel. Was it an easy feeling, she wondered, to be half of a set? Or did you automatically lose part of yourself when you joined with another?

She'd always thought of her parents as separate people, yet when she thought of one, the other came quickly to mind. Would it be a comfort to know you could reach out your hand and someone else's would curl around it?

She held out her own and remembered how hard, how strong, Jonas's had been. No, he wouldn't make a relationship a comfortable affair. Being joined with him would be demanding, even frightening. A woman would have to be strong enough to keep herself intact, and soft enough to allow herself to merge. A relationship with a man like Jonas would be a risk that would never ease.

For a moment, she found herself dreaming of it, dreaming of what it had been like to be held close and kissed as though nothing and no one else existed. To be kissed like that always, to be held like that whenever the need moved you—it might be worth taking chances for.

Stupid, she thought quickly, shaking herself out of it. Jonas wasn't looking for a partner, and she wasn't looking for a dream. Circumstances had tossed them together temporarily. Both of them had to deal with their own realities. But she felt a sense of regret and a stirring of wishes.

Because the feeling remained, just beyond her grasp, Liz concentrated hard on the little details that needed attending to before she could close up. The paperwork and the contents of the cash box were transferred to a canvas portfolio. She'd have to swing out of her way to make a night deposit, but she no longer felt safe taking the cash or the checks home. She spent an extra few minutes meticulously filling out a deposit slip.

It wasn't until she'd picked up her keys again that she remembered her tanks. Tucking the portfolio under the counter, she turned to deal with her own gear.

It was perhaps her only luxury. She'd spent more on her personal equipment than she had on all the contents of her closet and dresser. To Liz, the wet suit was more exciting than any French silks. All her gear was kept separate from the shop's inventory. Unlocking the door to the closet, Liz hung up her wet suit, stored her mask, weight belt, regulator. Her knife was sheathed and set on a shelf. After setting her tanks side by side, she shut the door and prepared to lock it again. After she'd taken two steps away she looked down at the keys again. Without knowing precisely why, she moved each one over the ring and identified it.

The shop door, the shop window, her bike, the lock for the chain, the cash box, the front and back doors of her house, her storage room. Eight keys for eight locks. But there was one more on her ring, a small silver key that meant nothing to her at all.

Puzzled, she counted off the keys again, and again found one extra. Why should there be a key on her ring that didn't belong to her? Closing her fingers over it, she tried to think if anyone had given her the key to hold. No, it didn't make sense. Brows drawn together, she studied the key again. Too small for a car or door key, she decided. It looked like the key to a locker, or a box or... Ridiculous, she decided on a long breath. It wasn't her key but it was on her ring. Why?

Because someone put it there, she realized, and opened her hand again. Her keys were often tossed in the drawer at the shop for easy access for Luis or one of the other men. They needed to open the cash box. And Jerry had often worked in the shop alone.

With a feeling of dread, Liz slipped the keys into her pocket. Jonas's words echoed in her head. *"You're involved, whether you want to be or not."*

Liz closed the shop early.

* * *

Jonas stepped into the dim bar to the scent of garlic and the wail of a squeaky jukebox. In Spanish, some-one sang of endless love. He stood for a moment, letting his eyes adjust, then skimmed his gaze over the narrow booths. As agreed, Erika sat all the way in the back, in the corner.

"You're late." She waved an unlit cigarette idly as he joined her.

"I passed it the first time. This place isn't exactly on the tourist route."

She closed her lips over the filter as Jonas lit her ciga-rette. "I wanted privacy."

Jonas glanced around. There were two men at the bar, each deep in separate bottles. Another couple squeezed themselves together on one side of a booth. The rest of the bar was deserted. "You've got it."

"But I don't have a drink."

Jonas slid out from the booth and bought two drinks at the bar. He set tequila and lime in front of Erika and set-tled for club soda. "You said you had something for me."

Erica twined a string of colored beads around her fin-ger. "You said you would pay fifty for a name."

In silence, Jonas took out his wallet. He set fifty on the table, but laid his hand over it. "You have the name."

Erika smiled and sipped at her drink. "Maybe. Maybe you want it bad enough to pay another fifty."

Jonas studied her coolly. This was the type his brother had always been attracted to. The kind of woman whose hard edge was just a bit obvious. He could give her an-other fifty, Jonas mused, but he didn't care to be taken for a sucker. Without a word, he picked up the bill and tucked it into his pocket. He was halfway out of the booth when Erika grabbed his arm.

"Okay, don't get mad. Fifty." She sent him an easy smile as he settled back again. Erika had been around too long to let an opportunity slip away. "A girl has to make a living, *sí?* The name is Pablo Manchez—he's the one with the face."

"Where can I find him?"

"I don't know. You got the name."

With a nod, Jonas took the bill out and passed it to her. Erika folded it neatly into her purse. "I'll tell you something else, because Jerry was a sweet guy." Her gaze skimmed the bar again as she leaned closer to Jonas. "This Manchez, he's bad. People got nervous when I asked about him. I heard he was mixed up in a couple of murders in Acapulco last year. He's paid, you know, to…" She made a gun out of her hand and pushed down her thumb. "When I hear that, I stop asking questions."

"What about the other one, the American?"

"Nothing. Nobody knows him. But if he hangs out with Manchez, he's not a Boy Scout." Erika tipped back her drink. "Jerry got himself in some bad business."

"Yeah."

"I'm sorry." She touched the bracelet on her wrist. "He gave me this. We had some good times."

The air in the bar was stifling him. Jonas rose and hesitated only a moment before he took out another bill and set it next to her drink. "Thanks."

Erika folded the bill as carefully as the first. *"De nada."*

She'd wanted him to be home. When Liz found the house empty, she made a fist over the keys in her hand

and swore in frustration. She couldn't sit still; her nerves had been building all during the drive home. Outside, Moralas's evening shift was taking over.

For how long? she wondered. How long would the police sit patiently outside her house and follow her through her daily routine? In her bedroom, Liz closed the canvas bag of papers and cash in her desk. She regretted not having a lock for it, as well. Sooner or later, she thought, Moralas would back off on the protection. Then where would she be? Liz looked down at the key again. She'd be alone, she told herself bluntly. She had to do something.

On impulse, she started into her daughter's room. Perhaps Jerry had left a case, a box of some kind that the police had overlooked. Systematically she searched Faith's closet. When she found the little teddy bear with the worn ear, she brought it down from the shelf. She'd bought it for Faith before she'd been born. It was a vivid shade of purple, or had been so many years before. Now it was faded a bit, a little loose at the seams. The ear had been worn down to a nub because Faith had always carried him by it. They'd never named it, Liz recalled. Faith had merely called it *mine* and been satisfied.

On a wave of loneliness that rocked her, Liz buried her face against the faded purple pile. "Oh, I miss you, baby," she murmured. "I don't know if I can stand it."

"Liz?"

On a gasp of surprise, Liz stumbled back against the closet door. When she saw Jonas, she put the bear behind her back. "I didn't hear you come in," she said, feeling foolish.

"You were busy." He came toward her to gently pry the bear from her fingers. "He looks well loved."

"He's old." She cleared her throat and took the toy

back again. But she found it impossible to stick it back on the top shelf. "I keep meaning to sew up the seams before the stuffing falls out." She set the bear down on Faith's dresser. "You've been out."

"Yes." He'd debated telling her of his meeting with Erika, and had decided to keep what he'd learned to himself, at least for now. "You're home early."

"I found something." Liz reached in her pocket and drew out her keys. "This isn't mine."

Jonas frowned at the key she indicated. "I don't know what you mean."

"I mean this isn't my key, and I don't know how it got on my ring."

"You just found it today?"

"I found it today, but it could have been put on anytime. I don't think I would've noticed." With the vain hope of distancing herself, Liz unhooked it from the others and handed it to Jonas. "I keep these in a drawer at the shop when I'm there. At home, I usually toss them on the kitchen counter. I can't think of any reason for someone to put it with mine unless they wanted to hide it."

Jonas examined the key. "'The Purloined Letter,'" he murmured.

"What?"

"It was one of Jerry's favorite stories when we were kids. I remember when he tested out the theory by putting a book he'd bought for my father for Christmas on the shelf in the library."

"So do you think it was his?"

"I think it would be just his style."

Liz picked up the bear again, finding it comforted her. "It doesn't do much good to have a key when you don't have the lock."

"It shouldn't be hard to find it." He held the key up by the stem. "Do you know what it is?"

"A key." Liz sat on Faith's bed. No, she hadn't distanced herself. The quicksand was bubbling again.

"To a safe-deposit box." Jonas turned it over to read the numbers etched into the metal.

"Do you think Captain Moralas can trace it?"

"Eventually," Jonas murmured. The key was warm in his hand. It was the next step, he thought. It had to be. "But I'm not telling him about it."

"Why?"

"Because he'd want it, and I don't intend to give it to him until I open the lock myself."

She recognized the look easily enough now. It was still revenge. Leaving the bear on her daughter's bed, Liz rose. "What are you going to do, go from bank to bank and ask if you can try the key out? You won't have to call the police, they will."

"I've got some connections—and I've got the serial number." Jonas pocketed the key. "With luck, I'll have the name of the bank by tomorrow afternoon. You may have to take a couple of days off."

"I can't take a couple of days off, and if I could, why should I need to?"

"We're going to Acapulco."

She started to make some caustic comment, then stopped. "Because Jerry told Erika he'd had business there?"

"If Jerry was mixed up in something, and he had something important or valuable, he'd tuck it away. A safe-deposit box in Acapulco makes sense."

"Fine. If that's what you believe, have a nice trip."

She started to brush past him. Jonas only had to shift his body to bar the door.

"We go together."

The word "together" brought back her thoughts on couples and comfort. And it made her remember her conclusion about Jonas. "Look, Jonas, I can't drop everything and follow you on some wild-goose chase. Acapulco is very cosmopolitan. You won't need an interpreter."

"The key was on your ring. The knife was at your throat. I want you where I can see you."

"Concerned?" Her face hardened, muscle by muscle. "You're not concerned with me, Jonas. And you're certainly not concerned *about* me. The only thing you care about is your revenge. I don't want any part of it, or you."

He took her by the shoulders until she was backed against the door. "We both know that's not true. We've started something." His gaze skimmed down, lingered on her lips. "And it's not going to stop until we're both finished with it."

"I don't know what you're talking about."

"Yes, you do." He pressed closer so that their bodies met and strained, one against the other. He pressed closer to prove something, perhaps only to himself. "Yes, you do," he repeated. "I came here to do something, and I intend to do it. I don't give a damn if you call it revenge."

Her heart was beating lightly at her throat. She wouldn't call it fear. But his eyes were cold and close. "What else?"

"Justice."

She felt an uncomfortable twinge, remembering her own feelings on justice. "You're not using your law books, Jonas."

"Law doesn't always equal justice. I'm going to find

out what happened to my brother and why." He skimmed his hand over her face and tangled his fingers in her hair. He didn't find silk and satin, but a woman of strength. "But there's more now. I look at you and I want you." He reached out, taking her face in his hand so that she had no choice but to look directly at him. "I hold you and I forget what I have to do. Damn it, you're in my way."

At the end of the words, his mouth was crushed hard on hers. He hadn't meant to. He hadn't had a choice. Before he'd been gentle with her because the look in her eyes requested it. Now he was rough, desperate, because the power of his own needs demanded it.

He frightened her. She'd never known fear could be a source of exhilaration. As her heart pounded in her throat, she let him pull her closer, still closer to the edge. He dared her to jump off, to let herself tumble down into the unknown. To risk.

His mouth drew desperately from hers, seeking passion, seeking submission, seeking strength. He wanted it all. He wanted it mindlessly from her. His hands were reaching for her as if they'd always done so. When he found her, she stiffened, resisted, then melted so quickly that it was nearly impossible to tell one mood from the next. She smelled of the sea and tasted of innocence, a combination of mystery and sweetness that drove him mad.

Forgetting everything but her, he drew her toward the bed and fulfillment.

"No." Liz pushed against him, fighting to bring herself back. They were in her daughter's room. "Jonas, this is wrong."

He took her by the shoulders. "Damn it, it may be the only thing that's right."

She shook her head, and though unsteady, backed away. His eyes weren't cold now. A woman might dream of having a man look at her with such fire and need. A woman might toss all caution aside if only to have a man want her with such turbulent desire. She couldn't.

"Not for me. I don't want this, Jonas." She reached up to push back her hair. "I don't want to feel like this."

He took her hand before she could back away. His head was swimming. There had been no other time, no other place, no other woman that had come together to make him ache. "Why?"

"I don't make the same mistake twice."

"This is now, Liz."

"And it's my life." She took a long, cleansing breath and found she could face him squarely. "I'll go with you to Acapulco because the sooner you have what you want, the sooner you'll go." She gripped her hands together tightly, the only outward sign that she was fighting herself. "You know Moralas will have us followed."

He had his own battles to fight. "I'll deal with that."

Liz nodded because she was sure he would. "Do what you have to do. I'll make arrangements for Luis to take over the shop for a day or two."

When she left him alone, Jonas closed his hands over the key again. It would open a lock, he thought. But there was another lock that mystified and frustrated him. Idly, he picked up the bear Liz had left on the bed. He looked from it to the key in his hand. Somehow he'd have to find a way to bring them together.

Chapter Six

Acapulco wasn't the Mexico Liz understood and loved. It wasn't the Mexico she'd fled to a decade before, nor where she'd made her home. It was sophisticated and ultra modern with spiraling high-rise hotels crowded together and gleaming in tropical sunlight. It was swimming pools and trendy shops. Perhaps it was the oldest resort in Mexico, and boasted countless restaurants and nightclubs, but Liz preferred the quietly rural atmosphere of her own island.

Still she had to admit there was something awesome about the city, cupped in the mountains and kissed by a magnificent bay. She'd lived all her life in flat land, from Houston to Cozumel. The mountains made everything else seem smaller, and somehow protected. Over the water, colorful parachutes floated, allowing the adventurous a bird's-eye view and a stunning ride. She wondered fleetingly if skimming through the sky would be as liberating as skimming through the water.

The streets were crowded and noisy, exciting in their own way. It occurred to her that she'd seen more people in the hour since they'd landed at the airport than she might in a week on Cozumel. Liz stepped out of the cab and wondered if she'd have time to check out any of the dive shops.

Jonas had chosen the hotel methodically. It was luxuriously expensive—just Jerry's style. The villas overlooked the Pacific and were built directly into the mountainside. Jonas took a suite, pocketed the key and left the luggage to the bellman.

"We'll go to the bank now." It had taken him two days to match the key with a name. He wasn't going to waste any more time.

Liz followed him out onto the street. True, she hadn't come to enjoy herself, but a look at their rooms and a bite of lunch didn't seem so much to ask. Jonas was already climbing into a cab. "I don't suppose you'd considered making that a request."

He gave her a brief look as she slammed the cab door. "No." After giving the driver their direction, Jonas settled back. He could understand Jerry drifting to Acapulco, with its jet-set flavor, frantic nightlife and touches of luxury. When Jerry landed in a place for more than a day, it was a city that had the atmosphere of New York, London, Chicago. Jerry had never been interested in the rustic, serene atmosphere of a spot like Cozumel. So since he'd gone there, stayed there, he'd had a purpose. In Acapulco, Jonas would find out what it was.

As to the woman beside him, he didn't have a clue. Was she caught up in the circumstances formed before

they'd ever met, or was he dragging her in deeper than
he had a right to? She sat beside him, silent and a little
sulky. Probably thinking about her shop, Jonas decided,
and wished he could send her safely back to it. He wished
he could turn around, go back to the villa and make love
with her until they were both sated.

She shouldn't have appealed to him at all. She wasn't
witty, flawlessly polished or classically beautiful. But
she did appeal to him, so much so that he was spending his nights awake and restless, and his days on the
edge of frustration. He wanted her, wanted to fully explore the tastes of passion she'd given him. He wanted
to arouse her until she couldn't think of accounts or customers or schedules. Perhaps it was a matter of wielding
power—he could no longer be sure. But mostly, inex-
plicably, he wanted to erase the memory of how she'd
looked when he'd walked into her daughter's room and
found her clutching a stuffed bear.

When the cab rolled up in front of the bank, Liz
stepped out on the curb without a word. There were shops
across the streets, boutiques where she could see bright,
wonderful dresses on cleverly posed mannequins. Even
with the distance, she caught the gleam and glimmer of
jewelry. A limousine rolled by, with smoked glass windows and quiet engine. Liz looked beyond the tall, glossy
buildings to the mountains, and space.

"I suppose this is the sort of place that appeals to you."

He'd watched her survey. She didn't have to speak for
him to understand that she'd compared Acapulco with her
corner of Mexico and found Acapulco lacking. "Under
certain circumstances." Taking her arm, Jonas led her
inside.

The bank was, as banks should be, quiet and sedate.

Clerks wore neat suits and polite smiles. What conversation there was, was carried on in murmurs. Jerry, he thought, had always preferred the ultraconservative in storing his money, just as he'd preferred the wild in spending it. Without hesitation, Jonas strolled over to the most attractive teller. "Good afternoon."

She glanced up. It only took a second for her polite smile to brighten. "Mr. Sharpe, *buenos días.* It's nice to see you again."

Beside him, Liz stiffened. He's been here before, she thought. Why hadn't he told her? She sent a long, probing look his way. Just what game was he playing?

"It's nice to see you." He leaned against the counter, urbane and, she noted, flirtatious. The little tug of jealousy was as unexpected as it was unwanted. "I wondered if you'd remember me."

The teller blushed before she glanced cautiously toward her supervisor. "Of course. How can I help you today?"

Jonas took the key out of his pocket. "I'd like to get into my box." He simply turned and stopped Liz with a look when she started to speak.

"I'll arrange that for you right away." The teller took a form, dated it and passed it to Jonas. "If you'll just sign here."

Jonas took her pen and casually dashed off a signature. Liz read: *Jeremiah C. Sharpe.* Though she looked up quickly, Jonas was smiling at the teller. Because her supervisor was hovering nearby, the teller stuck to procedure and checked the signature against the card in the files. They matched perfectly.

"This way, Mr. Sharpe."

"Isn't that illegal?" Liz murmured as the teller led them from the main lobby.

"Yes." Jonas gestured for her to precede him through the doorway.

"And does it make me an accessory?"

He smiled at her, waiting while the teller drew the long metal box from its slot. "Yes. If there's any trouble, I'll recommend a good lawyer."

"Great. All I need's another lawyer."

"You can use this booth, Mr. Sharpe. Just ring when you're finished."

"Thanks." Jonas nudged Liz inside, shut, then locked, the door.

"How did you know?"

"Know what?" Jonas set the box on a table.

"To go to that clerk? When she first spoke to you, I thought you'd been here before."

"There were three men and two women. The other woman was into her fifties. As far as Jerry would've been concerned, there would have been only one clerk there."

That line of thinking was clear enough, but his actions weren't. "You signed his name perfectly."

Key in hand, Jonas looked at her. "He was part of me. If we were in the same room, I could have told you what he was thinking. Writing his name is as easy as writing my own."

"And was it the same for him?"

It could still hurt, quickly and unexpectedly. "Yes, it was the same for him."

But Liz remembered Jerry's good-natured description of his brother as a stuffed shirt. The man Liz was beginning to know didn't fit. "I wonder if you understood each other as well as both of you thought." She looked down at the box again. None of her business, she thought, and wished it were as true as she'd once believed. "I guess you'd better open it."

He slipped the key into the lock, then turned it soundlessly. When he drew back the lid, Liz could only stare. She'd never seen so much money in her life. It sat in neat stacks, tidily banded, crisply American. Unable to resist, Liz reached out to touch.

"God, it looks like thousands." She swallowed. "Hundreds of thousands."

His face expressionless, Jonas flipped through the stacks. The booth became as quiet as a tomb. "Roughly three hundred thousand, in twenties and fifties."

"Do you think he stole it?" she murmured, too overwhelmed to notice Jonas's hands tighten on the money. "This must be the money the man who broke into my house wanted."

"I'm sure it is." Jonas set down a stack of bills and picked up a small bag. "But he didn't steal it." He forced his emotions to freeze. "I'm afraid he earned it."

"How?" she demanded. "No one earns this kind of money in a matter of days, and I'd swear Jerry was nearly broke when I hired him. I know Luis lent him ten thousand pesos before his first paycheck."

"I'm sure he was." He didn't bother to add that he'd wired his brother two hundred before Jerry had left New Orleans. Carefully, Jonas reached under the stack of money and pulled out a small plastic bag, dipped in a finger and tasted. But he'd already known.

"What is that?"

His face expressionless, Jonas sealed the bag. He couldn't allow himself any more grief. "Cocaine."

Horrified, Liz stared at the bag. "I don't understand.

He lived in my house. I'd have known if he were using drugs."

Jonas wondered if she realized just how innocent she was of the darker side of humanity. Until that moment, he hadn't fully realized just how intimate he was with it. "Maybe, maybe not. In any case, Jerry wasn't into this sort of thing. At least not for himself."

Liz sat down slowly. "You mean he sold it?"

"Dealt drugs?" Jonas nearly smiled. "No, that wouldn't have been exciting enough." In the corner of the box was a small black address book. Jonas took it out to leaf through it. "But smuggling," he murmured. "Jerry could have justified smuggling. Action, intrigue and fast money."

Her mind was whirling as she tried to focus back on the man she'd known so briefly. Liz had thought she'd understood him, categorized him, but he was more of a stranger now than when he'd been alive. It didn't seem to matter anymore who or what Jerry Sharpe had been. But the man in front of her mattered. "And you?" she asked. "Can you justify it?"

He glanced down at her, over the book in his hands. His eyes were cold, so cold that she could read nothing in them at all. Without answering, Jonas went back to the book.

"He'd listed initials, dates, times and some numbers. It looks as though he made five thousand a drop. Ten drops."

Liz glanced over at the money again. It no longer seemed crisp and neat but ugly and ill used. "That only makes fifty thousand. You said there was three hundred."

"That's right." Plus a bag of uncut cocaine with a hefty

street value. Jonas took out his own book and copied down the pages from his brother's.

"What are we going to do with this?"

"Nothing."

"Nothing?" Liz rose again, certain she'd stepped into a dream. "Do you mean just leave it here? Just leave it here in this box and walk away?"

With the last of the numbers copied, Jonas replaced his brother's book. "Exactly."

"Why did we come if we're not going to do anything with it?"

He slipped his own book into his jacket. "To find it."

"Jonas." Before he could close the lid she had her hand on his wrist. "You have to take it to the police. To Captain Moralas."

In a deliberate gesture, he removed her hand, then picked up the bag of coke. She understood rejection and braced herself against it. But it wasn't rejection she saw in his face; it was fury. "You want to take this on the plane, Liz? Any idea on what the penalty is in Mexico for carrying controlled substances?"

"No."

"And you don't want to." He closed the lid, locked it. "For now, just forget you saw anything. I'll handle this in my own way."

"No."

His emotions were raw and tangled, his patience thin. "Don't push me, Liz."

"Push you?" Infuriated, she grabbed his shirtfront and planted her feet. "You've pushed me for days. Pushed me right into the middle of something that's so opposed to the way I've lived I can't even take it all in. Now that I'm over my head in drug smuggling and something like a quarter of a million dollars, you tell me to forget it. What do you expect me to do, go quietly back and rent tanks? Maybe you've finished using me now, Jonas, but I'm not ready to be brushed aside. There's a murderer out there who thinks I know where the money is." She stopped as her skin iced over. "And now I do."

"That's just it," Jonas said quietly. For the second time, he removed her hands, but this time he held on to her wrists. Frightened, he thought. He was sure her pulse beat with fear as well as anger. "Now you do. The best thing for you to do now is stay out of it, let them focus on me."

"Just how am I supposed to do that?"

The anger was bubbling closer, the anger he'd wanted to lock in the box with what had caused it. "Go to Houston, visit your daughter."

"How can I?" she demanded in a whisper that vibrated in the little room. "They might follow me." She looked down at the long, shiny box. "They would follow me. I won't risk my daughter's safety."

She was right, and because he knew it, Jonas wanted to rage. He was boxed in, trapped between love and loyalty and right and wrong. Justice and the law. "We'll talk to Moralas when we get back." He picked up the box again, hating it.

"Where are we going now?"

Jonas unlocked the door. "To get a drink."

Rather than going with Jonas to the lounge, Liz took some time for herself. Because she felt he owed her, she went into the hotel's boutique, found a simple one-piece bathing suit and charged it to the room. She hadn't packed anything but a change of clothes and toiletries. If she was stuck in Acapulco for the rest of the evening, she was going to enjoy the private pool each villa boasted.

The first time she walked into the suite, she was dumbfounded. Her parents had been reasonably successful, and she'd been raised in a quietly middle-class atmosphere. Nothing had prepared her for the sumptuousness of the two-bedroom suite overlooking the Pacific. Her feet sank cozily into the carpet. Softly colored paintings were spaced along ivory-papered walls. The sofa, done in grays and greens and blues, was big enough for two to sprawl on for a lazy afternoon nap.

She found a phone in the bathroom next to a tub so wide and deep that she was almost tempted to take her dip there. The sink was a seashell done in the palest of pinks.

So this is how the rich play, she mused as she wandered to the bedroom where her overnight bag was set at the end of a bed big enough for three. The drapes of her balcony were open so that she could see the tempestuous surf of the Pacific hurl up and spray. She pulled the glass doors open, wanting the noise.

This was the sort of world Marcus had told her of so many years before. He'd made it seem like a fairy tale with gossamer edges. Liz had never seen his home, had never been permitted to, but he'd described it to her. The white pillars, the white balconies, the staircase that curved up and up. There were servants to bring you tea in the afternoons, a stable where grooms waited to saddle glossy horses. Champagne was drunk from French crystal. It had been a fairy tale, and she hadn't wanted it for herself. She had only wanted him.

A young girl's foolishness, Liz thought now. In her naive way, she'd made a prince out of a man who was weak and selfish and spoiled. But over the years she had thought of the house he'd talked of and pictured her daughter on those wide, curving stairs. That had been her sense of justice.

The image wasn't as clear now, not now that she'd seen wealth in a long metal box and understood where it had come from. Not when she'd seen Jonas's eyes when he'd spoken of his kind of justice. That hadn't been a fairy tale with gossamer edges, but grimly real. She had some thinking to do. But before she could plan for the rest of her life, and for her daughter's, she had to get through the moment.

Jonas. She was bound to him through no choice of her own. And perhaps he was bound to her in the same way. Was that the reason she was drawn to him? Because they were trapped in the same puzzle? If she could only explain it away, maybe she could stop the needs that kept swimming through her. If she could only explain it away, maybe she would be in control again.

But how could she explain the feelings she'd experienced on the silent cab ride back to the hotel? She had had to fight the desire to put her arms around him, to offer comfort when nothing in his manner had indicated he needed or wanted it. There were no easy answers—no answers at all to the fact that she was slowly, inevitably falling in love with him.

It was time to admit that, she decided, because you could never face anything until it was admitted. You could never solve anything until it was faced. She'd lived by that rule years before during the biggest crisis of her life. It still held true.

So she loved him, or very nearly loved him. She was no longer naive enough to believe that love was the beginning of any answer. He would hurt her. There were no ifs about that. He'd steal from her the one thing she'd managed to hold fast to for ten years. And once he'd taken her heart, what would it mean to him? She shook her head. No more than such things ever mean to those who take them.

Jonas Sharpe was a man on a mission, and she was no more to him than a map. He was ruthless in his own patient way. When he had finished what he'd come to do, he would turn away from her, go back to his life in Philadelphia and never think of her again.

Some women, Liz thought, were doomed to pick the men who could hurt them the most. Making her mind a blank, Liz stripped and changed to her bathing suit. But Jonas, thoughts of Jonas, kept slipping through the barriers.

Maybe if she talked to Faith—if she could touch her greatest link with normality, things would snap back into focus. On impulse, Liz picked up the phone beside her bed and began the process of placing the call. Faith would just be home from school, Liz calculated, growing more excited as she heard the clinks and buzzes on the receiver. When the phone began to ring, she sat on the bed. She was already smiling.

"Hello?"

"Mom?" Liz felt the twin surges of pleasure and guilt as she heard her mother's voice. "It's Liz."

"Liz!" Rose Palmer felt identical surges. "We didn't expect to hear from you. Your last letter just came this morning. Nothing's wrong, is it?"

"No, no, nothing's wrong." Everything's wrong. "I just wanted to talk to Faith."

"Oh, Liz, I'm so sorry. Faith's not here. She has her piano lesson today."

The letdown came, but she braced herself against it. "I forgot." Tears threatened, but she forced them back. "She likes the lessons, doesn't she?"

"She loves them. You should hear her play. Remember when you were taking them?"

"I had ten thumbs." She managed to smile. "I wanted to thank you for sending the pictures. She looks so grown up. Momma, is she…looking forward to coming back?"

Rose heard the need, felt the ache. She wished, not for the first time, that her daughter was close enough to hold. "She's marking off the days on her calendar. She bought you a present."

Liz had to swallow. "She did?"

"It's supposed to be a surprise, so don't tell her I told you."

"I won't." She dashed tears away, grateful she could keep her voice even. It hurt, but was also a comfort to be able to speak to someone who knew and understood Faith as she did. "I miss her. The last few weeks always seem the hardest."

Her voice wasn't as steady as she thought—and a mother hears what others don't. "Liz, why don't you come home? Spend the rest of the month here while she's in school?"

"No, I can't. How's Dad?"

Rose fretted impatiently at the change of subject, then subsided. She'd never known anyone as thoroughly stubborn as her daughter. Unless it was her granddaughter. "He's fine. Looking forward to coming down and doing some diving."

"We'll take one of the boats out—just the four of us. Tell Faith I…tell her I called," she finished lamely.

"Of course I will. Why don't I have her call you back when she gets home? The car pool drops her off at five."

"No. No, I'm not home. I'm in Acapulco—on business." Liz let out a long breath to steady herself. "Just tell her I miss her and I'll be waiting at the airport. You know I appreciate everything you're doing. I just—"

"Liz." Rose interrupted gently. "We love Faith. And we love you."

"I know." Liz pressed her fingers to her eyes. She did know, but was never quite sure what to do about it. "I love you, too. It's just that sometimes things get so mixed up."

"Are you all right?"

She dropped her hand again, and her eyes were dry. "I will be when you get there. Tell Faith I'm marking off the days, too."

"I will."

"Bye, Momma."

She hung up and sat until the churning emptiness had run its course. If she'd had more confidence in her parents' support, more trust in their love, would she have fled the States and started a new life on her own? Liz dragged a hand through her hair. She'd never be sure of that, nor could she dwell on it. She'd burned her own bridges. The only thing that was important was Faith, and her happiness.

An hour later, Jonas found her at the pool. She swam laps in long, smooth strokes, her body limber. She seemed tireless, and oddly suited to the private luxury. Her suit was a flashy red, but the cut so simple that it relied strictly on the form it covered for style.

He counted twenty laps before she stopped, and wondered how many she'd completed before he'd come down.

It seemed to him as if she swam to drain herself of some tension or sorrow, and that with each lap she'd come closer to succeeding. Waiting, he watched her tip her head back in the water so that her hair slicked back. The marks on her neck had faded. As she stood, water skimmed her thigh.

"I've never seen you relaxed," Jonas commented. But even as he said the words, he could see her muscles tense again. She turned away from her contemplation of the mountains and looked at him.

He was tired, she realized, and wondered if she should have seen it before. There was a weariness around his eyes that hadn't been there that morning. He hadn't changed his clothes, and had his hands tucked into the pockets of bone-colored slacks. She wondered if he'd been up to the suite at all.

"I didn't bring a suit with me." Liz pushed against the side of the pool and hitched herself out. Water rained from her. "I charged this one to the room."

The thighs were cut nearly to the waist. Jonas caught himself wondering just how the skin would feel there. "It's nice."

Liz picked up her towel. "It was expensive."

He only lifted a brow. "I could deduct it from the rent."

Her lips curved a little as she rubbed her hair dry. "No, you can't. But since you're a lawyer, I imagine you can find a way to deduct it from something else. I saved the receipt."

He hadn't thought he could laugh. "I appreciate it. You know, I get the impression you don't think much of lawyers."

Something came and went in her eyes. "I try not to think of them at all."

Taking the towel from her, he gently dried her face. "Faith's father's a lawyer?"

Without moving, she seemed to shift away from him. "Leave it alone, Jonas."

"You don't."

"Actually I do, most of the time. Maybe it's been on my mind the past few weeks, but that's my concern."

He draped the towel around her shoulders and, holding the ends, drew her closer. "I'd like you to tell me about it."

It was his voice, she thought, so calm, so persuasive, that nearly had her opening both mind and heart. She could almost believe as she looked at him that he really wanted to know, to understand. The part of her that was already in love with him needed to believe he might care. "Why?"

"I don't know. Maybe it's that look that comes into your eyes. It makes a man want to stroke it away."

Her chin came up a fraction. "There's no need to feel sorry for me."

"I don't think sympathy's the right word." Abruptly weary, he dropped his forehead to hers. He was tired of fighting demons, of trying to find answers. "Damn."

Uncertain, she stood very still. "Are you all right?"

"No. No, I'm not." He moved away from her to walk to the end of the path where a plot of tiny orange flowers poked up through white gravel. "A lot of things you said today were true. A lot of things you've said all along are true. I can't do anything about them."

"I don't know what you want me to say now."

"Nothing." Hideously tired, he ran both hands over his face. "I'm trying to live with the fact that my brother's dead, and that he was murdered because he decided to make some easy money drug-trafficking. He had a good brain, but he always chose to use it in the wrong way. Every time I look in the mirror, I wonder why."

Liz was beside him before she could cut off her feelings. He hurt. It was the first time she'd seen below the surface to the pain. She knew what it was like to live with pain. "He was different, Jonas. I don't think he was bad, just weak. Mourning him is one thing—blaming yourself for what he did, or for what happened to him, is another."

He hadn't known he needed comfort, but her hand resting on him had something inside him slowly uncurling. "I was the only one who could reach him, keep him on some kind of level. There came a point where I just got tired of running both our lives."

"Do you really believe you could have prevented him from doing what he did?"

"Maybe. That's something else I have to live with."

"Just a minute." She took his shirtfront in much the same way she had that afternoon. There was no sympathy now, but annoyance on her face. He hadn't known he needed that, as well. "You were brothers, twins, but you were separate people. Jerry wasn't a child to be guided and supervised. He was a grown man who made his decisions."

"That's the trouble. Jerry never grew up."

"And you did," she tossed back. "Are you going to punish yourself for it?"

He'd been doing just that, Jonas realized. He'd gone home, buried his brother, comforted his parents and blamed himself for not preventing something he knew in his heart had been inevitable. "I have to find out who killed him, Liz. I can't set the rest aside until I do."

"We'll find them." On impulse, she pressed her cheek

to his. Sometimes the slightest human contact could wash away acres of pain. "Then it'll be over."

He wasn't sure he wanted it to be, not all of it. He ran a hand down her arm, needing the touch of her skin. He found it chilled. "The sun's gone down." He wrapped the towel around her in a gesture that would have been mere politeness with another woman. With Liz, it was for protection. "You'd better get out of that wet suit. We'll have dinner."

"Here?"

"Sure. The restaurant's supposed to be one of the best."

Liz thought of the elegance of their suite and the contents of her overnight bag. "I didn't bring anything to wear."

He laughed and swung an arm around her. It was the first purely frivolous thing he'd heard her say. "Charge something else."

"But—"

"Don't worry, I've got the best crooked accountant in Philadelphia."

Chapter Seven

Because she'd been certain she would never sleep away from home, in a hotel bed, Liz was surprised to wake to full sunlight. Not only had she slept, she realized, she'd slept like a rock for eight hours and was rested and ready to go. True, it was just a little past six, and she had no business to run, but her body was tuned to wake at that hour. A trip to Acapulco didn't change that.

It had changed other things, she reminded herself as she stretched out in the too-big bed. Because of it, she'd become inescapably tangled in murder and smuggling. Putting the words together made her shake her head. In a movie, she might have enjoyed watching the melodrama. In a book, she'd have turned the page to read more. But in her own life, she preferred the more mundane. Liz was too practical to delude herself into believing she could distance herself from any part of the puzzle any longer.

For better or worse, she was personally involved in this melodrama. That included Jonas Sharpe. The only question now was which course of action to take.

She couldn't run. That had never been a choice. Liz had already concluded she couldn't hide behind Moralas and his men forever. Sooner or later the man with the knife would come back, or another man more determined or more desperate. She wouldn't escape a second time. The moment she'd looked into the safe-deposit box, she'd become a full-fledged player in the game. Which brought her back full circle to Jonas. She had no choice but to put her trust in him now. If he were to give up on his brother's murder and return to Philadelphia she would be that much more alone. However much she might wish it otherwise, Liz needed him just as much as he needed her.

Other things had changed, she thought. Her feelings for him were even more undefined and confusing than they had started out to be. Seeing him as she had the evening before, hurt and vulnerable, had touched off more than impersonal sympathy or physical attraction. It had made her feel a kinship, and the kinship urged her to help him, not only for her own welfare, but for his. He suffered, for his brother's loss, but also for what his brother had done. She'd loved once, and had suffered, not only because of loss but because of disillusionment.

A lifetime ago? Liz wondered. Did we ever really escape from one lifetime to another? It seemed years could pass, circumstances could change, but we carried our baggage with us through each phase. If anything, with each phase we had to carry a bit more. There was little use in thinking, she told herself as she climbed from the bed. From this point on, she had little choice but to act.

Jonas heard her the moment she got up. He'd been

awake since five, restless and prowling. For over an hour
he'd been racking his brain and searching his conscience
for a way to ease Liz out of a situation his brother, and
he himself had locked her into. He'd already thought of
several ways to draw attention away from her to himself,
but that wouldn't guarantee Liz's safety. She wouldn't go
to Houston, and he understood her feelings about endangering her daughter in any way.

As the days passed, he felt he was coming to understand her better and better. She was a loner, but only
because she saw it as the safest route. She was a busi-
nesswoman, but only because she looked to her daughter's welfare first. Inside, he thought, she was a woman
with dreams on hold and love held in bondage. She had
steered both toward her child and denied herself. And,
Jonas added, she'd convinced herself she was content.

That was something else he understood, because until
a few weeks before he had also convinced himself he
was content. It was only now, after he'd had the opportunity to look at his life from a distance, that he realized
he had merely been drifting. Perhaps, when the outward
trimmings were stripped away, he hadn't been so different from his brother. For both of them, success had been
the main target, they had simply aimed for it differently.
Though Jonas had a steady job, a home of his own, there
had never been an important woman. He'd put his career
first. Jonas wasn't certain he'd be able to do so again.
It had taken the loss of his brother to make him realize
he needed something more, something solid. Exploring
the law was only a job. Winning cases was only a tran-
sitory satisfaction. Perhaps he'd known it for some time.
After all, he'd bought the old house in Chadd's Ford to

give himself something permanent. When had he started thinking about sharing it?

Still, thinking about his own life didn't solve the problem of Liz Palmer and what he was going to do with her. She couldn't go to Houston, he thought again, but there were other places she could go until he could assure her that her life could settle back the way she wanted it. His parents were his first thought, and the quiet country home they'd retired to in Lancaster. If he could find a way to slip her out of Mexico, she would be safe there. It would even be possible to have her daughter join her. Then his conscience would ease. Jonas had no doubt that his parents would accept them both, then dote on them.

Once he'd done what he'd come to do, he could go to Lancaster himself. He'd like to see Liz there, in surroundings he was used to. He wanted time to talk with her about simple things. He wanted to hear her laugh again, as she had only once in all the days he'd known her. Once they were there, away from the ugliness, he might understand his feelings better. Perhaps by then he'd be able to analyze what had happened inside him when she'd pressed her cheek against his and had offered unconditional support.

He'd wanted to hold on to her, to just hold on and the hell with the world. There was something about her that made him think of lazy evenings on cool porches and long Sunday afternoon walks. He couldn't say why. In Philadelphia he rarely took time for such things. Even socializing had become business. And he'd seen for himself that she never gave herself an idle hour. Why should he, a man dedicated to his work, think of lazing days away with a woman obsessed by hers?

She remained a mystery to him, and perhaps that

was an answer in itself. If he thought of her too often, too deeply, it was only because while his understanding was growing, he still knew so little. If it sometimes seemed that discovering Liz Palmer was just as important as discovering his brother's killer, it was only because they were tied together. How could he take his mind off one without taking his mind off the other? Yet when he thought of her now, he thought of her stretched out on his mother's porch swing, safe, content and waiting for him.

Annoyed with himself, Jonas checked his watch. It was after nine on the East Coast. He'd call his office, he thought. A few legal problems might clear his mind. He'd no more than picked up the receiver when Liz came out from her bedroom.

"I didn't know you were up," she said, and fiddled nervously with her belt. Odd, she felt entirely different about sharing the plush little villa with him than she did her home. After all, she reasoned, at home he was paying rent.

"I thought you'd sleep longer." He replaced the receiver again. The office could wait.

"I never sleep much past six." Feeling awkward, she wandered to the wide picture window. "Terrific view."

"Yes, it is."

"I haven't stayed in a hotel in…in years," she finished. "When I came to Cozumel, I worked in the same hotel where I'd stayed with my parents. It was an odd feeling. So's this."

"No urge to change the linen or stack the towels?"

When she chuckled, some of the awkwardness slipped away. "No, not even a twinge."

"Liz, when we're finished with all this, when it's behind us, will you talk to me about that part of your life?"

She turned to him, away from the window, but they both felt the distance. "When we're finished with this, there won't be any reason to."

He rose and came to her. In a gesture that took her completely by surprise, he took both of her hands. He lifted one, then the other, to his lips and watched her eyes cloud. "I can't be sure of that," he murmured. "Can you?"

She couldn't be sure of anything when his voice was quiet, his hands gentle. For a moment, she simply absorbed the feeling of being a woman cared for by a man. Then she stepped back, as she knew she had to. "Jonas, you told me once we had the same problem. I didn't want to believe it then, but it was true. It is true. Once that problem is solved, there really isn't anything else between us. Your life and mine are separated by a lot more than miles."

He thought of his house and his sudden need to share it. "They don't have to be."

"There was a time I might have believed that."

"You're living in the past." He took her shoulders, but this time his hands weren't as gentle. "You're fighting ghosts."

"I may have my ghosts, but I don't live in the past. I can't afford to." She put her hands to his wrists, but let them lie there only a moment before she let go. "I can't afford to pretend to myself about you."

He wanted to demand, he wanted to pull her with him to the sofa and prove to her that she was wrong. He resisted. It wasn't the first time he'd used courtroom skill, courtroom tactics, to win on a personal level. "We'll leave it your way for now," he said easily. "But the case isn't closed. Are you hungry?"

Unsure whether she should be uneasy or relieved, Liz nodded. "A little."

"Let's have breakfast. We've got plenty of time before the plane leaves."

She didn't trust him. Though Jonas kept the conversation light and passionless throughout breakfast, Liz kept herself braced for a countermove. He was a clever man, she knew. He was a man, she was certain, who made sure he got his own way no matter how long it took. Liz considered herself a woman strong enough to keep promises made, even when they were to herself. No man, not even Jonas, was going to make her change the course she'd set ten years before. There was only room enough for two loves in her life. Faith and her work.

"I can't get used to eating something at this hour of the morning that's going to singe my stomach lining."

Liz swallowed the mixture of peppers, onions and eggs. "Mine's flame resistant. You should try my chili."

"Does that mean you're offering to cook for me?"

When Liz glanced up she wished he hadn't been smiling at her in just that way. "I suppose I could make enough for two as easily as enough for one. But you don't seem to have any trouble in the kitchen."

"Oh, I can cook. It's just that once I've finished, it never seems worth the bother." He leaned forward to run a finger down her hand from wrist to knuckle. "Tell you what—I'll buy the supplies and even clean up the mess if you handle the chili."

Though she smiled, Liz drew her hand away. "The question is, can you handle the chili? It might burn right through a soft lawyer's stomach."

Appreciating the challenge, he took her hand again. "Why don't we find out? Tonight."

"All right." She flexed her fingers, but he merely linked his with them. "I can't eat if you have my hand."

He glanced down. "You have another one."

He made her laugh when she'd been set to insist. "I'm entitled to two."

"I'll give it back. Later."

"Hey, Jerry!"

The easy smile on Jonas's face froze. Only his eyes changed, locking on to Liz's, warning and demanding. His hand remained on hers, but the grip tightened. The message was very clear—she was to do nothing, say nothing until he'd tallied the odds. He turned, flashing a new smile. Liz's stomach trembled. It was Jerry's smile, she realized. Not Jonas's.

"Why didn't you tell me you were back in town?" A tall, tanned man with sandy blond hair and a trim beard dropped a hand on Jonas's shoulder. Liz caught the glint of a diamond on his finger. He was young, she thought, determined to store everything she could, barely into his thirties, and dressed with slick, trendy casualness.

"Quick trip," Jonas said as, like Liz, he took in every detail. "Little business…" He cast a meaningful glance toward Liz. "Little pleasure."

The man turned and stared appreciatively at Liz. "Is there any other way?"

Thinking fast, Liz offered her hand. "Hello. Since Jerry's too rude to introduce us, we'll have to do it ourselves. I'm Liz Palmer."

"David Merriworth." He took her hand between both of his. They were smooth and uncallused. "Jerry might have trouble with manners, but he's got great taste."

She smiled, hoping she did it properly. "Thank you."

"Pull up a chair, Merriworth." Jonas took out a cigarette. "As long as you keep your hands off my lady." He said it in the good-natured, only-kidding tone Jerry had inevitably used, but his eyes were Jonas's, warning her to tread carefully.

"Wouldn't mind a quick cup of coffee." David pulled over a chair after he checked his watch. "Got a breakfast meeting in a few minutes. So how are things on Cozumel?" He inclined his head ever so slightly. "Getting in plenty of diving?"

Jonas allowed his lips to curve and kept his eyes steady. "Enough."

"Glad to hear it. I was going to check in with you myself, but I've been in the States for a couple weeks. Just got back in last night." He used two sugars after the waiter set a fresh cup of coffee beside him. "Business is good, buddy. Real good."

"What business are you in, Mr. Merriworth?"

He gave Liz a big grin before he winked at Jonas. "Sales, sweetheart. Imports, you might say."

"Really." Because her throat was dry she drank more coffee. "It must be fascinating."

"It has its moments." He turned in his chair so that he could study her face. "So where did Jerry find you?"

"On Cozumel." She sent Jonas a steady look. "We're partners."

David lowered his cup. "That so?"

They were in too deep, Jonas thought, for him to contradict her. "That's so," he agreed.

David picked up his cup again with a shrug. "If it's okay with the boss, it doesn't bother me."

"I do things my way," Jonas drawled. "Or I don't do them."

Amused, and perhaps admiring, David broke into a smile. "That never changes. Look, I've been out of touch for a few weeks. The drops still going smooth?"

With those words, Jonas's last hopes died. What he'd found in the safe-deposit box had been real, and it had been Jerry's. He buttered a roll as though he had all the time in the world. Beneath the table, Liz touched his leg once, hoping he'd take it as comfort. He never looked at her. "Why shouldn't they?"

"It's the classiest operation I've ever come across," David commented, taking a cautious glance around to other tables. "Wouldn't like to see anything screw it up."

"You worry too much."

"You're the one who should worry," David pointed out. "I don't have to deal with Manchez. You weren't around last year when he took care of those two Colombians. I was. You deal with supplies, I stick with sales. I sleep better."

"I just dive," Jonas said, and tapped out his cigarette. "And I sleep fine."

"He's something, isn't he?" David sent Liz another grin. "I knew Jerry here was just the man the boss was looking for. You keep diving, kid." He tipped his cup at Jonas. "It makes me look good."

"Sounds like you two have known each other for a while," Liz said with a smile. Under the table, she twisted the napkin in her lap.

"Go way back, don't we, Jer?"

"Yeah. We go back."

"First time we hooked up was six, no, seven years ago. We were working a pigeon drop in L.A. We'd have had that twenty thousand out of that old lady if her daughter hadn't caught on." He took out a slim cigarette case. "Your brother got you out of that one, didn't he? The East Coast lawyer."

"Yeah." Jonas remembered posting the bond and pulling the strings.

"Now I've been working out of here for almost five. A real businessman." He slapped Jonas's arm. "Hell of a lot better than the pigeon drop, huh, Jerry?"

"Pays better."

David let out a roar of laughter. "Why don't I show you two around Acapulco tonight?"

"Gotta get back." Jonas signaled for the check. "Business."

"Yeah, I know what you mean." He nodded toward the restaurant's entrance. "Here's my customer now. Next time you drop down, give a call."

"Sure."

"And give my best to old Clancy." With another laugh, David gave them each a quick salute. They watched him stride across the room and shake hands with a dark-suited man.

"Don't say anything here," Jonas murmured as he signed the breakfast check. "Let's go."

Liz's crumpled napkin slid to the floor as she rose to walk out with him. He didn't speak again until they had the door of the villa closed behind them.

"You had no business telling him we were partners."

Because she'd been ready for the attack, she shrugged it off. "He said more once I did."

"He'd have said just as much if you'd made an excuse and left the table."

She folded her arms. "We have the same problem, remember?"

He didn't care to have his own words tossed back at him. "The least you could have done was to give him another name."

"Why? They know who I am. Sooner or later he's going to talk to whoever's in charge and get the whole story."

She was right. He didn't care for that either. "Are you packed?"

"Yes."

"Then let's check out. We'll go to the airport."

"And then?"

"And then we go straight to Moralas."

"You've been very busy." Moralas held on to his temper as he rocked back in his chair. "Two of my men wasted their valuable time looking for you in Acapulco. You might have told me, Mr. Sharpe, that you planned to take Miss Palmer on a trip."

"I thought a police tail in Acapulco might be inconvenient."

"And now that you have finished your own investigation, you bring me this." He held up the key and examined it. "This which Miss Palmer discovered several days ago. As a lawyer, you must understand the phrase 'withholding evidence.'"

"Of course." Jonas nodded coolly. "But neither Miss Palmer nor myself could know the key was evidence. We speculated, naturally, that it might have belonged to my brother. Withholding a speculation is hardly a crime."

"Perhaps not, but it is poor judgment. Poor judgment often translates into an offense."

Jonas leaned back in his chair. If Moralas wanted to argue law, they'd argue law. "If the key belonged to my brother, as executor of his estate, it became mine. In any case, once it was proved to me that the key did indeed belong to Jerry, and that the contents of the safe-deposit box were evidence, I brought both the key and a description of the contents to you."

"Indeed. And do you also speculate as to how your brother came to possess those particular items?"

"Yes."

Moralas waited a beat, then turned to Liz. "And you, Miss Palmer—you also have your speculations?"

She had her hands gripped tightly in her lap, but her voice was matter-of-fact and reasonable. "I know that whoever attacked me wanted money, obviously a great deal of money. We found a great deal."

"And a bag of what Mr. Sharpe…speculates is cocaine." Moralas folded his hands on the desk with the key under them. "Miss Palmer, did you at any time see Mr. Jeremiah Sharpe in possession of cocaine?"

"No."

"Did he at any time speak to you of cocaine or drug-trafficking?"

"No, of course not. I would have told you."

"As you told me about the key?" When Jonas started to protest, Moralas waved him off. "I will need a list of your customers for the past six weeks, Miss Palmer. Names and, wherever possible, addresses."

"My customers? Why?"

"It's more than possible that Mr. Sharpe used your shop for his contacts."

"My shop." Outraged, she stood up. "My boats? Do

you think he could have passed drugs under my nose without me being aware?"

Moralas took out a cigar and studied it. "I very much hope you were unaware, Miss Palmer. You will bring me the list of clients by the end of the week." He glanced at Jonas. "Of course, you are within your rights to demand a warrant. It will simply slow down the process. And I, of course, am within my rights to hold Miss Palmer as a material witness."

Jonas watched the pale blue smoke circle toward the ceiling. It was tempting to call Moralas's bluff simply as an exercise in testing two ends of the law. And in doing so, he and the captain could play tug-of-war with Liz for hours. "There are times, Captain, when it's wiser not to employ certain rights. I think I'm safe in saying that the three of us in this room want basically the same thing." He rose and flicked his lighter at the end of Moralas's cigar. "You'll have your list, Captain. And more."

Moralas lifted his gaze and waited.

"Pablo Manchez," Jonas said, and was gratified to see Moralas's eyes narrow.

"What of Manchez?"

"He's on Cozumel. Or was," Jonas stated. "My brother met with him several times in local bars and clubs. You may also be interested in David Merriworth, an American working out of Acapulco. Apparently he's the one who put my brother onto his contacts in Cozumel. If you contact the authorities in the States, you'll find that Merriworth has an impressive rap sheet."

In his precise handwriting, Moralas noted down the names, though he wasn't likely to forget them. "I appreciate the information. However, in the future, Mr. Sharpe,

I would appreciate it more if you stayed out of my way. *Buenas tardes,* Miss Palmer."

Moments later, Liz strode out to the street. "I don't like being threatened. That's what he was doing, wasn't it?" she demanded. "He was threatening to put me in jail."

Very calm, even a bit amused, Jonas lit a cigarette. "He was pointing out his options, and ours."

"He didn't threaten to put you in jail," Liz muttered.

"He doesn't worry as much about me as he does about you."

"Worry?" She stopped with her hand gripping the handle of Jonas's rented car.

"He's a good cop. You're one of his people."

She looked back toward the police station with a scowl. "He has a funny way of showing it." A scruffy little boy scooted up to the car and gallantly opened the door for her. Even as he prepared to hold out a hand, Liz was digging for a coin.

"Gracias."

He checked the coin, grinned at the amount and nodded approval. *"Buenas tardes, señorita."* Just as gallantly he closed the door for her while the coin disappeared into a pocket.

"It's a good thing you don't come into town often," Jonas commented.

"Why?"

"You'd be broke in a week."

Liz found a clip in her purse and pulled back her hair. "Because I gave a little boy twenty-five pesos?"

"How much did you give the other kid before we went into Moralas?"

"I bought something from him."

"Yeah." Jonas swung away from the curb. "You

look like a woman who can't go a day without a box of Chiclets."

"You're changing the subject."

"That's right. Now tell me where I can find the best place for buying ingredients for chili."

"You want me to cook for you tonight?"

"It'll keep your mind off the rest. We've done everything we can do for the moment," he added. "Tonight we're going to relax."

She would have liked to believe he was right. Between nerves and anger, she was wound tight. "Cooking's supposed to relax me?"

"Eating is going to relax you. It's just an unavoidable circumstance that you have to cook it first."

It sounded so absurd that she subsided. "Turn left at the next corner. I tell you what to buy, you buy it, then you stay out of my way."

"Agreed."

"And you clean up."

"Absolutely."

"Pull over here," she directed. "And remember, you asked for it."

Liz never skimped when she cooked, even taking into account that authentic Mexican spices had more zing than the sort sold in the average American supermarket. She'd developed a taste for Mexican food and Yucatán specialties when she'd been a child, exploring the peninsula with her parents. She wasn't an elaborate cook, and when alone would often make do with a sandwich, but when her heart was in it, she could make a meal that would more than satisfy.

Perhaps, in a way, she wanted to impress him. Liz

found she was able to admit it while she prepared a Mayan salad for chilling. It was probably very natural and harmless to want to impress someone with your cooking. After peeling and slicing an avocado, she found, oddly enough, she was relaxing.

So much of what she'd done in the past few days had been difficult or strange. It was a relief to make a decision no more vital than the proper way to slice her fruits and vegetables. In the end, she fussed with the arrangement a bit more, pleased with the contrasting colors of greens and oranges and cherry tomatoes. It was, she recalled, the only salad she could get Faith to eat because it was the only one Faith considered pretty enough. Liz didn't realize she was smiling as she began to sauté onions and peppers. She added a healthy dose of garlic and let it all simmer.

"It already smells good," Jonas commented as he strode through the doorway.

She only glanced over her shoulder. "You're supposed to stay out of my way."

"You cook, I take care of the table."

Liz only shrugged and turned back to the stove. She measured, stirred and spiced until the kitchen was filled with a riot of scent. The sauce, chunky with meat and vegetables, simmered and thickened on low heat. Pleased with herself, she wiped her hands on a cloth and turned around. Jonas was sitting comfortably at the table watching her.

"You look good," he told her. "Very good."

It seemed so natural, their being together in the kitchen with a pot simmering and a breeze easing its way through the screen. It made her remember how hard it was not to want such simple things in your life. Liz set the cloth down and found she didn't know what to do with her hands. "Some men think a woman looks best in front of a stove."

"I don't know. It's a toss-up with the way you looked at the wheel of a boat. How long does that have to cook?"

"About a half hour."

"Good." He rose and went to the counter where he'd left two bottles. "We have time for some wine."

A little warning signal jangled in her brain. Liz decided she needed a lid for the chili. "I don't have the right glasses."

"I already thought of that." From a bag beside the bottle, he pulled out two thin-stemmed wineglasses.

"You've been busy," she murmured.

"You didn't like me hovering over you in the market. I had to do something." He drew out the cork, then let the wine breathe.

"These candles aren't mine."

He turned to see Liz fiddling with the fringe of one of the woven mats he'd set on the table. In the center were two deep blue tapers that picked up the color in the border of her dishes.

"They're ours," Jonas told her.

She twisted the fringe around one finger, let it go, then twisted it again. The last time she'd burned candles had been during a power failure. These didn't look sturdy, but slender and frivolous. "There wasn't any need to go to all this trouble. I don't—"

"Do candles and wine make you uneasy?"

Dropping the fringe, she let her hands fall to her sides. "No, of course not."

"Good." He poured rich red wine into both glasses.

Walking to her, he offered one. "Because I find them re-laxing. We did agree to relax."

She sipped, and though she wanted to back away, held her ground. "I'm afraid you may be looking for more than I can give."

"No." He touched his glass to hers. "I'm looking for exactly what you can give."

Recognizing when she was out of her depth, Liz turned toward the refrigerator. "We can start on the salad."

He lit the candles and dimmed the lights. She told her-self it didn't matter. Atmosphere was nothing more than a pleasant addition to a meal.

"Very pretty," Jonas told her when she'd mixed the dressing and arranged avocado slices. "What's it called?"

"It's a Mayan salad." Liz took the first nibble and was satisfied. "I learned the recipe when I worked at the hotel. Actually, that's where most of my cooking comes from."

"Wonderful," Jonas decided after the first bite. "It makes me wish I'd talked you into cooking before."

"A one time only." She relaxed enough to smile. "Meals aren't—"

"Included in the rent," Jonas finished. "We might ne-gotiate."

This time she laughed at him and chose a section of grapefruit. "I don't think so. How do you manage in Philadelphia?"

"I have a housekeeper who'll toss together a casse-role on Wednesdays." He took another bite, enjoying the contrast of crisp greens and spicy dressing. "And I eat out a lot."

"And parties? I suppose you go to a lot of parties."

"Some business, some pleasure." He'd almost forgotten what it was like to sit in a kitchen and enjoy a simple meal. "To be honest, it wears a bit. The cruising."

"Cruising?"

"When Jerry and I were teenagers, we might hop in the car on a Friday night and cruise. The idea was to see what teenage girls had hopped in their cars to cruise. The party circuit's just adult cruising."

She frowned a bit because it didn't seem as glamorous as she'd imagined. "It seems rather aimless."

"Doesn't seem. Is."

"You don't appear to be a man who does anything without a purpose."

"I've had my share of aimless nights," he murmured. "You come to a point where you realize you don't want too many more." That was just it, he realized. It wasn't the work, the hours spent closeted with law books or in a courtroom. It was the nights without meaning that left him wanting more. He lifted the wine to top off her glass, but his eyes stayed on hers. "I came to that realization very recently."

Her blood began to stir. Deliberately, Liz pushed her wine aside and rose to go to the stove. "We all make decisions at certain points in our lives, realign our priorities."

"I have the feeling you did that a long time ago."

"I did. I've never regretted it."

That much was true, he thought. She wasn't a woman for regrets. "You wouldn't change it, would you?"

Liz continued to spoon chili into bowls. "Change what?"

"If you could go back eleven years and take a different path, you wouldn't do it."

She stopped. From across the room he could see the flicker of candlelight in her eyes as she turned to him.

More, he could see the strength that softness and shadows couldn't disguise. "That would mean I'd have to give up Faith. No, I wouldn't do it."

When she set the bowls on the table, Jonas took her hand. "I admire you."

Flustered, she stared down at him. "What for?"

"For being exactly what you are."

Chapter Eight

No smooth phrases, no romantic words could have affected her more deeply. She wasn't used to flattery, but flattery, Liz was sure, could be brushed easily aside by a woman who understood herself. Sincere and simple approval was a different matter. Perhaps it was the candlelight, the wine, the intimacy of the small kitchen in the empty house, but she felt close to him, comfortable with him. Without being aware of it happening, Liz dropped her guard.

"I couldn't be anything else."

"Yes, you could. I'm glad you're not."

"What are you?" she wondered as she sat beside him.

"A thirty-five-year-old lawyer who's just realizing he's wasted some time." He lifted his glass and touched it to hers. "To making the best of whatever there is."

Though she wasn't certain she understood him, Liz drank, then waited for him to eat.

"You could fuel an engine with this stuff." Jonas dipped his spoon into the chili again and tasted. Hot spice danced on his tongue. "It's great."

"Not too hot for your Yankee stomach?"

"My Yankee stomach can handle it. You know, I'm surprised you haven't opened a restaurant, since you can cook like this."

She wouldn't have been human if the compliment hadn't pleased her. "I like the water more than I like the kitchen."

"I can't argue with that. So you picked this up in the kitchen when you worked at the hotel?"

"That's right. We'd take a meal there. The cook would show me how much of this and how much of that. He was very kind," Liz remembered. "A lot of people were kind."

He wanted to know everything—the small details, the feelings, the memories. Because he did, he knew he had to probe with care. "How long did you work there?"

"Two years. I lost count of how many beds I made."

"Then you started your own business?"

"Then I started the dive shop." She took a thin cracker and broke it in two. "It was a gamble, but it was the right one."

"How did you handle it?" He waited until she looked over at him. "With your daughter?"

She withdrew. He could hear it in her voice. "I don't know what you mean."

"I wonder about you." He kept the tone light, knowing she'd never respond to pressure. "Not many women could have managed all you've managed. You were alone, pregnant, making a living."

"Does that seem so unusual?" It made her smile to think of it. "There are only so many choices, aren't there?"

"A great many people would have made a different one."

With a nod, she accepted. "A different one wouldn't have been right for me." She sipped her wine as she let her mind drift back. "I was frightened. Quite a bit at first, but less and less as time when on. People were very good to me. It might have been different if I hadn't been lucky. I went into labor when I was cleaning room 328." Her eyes warmed as if she'd just seen something lovely. "I remember holding this stack of towels in my hand and thinking, 'Oh God, this is it, and I've only done half my rooms.'" She laughed and went back to her meal. Jonas's bowl sat cooling.

"You worked the day your baby was born?"

"Of course. I was healthy."

"I know men who take the day off if they need a tooth filled."

She laughed again and passed him the crackers. "Maybe women take things more in stride."

Only some women, he thought. Only a few exceptional women. "And afterward?"

"Afterward I was lucky again. A woman I worked with knew Señora Alderez. When Faith was born, her youngest had just turned five. She took care of Faith during the day, so I was able to go right back to work."

The cracker crumbled in his hand. "It must have been difficult for you."

"The only hard part was leaving my baby every morning, but the señora was wonderful to Faith and to me. That's how I found this house. Anyway, one thing led to another. I started the dive shop."

He wondered if she realized that the more simply she

described it, the more poignant it sounded. "You said the dive shop was a gamble."

"Everything's a gamble. If I'd stayed at the hotel, I never would have been able to give Faith what I wanted to give her. And I suppose I'd have felt cheated myself. Would you like some more?"

"No." He rose to take the bowls himself while he thought out how to approach her. If he said the wrong thing, she'd pull away again. The more she told him, the more he found he needed to know. "Where did you learn to dive?"

"Right here in Cozumel, when I was just a little older than Faith." As a matter of habit she began to store the leftovers while Jonas ran water in the sink. "My parents brought me. I took to it right away. It was like, I don't know, learning to fly I suppose."

"Is that why you came back?"

"I came back because I'd always felt peaceful here. I needed to feel peaceful."

"But you must have still been in school in the States."

"I was in college." Crouching, Liz shifted things in the refrigerator to make room. "My first year. I was going to be a marine biologist, a teacher who'd enlighten class after class on the mysteries of the sea. A scientist who'd find all the answers. It was such a big dream. It over-whelmed everything else to the point where I studied constantly and rarely went out. Then I—" She caught herself. Straightening slowly, she closed the refrigerator. "You'll want the lights on to do those dishes."

"Then what?" Jonas demanded, taking her shoulder as she hit the switch.

She stared at him. Light poured over them without the

shifting shadows of candles. "Then I met Faith's father, and that was the end of dreams."

The need to know eclipsed judgment. He forgot to be careful. "Did you love him?"

"Yes. If I hadn't, there'd have been no Faith."

It wasn't the answer he'd wanted. "Then why are you raising her alone?"

"That's obvious, isn't it?" Anger surged as she shoved his hand aside. "He didn't want me."

"Whether he did or didn't, he was responsible to you and the child."

"Don't talk to me about responsibility. Faith's my responsibility."

"The law sees things otherwise."

"Keep your law," she snapped. "He could quote it chapter and verse, and it didn't mean a thing. We weren't wanted."

"So you let pride cut you off from your rights?" Impatient with her, he stuck his hands in his pockets and strode back to the sink. "Why didn't you fight for what you were entitled to?"

"You want the details, Jonas?" Memory brought its own particular pain, its own particular shame. Liz concentrated on the anger. Going back to the table, she picked up her glass of wine and drank deeply.

"I wasn't quite eighteen. I was going to college to study exactly what I wanted to study so I could do exactly what I wanted to do. I considered myself a great deal more mature than some of my classmates who flitted around from class to class more concerned about where the action would be that night. I spent most of my evenings in the library. That's where I met him. He was in his last year and knew if he didn't pass the bar there'd be hell to pay at home. His family had been in law or politics since the Revolution. You'd understand about family honor, wouldn't you?"

The arrow hit the mark, but he only nodded.

"Then you should understand the rest. We saw each other every night in the library, so it was natural that we began to talk, then have a cup of coffee. He was smart, attractive, wonderfully mannered and funny." Almost violently, she blew out the candles. The scent carried over and hung in the room. "I fell hard. He brought me flowers and took me for long quiet drives on Saturday nights. When he told me he loved me, I believed him. I thought I had the world in the palm of my hand."

She set the wine down again, impatient to be finished. Jonas said nothing. "He told me we'd be married as soon as he established himself. We'd sit in his car and look at the stars and he'd tell me about his home in Dallas and the wonderful rooms. The parties and the servants and the chandeliers. It was like a story, a lovely happily-ever-after story. Then one day his mother came." Liz laughed, but gripped the back of her chair until her knuckles were white. She could still feel the humiliation.

"Actually, she sent her driver up to the dorm to fetch me. Marcus hadn't said a thing about her visiting, but I was thrilled that I was going to meet her. At the curb was this fabulous white Rolls, the kind you only see in movies. When the driver opened the door for me, I was floating. Then I got in and she gave me the facts of life. Her son had a certain position to maintain, a certain image to project. She was sure I was a very nice girl, but hardly suitable for a Jensann of Dallas."

Jonas's eyes narrowed at the name, but he said nothing. Restless, Liz went to the stove and began to scrub the surface. "She told me she'd already spoken with her son and he understood the relationship had to end. Then she offered me a check as compensation. I was humiliated, and worse, I was pregnant. I hadn't told anyone yet, because I'd just found out that morning. I didn't take her money. I got out of the Rolls and went straight to Marcus. I was sure he loved me enough to toss it all aside for me, and for our baby. I was wrong."

Her eyes were so dry that they hurt. Liz pressed her fingers to them a moment. "When I went to see him, he was very logical. It had been nice; now it was over. His parents held the purse strings and it was important to keep them happy. But he wanted me to know we could still see each other now and again, as long as it was on the side. When I told him about the baby, he was furious. How could I have done such a thing? *I.*"

Liz tossed the dishrag into the sink so that hot, soapy water heaved up. "It was as though I'd conceived the baby completely on my own. He wouldn't have it, he wouldn't have some silly girl who'd gotten herself pregnant messing up his life. He told me I had to get rid of it. It—as though Faith were a thing to be erased and forgotten. I was hysterical. He lost his temper. There were threats. He said he'd spread word that I was sleeping around and his friends would back him up. I'd never be able to prove the baby was his. He said my parents would be embarrassed, perhaps sued if I tried to press it. He tossed around a lot of legal phrases that I couldn't understand, but I understood he was finished with me. His family had a lot of pull at the college, and he said he'd see that I was dismissed.

Because I was foolish enough to believe everything he said, I was terrified. He gave me a check and told me to go out of state—better, out of the country—to take care of things. That way no one would have to know.

"For a week I did nothing. I went through my classes in a daze, thinking I'd wake up and find out it had all been a bad dream. Then I faced it. I wrote my parents, telling them what I could. I sold the car they'd given me when I graduated from high school, took the check from Marcus and came to Cozumel to have my baby."

He'd wanted to know, even demanded, but now his insides were raw. "You could have gone to your parents."

"Yes, but at the time Marcus had convinced me they'd be ashamed. He told me they'd hate me and consider the baby a burden."

"Why didn't you go to his family? You were entitled to be taken care of."

"Go to them?" He'd never heard venom in her voice before. "Be taken care of by them? I'd have gone to hell first."

He waited a moment, until he was sure he could speak calmly. "They don't even know, do they?"

"No. And they never will. Faith is mine."

"And what does Faith know?"

"Only what she has to know. I'd never lie to her."

"And do you know that Marcus Jensann has his sights set on the senate, and maybe higher?"

Her color drained quickly and completely. "You know him?"

"By reputation."

Panic came and went, then returned in double force. "He doesn't know Faith exists. None of them do. They can't."

Watching her steadily, he took a step closer. "What are you afraid of?"

"Power. Faith is mine, she's going to stay mine. None of them will ever touch her."

"Is that why you stay here? Are you hiding from them?"

"I'll do whatever's necessary to protect my child."

"He's still got you running scared." Furious for her, Jonas took her arms. "He's got a frightened teenager strapped inside of you who's never had the chance to stretch and feel alive. Don't you know a man like that wouldn't even remember who you are? You're still running away from a man who wouldn't recognize you on the street."

She slapped him hard enough to make his head snap back. Breathing fast, she backed away from him, appalled by a show of violence she hadn't been aware of possessing. "Don't tell me what I'm running from," she whispered. "Don't tell me what I feel." She turned and fled. Before she'd reached the front door he had her again, whirling her around, gripping her hard. He no longer knew why his anger was so fierce, only that he was past the point of controlling it.

"How much have you given up because of him?" Jonas demanded. "How much have you cut out of your life?"

"It's my life!" she shouted at him.

"And you won't share it with anyone but your daughter. What the hell are you going to do when she's grown? What the hell are you going to do in twenty years when you have nothing but your memories?"

"Don't." Tears filled her eyes too quickly to be blinked away.

He grabbed her close again, twisting until she had to

look at him. "We all need someone. Even you. It's about time someone proved it to you."

"No."

She tried to turn her head but he was quick. With his mouth crushed on hers she struggled, but her arms were trapped between their bodies and his were ironlike around her. Emotions already mixed with fear and anger became more confused with passion. Liz fought not to give in to any of them as his mouth demanded both submission and response.

"You're not fighting me," he told her. His eyes were close, searing into hers. "You're fighting yourself. You've been fighting yourself since the first time we met."

"I want you to let me go." She wanted her voice to be strong, but it trembled.

"Yes. You want me to let you go just as much as you want me not to. You've been making your own decisions for a long time, Liz. This time I'm making one for you."

Her furious protest was lost against his mouth as he pressed her down to the sofa. Trapped under him, her body began to heat, her blood began to stir. Yes, she was fighting herself. She had to fight herself before she could fight him. But she was losing.

She heard her own moan as his lips trailed down her throat, and it was a moan of pleasure. She felt the hard line of his body against hers as she arched under him, but it wasn't a movement of protest. *Want me,* she seemed to say. *Want me for what I am.*

Her pulse began to thud in parts of her body that had been quiet for so many years. Life burst through her like a torrid wind through thin glass until every line of defense was shattered. With a desperate groan, she took his face in her hands and dragged his mouth back to hers.

She could taste the passion, the life, the promises. She wanted them all. Recklessness, so long chained within, tore free and ruled. A sound bubbled in her throat she wasn't even aware was a laugh as she wrapped herself around him. She wanted. He wanted. The hell with the rest.

He wasn't sure what had driven him—anger, need, pain. All he knew now was that he had to have her, body, soul and mind. She was wild beneath him, but no longer in resistance. Every movement was a demand that he take more, give more, and nothing seemed fast enough. She was a storm set to rage, a fire desperate to consume. Whatever he'd released inside of her had whipped out and taken him prisoner.

He pulled the shirt over her head and tossed it aside. His heartbeat thundered. She was so small, so delicate. But he had a beast inside him that had been caged too long. He took her breast in his mouth and sent them both spinning. She tasted so fresh: a cool, clear glass of water. She smelled of woman at her most unpampered and most seductive. He felt her body arch against his, taut as a bowstring, hot as a comet. The innocence that remained so integral a part of her trembled just beneath wanton passion. No man alive could have resisted it; any man alive might have wished for it. His mouth was buried at her throat when he felt the shirt rip away from his back.

She hardly knew what she was doing. Touching him sent demands to her brain that she couldn't deny. She wanted to feel him against her, flesh to flesh, to experience an intimacy she'd so long refused to allow herself. There'd been no one else. As Liz felt her skin fused to his she understood why. There was only one Jonas. She pulled his mouth back to hers to taste him again.

He drew off her slacks so that she was naked, but she didn't feel vulnerable. She felt invulnerable. Hardly able to breathe, she struggled with his. Then she gave him no choice. Desperate for that final release, she wrapped her legs around him and drew him into her until she was filled. At the shock of that first ragged peak, her eyes flew open. Inches away, he watched her face. Her mouth trembled open, but before she could catch her breath, he was driving her higher, faster. She couldn't tell how long they balanced on the edge, trapped between pleasure and fulfillment. Then his arms came around her, hers around his. Together, they broke free.

She didn't speak. Her system leveled slowly, and she was helpless to hurry it. He didn't move. He'd shifted his weight, but his arms had come around her and stayed there. She needed him to speak, to say something that would put what had happened in perspective. She'd only had one other lover and had learned not to expect.

Jonas rested his forehead against her shoulder a moment. He was wrestling with his own demons. "I'm sorry, Liz."

He could have said nothing worse. She closed her eyes and forced her emotions to drain. She nearly succeeded. Steadier, she reached for the tangle of clothes on the floor. "I don't need an apology." With her clothes in a ball in her arm, she walked quickly to the bedroom.

On a long breath, Jonas sat up. He couldn't seem to find the right buttons on Liz Palmer. Every move he made seemed to be a move in reverse. It still stunned him that he'd been so rough with her, left her so little choice in the final outcome. He'd be better off hiring her a private bodyguard and moving himself back to the hotel. It was true he didn't want to see her hurt and felt a certain responsibility for her welfare, but he didn't seem to be able to act on it properly. When she'd stood in the kitchen telling him what she'd been through, something had begun to boil in him. That it had taken the form of passion in the end wasn't something easily explained or justified. His apology had been inadequate, but he had little else.

Drawing on his pants, Jonas started for his room. It snouldn't have surprised him to find himself veering toward Liz's. She was just pulling on a robe. "It's late, Jonas."

"Did I hurt you?"

She sent him a look that made guilt turn over in his stomach. "Yes. Now I want to take a shower before I go to bed."

"Liz, there's no excuse for being so rough, and there's no making it up to you, but—"

"Your apology hurt me," she interrupted. "Now if you've said all you have to say, I'd like to be alone."

He stared at her a moment, then dragged a hand through his hair. How could he have convinced himself he understood her when she was now and always had been an enigma? "Damn it, Liz, I wasn't apologizing for making love to you, but for the lack of finesse. I practically tossed you on the ground and ripped your clothes off."

She folded her hands and tried to keep calm. "I ripped yours."

His lips twitched, then curved. "Yeah, you did."

Humor didn't come into her eyes. "And do you want an apology?"

He came to her then and rested his hands on her shoulders. Her robe was cotton and thin and whirling with bright color. "No. I guess what I'd like is for you to say you wanted me as much as I wanted you."

Her courage weakened, so she looked beyond him. "I'd have thought that was obvious."

"Liz." His hand was gentle as he turned her face back to his.

"All right. I wanted you. Now—"

"Now," he interrupted. "Will you listen?"

"There's no need to say anything."

"Yes, there is." He walked with her to the bed and drew her down to sit. Moonlight played over their hands as he took hers. "I came to Cozumel for one reason. My feelings on that haven't changed but other things have. When I first met you I thought you knew something, were hiding something. I linked everything about you to Jerry. It didn't take long for me to see there was something else. I wanted to know about you, for myself."

"Why?"

"I don't know. It's impossible not to care about you." At her look of surprise, he smiled. "You project this image of pure self-sufficiency and still manage to look like a waif. Tonight, I purposely maneuvered you into talking about Faith and what had brought you here. When you told me I couldn't handle it."

She drew her hand from his. "That's understandable. Most people have trouble handling unwed mothers."

Anger bubbled as he grabbed her hand again. "Stop putting words in my mouth. You stood in the kitchen talking and I could see you, young, eager and trusting, being betrayed and hurt. I could see what it had done to you, how it had closed you off from things you wanted to do."

"I told you I don't have any regrets."

"I know." He lifted her hand and kissed it. "I guess for a moment I needed to have them for you."

"Jonas, do you think anyone's life turns out the way they plan it as children?"

He laughed a little as he slipped an arm around her and drew her against him. Liz sat still a moment, unsure how to react to the casual show of affection. Then she leaned her head against his shoulder and closed her eyes. "Jerry and I were going to be partners."

"In what?"

"In anything."

She touched the coin on the end of his chain. "He had one of these."

"Our grandparents gave them to us when we were kids. They're identical five-dollar gold pieces. Funny, I always wore mine heads up. Jerry wore his heads down." He closed his fingers over the coin. "He stole his first car when we were sixteen."

Her fingers crept up to his. "I'm sorry."

"The thing was he didn't need to—we had access to any car in the garage. He told me he just wanted to see if he could get away with it."

"He didn't make life easy for you."

"No, he didn't make life easy. Especially for himself. But he never did anything out of meanness. There were times I hated him, but I never stopped loving him."

Liz drew closer. "Love hurts more than hate."

He kissed the top of her head. "Liz, I don't suppose you've ever talked to a lawyer about Faith."

"Why should I?"

"Marcus has a responsibility, a financial responsibility, at the least, to you and Faith."

"I took money from Marcus once. Not again."

"Child support payments could be set up very quietly. You could stop working seven days a week."

Liz took a deep breath and pulled away until she could see his face. "Faith is my child, has been my child only since the moment Marcus handed me a check. I could have had the abortion and gone back to my life as I'd planned it. I chose not to. I chose to have the baby, to raise the baby, to support the baby. She's never given me anything but pleasure from the moment she was born, and I have no intention of sharing her."

"One day she's going to ask you for his name."

Liz moistened her lips, but nodded. "Then one day I'll tell her. She'll have her own choice to make."

He wouldn't press her now, but there was no reason he couldn't have his law clerk begin to investigate child support laws and paternity cases. "Are you going to let me meet her? I know the deal is for me to be out of the house and out of your life when she gets back. I will, but I'd like the chance to meet her."

"If you're still in Mexico."

"One more question."

The smile came more easily. "One more."

"There haven't been any other men, have there?"

The smile faded. "No."

He felt twin surges of gratitude and guilt. "Then let me show you how it should be."

"There's no need—"

Gently, he brushed the hair back from her face. "Yes, there is. For both of us." He kissed her eyes closed. "I've wanted you from the first." His mouth on hers was as sweet as spring rain and just as gentle. Slowly, he slipped the robe from her shoulders, following the trail with warm lips. "Your skin's like gold," he murmured, then traced a finger over her breasts where the tone changed. "And so pale. I want to see all of you."

"Jonas—"

"All of you," he repeated, looking into her eyes until the heat kindled again. "I want to make love with all of you."

She didn't resist. Never in her life had anyone ever touched her with such reverence, looked at her with such need. When he urged her back, Liz lay on the bed, naked and waiting.

"Lovely," Jonas murmured. Her body was milk and honey in the moonlight. And her eyes were dark—dark and open and uncertain. "I want you to trust me." He began a slow journey of exploration at her ankles. "I want to know when I look at you that you're not afraid of me."

"I'm not afraid of you."

"You have been. Maybe I've even wanted you to be. No more."

His tongue slid over her skin and teased the back of her knees. The jolt of power had her rising up and gasping. "Jonas."

"Relax." He ran a hand lightly up her hip. "I want to feel your bones melt. Lie back, Liz. Let me show you how much you can have."

She obeyed, only because she hadn't the strength to resist. He murmured to her, stroking, nibbling, until she was too steeped in what he gave to give in return. But he wanted her that way, wanted to take her as though she hadn't been touched before. Not by him, not by anyone. Slowly, thoroughly and with great, great patience he seduced and pleasured. He thought as his mouth skimmed up her thigh that he could hear her skin hum.

She'd never known anything could be like this—so

deep, so dark. There was a freedom here, she discovered, that she'd once only associated with diving down through silent fathoms. Her body could float, her limbs could be weightless, but she could feel every touch, every movement. Dreamlike, sensations drifted over her, so soft, so misty, each blended into the next. How long could it go on? Perhaps, after all, there were forevers.

She was lean, with muscles firm in her legs. Like a dancer's he thought, disciplined and trained. The scent from the bowl on her dresser spiced the air, but it was her fragrance, cool as a waterfall, that swam in his head. His mind emptied of everything but the need to delight her. Love, when unselfish, has incredible power.

His tongue plunged into the heat and his hands gripped hers as she arched, stunned at being flung from a floating world to a churning one. He drew from her, both patient and relentless, until she shuddered to climax and over. When her hands went limp in his, he brought them back to his body and pleasured himself.

She hadn't known passion could stretch so far or a body endure such a barrage of sensations. His hands, rough at the palm, showed her secrets she'd never had the chance to imagine. His lips, warmed from her own skin, opened mysteries and whispered the answers. He gentled her, he enticed her, he stroked with tenderness and he devoured. Gasping for air, she had no choice but to allow him whatever he wanted, and to strain for him to show her more.

When he was inside of her she thought it was all, and more, than she could ever want. If this was love, she'd never tasted it. If this was passion, she'd only skimmed its surface. Now it was time to risk the depths. Willing, eager, she held on to him.

It was trust he felt from her, and trust that moved him unbearably. He thought he'd needed before, desired before, but never so completely. Though he knew what it was to be part of another person, he'd never expected to feel the merger again. Strong, complex, unavoidable, the emotion swamped him. He belonged to her as fully as he'd wanted her to belong to him.

He took her slowly, so that the thrill that coursed through her seemed endless. His skin was moist when she pressed her lips to his throat. The pulse there was as quick as her own. A giddy sense of triumph moved through her, only to be whipped away with passion before it could spread.

Then he drew her up to him, and her body, liquid and limber with emotion, rose like a wave to press against his. Wrapped close, mouths fused, they moved together. Her hair fell like rain down her back. She could feel his heartbeat fast against her breast.

Still joined, they lowered again. The rhythm quickened. Desperation rose. She heard him breathe her name before the gates burst open and she was lost in the flood.

Chapter Nine

She woke slowly, with a long, lazy stretch. Keeping her eyes closed, Liz waited for the alarm to ring. It wasn't often she felt so relaxed, even when waking, so she pampered herself and absorbed the luxury of doing nothing. In an hour, she mused, she'd be at the dive shop shifting through the day's schedule. The glass bottom, she thought, frowning a little. Was she supposed to take it out? Odd that she couldn't remember. Then with a start, it occurred to her that she didn't remember because she didn't know. She hadn't handled the schedule in two days. And last night…

She opened her eyes and looked into Jonas's.

"I could watch your mind wake up." He bent over and kissed her. "Fascinating."

Liz closed her fingers over the sheet and tugged it a little higher. What was she supposed to say? She'd never spent the night with a man, never awoken with one. She cleared her throat and wondered if every man awoke as sexily disheveled as Jonas Sharpe. "How did you sleep?" she managed, and felt ridiculous.

"Fine." He smiled as he brushed her hair from her cheek with a fingertip. "And you?"

"Fine." Her fingers moved restlessly on the sheet until he closed his hands over them. His eyes were warm and heavy and made her heart pound.

"It's a little late to be nervous around me, Elizabeth."

"I'm not nervous." But color rose to her cheeks when he pressed his lips to her naked shoulder.

"Still, it's rather flattering. If you're nervous…" He turned his head so the tip of his tongue could toy with her ear. "Then you're not unmoved. I wouldn't like to think you felt casually about being with me—yet."

Was it possible to want so much this morning what she'd sated herself with the night before? She didn't think it should be, and yet her body told her differently. She would, as she always did, listen to her intellect first. "It must be almost time to get up." One hand firmly on the sheets, she rose on her elbows to look at the clock. "That's not right." She blinked and focused again. "It can't be eight-fifteen."

"Why not?" He slipped a hand beneath the sheet and stroked her thigh.

"Because." His touch had her pulses speeding. "I always set it for six-fifteen."

Finding her a challenge, Jonas brushed light kisses over her shoulder, down her arm. "You didn't set it last night."

"I always—" She cut herself off. It was hard enough to try to think when he was touching her, but when she remembered the night before, it was nearly impossible to understand why she had to think. Her mind hadn't been on alarms and schedules and customers when her body had curled into Jonas's to sleep. Her mind, as it was now, had been filled with him.

"Always what?"

She wished he wouldn't distract her with fingertips sliding gently over her skin. She wished he could touch her everywhere at once. "I always wake up at six, whether I set it or not."

"You didn't this time." He laughed as he eased her back down. "I suppose I should be flattered again."

"Maybe I flatter you too much," she murmured and started to shift away. He simply rolled her back to him. "I have to get up."

"No, you don't."

"Jonas, I'm already late. I have to get to work."

Sunlight dappled over her face. He wanted to see it over the rest of her. "The only thing you have to do is make love with me." He kissed her fingers, then slowly drew them from the sheet. "I'll never get through the day without you."

"The boats—"

"Are already out, I'm sure." He cupped her breast, rubbing his thumb back and forth over the nipple. "Luis seems competent."

"He is. I haven't been in for two days."

"One more won't hurt."

Her body vibrated with need that slowly wound itself into her mind. Her arms came up to him, around him. "No, I guess it won't."

She hadn't stayed in bed until ten o'clock since she'd been a child. Liz felt as irresponsible as one as she started the coffee. True, Luis could handle the shop and the boats as well as she, but it wasn't his job. It was hers. Here she was, brewing coffee at ten o'clock, with her body still warm from loving. Nothing had been the same since Jonas Sharpe had arrived on her doorstep.

"It's useless to give yourself a hard time for taking a morning off," Jonas said from behind her.

Liz popped bread into the toaster. "I suppose not, since I don't even know today's schedule."

"Liz." Jonas took her by the arms and firmly turned her around. He studied her, gauging her mood before he spoke. "You know, back in Philadelphia I'm considered a workaholic. I've had friends express concern over the workload I take on and the hours I put in. Compared to you, I'm retired."

Her brows drew together as they did when she was concentrating. Or annoyed. "We each do what we have to do."

"True enough. It appears what I have to do is harass you until you relax."

She had to smile. He said it so reasonably and his eyes were laughing. "I'm sure you have a reputation for being an expert on harassment."

"I majored in it at college."

"Good for you. But I'm an expert at budgeting my own time. And there's my toast." He let her pluck it out, waited until she'd buttered it, then took a piece for himself.

"You mentioned diving lessons."

She was still frowning at him when she heard the coffee begin to simmer. She reached for one cup, then relented and took two. "What about them?"

"I'll take one. Today."

"Today?" She handed him his coffee, drinking her

own standing by the stove. "I'll have to see what's scheduled. The way things have been going, both dive boats should already be out."

"Not a group lesson, a private one. You can take me out on the *Expatriate*."

"Luis usually takes care of the private lessons."

He smiled at her. "I prefer dealing with the management."

Liz dusted crumbs from her fingers. "All right then. It'll cost you."

He lifted his cup in salute. "I never doubted it."

Liz was laughing when Jonas pulled into a narrow parking space at the hotel. "If he'd picked your pocket, why did you defend him?"

"Everyone's entitled to representation," Jonas reminded her. "Besides, I figured if I took him on as a client, he'd leave my wallet alone."

"And did he?"

"Yeah." Jonas took her hand as they crossed the sidewalk to the sand. "He stole my watch instead."

She giggled, a foolish, girlish sound he'd never heard from her. "And did you get him off?"

"Two years probation. There, it looks like business is good."

Liz shielded her eyes from the sun and looked toward the shop. Luis was busily fitting two couples with snorkel gear. A glance to the left showed her only the *Expatriate* remained in dock. "Cozumel's becoming very popular," she murmured.

"Isn't that the idea?"

"For business?" She moved her shoulders. "I'd be a fool to complain."

"But?"

"But sometimes I think it would be nice if I could block out the changes. I don't want to see the water choked with suntan oil. *Hola,* Luis."

"Liz!" His gaze passed over Jonas briefly before he grinned at her. "We thought maybe you deserted us. How did you like Acapulco?"

"It was…different," she decided, and was already scooting behind the counter to find the daily schedule. "Any problems?"

"Jose took care of a couple repairs. I brought Miguel back to fill in, but I keep an eye on him. Got this—what do you call it—brochure on the aqua bikes." He pulled out a colorful pamphlet, but Liz only nodded.

"The Brinkman party's out diving. Did we take them to Palancar?"

"Two days in a row. Miguel likes them. They tip good."

"Hmm. You're handling the shop alone."

"No problem. Hey, there was a guy." He screwed up his face as he tried to remember the name. "Skinny guy, American. You know the one you took out on the beginners' trip?"

She flipped through the receipts and was satisfied. "Trydent?"

"*Sí,* that was it. He came by a coupla times."

"Rent anything?"

"No." Luis wiggled his eyebrows at her. "He was looking for you."

Liz shrugged it off. If he hadn't rented anything, he didn't interest her. "If everything's under control here, I'm going to take Mr. Sharpe out for a diving lesson."

Luis looked quickly at Jonas, then away. The man

made him uneasy, but Liz looked happier than she had in weeks. "Want me to get the gear?"

"No, I'll take care of it." She looked up and smiled at Jonas. "Write Mr. Sharpe up a rental form and give him a receipt for the gear, the lesson and the boat trip. Since it's…" She trailed off as she checked her watch. "Nearly eleven, give him the half-day rate."

"You're all heart," Jonas murmured as she went to the shelves to choose his equipment.

"You got the best teacher," Luis told him, but couldn't manage more than another quick look at Jonas.

"I'm sure you're right." Idly, Jonas swiveled the newspaper Luis had tossed on the counter around to face him. He missed being able to sit down with the morning paper over coffee. The Spanish headlines told him nothing. "Anything going on I should know about?" Jonas asked, indicating the paper.

Luis relaxed a bit as he wrote. Jonas's voice wasn't so much like Jerry's when you weren't looking at him. "Haven't had a chance to look at it yet. Busy morning."

Going with habit, Jonas turned the paper over. There, in a faded black-and-white picture, was Erika. Jonas's fingers tightened. He glanced back and saw that Liz was busy, her back to him. Without a word, he slid the paper over the receipt Luis was writing.

"Hey, that's the—"

"I know," Jonas said in an undertone. "What does it say?"

Luis bent over the paper to read. He straightened again very slowly, and his face was ashen. "Dead," he whispered. "She's dead."

"How?"

Luis's fingers opened and closed on the pen he held. "Stabbed."

Jonas thought of the knife held at Liz's throat. "When?"

"Last night." Luis had to swallow twice. "They found her last night."

"Jonas," Liz called from the back, "how much do you weigh?"

Keeping his eyes on Luis, Jonas turned the paper over again. "One seventy. She doesn't need to hear this now," he added under his breath. He pulled bills from his wallet and laid them on the counter. "Finish writing the receipt."

After a struggle, Luis mastered his own fear and straightened. "I don't want anything to happen to Liz."

Jonas met the look with a challenge that held for several humming seconds before he relaxed. The smaller man was terrified, but he was thinking of Liz. "Neither do I. I'm going to see nothing does."

"You brought trouble."

"I know." His gaze shifted beyond Luis to Liz. "But if I leave, the trouble doesn't."

For the first time, Luis forced himself to study Jonas's face. After a moment, he blew out a long breath. "I liked your brother, but I think it was him who brought trouble."

"It doesn't matter anymore who brought it. I'm going to look out for her."

"Then you look good," Luis warned softly. "You look real good."

"First lesson," Liz said as she unlocked her storage closet. "Each diver carries and is responsible for his own gear." She jerked her head back to where Jonas's was stacked. With a last look at Luis, he walked through the doorway to gather it up.

"Preparing for a dive is twice as much work as diving itself," she began as she hefted her tanks. "It's a good thing it's worth it. We'll be back before sundown, Luis. *Hasta luego.*"

"Liz." She stopped, turning back to where Luis hovered in the doorway. His gaze passed over Jonas, then returned to her. *"Hasta luego,"* he managed, and closed his fingers over the medal he wore around his neck.

The moment she was on board, Liz restacked her gear. As a matter of routine, she checked all the *Expatriate*'s gauges. "Can you cast off?" she asked Jonas.

He ran a hand down her hair, surprising her. She looked so competent, so in charge. He wondered if by staying close he was protecting or endangering. It was becoming vital to believe the first. "I can handle it."

She felt her stomach flutter as he continued to stare at her. "Then you'd better stop looking at me and do it."

"I like looking at you." He drew her close, just to hold her. "I could spend years looking at you."

Her arms came up, hesitated, then dropped back to her sides. It would be so easy to believe. To trust again, give again, be hurt again. She wanted to tell him of the love growing inside her, spreading and strengthening with each moment. But if she told him she'd no longer have even the illusion of control. Without control, she was defenseless.

"I clocked you on at eleven," she said, but couldn't resist breathing deeply of his scent and committing it to memory.

Because she made him smile again, he drew her back. "I'm paying the bill, I'll worry about the time."

"Diving lesson," she reminded him. "And you can't dive until you cast off."

"Aye, aye, sir." But he gave her a hard, breath-stealing kiss before he jumped back on the dock.

Liz drew air into her lungs and let it out slowly before she turned on the engines. All she could hope was that she looked more in control than she felt. He was winning a battle, she mused, that he didn't even know he was fighting. She waited for Jonas to join her again before she eased the throttle forward.

"There are plenty of places to dive where we don't need the boat, but I thought you'd enjoy something away from the beaches. Palancar is one of the most stunning reefs in the Caribbean. It's probably the best place to start because the north end is shallow and the wall slopes rather than having a sheer vertical drop-off. There are a lot of caves and passageways, so it makes for an interesting dive."

"I'm sure, but I had something else in mind."

"Something else?"

Jonas took a small book out of his pocket and flipped through it. "What do these numbers look like to you?"

Liz recognized the book. It was the same one he'd used in Acapulco to copy down the numbers from his brother's book in the safe-deposit box. He still had his priorities, she reminded herself, then drew back on the throttle to let the boat idle.

The numbers were in precise, neat lines. Any child who'd paid attention in geography class would recognize them. "Longitude and latitude."

He nodded. "Do you have a chart?"

He'd planned this since he'd first seen the numbers, she realized. Their being lovers changed nothing else. "Of course, but I don't need it for this. I know these waters. That's just off the coast of Isla Mujeres." Liz adjusted her course and picked up speed. Perhaps, she thought, the course had already been set for both of them long before this. They had no choice but to see it through. "It's a long trip. You might as well relax."

He put his hands on her shoulders to knead. "We won't find anything, but I have to go."

"I understand."

"Would you rather I go alone?"

She shook her head violently, but said nothing.

"Liz, this had to be his drop point. By tomorrow, Moralas will have the numbers and send his own divers down. I have to see for myself."

"You're chasing shadows, Jonas. Jerry's gone. Nothing you can do is going to change that."

"I'll find out why. I'll find out who. That'll be enough."

"Will it?" With her hand gripping the wheel hard, she looked over her shoulder. His eyes were close, but they held that cool, set look again. "I don't think so—not for you." Liz turned her face back to the sea. She would take him where he wanted to go.

Isla Mujeres, Island of Women, was a small gem in the water. Surrounded by reefs and studded with untouched lagoons, it was one of the perfect retreats of the Caribbean. Party boats from the continental coast or one of the other islands cruised there daily to offer their customers snorkeling or diving at its best. It had once been known by pirates and blessed by a goddess. Liz anchored the boat off the southwest coast. Once again, she became the teacher.

"It's important to know and understand both the name and the use of every piece of equipment. It's not just a matter of stuffing in a mouthpiece and strapping on a tank. No smoking," she added as Jonas took out a cigarette. "It's ridiculous to clog up your lungs in the first place, and absurd to do it before a dive."

Jonas set the pack on the bench beside him. "How long are we going down?"

"We'll keep it under an hour. The depth here ranges to eighty feet. That means the nitrogen in your air supply will be over three times denser than what your system's accustomed to. In some people at some depths, this can cause temporary imbalances. If you begin to feel light-headed, signal to me right away. We'll descend in stages to give your body time to get used to the changes in pressure. We ascend the same way in order to give the nitrogen time to expel. If you come up too quickly, you risk decompression sickness. It can be fatal." As she spoke, she spread out the gear with the intention of explaining each piece. "Nothing is to be taken for granted in the water. It is not your milieu. You're dependent on your equipment and your own good sense. It's beautiful and it's exciting, but it's not an amusement park."

"Is this the same lecture you give on the dive boat?"

"Basically."

"You're very good."

"Thank you." She picked up a gauge. "Now—"

"Can we get started?" he asked and reached for his wet suit.

"We are getting started. You can't dive without a working knowledge of your equipment."

"That's a depth gauge." He nodded toward her hand as he stripped down to black briefs. "A very sophisticated one. I wouldn't think most dive shops would find it necessary to stock that quality."

"This is mine," she murmured. "But I keep a handful for rentals."

"I don't think I mentioned that you have the best-tended equipment I've ever seen. It isn't in the same league with your personal gear, but it's quality. Give me a hand, will you?"

Liz rose to help him into the tough, stretchy suit. "You've gone down before."

"I've been diving since I was fifteen." Jonas pulled up the zipper before bending over to check the tanks himself.

"Since you were fifteen." Liz yanked off her shirt and tossed it aside. Fuming, she pulled off her shorts until she wore nothing but a string bikini and a scowl. "Then why did you let me go on that way?"

"I liked hearing you." Jonas glanced up and felt his blood surge. "Almost as much as I like looking at you."

She wasn't in the mood to be flattered, less in the mood to be charmed. Without asking for assistance, she tugged herself into her wet suit. "You're still paying for the lesson."

Jonas grinned as he examined his flippers. "I never doubted it."

She strapped on the rest of her gear in silence. It was difficult even for her to say if she were really angry. All she knew was the day, and dive, weren't as simple as they had started out to be. Lifting the top of a bench, she reached into a compartment and took out two short metal sticks shaped like bats.

"What's this for?" Jonas asked as she handed him one.

"Insurance." She adjusted her mask. "We're going down to the caves where the sharks sleep."

"Sharks don't sleep."

"The oxygen content in the water in the cave keeps them quiescent. But don't think you can trust them."

Without another word, she swung over the side and down the ladder.

The water was as clear as glass, so she could see for more than a hundred feet. As she heard Jonas plunge in beside her, Liz turned to assure herself he did indeed know what he was doing. Catching her skeptical look, Jonas merely circled his thumb and forefinger, then pointed down.

He was tense. Liz could feel it from him, though she understood it had nothing to do with his skill underwater. His brother had dived here once—she was as certain of it as Jonas. And the reason for his dives had been the reason for his death. She no longer had to think whether she was angry. In a gesture as personal as a kiss, she reached out a hand and took his.

Grateful, Jonas curled his fingers around hers. He didn't know what he was looking for, or even why he continued to look when already he'd found more than he'd wanted to. His brother had played games with the rules and had lost. Some would say there was justice in that. But they'd shared birth. He had to go on looking, and go on hoping.

Liz saw the first of the devilfish and tugged on Jonas's hand. Such things never failed to touch her spirit. The giant manta rays cruised together, feeding on plankton and unconcerned with the human intruders. Liz kicked forward, delighted to swim among them. Their huge mouths could crush and devour crustaceans. Their wingspan of twenty feet and more was awesome. Without fear, Liz reached out to touch. Pleasure came easily, as it always did to her in the sea. Her eyes were laughing as she reached out again for Jonas.

They descended farther, and some of his tension began

to dissolve. There was something different about her here, a lightness, an ease that dissolved the sadness that always seemed to linger in her eyes. She looked free, and more, as happy as he'd ever seen her. If it were possible to fall in love in a matter of moments, Jonas fell in love in those, forty feet below the surface with a mermaid who'd forgotten how to dream.

Everything she saw, everything she could touch fascinated her. He could see it in the way she moved, the way she looked at everything as though it were her first dive. If he could have found a way, he would have stayed with her there, surrounded by love and protected by fathoms.

They swam deeper, but leisurely. If something evil had been begun, or been ended there, it had left no trace. The sea was calm and silent and full of life too lovely to exist in the air.

When the shadow passed over, Liz looked up. In all her dives, she'd never seen anything so spectacular. Thousands upon thousands of silvery grunts moved together in a wave so dense that they might have been one creature. Eyes wide with the wonder of it, Liz lifted her arms and took her body up. The wave swayed as a unit, avoiding intrusion. Delighted, she signaled for Jonas to join her. The need to share the magic was natural. This was the pull of the sea that had driven her to study, urged to explore and invited her once to dream. With her fingers linked with Jonas's, she propelled them closer. The school of fish split in half so that it became two unified forms swirling on either side of them. The sea teemed with them, thick clouds of silver so tightly grouped that they seemed fused together.

For a moment she was as close to her own fantasies as she had ever been, floating free, surrounded by magic, with her lover's hand in hers. Impulsively, she wrapped her arms around Jonas and held on. The clouds of fish swarmed around them, linked into one, then swirled away.

He could feel her pulse thud when he reached for her wrist. He could see the fascinated delight in her eyes. Hampered by his human frailty in the water, he could only touch his hand to her cheek. When she lifted her own to press it closer, it was enough. Side by side they swam toward the seafloor.

The limestone caves were eerie and compelling. Once Jonas saw the head of a moray eel slide out and curve, either in curiosity or warning. An old turtle with barnacles crusting his back rose from his resting place beneath a rock and swam between them. Then at the entrance to a cave, Liz pointed and shared another mystery.

The shark moved across the sand, as a dog might on a hearth rug. His small, black eyes stared back at them as his gills slowly drew in water. While they huddled just inside the entrance, their bubbles rising up through the porous limestone and toward the surface, the shark shifted restlessly. Jonas reached for Liz's hand to draw her back, but she moved a bit closer, anxious to see.

In a quick move, the shark shot toward the entrance. Jonas was grabbing for Liz and his knife, when she merely poked at the head with her wooden bat. Without pausing, the shark swam toward the open sea and vanished.

He wanted to strangle her. He wanted to tell her how fascinating she was to watch. Since he could do neither, Jonas merely closed a hand over her throat and gave her a mock shake. Her laughter had bubbles dancing.

They swam on together, parting from time to time to

explore separate interests. He decided she'd forgotten his purpose in coming, but thought it was just as well. If she could take this hour for personal freedom, he was glad of it. For him, there were demands.

The water and the life in it were undeniably beautiful, but Jonas noticed other things. They hadn't seen another diver and their down time was nearly up. The caves where the sharks slept were also a perfect place to conceal a cache of drugs. Only the very brave or the very foolish would swim in their territory at night. He thought of his brother and knew Jerry would have considered it the best kind of adventure. A man with a reason could swim into one of the caves while the sharks were out feeding, and leave or take whatever he liked.

Liz hadn't forgotten why Jonas had come. Because she thought she could understand a part of what he was feeling, she gave him room. Here, eighty feet below the surface, he was searching for something, anything, to help him accept his brother's death. And his brother's life.

It would come to an end soon, Liz reflected. The police had the name of the go-between in Acapulco. And the other name that Jonas had given them, she remembered suddenly. Where had he gotten that one? She looked toward him and realized there were things he wasn't telling her. That, too, would end soon, she promised herself. Then she found herself abruptly out of air.

She didn't panic. Liz was too well trained to panic. Immediately, she checked her gauge and saw that she had ten full minutes left. Reaching back, she ran a hand down her hose and found it unencumbered. But she couldn't draw air.

Whatever the gauge said, her life was on the line. If she swam toward the surface, her lungs would be crushed by the pressure. Forcing herself to stay calm, she swam in a diagonal toward Jonas. When she caught his ankle, she tugged sharply. The smile he turned with faded the moment he saw her eyes. Recognizing her signal, he immediately removed his regulator and passed it to her. Liz drew in air. Nodding, she handed it back to him. Their bodies brushing, her hand firm on his shoulder, they began their slow ascent.

Buddy-breathing, they rose closer to the surface, restraining themselves from rushing. What took only a matter of minutes seemed to drag on endlessly. The moment Liz's head broke water, she pushed back her mask and gulped in fresh air.

"What happened?" Jonas demanded, but when he felt her begin to shake, he only swore and pulled her with him to the ladder. "Take it easy." His hand was firm at her back as she climbed up.

"I'm all right." But she collapsed on a bench, without the energy to draw off her tanks. Her body shuddered once with relief as Jonas took the weight from her. With her head between her knees, she waited for the mists to clear. "I've never had anything like that happen," she managed. "Not at eighty feet."

He was rubbing her hands to warm them. "What did happen?"

"I ran out of air."

Enraged, he took her by the shoulders and dragged her back to a sitting position. "Ran out of air? That's unforgivably careless. How can you give lessons when you haven't the sense to watch your own gauges?"

"I watched my gauge." She drew air in and let it out slowly. "I should have had another ten minutes."

"You rent diving equipment, for God's sake! How can you be negligent with your own? You might've died."

The insult to her competence went a long way toward smothering the fear. "I'm never careless," she snapped at him. "Not with rental equipment or my own." She dragged the mask from her head and tossed it on the bench. "Look at my gauge. I should have had ten minutes left."

He looked, but it didn't relieve his anger. "Your equipment should be checked. If you go down with a faulty gauge you're inviting an accident."

"My equipment has been checked. I check it myself after every dive, and it was fine before I stored it. I filled those tanks myself." The alternative came to her even as she finished speaking. Her face, already pale, went white. "God, Jonas, I filled them myself. I checked every piece of equipment the last time I went down."

He closed a hand over hers hard enough to make her wince. "You keep it in the shop, in that closet."

"I lock it up."

"How many keys?"

"Mine—and an extra set in the drawer. They're rarely used because I always leave mine there when I go out on the boats."

"But the extra set would have been used when we were away?"

The shaking was starting again. This time it wasn't as simple to control it. "Yes."

"And someone used the key to the closet to get in and tamper with your equipment."

She moistened her lips. "Yes."

The rage ripped inside him until he was nearly blind with it. Hadn't he just promised to watch out for her, to keep her safe? With intensely controlled movements, he pulled off his flippers and discarded his mask. "You're going back. You're going to pack, then I'm putting you on a plane. You can stay with my family until this is over."

"No."

"You're going to do exactly what I say."

"No," she said again and managed to draw the strength to stand. "I'm not going anywhere. This is the second time someone's threatened my life."

"And they're not going to have a chance to do it again."

"I'm not leaving my home."

"Don't be a fool." He rose. Knowing he couldn't touch her, he unzipped his wet suit and began to strip it off. "Your business isn't going to fall apart. You can come back when it's safe."

"I'm not leaving." She took a step toward him. "You came here looking for revenge. When you have it, you can leave and be satisfied. Now I'm looking for answers. I can't leave because they're here."

Struggling to keep his hands gentle, he took her face between them. "I'll find them for you."

"You know better than that, don't you, Jonas? Answers don't mean anything unless you find them yourself. I want my daughter to be able to come home. Until I find those answers, until it's safe, she can't." She lifted her hands to his face so that they stood as a unit. "We both have reasons to look now."

He sat, took his pack of cigarettes and spoke flatly. "Erika's dead."

The anger that had given her the strength to stand wavered. "What?"

"Murdered." His voice was cold again, hard again. "A few days ago I met her, paid her for a name."

Liz braced herself against the rail. "The name you gave to the captain."

Jonas lit his cigarette, telling himself he was justified to put fear back into her eyes. "That's right. She asked some questions, got some answers. She told me this Pablo Manchez was bad, a professional killer. Jerry was killed by a pro. So, it appears, was Erika."

"She was shot?"

"Stabbed," Jonas corrected and watched Liz's hand reach involuntarily for her own neck. "That's right." He drew violently on the cigarette then hurled it overboard before he rose. "You're going back to the States until this is all over."

She turned her back on him a moment, needing to be certain she could be strong. "I'm not leaving, Jonas. We have the same problem."

"Liz—"

"No." When she turned back her chin was up and her eyes were clear. "You see, I've run from problems before, and it doesn't work."

"This isn't a matter of running, it's a matter of being sensible."

"You're staying."

"I don't have a choice."

"Then neither do I."

"Liz, I don't want you hurt."

She tilted her head as she studied him. She could believe that, she realized, and take comfort in it. "Will you go?"

"I can't. You know I can't."

"Neither can I." She wrapped her arms around him,

pressed her cheek to his shoulder in a first spontaneous show of need or affection. "Let's go home," she murmured. "Let's just go home."

Chapter Ten

Every morning when Liz awoke she was certain Captain Moralas would call to tell her it was all over. Every night when she closed her eyes, she was certain it was only a matter of one more day. Time went on.

Every morning when Liz awoke she was certain Jonas would tell her he had to leave. Every night when she slept in his arms, she was certain it was the last time. He stayed.

For over ten years her life had had a certain purpose. Success. She'd started the struggle toward it in order to survive and to provide for her child. Somewhere along the way she'd learned the satisfaction of being on her own and making it work. In over ten years, Liz had gone steadily forward without detours. A detour could mean failure and the loss of independence. It had been barely a month since Jonas had walked into her house and her life. Since that time the straight road she had followed had forked. Ignoring the changes hadn't helped, fighting them hadn't worked. Now it no longer seemed she had the choice of which path to follow.

Because she had to hold on to something, she worked every day, keeping stubbornly to her old routine. It was the only aspect of her life that she could be certain she could control. Though it brought some semblance of order to her life, it didn't keep Liz's mind at rest. She found herself studying her customers with suspicion. Business thrived as the summer season drew closer. It didn't seem as important as it had even weeks before, but she kept the shop open seven days a week.

Jonas had taken the fabric of her life, plucked at a few threads and changed everything. Liz had come to the point that she could admit nothing would ever be quite the same again, but she had yet to come to the point that she knew what to do about it. When he left, as she knew he would, she would have to learn all over again how to suppress longings and black out dreams.

They would find Jerry Sharpe's killer. They would find the man with the knife. If she hadn't believed that, Liz would never have gone on day after day. But after the danger was over, after all questions were answered, her life would never be as it had been. Jonas had woven himself into it. When he went away, he'd leave a hole behind that would take all her will to mend.

Her life had been torn before. Liz could comfort herself that she had put it together again. The shape had been different, the texture had changed, but she had put it together. She could do so again. She would have to.

There were times when she lay in bed in the dark, in

the early hours of the morning, restless, afraid she would have to begin those repairs before she was strong enough.

Jonas could feel her shift beside him. He'd come to understand she rarely slept peacefully. Or she no longer slept peacefully. He wished she would lean on him, but knew she never would. Her independence was too vital, and opposingly, her insecurity was too deep to allow her to admit a need for another. Even the sharing of a burden was difficult for her. He wanted to soothe. Through his adult life, Jonas had carefully chosen companions who had no problems, required no advice, no comfort, no support. A woman who required such things required an emotional attachment he had never been willing to make. He wasn't a selfish man, simply a cautious one. Throughout his youth, and through most of his adult life, he'd picked up the pieces his brother had scattered. Consciously or unconsciously, Jonas had promised himself he'd never be put in the position of having to do so for anyone else.

Now he was drawing closer and closer to a woman who elicited pure emotion, then tried to deflect it. He was falling in love with a woman who needed him but refused to admit it. She was strong and had both the intelligence and the will to take care of herself. And she had eyes so soft, so haunted, that a man would risk anything to protect her from any more pain.

She had completely changed his life. She had altered the simple, tidy pattern he'd been weaving for himself. He *needed* to soothe, to protect, to share. There was nothing he could do to change that. Whenever he touched her, he came closer to admitting there was nothing he would do.

The bed was warm and the room smelled of the flowers that grew wild outside the open window. Their scent mixed with the bowl of potpourri on Liz's dresser. Now and then the breeze ruffled through palm fronds so that the sound whispered but didn't disturb. Beside him was a woman whose body was slim and restless. Her hair spread over her pillow and onto his, carrying no more fragrance than wind over water. The moonlight trickled in, dipping into corners, filtering over the bed so he could trace her silhouette. As she tossed in sleep, he drew her closer. Her muscles were tense, as though she were prepared to reject the gift of comfort even before it was offered. Slowly, as her breath whispered at his throat, he began to massage her shoulders. Strong shoulders, soft skin. He found the combination irresistible. She murmured, shifting toward him, but he didn't know if it was acceptance or request. It didn't matter.

She felt so good there; she felt right there. All questions, all doubts could wait for the sunrise. Before dawn they would share the need that was in both of them. In the moonlight, in the quiet hours, each would have what the other could offer. He touched his mouth lightly, ever so lightly, to hers.

She sighed, but it was only a whisper of a sound— a sigh in sleep as her body relaxed against his. If she dreamed now, she dreamed of easy things, calm water, soft grass. He trailed a hand down her back, exploring the shape of her. Long, lean, slender and strong. He felt his own body warm and pulse. Passion, still sleepy, began to stir.

She seemed to wake in stages. First her skin, then her blood, then muscle by muscle. Her body was alert and throbbing before her mind raced to join it. She found herself wrapped around Jonas, already aroused, already

hungry. When his mouth came to hers again, she answered him.

There was no hesitation in her this time, no moment
of doubt before desire overwhelmed reason. She wanted
to give herself to him as fully as it was possible to give.
It wouldn't be wise to speak her feelings out loud. It
couldn't be safe to tell him with words that her heart
was stripped of defenses and open for him. But she could
show him, and by doing so give them both the pleasure
of love without restrictions.

Her arms tightened around him as her mouth roamed
madly over his. She drew his bottom lip inside the heat,
inside the moistness of her mouth and nibbled, sucked
until his breath came fast and erratic. She felt the abrupt
tension as his body pressed against hers and realized he,
too, could be seduced. He, too, could be aroused beyond
reason. And she realized with a heady sort of wonder that
she could be the seducer, she could arouse.

She shifted her body under his, tentatively, but with
a slow rhythm that had him murmuring her name and
grasping for control. Instinctively she sought out vulnerabilities, finding them one by one, learning from them,
taking from them. Her tongue flicked over his throat,
seeking then enjoying the subtle, distinct taste of man.
His pulse was wild there, as wild as hers. She shifted
again until she lay across him and his body was hers for
the taking.

Her hands were inexperienced so that her stroking
was soft and hesitant. It drove him mad. No one had
ever been so sweetly determined to bring him pleasure.
She pressed kisses over his chest, slowly, experimentally,
then rubbed her cheek over his skin so that the touch both
soothed and excited.

His body was on fire, yet it seemed to float free so that he could feel the passage of air breathe cool over his flesh. She touched, and the heat spread like brushfire. She tasted and the moistness from her lips was like the whisper of a night breeze, cooling, calming.

"Tell me what you want." She looked up and her eyes were luminous in the moonlight, dark and beautiful. "Tell me what to do."

It was almost more than he could bear, the purity of the request, the willingness to give. He reached up so that his hands were lost in her hair. He could have kept her there forever, arched above him with her skin glowing gold in the thin light, her hair falling pale over her shoulders, her eyes shimmering with need. He drew her down until their lips met again. Hunger exploded between them. She didn't need to be told, she didn't need to be taught. Her body took over so that her own desire drove them both.

Jonas let reason go, let control be damned. Gripping her hips, he drew her up, then brought her to him, brought himself into her with a force that had her gasping in astonished pleasure. As she shuddered again, then again, he reached for her hands. Their fingers linked as she arched back and let her need set the pace. Frantic. Desperate. Uncontrollable. Pleasure, pain, delight, terror all whipped through her, driving her on, thrusting her higher.

He couldn't think, but he could feel. Until that moment, he wouldn't have believed it possible to feel so much so intensely. Sensations racked him, building and building and threatening to explode until the only sound he could hear was the roar of his own heart inside his head. With his eyes half open he could see her above him, naked and glorious in the moonlight. And when she plunged him beyond sensation, beyond sight and reason, he could still see her. He always would.

It didn't seem possible. It didn't, Liz thought, seem reasonable that she could be managing the shop, dealing with customers, stacking equipment when her system was still soaking up every delicious sensation she'd experienced just before dawn. Yet she was there, filling out forms, giving advice, quoting prices and making change. Still it was all mechanical. She'd been wise to delegate the diving tours and remain on shore.

She greeted her customers, some old and some new, and tried not to think too deeply about the list she'd been forced to give Moralas. How many of them would come to the Black Coral for equipment or lessons if they knew that by doing only that they were under police investigation? Jerry Sharpe's murder, and her involvement in it, could endanger her business far more than a slow season or a rogue hurricane.

Over and above her compassion, her sympathy and her hopes that Jonas could put his mind and heart at rest was a desperate need to protect her own, to guard what she'd built from nothing for her daughter. No matter how she tried to bury it, she couldn't completely block out the resentment she felt for being pulled into a situation that had been none of her making.

Yet there was a tug-of-war waging inside of her. Resentment for the disruption of her life battled against the longing to have Jonas remain in it. Without the disruption, he never would have come to her. No matter how much she tried, she could never regret the weeks they'd had together. She promised herself that she never would. It was time to admit that she had a great scope of love that had been trapped inside her. Rejected once, it had refused to risk again. But Jonas had released it, or perhaps she'd released it herself. Whatever happened, however it ended, she'd been able to love again.

"You're a hard lady to pin down."

Startled out of her own thoughts, Liz looked up. It took her a moment to remember the face, and a moment still to link a name with it. "Mr. Trydent." She rose from her desk to go to the counter. "I didn't realize you were still on the island."

"I only take one vacation a year, so I like to make the most of it." He set a tall paper cup that bounced with ice on the counter. "I figured this was the only way to get you to have a drink with me."

Liz glanced at the cup and wondered if she'd been businesslike or rude. At the moment she would have liked nothing better than to be alone with her own thoughts, but a customer was a customer. "That's nice of you. I've been pretty tied up."

"No kidding." He gave her a quick smile that showed straight teeth and easy charm. "You're either out of town or out on a boat. So I thought about the mountain and Mohammed." He glanced around. "Things are pretty quiet now."

"Lunchtime," Liz told him. "Everyone who's going out is already out. Everyone else is grabbing some food or a siesta before they decide how to spend the afternoon."

"Island living."

She smiled back. "Exactly. Tried any more diving?"

He made a face. "I let myself get talked into a night dive with Mr. Ambuckle before he headed back to Texas. I'm planning on sticking to the pool for the rest of my vacation."

"Diving's not for everyone."

"You can say that again." He drank from the second cup he'd brought, then leaned on the counter. "How about dinner? Dinner's for everyone."

She lifted a brow, a little surprised, a little flattered that he seemed bent on a pursuit. "I rarely eat out."

"I like home cooking."

"Mr. Trydent—"

"Scott," he corrected.

"Scott, I appreciate the offer, but I'm…" How did she put it? Liz wondered. "I'm seeing someone."

He laid a hand on hers. "Serious?"

Not sure whether she was embarrassed or amused, Liz drew her hand away. "I'm a serious sort of person."

"Well." Scott lifted his cup, watching her over the rim as he drank. "I guess we'd better stick to business then. How about explaining the snorkeling equipment to me?"

With a shrug, Liz glanced over her shoulder. "If you can swim, you can snorkel."

"Let's just say I'm cautious. Mind if I come in and take a look?"

She'd been ungracious enough for one day, Liz decided. She sent him a smile. "Sure, look all you want." When he'd skirted around the counter and through the door, she walked with him to the back shelves. "The snorkel's just a hollow tube with a mouthpiece," she began as she took one down to offer it. "You put this lip between your teeth and breathe normally through your mouth. With the tube attached to a face mask, you can paddle around on the surface indefinitely."

"Okay. How about all the times I see these little tubes disappear under the water?"

"When you want to go down, you hold your breath

and let out a bit of air to help you descend. The trick is to blow out and clear the tube of water when you surface. Once you get the knack, you can go down and up dozens of times without ever taking your face out of the water."

Scott turned the snorkel over in his hand. "There's a lot to see down there."

"A whole world."

He was no longer looking at the snorkel, but at her. "I guess you know a lot about the water and the reefs in this area. Know much about Isla Mujeres?"

"Excellent snorkeling and diving." Absently, Liz took down a mask to show him how to attach the snorkel. "We offer full- and half-day trips. If you're adventurous enough, there are caves to explore."

"And some are fairly remote," he said idly.

"For snorkeling you'd want to stay closer to the reefs, but an experienced diver could spend days around the caves."

"And nights." Scott passed the snorkel through his fingers as he watched her. "I imagine a diver could go down there at night and be completely undisturbed."

She wasn't certain why she felt a trickle of alarm. Automatically, she glanced over his shoulder to where her police guard half dozed in the sun. Silly, she told herself with a little shrug. She'd never been one to jump at shadows. "It's a dangerous area for night diving."

"Some people prefer danger, especially when it's profitable."

Her mouth was dry, so she swallowed as she replaced the mask on the shelf. "Perhaps. I don't."

This time his smile wasn't so charming or his eyes so friendly. "Don't you?"

"I don't know what you mean."

"I think you do." His hand closed over her arm. "I think you know exactly what I mean. What Jerry Sharpe skimmed off the top and dumped in that safe-deposit box in Acapulco was petty cash, Liz." He leaned closer as his voice lowered. "There's a lot more to be made. Didn't he tell you?"

She had a sudden, fierce memory of a knife probing against her throat. "He didn't tell me anything. I don't know anything." Before she could evade, he had her backed into a corner. "If I scream," she managed in a steady voice, "there'll be a crowd of people here before you can take a breath."

"No need to scream." He held up both hands as if to show her he meant no harm. "This is a business discussion. All I want to know is how much Jerry told you before he made the mistake of offending the wrong people."

When she discovered she was trembling, Liz forced herself to stop. He wouldn't intimidate her. What weapon could he hide in a pair of bathing trunks and an open shirt? She straightened her shoulders and looked him directly in the eye. "Jerry didn't tell me anything. I said the same thing to your friend when he had the knife at my throat. It didn't satisfy him, so he put a damaged gauge on my tanks."

"My partner doesn't understand much about finesse," Scott said easily. "I don't carry knives, and I don't know enough about your diving equipment to mess with the gauges. What I know about is you, and I know plenty. You work too hard, Liz, getting up at dawn and hustling until sundown. I'm just trying to give you some options. Business, Liz. We're just going to talk business."

It was his calm, reasonable attitude that had her temper whipping out. He could be calm, he could be reasonable, and people were dead. "I'm not Jerry and I'm not Erika, so keep that in mind. I don't know anything about the filthy business you're into, but the police do, and they'll know more. If you think you can frighten me by threatening me with a knife or damaging my equipment, you're right. But that doesn't stop me from wishing every one of you to hell. Now get out of my shop and leave me alone."

He studied her face for a long ten seconds, then backed an inch or two away. "You've got me wrong, Liz. I said this was a business discussion. With Jerry gone, an experienced diver would come in handy, especially one who knows the waters around here. I'm authorized to offer you five thousand dollars. Five thousand American dollars for doing what you do best. Diving. You go down, drop off one package and pick up another. No names, no faces. Bring the package back to me unopened and I hand you five thousand in cash. Once or twice a week, and you can build up a nice little nest egg. I'd say a woman raising a kid alone could use some extra money."

Fear had passed into fury; she clenched her hands together. "I told you to get out," she repeated. "I don't want your money."

He smiled and touched a finger to her cheek. "Give it some thought. I'll be around if you change your mind."

Liz waited for her breathing to level as she watched him walk away. With deliberate movements, she locked the shop, then walked directly to her police guard. "I'm going home," she told him as he sprang to attention. "Tell Captain Moralas to meet me there in half an hour." Without waiting for a reply, she strode across the sand.

Fifteen minutes later, Liz slammed into her house. The ride home hadn't calmed her. At every turn she'd

been violated. At every turn, her privacy and peace had
been disrupted. This last incident was the last she'd accept. She might have been able to handle another threat,
another demand. But he'd offered her a job. Offered to
pay her to smuggle cocaine, to take over the position of
a man who'd been murdered. Jonas's brother.

A nightmare, Liz thought as she paced from window
to window. She wished she could believe it was a nightmare. The cycle was drawing to a close, and she felt
herself being trapped in the center. What Jerry Sharpe
had started, she and Jonas would be forced to finish, no
matter how painful. No matter how deadly. Finish it she
would, Liz promised herself. The cycle would be broken,
no matter what she had to do. She would be finished with
it so her daughter could come home safely. Whatever she
had to do, she would see to that.

At the sound of a car approaching, Liz went to the
front window. Jonas, she thought, and felt her heart sink.
Did she tell him now that she'd met face-to-face with the
man who might have killed his brother? If he had the
name, if he knew the man, would he race off in a rage for
the revenge he'd come so far to find? And if he found his
revenge, could the cycle ever be broken? Instead, she was
afraid it would revolve and revolve around them, smothering everything else. She saw Jonas, a man of the law, a
man of patience and compassion, shackled forever within
the results of his own violence. How could she save him
from that and still save herself?

Her hand was cold as she reached for the door and
opened it to meet him. He knew there was something
wrong before he touched her. "What are you doing home?
I went by the shop and it was closed."

"Jonas." She did the only thing she knew how. She

drew him against her and held on. "Moralas is on his way here."

"What happened?" A little skip of panic ran through him before he could stop it. He held her away, searching her face. "Did something happen to you? Were you hurt?"

"No, I'm not hurt. Come in and sit down."

"Liz, I want to know what happened."

She heard the sound of a second engine and looked down the street to see the unmarked car. "Moralas is here," she murmured. "Come inside, Jonas. I'd rather go through this only once."

There was really no decision to be made, Liz told herself as she moved away from the door to wait. She would give Moralas and Jonas the name of the man who had approached her. She would tell them exactly what he'd said. By doing so she would take herself one step further away from the investigation. They would have a name, a face, a location. They would have motive. It was what the police wanted, it was what she wanted. She glanced at Jonas as Moralas came up the front walk. It was what Jonas wanted. What he needed. And by giving it to him, she would take herself one step further way from him.

"Miss Palmer." Moralas took off his hat as he entered, glanced briefly at Jonas and waited.

"Captain." She stood by a chair but didn't sit. "I have some information for you. There's an American, a man named Scott Trydent. Less than an hour ago he offered me five thousand dollars to smuggle cocaine off the reef of Isla Mujeres."

Moralas's expression remained impassive. He tucked his hat under his arm. "And have you had previous dealings with this man?"

"He joined one of my diving classes. He was friendly.

Today he came by the shop to talk to me. Apparently he believed that I…" She trailed off to look at Jonas. He stood very still and very quiet just inside the door. "He thought that Jerry had told me about the operation. He'd found out about the safe-deposit box. I don't know how. It was as though he knew every move I've made for weeks." As her nerves began to fray, she dragged a hand through her hair. "He told me that I could take over Jerry's position, make the exchange in the caves near Isla Mujeres and be rich. He knows…" She had to swallow to keep her voice from trembling. "He knows about my daughter."

"You would identify him?"

"Yes. I don't know if he killed Jerry Sharpe." Her gaze shifted to Jonas again and pleaded. "I don't know, but I could identify him."

Moralas watched the exchange before crossing the room. "Please sit down, Miss Palmer."

"You'll arrest him?" She wanted Jonas to say something, anything, but he continued to stand in silence. "He's part of the cocaine ring. He knows about Jerry's Sharpe's murder. You have to arrest him."

"Miss Palmer." Moralas urged her down on the sofa, then sat beside her. "We have names. We have faces. The smuggling ring currently operating in the Yucatan Peninsula is under investigation by both the Mexican and the American governments. The names you and Mr. Sharpe have given me are not unfamiliar. But there is one we don't have. The person who organizes, the person who undoubtedly ordered the murder of Jerry Sharpe. This is the name we need. Without it, the arrest of couriers, of salesmen, is nothing. We need this name, Miss Palmer. And we need proof."

"I don't understand. You mean you're just going

to let Trydent go? He'll just find someone else to make the drops."

"It won't be necessary for him to look elsewhere if you agree."

"No." Before Liz could take in Moralas's words, Jonas was breaking in. He said it quietly, so quietly that chills began to race up and down her spine. He took out a cigarette. His hands were rock steady. Taking his time, he flicked his lighter and drew until the tip glowed red. He blew out a stream of smoke and locked his gaze on Moralas. "You can go to hell."

"Miss Palmer has the privilege to tell me so herself."

"You're not using her. If you want someone on the inside, someone closer to the names and proof, I'll make the drop."

Moralas studied him, saw the steady nerves and untiring patience along with simmering temper. If he'd had a choice, he'd have preferred it. "It isn't you who has been asked."

"Liz isn't going down."

"Just a minute." Liz pressed both hands to her temples. "Are you saying you want me to see Trydent again, to tell him I'll take the job? That's crazy. What purpose could there be?"

"You would be a decoy." Moralas glanced down at her hands. Delicate, yes, but strong. There was nothing about Elizabeth Palmer he didn't know. "The investigation is closing in. We don't want the ring to change locations at this point. If the operation appears to go smoothly, there should be no move at this time. You've been the stumbling block, Miss Palmer, for the ring, and the investigation."

"How?" Furious, she started to stand. Moralas merely put a hand on her arm.

"Jerry Sharpe lived with you, worked for you. He had a weakness for women. Neither the police nor the smugglers have been sure exactly what part you played. Jerry Sharpe's brother is now living in your home. The key to the safe-deposit box was found by you."

"Guilty by association, Captain?" Her voice took on that ice-sharp edge Jonas had heard only once or twice before. "Have I had police protection, or have I been under surveillance?"

Moralas's tone never altered. "One serves the same purpose as the other."

"If I'm under suspicion, haven't you considered that I might simply take the money and run?"

"That's precisely what we want you to do."

"Very clever." Jonas wasn't certain how much longer he could hold on to his temper. It would have given him great satisfaction to have picked Moralas up bodily and thrown him out of the house. Out of Liz's life. "Liz double-crosses them, annoying the head of the operation. It's then necessary to eliminate her the way my brother was eliminated."

"Except that Miss Palmer will be under police protection at all times. If this one drop goes as we plan, the investigation will end, and the smugglers, along with your brother's killer, will be caught and punished. This is what you want?"

"Not if it means risking Liz. Plant your own pigeon, Moralas."

"There isn't time. With your cooperation, Miss Palmer, we can end this. Without it, it could take months."

Months? she thought. Another day would be a life-time. "I'll do it."

Jonas was beside her in a heartbeat, pulling her off the couch. "Liz—"

"My daughter comes home in two weeks." She put her hands on his arms. "She won't come back to any-thing like this."

"Take her someplace else." Jonas gripped her shoul-ders until his fingers dug into flesh. "We'll go some-place else."

"Where?" she demanded. "Every day I tell myself I'm pulling away from this thing and every day it's a lie. I've been in it since Jerry walked in the door. We can't change that. Until it's over, really over, nothing's going to be right."

He knew she was right, had known it from the first moment. But too much had changed. There was a des-peration in him now that he'd never expected to feel. It was all for her. "Come back to the States with me. It will be over."

"Will it? Will you forget your brother was murdered? Will you forget the man who killed him?" His fingers tightened, his eyes darkened, but he said nothing. Her breath came out in a sigh of acceptance. "No, it won't be over until we finish it. I've run before, Jonas. I promised myself I'd never run again."

"You could be killed."

"I've done nothing and they've nearly killed me twice." She dropped her head on his chest. "Please help me."

He couldn't force her to bend his way. Two of the things he most admired in her were her capacity to give and her will to stand firm. He could plead with her, he could argue, but he could never lie. If she ran, if they ran, they'd never be free of it. His arm came around her. Her hair smelled of summer and sea air. And before the summer ended, he promised himself, she'd be free. They'd both be free.

"I go with her." He met Moralas's eyes over her head.

"That may not be possible."

"I'll make it possible."

Chapter Eleven

She'd never been more frightened in her life. Every day she worked in the shop, waiting for Scott Trydent to approach. Every evening she locked up, went home and waited for the phone to ring. Jonas said little. She no longer knew what he did with the hours they were apart, but she was aware that he was planning his own move, in his own time. It only frightened her more.

Two days passed until her nerves were stretched thinner and tighter than she would have believed possible. On the beach, people slept or read novels, lovers walked by arm in arm. Children chattered and ran. Snorkelers splashed around the reef. She wondered why nothing seemed normal, or if it ever would again. At sundown she emptied her cash box, stacked gear and began to lock up.

"How about that drink?"

Though she'd thought she'd braced herself for the

moment when it would begin, Liz jolted. Her head began to throb in a slow, steady rhythm she knew would last for hours. In the pit of her stomach she felt the twist come and go from panicked excitement. From this point on, she reminded herself, she had no room to panic. She turned and looked at Scott. "I was wondering if you'd come back."

"Told you I'd be around. I always figure people need a couple of days to mull things over."

She had a part to play, Liz reminded herself. She had to do it well. Carefully, she finished locking up, then turned back to him. She didn't smile. It was to be a business discussion, cut-and-dried. "We can get a drink over there." She pointed to the open-air thatched-roof restaurant overhanging the reef. "It's public."

"Suits me." Though he offered his hand, she ignored it and began to walk.

"You used to be friendlier."

"You used to be a customer." She sent him a sideways look. "Not a business partner."

"So..." She saw him glance right, then left. "You've mulled."

"You need a diver, I need money." Liz walked up the two wooden stairs and chose a chair that had her back to the water. Seconds after she sat, a man settled himself into a corner table. One of Moralas's, she thought, and ordered herself to be calm. She'd been briefed and rebriefed. She knew what to say, how to say it, and that the waiter who would serve them carried a badge and a gun. "Jerry didn't tell me a great deal," she began, and ordered an American soft drink. "Just that he made the drop and collected the money."

"He was a good diver."

Liz swallowed the little bubble of fear. "I'm better."

Scott grinned at her. "So I'm told."

A movement beside her had her glancing over, then freezing. A dark man with a pitted face took the chair beside her. Liz knew he wore a thin silver band on his wrist before she looked for it.

"Pablo Manchez, Liz Palmer. Though I think you two have met."

"Señorita." Manchez's thin mouth curved as he took her hand.

"Tell your friend to keep his hands to himself." Calmly, Jonas pulled a chair up to the table. "Why don't you introduce me, Liz?" When she could do no more than stare at him, he settled back. "I'm Jonas Sharpe. Liz and I are partners." He leveled his gaze to Manchez. This was the man, he thought, whom he'd come thousands of miles to see. This was the man he'd kill. Jonas felt the hatred and the fury rise. But he knew how to strap the emotions and wait. "I believe you knew my brother."

Manchez's hand dropped from Liz's and went to his side. "Your brother was greedy and stupid."

Liz held her breath as Jonas reached in his pocket. Slowly, he pulled out his cigarettes. "I'm greedy," he said easily as he lit one. "But I'm not stupid. I've been looking for you." He leaned across the table. With a slow smile, he offered Manchez the cigarettes.

Manchez took one and broke off the filter. His hands were beautiful, with long spidery fingers and narrow palms. Liz fought back a shudder as she looked at them. "So you found me."

Jonas was still smiling as he ordered a beer. "You need a diver."

Scott sent Manchez a warning look. "We have a diver."

"What you have is a team. Liz and I work together."
Jonas blew out a stream of smoke. "Isn't that right, Liz?"

He wanted them. He wasn't going to back off until he
had them. And she had no choice. "That's right."

"We don't need no team." Manchez started to rise.

"You need us." Jonas took his beer as it was served.
"We already know a good bit about your operation. Jerry
wasn't good at keeping secrets." Jonas took a swig from
the bottle. "Liz and I are more discreet. Five thousand
a drop?"

Scott waited a beat, then held a hand up, signaling
Manchez. "Five. If you want to work as a team, it's your
business how you split it."

"Fifty-fifty." Liz spread her fingers around Jonas's
beer. "One of us goes down, one stays in the dive boat."

"Tomorrow night. Eleven o'clock. You come to the
shop. Go inside. You'll find a waterproof case. It'll be
locked."

"So will the shop," Liz put in. "How does the case
get inside?"

Manchez blew smoke between his teeth. "I got no
problem getting in."

"Just take the case," Scott interrupted. "The coordinates will be attached to the handle. Take the boat out,
take the case down, leave it. Then come back up and wait
exactly an hour. That's when you dive again. All you have
to do is take the case that's waiting for you back to the
shop and leave it."

"Sounds smooth," Jonas decided. "When do we get
paid?"

"After you do the job."

"Half up front." Liz took a long swallow of beer and

hoped her heart would settle. "Leave twenty-five hundred with the case or I don't dive."

Scott smiled. "Not as trusting as Jerry."

She gave him a cold, bitter look. "And I intend to stay alive."

"Just follow the rules."

"Who makes them?" Jonas took the beer back from Liz. Her hand slipped down to his leg and stayed steady.

"You don't want to worry about that," Manchez advised. The cigarette was clamped between his teeth as he smiled. "He knows who you are."

"Just follow the coordinates and keep an eye on your watch." Scott dropped bills on the table as he rose. "The rest is gravy."

"Stay smart, Jerry's brother." Manchez gave them both a slow smile. *"Adios, señorita."*

Jonas calmly finished his beer as the two men walked away.

"You weren't supposed to interfere during the meeting," Liz began in a furious undertone. "Moralas said—"

"The hell with Moralas." He crushed out his cigarette, watching as the smoke plumed up. "Is that the man who put the bruises on your neck?"

Her hand moved up before she could stop it. Halfway to her throat, Liz curled her fingers into a ball and set her hand on the table. "I told you I didn't see him."

Jonas turned his head. His eyes, as they had before, reminded her of frozen smoke. "Was it the man?"

He didn't need to be told. Liz leaned closer and spoke softly. "I want it over, Jonas. And I don't need revenge. You were supposed to let me meet with Scott and set things up by myself."

In an idle move, he tilted the candle on the table toward him and lit it. "I changed my mind."

"Damn you, you could've messed everything up. I don't want to be involved but I am. The only way to get uninvolved is to finish it. How do we know they won't just back off now that you've come into it?"

"Because you're right in the middle, and you always have been." Before she could speak, he took her arm. His face was close, his voice cool and steady. "I was going to use you. From the minute I walked into your house, I was going to use you to get to Jerry's killer. If I had to walk all over you, if I had to knock you out of the way or drag you along with me, I was going to use you. Just the way Moralas is going to use you. Just the way the others are going to use you." The heat of the candle flickered between them as he drew her closer. "The way Jerry used you."

She swallowed the tremor and fought against the pain. "And now?"

He didn't speak. They were so close that he could see himself reflected in her eyes. In them, surrounding his own reflection, he saw the doubts and the defiance. His hand came to the back of her neck, held there until he could feel the rhythm of her pulse. With a simmering violence, he pulled her against him and covered her mouth with his. A flare that was passion, a glimmer that was hope—he didn't know which to reach for. So he let her go.

"No one's going to hurt you again," he murmured. "Especially not me."

It was the longest day of her life. Liz worked and waited as the hours crawled by. Moralas's men mixed with the vacationers on the beach. So obviously, it seemed to Liz, that she wondered everyone else didn't notice them as though they wore badges around their necks. Her boats went out, returned and went out again. Tanks and equipment were checked and rented. She filled out invoices and accepted credit cards as if there were some importance to daily routine. She wished for the day to end. She hoped the night would never come.

A thousand times she thought of telling Moralas she couldn't go through with it. A thousand times she called herself a coward. But as the sun went down and the beach began to clear, she realized courage wasn't something that could be willed into place. She would run, if she had the choice. But as long as she was in danger, Faith was in danger. When the sun went down, she locked the shop as if it were the end of any ordinary day. Before she'd pocketed her keys, Jonas was beside her.

"There's still time to change your mind."

"And do what? Hide?" She looked out at the beach, at the sea, at the island that was her home. And her prison. Why had she never seen it as a prison until Jonas had come to it? "You've already told me how good I am at hiding."

"Liz—"

She shook her head to stop him. "I can't talk about it. I just have to do it."

They drove home in silence. In her mind, Liz went over her instructions, every point, every word Moralas had pushed at her. She was to follow the routine, make the exchange, then turn the case with the money over to the police who'd be waiting near the dock. She'd wait for the next move. And while she waited, she'd never be more than ten feet away from a cop. It sounded foolproof. It made her stomach churn.

There was a man walking a dog along the street in front of her house. One of Moralas's men. The man whittling on her neighbor's porch had a gun under his denim vest. Liz tried to look at neither of them.

"You're going to have a drink, some food and a nap," Jonas ordered as he steered her inside.

"Just the nap."

"The nap first then." After securing the lock, Jonas followed her into the bedroom. He lowered the shades. "Do you want anything?"

It was still so hard to ask. "Would you lie down with me?"

He came to her. She was already curled on her side, so he drew her back against him and wrapped her close. "Will you sleep?"

"I think so." In sleep she could find escape, if only temporarily. But she didn't close her eyes. "Jonas?"

"Hmm?"

"After tonight—after we've finished, will you hold me like this again?"

He pressed his lips to her hair. He didn't think he could love her any more. He was nearly certain if he told her she'd pull away. "As long as you want. Just sleep."

Liz let her eyes close and her mind empty.

The case was small, the size of an executive briefcase. It seemed too inconspicuous to be the catalyst for so much danger. Beside it, on the counter of Liz's shop, was an envelope. Inside was a slip of paper with longitude and latitude printed. With the slip of paper were twenty-five one-hundred-dollar bills.

"They kept their part of the bargain," Jonas commented.

Liz merely shoved the envelope into a drawer. "I'll get my equipment."

Jonas watched her. She'd rather do this on her own, he reflected. She'd rather not think she had someone to lean on, to turn to. He took her tanks before she could heft them. She was going to learn, he reminded himself, that she had a great deal more than that. "The coordinates?"

"The same that were in Jerry's book." She found herself amazingly calm as she waited to lock the door behind him. They were being watched. She was aware that Moralas had staked men in the hotel. She was just as certain Manchez was somewhere close. She and Jonas didn't speak again until they were on the dive boat and had cast off. "This could end it." She glanced at him as she set her course.

"This could end it."

She was silent for a moment. All during the evening hours she'd thought about what she would say to him, how she would say it. "Jonas, what will you do?"

The flame of his lighter hissed, flared, then was quiet. "What I have to do."

The fear tasted like copper in her mouth, but it had nothing to do with herself and everything to do with Jonas. "If we make the exchange tonight, turn the second case over to Moralas. They'll have to come out in the open. Manchez, and the man who gives the orders."

"What are you getting at, Liz?"

"Manchez killed your brother."

Jonas looked beyond her. The sea was black. The sky was black. Only the hum of the motor broke the silence. "He was the trigger."

"Are you going to kill him?"

Slowly, he turned back to her. The question had been quiet, but her eyes weren't. They sent messages, posed argument, issued pleas. "It doesn't involve you."

That hurt deeply, sharply. With a nod, she followed the shimmer of light on the water. "Maybe not. But if you let hate rule what you do, how you think, you'll never be free of it. Manchez will be dead, Jerry will still be dead and you…" She turned to look at him again. "You'll never really be alive again."

"I didn't come all this way, spend all this time, to let Manchez walk away. He kills for money and because he enjoys it. He enjoys it," Jonas repeated viciously. "You can see it in his eyes."

And she had. But she didn't give a damn about Manchez. "Do you remember telling me once that everyone was entitled to representation?"

He remembered. He remembered everything he'd once believed in. He remembered how Jerry had looked in the cold white light of the morgue. "It didn't have anything to do with this."

"I suppose you change the rules when it's personal."

"He was my brother."

"And he's dead." With a sigh she lifted her face so that the wind could cool her skin. "I'm sorry, Jonas. Jerry's dead and if you go through with what you've planned, you're going to kill something in yourself." And, though she couldn't tell him, something in her. "Don't you trust the law?"

He tossed his cigarette into the water, then leaned on the rail. "I've been playing with it for years. It's the last thing I'd trust."

She wanted to go to him but didn't know how. Still,

no matter what he did, she was beside him. "Then you'll have to trust yourself. And so will I."

Slowly, he crossed to her. Taking her face in his hands, he tried to understand what she was telling him, what she was still holding back. "Will you?"

"Yes."

He leaned to press a kiss to her forehead. Inside there was a need, a fierce desire to tell her to head the boat out to sea and keep going. But that would never work, not for either of them. They stood on the boat together, and stood at the crossroads. "Then start now." He kissed her again before he turned and lifted one of the compartment seats. Liz frowned as she saw the wet suit.

"What are you doing?"

"I arranged to have Luis leave this here for me."

"Why? We can't both go down."

Jonas stripped down to his trunks. "That's right. I'm diving, you're staying with the boat."

Liz stood very straight. It wouldn't do any good to lose her temper. "The arrangements were made on all sides, Jonas. I'm diving."

"I'm changing the arrangements." He tugged the wet suit up to his waist before he looked at her. "I'm not taking any more chances with you."

"You're not taking chances with me. I am. Jonas, you don't know these waters. I do. You've never gone down here at night. I have."

"I'm about to."

"The last thing we need right now is for you to start behaving like an overprotective man."

He nearly laughed as he snapped the suit over his shoulders. "That's too bad, then, because that's just what we've got."

"I told Manchez and Trydent I was going down."

"I guess your reputation's shot when you lie to murderers and drug smugglers."

"Jonas, I'm not in the mood for jokes."

He strapped on his diver's knife, adjusted his weight belt, then reached for his mask. "Maybe not. And maybe you're not in the mood to hear this. I care about you. Too damn much." He reached out, gripping her chin. "My brother dragged you into this because he never wasted two thoughts about anyone else in his life. I pulled you in deeper because all I was thinking about was payback. Now I'm thinking about you, about us. You're not going down. If I have to tie you to the wheel, you're not going down."

"I don't want you to go." She balled her fists against his chest. "If I was down, all I'd think about was what I was doing. If I stay up here, I won't be able to stop thinking about what could happen to you."

"Time me." He lifted the tanks and held them out to her. "Help me get them on."

Hadn't she told herself weeks before that he wasn't a man who'd lose an argument? Her hands trembled a bit as she slipped the straps over his shoulders. "I don't know how to handle being protected."

He hooked the tanks as he turned back to her. "Practice."

She closed her eyes. It was too late for talk, too late for arguments. "Bear northeast as you dive. The cave's at eighty feet." She hesitated only a moment, then picked up a spear gun. "Watch out for sharks."

When he was over the side, she lowered the case to him. In seconds, he was gone and the sea was black and still. In her mind, Liz followed him fathom by fathom.

The water would be dark so that he would be dependent on his gauges and the thin beam of light. Night creatures would be feeding. Squid, the moray, barracuda. Sharks. Liz closed her mind to it.

She should have forced him to let her go. How? Pacing the deck, she pushed the hair back from her face. He'd gone to protect her. He'd gone because he cared about her. Shivering, she sat down to rub her arms warm again. Was this what it was like to be cared for by a man? Did it mean you had to sit and wait? She was up again and pacing. She'd lived too much of her life doing to suddenly become passive. And yet... To hear him say he cared. Liz sat again and waited.

She'd checked her watch four times before she heard him at the ladder. On a shudder of relief, she dashed over to the side to help him. "I'm going down the next time," she began.

Jonas pulled off his light, then his tanks. "Forget it." Before she could protest, he dragged her against him. "We've got an hour," he murmured against her ear. "You want to spend it arguing?"

He was wet and cold. Liz wrapped herself around him. "I don't like being bossed around."

"Next time you can boss me around." He dropped onto a bench and pulled her with him. "I'd forgotten what it was like down there at night. Fabulous." And it was nearly over, he told himself. The first step had been taken, the second one had to follow. "I saw a giant squid. Scared the hell out of him with the light. I swear he was thirty feet long."

"They get bigger." She rested her head on his shoulder and tried to relax. They had an hour. "I was diving with my father once. We saw one that was nearly sixty."

"Made you nervous?"

"No. I was fascinated. I remember I swam close enough to touch the tentacles. My father gave me a twenty-minute lecture when we surfaced."

"I imagine you'd do the same thing with Faith."

"I'd be proud of her," Liz began, then laughed. "Then I'd give her a twenty-minute lecture."

For the first time that night he noticed the stars. The sky was alive with them. It made him think of his mother's porch swing and long summer nights. "Tell me about her."

"You don't want to get me started."

"Yes, I do." He slipped an arm around her shoulder. "Tell me about her."

With a half smile, Liz closed her eyes. It was good to think of Faith, to talk of Faith. A picture began to emerge for Jonas of a young girl who liked school because there was plenty to do and lots of people. He heard the love and the pride, and the wistfulness. He saw the dark, sunny-faced girl in the photo and learned she spoke two languages, liked basketball and hated vegetables.

"She's always been sweet," Liz reflected. "But she's no angel. She's very stubborn, and when she's crossed, her temper isn't pretty. Faith wants to do things herself. When she was two she'd get very annoyed if I wanted to help her down the stairs."

"Independence seems to run in the family."

Liz moved her shoulders. "We've needed it."

"Ever thought about sharing?"

Her nerves began to hum. Though she shifted only a bit, it was away from him. "When you share, you have to give something up. I've never been able to afford to give up anything."

It was an answer he'd expected. It was an answer he intended to change. "It's time to go back down."

Liz helped him back on with his tanks. "Take the spear gun. Jonas…" He was already at the rail before she ran to him. "Hurry back," she murmured. "I want to go home. I want to make love with you."

"Hell of a time to bring that up." He sent her a grin, curled and fell back into the water.

Within five minutes Liz was pacing again. Why hadn't she thought to bring any coffee? She'd concentrate on that. In little more than an hour they could be huddled in her kitchen with a pot brewing. It wouldn't matter that there would be police surrounding the house. She and Jonas would be inside. Together. Perhaps she was wrong about sharing. Perhaps… When she heard the splash at the side of the boat, she was at the rail like a shot.

"Jonas, did something happen? Why—" She found herself looking down the barrel of a .22.

"Señorita." Manchez tossed his mask and snorkel onto a bench as he climbed over the side. *"Buenas noches."*

"What are you doing here?" She struggled to sound indignant as the blood rushed from her face. No, she wasn't brave, she realized. She wasn't brave at all. "We had a deal."

"You're an amateur," he told her. "Like Sharpe was an amateur. You think we'd just forget about the money?"

"I don't know anything about the money Jerry took." She gripped the rail. "I've told you that all along."

"The boss decided you were a loose end, pretty lady. You do us a favor and make this delivery. We do you a favor. We kill you quickly."

She didn't look at the gun again. She didn't dare. "If

you keep killing your divers, you're going to be out of business."

"We're finished in Cozumel. When your friend brings up the case, I take it and go to Merida. I live in style. You don't live at all."

She wanted to sit because her knees were shaking. She stood because she thought she might never be able to again. "If you're finished in Cozumel, why did you set up this drop?"

"Clancy likes things tidy."

"Clancy?" The name David Merriworth had mentioned, Liz remembered, and strained to hear any sound from the water.

"There's a few thousand in cocaine down there, that's all. A few thousand dollars in the case coming up. The boss figures it's worth the investment to make it look like you were doing the dealing with Sharpe. Then you two have an argument and shoot each other. Case closed."

"You killed Erika, too, didn't you?"

"She asked too many questions." He lowered the gun. "You ask too many questions."

Light flooded the boat and the water so quickly that Liz's first instinct was to freeze. Before the next reaction had fully registered, she was tumbling into the water and diving blind.

How could she warn Jonas? Liz groped frantically in the water as lights played on the surface above her. She had no tanks, no mask, no protection. Any moment he'd be surfacing, unaware of any danger. He had no protection but her.

Without equipment, she'd be helpless in a matter of moments. She fought to stay down, keeping as close to the ladder as she dared. Her lungs were ready to burst when she felt the movement in the water. Liz turned toward the beam of light.

When he saw her, his heart nearly stopped. She looked like a ghost clinging to the hull of the boat. Her hair was pale and floating out in the current, her face was nearly as white as his light. Before his mind could begin to question, he was pushing his mouthpiece between her lips and giving her air. There could be no communication but emotion. He felt the fear. Jonas steadied the spear gun in his arm and surfaced.

"Mr. Sharpe." Moralas caught him in the beam of a spotlight. Liz rose up beside him. "We have everything under control." On the deck of her boat, Liz saw Manchez handcuffed and flanked by two divers. "Perhaps you will give my men and their prisoner a ride back to Cozumel."

She felt Jonas tense. The spear gun was set and aimed. Even through the mask, she could see his eyes burning, burning as only ice can. "Jonas, please." But he was already starting up the ladder. She hauled herself over the rail and tumbled onto the deck, cold and dripping. "Jonas, you can't. Jonas, it's over."

He barely heard her. All his emotion, all his concentration was on the man who stood only feet away. Their eyes were locked. It gave him no satisfaction to watch the blood drain from Manchez's face, or the knowledge leap frantically into his eyes. It was what he'd come for, what he'd promised himself. The medallion on the edge of his chain dangled and reminded him of his brother. His brother was dead. No satisfaction. Jonas lowered the gun.

Manchez tossed back his head. "I'll get out," he said quietly. The smile started to spread. "I'll get out."

The spear shot out and plowed into the deck between

Manchez's feet. Liz saw the smile freeze on his face an instant before one formed on Jonas's. "I'll be waiting."

Could it really be over? It was all Liz could think when she awoke, warm and dry, in her own bed. She was safe, Jonas was safe and the smuggling ring on Cozumel was broken. Of course, Jonas had been furious. Manchez had been watched, they had been watched, but the police had made their presence known only after Liz had been held at gunpoint.

But he'd gotten what he'd come for, she thought. His brother's killer was behind bars. He'd face a trial and justice. She hoped it was enough for Jonas.

The morning was enough for her. The normality of it. Happy, she rolled over and pressed her body against Jonas's. He only drew her closer.

"Let's stay right here until noon."

She laughed and nuzzled against his throat. "I have—"

"A business to run," he finished.

"Exactly. And for the first time in weeks I can run it without having this urge to look over my shoulder. I'm happy." She looked at him, then tossed her arms around his neck and squeezed. "I'm so happy."

"Happy enough to marry me?"

She went still as a stone, then slowly, very slowly drew away. "What?"

"Marry me. Come home with me. Start a life with me."

She wanted to say yes. It shocked her that her heart burned to say yes. Pulling away from him was the hardest thing she'd ever done. "I can't."

He stopped her before she could scramble out of bed. It hurt, he realized, more than he could possibly have anticipated. "Why?"

"Jonas, we're two different people with two totally separate lives."

"We stopped having separate lives weeks ago." He took her hands. "They're not ever going to be separate again."

"But they will." She drew her hands away. "After you're back in Philadelphia for a few weeks, you'll barely remember what I look like."

He had her wrists handcuffed in his hands. The fury that surfaced so seldom in him seemed always on simmer when he was around her. "Why do you do that?" he demanded. "Why can't you ever take what you're given?" He swung her around until she was beneath him on the bed. "I love you."

"Don't." She closed her eyes as the wish nearly eclipsed the reason. "Don't say that to me."

Shut out. She was shutting him out. Jonas felt the panic come first, then the anger. Then the determination. "I will say it. If I say it enough, sooner or later you'll start to believe it. Do you think all these nights have been a game? Haven't you felt it? Don't you feel anything?"

"I thought I felt something once before."

"You were a child." When she started to shake her head, he gripped her tighter. "Yes, you were. In some ways you still are, but I know what goes through you when you're with me. I know. I'm not a ghost, I'm not a memory. I'm real and I want you."

"I'm afraid of you," she whispered. "I'm afraid because you make me want what I can't have. I won't marry you, Jonas, because I'm through taking chances with my life and I won't take chances with my child's life. Please let me go."

He released her, but when she stood, his arms went around her. "It isn't over for us."

She dropped her head against his chest, pressed her cheek close. "Let me have the few days we have left. Please let me have them."

He lifted her chin. Everything he needed to know was in her eyes. A man who knew and who planned to win could afford to wait. "You haven't dealt with anyone as stubborn as you are before this. And you haven't nearly finished dealing with me." Then his hand gentled as he stroked her hair. "Get dressed. I'll take you to work."

Because he acted as though nothing had been said, Liz relaxed. It was impossible, and she knew it. They'd known each other only weeks, and under circumstances that were bound to intensify any feelings. He cared. She believed that he cared, but love—the kind of love needed to build a marriage—was too much to risk.

She loved. She loved so much that she pushed him away when she wanted to pull him closer. He needed to go back to his life, back to his world. After time had passed, if he thought of her he'd think with gratitude that she had closed a door he'd opened on impulse. She would think of him. Always.

By the time Liz was walking toward the shop, she'd settled her mind. "What are you going to do today?"

"Me?" Jonas, too, had settled his mind. "I'm going to sit in the sun and do nothing."

"Nothing?" Incredulous, Liz stared at him. "All day?"

"It's known as relaxing, or taking a day off. If you do it several days running, it's called a vacation. I was supposed to have one in Paris."

Paris, she thought. It would suit him. She wondered

briefly how the air smelled in Paris. "If you get bored, I'm sure one of the boats could use the extra crew."

"I've had enough diving for a few days, thanks." Jonas plopped down on a chaise in front of the shop. It was the best place to keep an eye on her.

"Miguel." Liz automatically looked around for Luis. "You're here early."

"I came with Luis. He's checking out the dive boat— got an early tour."

"Yes, I know." But she wouldn't trust Miguel to run the shop alone for long. "Why don't you help him? I'll take care of the counter."

"*Bueno.* Oh, there were a couple of guys looking at the fishing boat. Maybe they want to rent."

"I'll take a look. You go ahead." Walking back, she crouched beside Jonas. "Keep an eye on the shop for me, will you? I've got a couple of customers over by the *Expatriate.*"

Jonas adjusted his sunglasses. "What do you pay per hour?"

Liz narrowed her eyes. "I might cook dinner tonight."

With a smile, he got up to go behind the counter. "Take all the time you need."

He made her laugh. Liz strolled down the walkway and to the pier, drinking up the morning. She could use a good fishing cruise. The aqua bikes had been ordered, but they still had to be paid for. Besides, she'd like the ride herself. It made her think of Jonas and his unwanted catch a few weeks before. Liz laughed again as she approached the men beside her boat.

"*Buenos días,*" she began. "Mr. Ambuckle." Beaming a smile, Liz held out a hand. "I didn't know you were back. Is this one of your quick weekend trips?"

"That's right." His almost bald head gleamed in the sun as he patted her hand. "When the mood strikes me I just gotta move."

"Thinking about some big-game fishing this time around?"

"Funny you should mention it. I was just saying to my associate here that I only go for the big game."

"Only the big game." Scott Trydent turned around and pushed back his straw hat. "That's right, Clancy."

"Now don't turn around, honey." Ambuckle's fingers clamped over hers before she could move. "You're going to get on the boat, nice and quiet. We have some talking to do, then we might just take a little ride."

"How long have you been using my dive shop to smuggle?" Liz saw the gun under Scott's jacket. She couldn't signal to Jonas, didn't dare.

"For the past couple of years I've found your shop's location unbeatable. You know, they ship that stuff up from Colombia and dump in Miami. The way the heat's been on the past few years, you take a big chance using the regular routes. It takes longer this way, but I lose less merchandise."

"And you're the organizer," she murmured. "You're the man the police want."

"I'm a businessman," he said with a smile. "Let's get on board, little lady."

"The police are watching," Liz told him as she climbed on deck.

"The police have Manchez. If he hadn't tried to pull a double cross, the last shipment would have gone down smooth."

"A double cross?"

"That's right," Scott put in as he flanked her. "Pablo

decided he could make more free-lancing than by being a company man."

"And by reporting on his fellow employee, Mr. Trydent moves up in rank. I work my organization on the incentive program."

Scott grinned at Ambuckle. "Can't beat the system."

"You had Jerry Sharpe killed." Struggling to believe what was happening, Liz stared at the round little man who'd chatted with her and rented her tanks. "You had him shot."

"He stole a great deal of money from me." Ambuckle's face puckered as he thought of it. "A great deal. I had Manchez dispose of him. The truth is, I'd considered you as a liaison for some time. It seemed simpler, however, just to use your shop. My wife's very fond of you."

"Your wife." Liz thought of the neat, matronly woman in skirted bathing suits. "She knows you smuggle drugs, and she knows you kill people?"

"She thinks we have a great stockbroker." Ambuckle grinned. "I've been moving snow for ten years, and my wife wouldn't know coke from powdered sugar. I like to keep business and family separate. The little woman's going to be sick when she finds out you had an accident. Now we're going to take a little ride. And we're going to talk about the three hundred thousand our friend Jerry slipped out from under my nose. Cast off, Scott."

"No!" Thinking only of survival, Liz made a lunge toward the dock. Ambuckle had her on the deck with one shove. He shook his head, dusted his hands and turned to her. "I'd wanted to keep this from getting messy. You know, I switched gauges on your tanks, figuring you'd back off. Always had a soft spot for you, little lady. But business is business." With a wheezy sigh, he turned to

Scott. "Since you've taken over Pablo's position, I assume you know how to deal with this."

"I certainly do." He took out a revolver. His eyes locked on Liz's. When she caught her breath, he turned the barrel toward Ambuckle. "You're under arrest." With his other hand, he pulled out a badge. "You have the right to remain silent…" It was the last thing Liz heard before she buried her face in her hands and wept.

Chapter Twelve

"I want to know what the hell's been going on." They were in Moralas's office, but Jonas wouldn't sit. He stood behind Liz's chair, his fingers curled tight over the back rung. If anyone had approached her, he would have struck first and asked questions later. He'd already flattened the unfortunate detective who'd tried to hold him back when he'd seen Liz on the deck of the *Expatriate* with Scott.

With his hands folded on his desk, Moralas gave Jonas a long, quiet look. "Perhaps the explanation should come from your countryman."

"Special Agent Donald Scott." The man Liz had known as Scott Trydent sat on the corner of Moralas's desk. "Sorry for the deception, Liz." Though his voice was calm and matter-of-fact, it couldn't mask the excitement that bubbled from him. As he sipped his coffee, he glanced up at Jonas. Explanations wouldn't go over easily with this one, he thought. But he'd always believed the ends justified the means. "I've been after that son of a bitch for three years." He drank again, savoring triumph. "It took us two before we could infiltrate the ring, and even then I couldn't make contact with the head man. To get to him I had to go through more channels than you do with the Company. He's been careful. For the past eight months I've been working with Manchez as Scott Trydent. He was the closest I could get to Ambuckle until two days ago."

"You used her." Jonas's hand went to Liz's shoulder. "You put her right in the middle."

"Yeah. The problem was, for a long time we weren't sure just how involved she was. We knew about your shop, Liz. We knew you were an experienced diver. In fact, there isn't anything about you my organization didn't know. For some time, you were our number-one suspect."

"Suspect?" She had her hands folded neatly in her lap, but the anger was boiling. "You suspected me."

"You left the U.S. over ten years ago. You've never been back. You have both the contacts and the means to have run the ring. You keep your daughter off the island for most of the year and in one of the best schools in Houston."

"That's my business."

"Details like that become our business. When you took Jerry Sharpe in and gave him a job, we leaned even further toward you. He thought differently, but then we weren't using him for his opinions."

She felt Jonas's fingers tighten and reached up to them as she spoke. "Using him?"

"I contacted Jerry Sharpe in New Orleans. He was

someone else we knew everything about. He was a con, an operator, but he had style." He took another swig of coffee as he studied Jonas. "We made him a deal. If he could get on the inside, feed us information, we'd forget about a few…indiscretions. I liked your brother," Scott said to Jonas. "Really liked him. If he'd been able to settle a bit, he'd have made a hell of a cop. 'Conning the bad guys,' he called it."

"Are you saying Jerry was working for you?" Jonas felt his emotions race toward the surface. The portrait he'd barely been able to force himself to accept was changing.

"That's right." Scott took out a cigarette and watched the match flare as he struck it. "I liked him—I mean that. He had a way of looking at things that made you forget they were so lousy."

That was Jerry, Jonas thought. To give himself a moment, he walked to the window. He could see the water lapping calmly against the hulls of boats. He could see the sun dancing down on it and children walking along the sea wall. The scene had been almost the same the day he'd arrived on Cozumel. Some things remained the same; others altered constantly. "What happened?"

"He had a hard time following orders. He wanted to push them too fast too far. He told me once he had something to prove, to himself and to the other part of him. The better part of him."

Jonas turned slowly. The pain came again, an ache. Liz saw it in his eyes and went to stand with him. "Go on."

"He got the idea into his head to rip off the money from a shipment. I didn't know about it until he called me from Acapulco. He figured he'd put the head man in a position where he'd have to deal personally. I told him to stay put, that we were scrubbing him. He'd have been taken back to the States and put somewhere safe until the job was over." He tossed the match he'd been holding into an ashtray on Moralas's desk. "He didn't listen. He came back to Cozumel and tried to deal with Manchez himself. It was over before I knew. Even if I'd have known, I can't be sure I could've stopped it. We don't like to lose civilians, Mr. Sharpe. I don't like to lose friends."

The anger drained from him degree by degree. It would have been so like Jerry, Jonas thought. An adventure, the excitement, the impulsiveness. "Go on."

"Orders came down to put the pressure on Liz." Scott gave a half laugh that had nothing to do with humor. "Orders from both sides. It wasn't until after your trip to Acapulco that we were sure you weren't involved in the smuggling. You stopped being a suspect and became the decoy."

"I came to the police." She looked at Moralas. "I came to you. You didn't tell me."

"I wasn't aware of Agent Scott's identity until yesterday. I knew only that we had a man on the inside and that it was necessary to use you."

"You were protected," Scott put in. "There wasn't a day you weren't guarded by Moralas's men and by mine. Your being here complicated things," he said to Jonas. "You were pushing too close to the bone. I guess you and Jerry had more in common than looks."

Jonas felt the weight on the chain around his neck. "Maybe we did."

"Well, we'd come to the point where we had to settle for Manchez and a few others or go for broke. We went for broke."

"The drop we made. It was a setup."

"Manchez had orders to do whatever he had to to get

back the money Jerry had taken. They didn't know about the safe-deposit box." He blew out a stream of smoke. "I had to play it pretty fast and loose to keep that under wraps. But then we didn't know about it either, until you led us to it. As far as Ambuckle was concerned, you had the money, and he was going to get it back. He wanted it to look as though you'd been running the smuggling operation together. When you were found dead, the heat would be off of him. He planned to lie low awhile, then pick up business elsewhere. I had that from Manchez. You were set up," he agreed. "So was he. I got to Merriworth, made enough noise about how Manchez was about to double-cross to set him off. When Manchez was snorkeling to your boat, I was on the phone with the man I knew as Clancy. I got a promotion, and Clancy came back to deal with you himself."

Liz tried to see it as he did, as a chess game, as any game with pawns. She couldn't. "You knew who he was yesterday morning and you still had me get on that boat."

"There were a dozen sharpshooters in position. I had a gun, Ambuckle didn't. We wanted him to order Liz's murder, and we wanted him to tell her as much as possible. When this goes to court, we want it tidy. We want him put away for a long time. You're a lawyer, Sharpe. You know how these things can go. We can make a clean collar, have a stack of evidence and lose. I've watched too many of these bastards walk." He blew out smoke between set teeth. "This one's not walking anywhere but into federal prison."

"There is still the question of whether these men will be tried in your country or mine." Moralas spoke softly, and didn't move when Scott whirled on him.

"Look, Moralas—"

"This will be discussed later. You have my thanks and my apologies," he said to Jonas and Liz. "I regret we saw no other way."

"So do I," Liz murmured, then turned to Scott. "Was it worth it?"

"Ambuckle brought thousands of pounds of cocaine into the States. He's responsible for more than fifteen murders in the U.S. and Mexico. Yeah, it was worth it."

She nodded. "I hope you understand that I never want to see you again." After closing her hand around Jonas's she managed a smile. "You were a lousy student."

"Sorry we never had that drink." He looked back at Jonas. "Sorry about a lot of things."

"I appreciate what you told me about my brother. It makes a difference."

"I'm recommending him for a citation. They'll send it to your parents."

"It'll mean a great deal to them." He offered his hand and meant it. "You were doing your job—I understand that. We all do what we have to do."

"That doesn't mean I don't regret it."

Jonas nodded. Something inside him was free, completely free. "As to putting Liz through hell for the past few weeks…" Very calmly, Jonas curled his hand into a fist and planted it solidly on Scott's jaw. The thin man snapped a chair in half as he crashed into it on his way to the floor.

"Jonas!" Stunned, Liz could do no more than stare. Then, incredibly, she felt the urge to giggle. With one hand over her mouth, she leaned into Jonas and let the laughter come. Moralas remained contentedly at his desk, sipping coffee.

Scott rubbed his jaw gingerly. "We all do what we have to do," he murmured.

Jonas only turned his back. "Goodbye, Captain."

Moralas stayed where he was. "Goodbye, Mr. Sharpe." He rose and, in a rare show of feeling, took Liz's hand and kissed it. *"Vaya con dios."*

He waited until the door had shut behind them before he looked down at Scott again. "Your government will, of course, pay for the chair."

He was gone. She'd sent him away. After nearly two weeks, Liz awoke every morning with the same thoughts. Jonas was gone. It was for the best. After nearly two weeks she awoke every morning struggling to convince herself. If she'd followed her heart, she would have said yes the moment he'd asked her to marry him. She would have left everything she'd built behind and gone with him. And ruined his life, perhaps her own.

He was already back in his own world, poring through law books, facing juries, going to elegant dinner parties. By now, she was sure his time in Cozumel was becoming vague. After all, he hadn't written. He hadn't called. He'd left the day after Ambuckle had been taken into custody without another word about love. He'd conquered his ghosts when he'd faced Manchez and had walked away whole.

He was gone, and she was once more standing on her own. As she was meant to, Liz thought. She'd have no regrets. That she'd promised herself. What she'd given to Jonas had been given without conditions or expectations. What he'd given to her she'd never lose.

The sun was high and bright, she thought. The air was as mellow as quiet music. Her lover was gone, but she, too, was whole. A month of memories could be stretched to last a lifetime. And Faith was coming home.

Liz pulled her bike into a parking space and listened to the thunder of a plane taking off. Even now Faith and her parents were crossing the Gulf. Liz left her bike and walked toward the terminal. It was ridiculous to feel nervous, she told herself, but she couldn't prevent it. It was ridiculous to arrive at the airport nearly an hour early, but she'd have gone mad at home. She skirted around a bed of marigolds and geraniums. She'd buy flowers, she decided. Her mother loved flowers.

Inside the terminal, the air was cool and full of noise. Tourists came and went but rarely passed the shops without a last-minute purchase. Liz started in the first store and worked her way down, buying consistently and strictly on impulse. By the time she arrived at the gate, she carried two shopping bags and an armful of dyed carnations.

Any minute, she thought. She'd be here any minute. Liz shifted both bags to one hand and nervously brushed at her hair. Passengers waited for their flights by napping in the black plastic chairs or reading guidebooks. She watched a woman check her lipstick in a compact mirror and wondered if she had time to run into the ladies room to examine her own face. Gnawing on her lip, she decided she couldn't leave, even for a moment. Neither could she sit, so she paced back and forth in front of the wide windows and watched the planes come and go. It was late. Planes were always late when you were waiting for them. The sky was clear and blue. She knew it was equally clear in Houston because she'd been checking the weather for days. But the plane was late. Impatient, she walked back to security to ask about the status. She should have known better.

Liz got a shrug and the Mexican equivalent of *It'll be here when it comes.* In another ten minutes, she was ready to scream. Then she saw it. She didn't have to hear the flight announcement to know. With her heart thudding dully, she waited by the door.

Faith wore blue striped pants and a white blouse. Her hair's grown, Liz thought as she watched her daughter come down the steps. She's grown—though she knew it would never do to tell Faith so. She'd just wrinkle her nose and roll her eyes. Her palms were wet. *Don't cry, don't cry,* Liz ordered herself. But the tears were already welling. Then Faith looked up and saw her. With a grin and a wave she was racing forward. Liz dropped her bags and reached out for her daughter.

"Mom, I got to sit by the window, but I couldn't see our house." As she babbled, Faith held her mother's neck in a stranglehold. "I brought you a present."

With her face buried against Faith's throat, Liz drew in the scents—powder, soap and chocolate from the streak on the front of the white blouse. "Let me look at you." Drawing her back, Liz soaked up the sight of her. *She's beautiful,* Liz realized with a jolt. Not just cute or sweet or pretty any longer. Her daughter was beautiful.

I can't let her go again. It hit her like a wall. *I'll never be able to let her go again.* "You've lost a tooth," Liz managed as she brushed back her daughter's hair.

"Two." Faith grinned to show the twin spaces. "Grandma said I could put them under my pillow, but I brought them with me so I can put them under my real pillow. Will I get pesos?"

"Yes." Liz kissed one cheek, then the other. "Welcome home."

With her hand firmly in Faith's, Liz rose to greet her parents. For a moment she just looked at them, trying to see them as a stranger would. Her father was tall and still slim, though his hairline was creeping back. He was grinning at her the way he had whenever she'd done something particularly pleasing to him. Her mother stood beside him, lovely in her tidy way. She looked now, as she'd always looked to Liz, like a woman who'd never had to handle a crisis more stressful than a burned roast. Yet she'd been as solid and as sturdy as a rock. There were tears in her eyes. Liz wondered abruptly if the beginning of the summer left her mother as empty as the end of the summer left her.

"Momma." Liz reached out and was surrounded. "Oh, I've missed you. I've missed you all so much." *I want to go home.* The thought surged up inside her and nearly poured out. She needed to go home.

"Mom." Faith tugged on the pocket of her jeans. "Mom."

Giddy, Liz turned and scooped her up. "Yes." She covered her face with kisses until Faith giggled. "Yes, yes, yes!"

Faith snuggled in. "You have to say hello to Jonas."

"What?"

"He came with us. You have to say hi."

"I don't—" Then she saw him, leaning against the window, watching—waiting patiently. The blood rushed out of her head to her heart until she was certain something would burst. Holding onto Faith, Liz stood where she was. Jonas walked to her, took her face in both hands and kissed her hard.

"Nice to see you," he murmured, then bent down to pick up the bags Liz had dropped. "I imagine these are for you," he said as he handed Liz's mother the flowers.

"Yes." Liz tried to gather the thoughts stumbling through her mind. "I forgot."

"They're lovely." She sent her daughter a smile. "Jonas is going to drive us to the hotel. I invited him to dinner tonight. I hope you don't mind. You always make enough."

"No, I... Of course."

"We'll see you then." She gave Liz another brief kiss. "I know you want to get Faith home and have some time together. We'll see you tonight."

"But I—"

"Our bags are here. We're going to deal with customs."

Before Liz could say another word, she was alone with her daughter.

"Can we stop by and see Señor Pessado?"

"Yes," Liz said absently.

"Can I have some candy?"

Liz glanced down to the chocolate stain on Faith's blouse. "You've already had some."

Faith just smiled. She knew she could depend on Señor Pessado. "Let's go home now."

Liz waited until Faith was unpacked, until the crystal bird Faith had bought her was hanging in the window and her daughter had consumed two tacos and a pint of milk.

"Faith..." She wanted her voice to be casual. "When did you meet Mr. Sharpe?"

"Jonas? He came to Grandma's house." Faith turned the doll Liz had brought her this way and that for inspection.

"To Grandma's? When?"

"I don't know." She decided to call the doll Cassandra because it was pretty and had long hair. "Can I have my ice cream now?"

"Oh—yes." Liz walked over to get it out of the freezer. "Faith, do you know why he went to Grandma's?"

"He wanted to talk to her, I guess. To Grandpa, too. He stayed for dinner. I knew Grandma liked him because she made cherry pies. I liked him, too. He can play the piano really good." Faith eyed the ice cream and was satisfied when her mother added another scoop. "He took me to the zoo."

"What?" The bowl nearly slipped out of Liz's hand as she set it down. "Jonas took you to the zoo?"

"Last Saturday. We fed popcorn to the monkeys, but mostly we ate it." She giggled as she shoveled in ice cream. "He tells funny stories. I scraped my knee." Remembering suddenly, Faith pulled up her slacks to show off her wound.

"Oh, baby." It was small and already scabbed over, but Liz brushed a kiss over it anyway. "How'd you do this?"

"At the zoo. I was running. I can run really fast in my new sneakers, but I fell down. I didn't cry."

Liz rolled the slacks down. "I'm sure you didn't."

"Jonas didn't get mad or anything. He cleaned it all up with his handkerchief. It was pretty messy. I bled a lot." She smiled at that, pleased with herself. "He said I have pretty eyes just like you."

A little thrill of panic raced through her, but she couldn't stop herself. "Did he? What else did he say?"

"Oh, we talked about Mexico and about Houston. He wondered which I liked best."

Liz rested her hands on her daughter's knees. *This is*

what matters, she realized. This was all that really mattered. "What did you tell him?"

"I like it best where you are." She scraped the bottom of the bowl. "He said he liked it best there, too. Is he going to be your boyfriend?"

"My—" Liz managed, just barely, to suppress the laugh. "No."

"Charlene's mother has a boyfriend, but he isn't as tall as Jonas and I don't think he ever took Charlene to the zoo. Jonas said sometime maybe we could go see the Liberty Bell. Do you think we can?"

Liz picked up the ice cream dish and began to wash it. "We'll see," she muttered.

"Listen, someone's coming." Faith was up like a shot and dashing for the front door. "It's Jonas!" With a whoop, she was out of the door and running full steam.

"Faith!" Liz hurried from the kitchen and reached the porch in time to see Faith hurl herself at Jonas. With a laugh, he caught her, tossed her in the air then set her down again in a move so natural that it seemed he'd been doing so all his life. Liz knotted the dishcloth in her hands.

"You came early." Pleased, Faith hung on to his hand. "We were talking about you."

"Were you?" He tousled Faith's hair but looked up at Liz. "That's funny, because I was thinking about you."

"We're going to make paella because that's what Grandpa likes best. You can help."

"Faith—"

"Love to," Jonas interrupted. "After I talk to your mother." At the foot of the stairs he crouched down to Faith's level. "I'd really like to talk to your mom alone."

Faith's mouth screwed up. "Why?"

"I have to convince her to marry me."

He ignored Liz's gasp and watched for Faith's reaction. Her eyes narrowed and her mouth pursed. "She said you weren't her boyfriend. I asked."

He grinned and leaned closer. "I just have to talk her into it."

"Grandma says nobody can ever talk my mom into anything. She has a hard head."

"So do I, and I make a living talking people into things. But maybe you could put in a few good words for me later."

As Faith considered, her eyes brightened. "Okay. Mom, can I see if Roberto's home? You said he had new puppies."

Liz stretched out the cloth then balled it again. "Go ahead, but just for a little while."

Jonas straightened as he watched Faith race toward the house across the street. "You've done an excellent job with your daughter, Elizabeth."

"She's done a great deal of it herself."

He turned and saw the nerves on her face. It didn't displease him. But he remembered the way she'd looked when she had opened her arms to Faith at the airport. He wanted, he would, see her look that way again. "Do you want to talk inside?" he began as he walked up the steps. "Or right here?"

"Jonas, I don't know why you've come back, but—"

"Of course you know why I've come back. You're not stupid."

"We don't have anything to talk about."

"Fine." He closed the distance quickly. She didn't resist, though she told herself she would. When he dragged her against him, she went without hesitation. Her mouth locked hungrily to his, and for a moment, just for a moment, the world was right again. "If you don't want to talk, we'll go inside and make love until you see things a little more clearly."

"I see things clearly." Liz put her hands on his arms and started to draw away.

"I love you."

He felt the shudder, saw the flash of joy in her eyes before she looked away. "Jonas, this isn't possible."

"Wrong. It's entirely possible—in fact, it's already done. The point is, Liz, you need me."

Her eyes narrowed to slits. "What I need I take care of."

"That's why I love you," he said simply and took the wind out of her sails.

"Jonas—"

"Are you going to tell me you haven't missed me?" She opened her mouth, then shut it again. "Okay, so you take the Fifth on that one." He stepped back from her. "Are you going to deny that you've spent some sleepless nights in the past couple of weeks, that you've thought about what happened between us? Are you going to stand here and look at me now and tell me you're not in love with me?"

She'd never been able to lie well. Liz turned and meticulously spread the dishcloth over the porch rail. "Jonas, I can't run my life on my feelings."

"From now on you can. Did you like the present Faith brought you?"

"What?" Confused, she turned back. "Yes, of course I did."

"Good. I brought you one, too." He took a box out of his pocket. Liz saw the flash of diamond and nearly had her hand behind her back before he caught it in his. Firmly, he slipped the ring on. "It's official."

She wouldn't even look at it. She couldn't stop herself. The diamond was shaped in a teardrop and as white and glossy as a wish. "You're being ridiculous," she told him, but couldn't make herself take it off.

"You're going to marry me." He took her shoulders and leaned her back against a post. "That's not negotiable. After that, we have several options. I can give up my practice and live in Cozumel. You can support me."

She let out a quick breath that might have been a laugh. "Now you're really being ridiculous."

"You don't like that one. Good, I didn't care for it either. You can come back to Philadelphia with me. I'll support you."

Her chin went up. "I don't need to be supported."

"Excellent. We agree on the first two options." He ran his hands through her hair and discovered he wasn't feeling as patient as he'd thought he would. "Now, you can come back to the States. We'll take a map and you can close your eyes and pick a spot. That's where we'll live."

"We can't run our lives this way." She pushed him aside to walk down the length of the porch and back. But part of her was beginning to believe they could. "Don't you see how impossible it is?" she demanded as much of herself as of him. "You have your career. I have my business. I'd never be a proper wife for someone like you."

"You're the only wife for someone like me." He grabbed her shoulders again. No, he wasn't feeling patient at all. "Damn it, Liz, you're the only one. If the business is important to you, keep it. Have Luis run it. We can come back a half a dozen times a year if you want. Start another business. We'll go to Florida, to California, anywhere you want where they need a good dive shop. Or…" He waited until he was sure he had her full attention. "You could go back to school."

He saw it in her eyes—the surprise, the dream, then the denial. "That's over."

"The hell it is. Look at you—it's what you want. Keep the shop, build another, build ten others, but give yourself something for yourself."

"It's been more than ten years."

He lifted a brow. "You said once you wouldn't change anything."

"And I meant it, but to go back now, after all this time."

"Afraid?"

Her eyes narrowed; her spine stiffened. "Yes."

He laughed, delighted with her. "Woman, in the past few weeks, you've been through hell and out again. And you're afraid of a few college courses?"

With a sigh, she turned away. "I might not be able to make it."

"So what?" He whirled her back again. "So you fall flat on your face. I'll be right there falling down with you. It's time for risking, Liz. For both of us."

"Oh, I want to believe you." She lifted a hand to rest it on his face. "I want to. I do love you, Jonas. So much."

She was locked against him again, lost in him. "I need you, Liz. I'm not going back without you."

She clung to him a moment, almost ready to believe. "But it's not just me. You have to understand I can't do whatever I'd like."

"Faith?" He drew her back again. "I've spent the past weeks getting to know her. My main objective when I started was to ingratiate myself. I figured the only way to get to you was through her."

So she'd already surmised. "Afternoons at the zoo?"

"That's right. Thing was, I didn't know she was as easy to fall for as her mother. I want her."

The hand Liz had lifted to her hair froze. "I don't understand."

"I want her to be mine—legally, emotionally. I want you to agree to let me adopt her."

"Adopt…" Whatever she might have expected from him, it hadn't been this. "But she's—"

"Yours?" he interrupted. "No, she's going to be ours. You're going to have to share her. And if you're set on her going to school in Houston, we'll live in Houston. Within the year I expect she should have a brother or sister because she needs family as much as we do."

He was offering her everything, everything she'd ever wanted and had refused to believe in. She had only to hold out her hand. The idea terrified her. "She's another man's child. How will you be able to forget that?"

"She's your child," he reminded her. "You told me yourself she was your child only. Now she's going to be mine." Taking her hands, he kissed them. "So are you."

"Jonas, do you know what you're doing? You're asking for a wife who'll have to start from scratch and a half-grown daughter. You're complicating your life."

"Yeah, and maybe I'm saving it."

And hers. Her blood was pumping again, her skin was tingling. For the first time in years she could look at her life and see no shadows. She closed her eyes and breathed deeply before she turned. "Be sure," she whispered. "Be absolutely sure. If I let myself go, if I say yes and you change your mind, I'll hate you for the rest of my life."

He took her by the shirtfront. "In one week, we're going to my parents' farm in Lancaster, calling the local minister, justice of the peace or witch doctor and we're getting married. Adoption papers are being drawn up. When we settle in as a family, we're all having the same name. You and Faith and I."

With a sigh, Liz leaned back again against the post and studied his face. It was beautiful, she decided. Strong, passionate, patient. Her life was going to be bound up with that face. It was as real as flesh and blood and as precious as dreams. Her lover was back, her child was with her and nothing was impossible.

"When I first met you, I thought you were the kind of man who always got what he wanted."

"And you were right." He took her hands again and held them. "Now what are we going to tell Faith?" he demanded.

Her lips curved slowly. "I guess we'd better tell her you talked me into it."

* * * * *

BOUNDARY LINES

For Ruth Langan,
for all the years.

Chapter One

The wind whipped against her cheeks. It flowed through her hair, smelling faintly of spring and growing things. Jillian lifted her face to it, as much in challenge as in appreciation. Beneath her, the sleek mare strained for more speed. They'd ride, two free spirits, as long as the sun stayed high.

Short, tough grass was crushed under hooves, along with stray wildflowers. Jillian gave no thought to the buttercups as she crossed to the path. Here the soil was hard, chestnut in color and bordered by the silver-gray sage.

There were no trees along this rough, open plain, but Jillian wasn't looking for shade. She galloped by a field of wheat bleaching in the sun with hardly a stray breeze to rustle it. Farther on there was hay, acres of it, nearly ready for the first harvesting. She heard and recognized the call of a meadowlark. But she wasn't a farmer. If someone had termed her one, Jillian would have laughed or bristled, depending on her mood.

The crops were grown because they were needed, in the same way the vegetable patch was sown and tended. Growing your own feed made you self-reliant. There was nothing more important than that in Jillian's estimation. In a good year there were enough crops left over to bring in a few extra dollars. The few extra dollars would buy more cattle. It was always the cattle.

She was a rancher—like her grandfather had been, and his father before him.

The land stretched as far as she could see. Her land. It was rolling and rich. Acre after acre of grain sprouted up, and beyond it were the plains and pastures where the cattle and horses grazed. But she wasn't riding fence today, counting head or poring over the books in her grandfather's leather-and-oak office. Today she wanted freedom, and was taking it.

Jillian hadn't been raised on the rugged, spacious plains of Montana. She hadn't been born in the saddle. She'd grown up in Chicago because her father had chosen medicine over ranching, and east over west. Jillian hadn't blamed him as her grandfather had—it was a matter of choice. Everyone was entitled to the life they chose. That was why she'd come here, back to her heritage, five years before when she'd turned twenty.

At the top of the hill Jillian stopped the mare. From here she could see over the planted fields to the pastures, fenced in with wire that could hardly be seen from that distance. It gave the illusion of open range where the cattle could roam at will. Once, it would've been like that, she mused as she tossed her hair back over her shoulder. If she narrowed her eyes, she could almost see it—open, free—the way it had been when her ancestors had first come to settle. The gold rush had brought them, but the land had kept them. It kept her.

Gold, she thought with a shake of her head. Who needed gold when there was priceless wealth in space alone? She preferred the spread of land with its isolated mountains and valleys. If her people had gone farther west, into the higher mountains, her great-great-grandparents might have toiled in the streams and the mines. They might have staked their claim there, plucking out nuggets and digging out gold dust, but they would never have found anything richer than this. Jillian had understood the land's worth and its allure the first moment she'd seen it.

She'd been ten. At her grandfather's invitation—command, Jillian corrected with a smirk—both she and her brother, Marc, had made the trip west, to Utopia. Marc had been there before, of course. He'd been sixteen and quietly capable in the way of their father. And no more interested in ranching than his father had been.

Her first glimpse of the ranch hadn't surprised her, though it wasn't what many children might've expected after years of exposure to western cinema. It was vast, and somehow tidy. Paddocks, stables, barns and the sturdy charm of the ranch house itself. Even at ten, even after one look, Jillian had known she hadn't been meant for the streets and sidewalks of Chicago, but for this open sky and endless land. At ten, she'd had her first experience with love at first sight.

But it wasn't love at first sight with her grandfather. He'd been a tough, weathered, opinionated old man. The ranch and his herd had been his life. He hadn't the least idea what to do with a spindly girl who happened to be his son's daughter. They'd circled each other warily for days, until he'd made the mistake of letting out some caustic remark about her father and his choice of pills and needles. Quick tempered, Jillian had flown to her father's defense. They'd ended up shouting at each other, Jillian red-faced and dry-eyed even after being threatened with a razor strap.

They'd parted at the end of that visit with a combination of mutual respect and dislike. Then he'd sent her a custom-made, buff-colored Stetson for her birthday. And it began…

Perhaps they'd grown to love one another so deeply because they'd taken their time about it. Those sporadic weeks during her adolescence he'd taught her everything, hardly seeming to teach at all: how to gauge the weather by the smell of the air, the look of the sky; how to deliver a breech calf; how to ride fence and herd a steer. She'd called him Clay because they'd been friends. And when she'd tried her first and only plug of tobacco, he'd held her head when she'd been sick. He hadn't lectured.

When his eyes had grown weak, Jillian had taken over the books. They'd never discussed it—just as they'd never discussed that her move there in the summer of her twentieth year would be permanent. When his illness had begun to take over, she'd gradually assumed the responsibilities of the ranch, though no words had passed between them to make it official.

When he died, the ranch was hers. Jillian hadn't needed to hear the will read to know it. Clay had known she would stay. She'd left the east behind—and if there were memories from there that still twisted inside her, she buried them. More easily than she'd buried her grandfather.

It was herself she grieved for, and knowing it made her impatient. Clay had lived long and hard, doing as he chose the way he chose. His illness had wasted him, and would have brought him pain and humiliation had it continued. He would have hated that, would have railed at her if he could have seen how she'd wept over him.

God Almighty, girl! What're you wasting time here for? Don't you know there's a ranch to run? Get some hands out to check the fence in the west forty before we've got cattle roaming all over Montana.

Yes, she thought with a half smile. He'd have said something like that—cursed her a bit, then would've turned away with a grunt. Of course, she'd have cursed right back at him.

"You mangy old bear," she muttered. "I'm going to turn Utopia into the best ranch in Montana just to spite you." Laughing, she threw her face up to the sky. "See if I don't!"

Sensing her change of mood, the mare began to dance impatiently, tossing her head. "All right, Delilah." Jillian leaned over to pat her creamy neck. "We've got all afternoon." In a deft move she turned the mare around and started off at an easy lope.

There weren't many free hours like this, so they were prized. As it was, Jillian knew she'd stolen them. That made it all the sweeter. If she had to work eighteen hours tomorrow to make up for it, she'd do it without complaint. Even the bookwork, she thought with a sigh. Though there was that sick heifer that needed watching, and the damn Jeep that'd broken down for the third time this month. And the fence along the boundary line. The Murdock boundary line, she thought with a grimace.

The feud between the Barons and the Murdocks

stretched back to the early 1900s when Noah Baron, her great-grandfather, came to southeast Montana. He'd meant to go on, to the mountains and the gold, but had stayed to homestead. The Murdocks had already been there, with their vast, rich ranch. The Barons had been peasants to them, intruders doomed to fail—or to be driven out. Jillian gritted her teeth as she remembered the stories her grandfather had told her: cut fences, stolen cattle, ruined crops.

But the Barons had stayed, survived, and succeeded. No, they didn't have the amount of land the Murdocks did, or the money, but they knew how to make the best use of what they did have. If her grandfather had struck oil as the Murdocks had, Jillian thought with a smirk, they could have afforded to specialize in purebred beef, as well. That had been a matter of chance, not skill.

She told herself she didn't care about the purebred part of it. Let the Murdock clan wave their blue ribbons and shout about improving the line. She'd raise her Herefords and shorthorns and get the best price for them at the Exchange. Baron beef was prime, and everyone knew it.

When was the last time one of the high-and-mighty Murdocks rode the miles of fence, sweating under the sun while checking for a break? When was the last time one of them had eaten dust on a drive? Jillian knew for a fact that Paul J. Murdock, her grandfather's contemporary, hadn't bothered to ride fence or flank cattle in more than a year.

She let out a short, derisive laugh. All they knew about was the figures in the account books and politicking. By the time she was finished, Utopia would make the Double M look like a dude ranch.

The idea put her in a better mood, so that the line

between her brows vanished. She wouldn't think of the Murdocks today, or of the back-breaking work that promised to begin before the sun came up tomorrow. She would think only of the sweetness of these stolen hours, of the rich smell of spring…and the endless hard blue of the sky.

Jillian knew this path well. It ran along the westernmost tip of her land. Too tough for the plow, too stubborn for grazing, it was left alone. It was here she always came when she wanted both a sense of solitude and excitement. No one else came here, from her own ranch or from the Murdock spread that ran parallel to it. Even the fence that had once formed the boundary had fallen years before, and had been forgotten. No one cared about this little slice of useless land but her, which made her care all the more.

Now there were a few trees, the cottonwood and aspen just beginning to green. Over the sound of the mare's hooves she heard a warbler begin to sing. There might be coyotes, too, and certainly rattlesnakes. Jillian wasn't so enchanted she didn't remember that. There was a rifle, oiled and loaded, strapped to the back of her saddle.

The mare scented the water from the pond, and Jillian let her have her head. The thought of stripping off her sweaty clothes and diving in appealed immensely. Five minutes in that clear, icy water would be exhilarating, and Delilah could rest and drink before they began the long trip back. Spotting the glistening water, Jillian let the reins drop, relaxing. Her grandfather would have cursed her for her lack of attention, but she was already thinking about the luxury of sliding naked into the cold water, then drying in the sun.

But the mare scented something else. Abruptly she

reared, plunging so that Jillian's first thought was rattler. While she struggled to control Delilah with one hand, she reached behind for the rifle. Before she could draw a breath, she was hurtling through space. Jillian only had time for one muttered oath before she landed bottom first in the pond. But she'd seen that the rattlesnake had legs.

Sputtering and furious, she struggled to her feet, wiping her wet hair out of her eyes so that she could glare at the man astride a buckskin stallion. Delilah danced nervously while he held the glistening stallion still.

He didn't need to have his feet on the ground for her to see that he was tall. His hair was dark, waving thick and long beneath a black Stetson that shadowed a raw-boned, weathered face. His nose was straight and aristocratic, his mouth well shaped and solemn. Jillian didn't take the time to admire the way he sat the stallion—with a casual sort of control that exuded confidence and power. What she did see was that his eyes were nearly as black as his hair. And laughing.

Narrowing her own, she spat at him, "What the hell are you doing on my land?"

He looked at her in silence, the only movement a very slow lifting of his left brow. Unlike Jillian, he was taking the time to admire. Her fiery hair was darkened almost to copper with the water and clung wetly to accent the elegance of bone and skin—fine boned, honey-toned skin. He could see the flash of green that was her eyes, dark as jade and dangerous as a cat's. Her mouth, clamped together in fury, had a luxuriously full, promising lower lip that contrasted with the firm stubborn chin.

Casually he let his gaze slide down. She was a long one, he thought, with hardly more curves than a boy. But just now, with the shirt wet and snug as a second skin…

Slowly his gaze climbed back to hers. She didn't blush at the survey, though she recognized it. There wasn't apprehension or fear in her eyes. Instead, she shot him a hard look that might have withered another man.

"I said," Jillian began in a low, clipped voice, "what the hell are you doing on my land?"

Instead of answering he swung out of the saddle—the move smooth and economic enough to tell her he'd been in and out of one most of his life. He walked toward her with a loose, easy stride that still carried the air of command. Then he smiled. In one quick flash his face changed from dangerously sexy to dangerously charming. It was a smile that said, you can trust me...for the moment. He held out a hand.

"Ma'am."

Jillian drew in one deep breath and let it out again. Ignoring the offered hand, she climbed out of the water by herself. Dripping, cold, but far from cooled off, Jillian stuck her hands on her hips. "You haven't answered my question."

Nerve, he thought, still studying her. She's got plenty of that. Temper and—he noticed the way her chin was thrown up in challenge—arrogance. He liked the combination. Hooking his thumbs in his pockets, he shifted his weight, thinking it was a shame she'd dry off quickly in the full sun.

"This isn't your land," he said smoothly, with only a hint of a Western drawl. "Miss..."

"Baron," Jillian snapped. "And who the hell are you to tell me this isn't my land?"

He tipped his hat with more insolence than respect.

"Aaron Murdock." His lips twitched at her hiss of breath. "Boundary runs straight up through here." He looked down at the toes of his boots inches away from the toes of hers as if he could see the line drawn there. "Cuts about clean down the middle of the pond." He brought his gaze back to hers—mouth solemn, eyes laughing. "I think you landed on my side."

Aaron Murdock, son and heir. Wasn't he supposed to be out in Billings playing in their damn oil fields? Frowning, Jillian decided he didn't look like the smooth college boy her grandfather had described to her. That was something she'd think about later. Right now, it was imperative she make her stand, and make it stick.

"*If* I landed on your side," she said scathingly, "it was because you were lurking around with that." She jerked her thumb at his horse. Gorgeous animal, she thought with an admiration she had to fight to conceal.

"Your hands were slack on the reins," he pointed out mildly.

The truth of it only added fuel to the fire. "His scent spooked Delilah."

"Delilah." A flicker of amusement ran over his face as he pushed back his hat and studied the smooth clean lines of Jillian's mare. "Must've been fate," he murmured. "Samson." At the sound of his name the stallion walked over to nuzzle Aaron's shoulder.

Jillian choked back a chuckle, but not in time to conceal the play of a small dimple at the side of her mouth. "Just remember what Samson's fate was," she retorted. "And keep him away from my mare."

"A mighty pretty filly," Aaron said easily. While he stroked his horse's head his eyes remained on Jillian. "A bit high strung," he continued, "but well built. She'd breed well."

Jillian's eyes narrowed again. Aaron found he liked the

way they glinted through the thick, luxurious lashes. "I'll worry about her breeding, Murdock." She planted her feet in the ground that soaked up the water still dripping from her. "What're you doing up here?" she demanded. "You won't find any oil."

Aaron tilted his head. "I wasn't looking for any. I wasn't looking for a woman either." Casually he reached over and lifted a strand of her heavy hair. "But I found one."

Jillian felt that quick, breathless pressure in her chest and recognized it. Oh, no, she'd let that happen to her once before. She let her gaze drop down to where his long brown fingers toyed with the ends of her hair, then lifted it to his face again. "You wouldn't want to lose that hand," she said softly.

For a moment, his fingers tightened, as if he considered picking up the challenge she'd thrown down. Then, as casually as he'd captured her hair, he released it. "Testy, aren't you?" Aaron said mildly. "But then, you Barons've always been quick to draw."

"To defend," Jillian corrected, standing her ground.

They measured each other a moment, both surprised to find the opposition so attractive. Tread carefully. The command went through each of their minds, though it was an order both habitually had trouble carrying out.

"I'm sorry about the old man," Aaron said at length. "He'd have been your—grandfather?"

Jillian's chin stayed up, but Aaron saw the shadow that briefly clouded her eyes. "Yes."

She'd loved him, Aaron thought with some surprise. From his few run-ins with Clay Baron, he'd found a singularly unlovable man. He let his memory play back with the snatches of information he'd gleaned since his return to the Double M. "You'd be the little girl who spent some summers here years back," he commented, trying to remember if he'd ever caught sight of her before. "From back east." His hand came back to stroke his chin, a bit rough from the lack of razor that morning. "Jill, isn't it?"

"Jillian," she corrected coldly.

"Jillian." The swift smile transformed his face again. "It suits you better."

"Miss Baron suits me best," she told him, damning his smile.

Aaron didn't bother to acknowledge her deliberate unfriendliness, instead giving in to the urge to let his gaze slip briefly to her mouth again. No, he didn't believe he'd seen her before. That wasn't a mouth a man forgot. "If Gil Haley's running things at Utopia, you should do well enough."

She bristled. He could almost see her spine snap straight. "I run things at Utopia," she said evenly.

His mouth tilted at one corner. "You?"

"That's right, Murdock, me. I haven't been pushing papers in Billings for the last five years." Something flashed in his eyes, but she ignored it and plunged ahead. "Utopia's mine, every inch of ground, every blade of grass. The difference is I work it instead of strutting around the State Fair waving my blue ribbons."

Intrigued, he took her hands, ignoring her protest as he turned them over to study the palms. They were slender, but hard and capable. Running his thumb over a line of callus, Aaron felt a ripple of admiration—and desire. He'd grown very weary of pampered helpless hands in Billings. "Well, well," he murmured, keeping her hands in his as he looked back into her eyes.

She was furious—that his hands were so strong, that

they held hers so effortlessly. That her heartbeat was roaring in her ears. The warbler had begun to sing again and she could hear the gentle swish of the horses' tails as they stood.

He smelled pleasantly of leather and sweat. Too pleasantly. There was a rim of amber around the outside of his irises that only accented the depth of brown. A scar, very thin and white, rode along the edge of his jaw. You wouldn't notice it unless you looked very closely. Just as you might not notice how strong and lean his hands were unless yours were caught in them.

Jillian snapped back quickly. It didn't pay to notice things like that. It didn't pay to listen to that roaring in your head. She'd done that once before and where had it gotten her? Dewy-eyed, submissive and soft-headed. She was a lot smarter than she'd been five years before. The most important thing was to remember who he was—a Murdock. And who she was—a Baron.

"I warned you about your hands before," she said quietly.

"So you did," Aaron agreed, watching her face. "Why?"

"I don't like to be touched."

"No?" His brow lifted again, but he didn't yet release her hands. "Most living things do—if they're touched properly." His eyes locked on hers abruptly, very direct, very intuitive. "Someone touch you wrong once, Jillian?"

Her gaze didn't falter. "You're trespassing, Murdock."

Again, that faint inclination of the head. "Maybe. We could always string the fence again."

She knew he hadn't misunderstood her. This time, when she tugged on her hands, he released them. "Just stay on your side," she suggested.

He adjusted his hat so that the shadow fell over his face again. "And if I don't?"

Her chin came up. "Then I'll have to deal with you." Turning her back, she walked to Delilah and gathered the reins. It took an effort not to pass her hand over the buckskin stallion, but she resisted. Without looking at Aaron, Jillian swung easily into the saddle, then fit her own damp, flat-brimmed hat back on her head. Now she had the satisfaction of being able to look down at him.

In a better humor, Jillian leaned on the saddle horn. Leather creaked easily beneath her as Delilah shifted her weight. Her shirt was drying warm on her back. "You have a nice vacation, Murdock," she told him with a faint smile. "Don't wear yourself out while you're here."

He reached up to stroke Delilah's neck. "Now, I'm going to try real hard to take your advice on that, Jillian."

She leaned down a bit closer. "Miss Baron."

Aaron surprised her by tugging the brim of her hat down to her nose. "I like Jillian." He grabbed the string tie of the hat before she could straighten, then gave her a long, odd look. "I swear," he murmured, "you smell like something a man could just close his eyes and wallow in."

She was amused. Jillian told herself she was amused while she pretended not to feel the quick trip of her pulse. She removed his hand from the string of her hat, straightened and smiled. "You disappoint me. I'd've thought a man who'd spent so much time in college and the big city would have a snappier line and a smoother delivery."

He slipped his hands into his back pockets as he looked up at her. It was fascinating to watch the way the sun shot into her eyes without drawing out the smallest fleck of gold or gray in that cool, deep green. The eyes were too stubborn to allow for any interference; they suited the woman. "I'll practice," Aaron told her with the hint of a smile. "I'll do better next time."

She gave a snort of laughter and started to turn her horse. "There won't be a next time."

His hand was firm on the bridle before she could trot off. The look he gave her was calm, and only slightly amused. "You look smarter than that Jillian. We'll have a number of next times before we're through."

She didn't know how she'd lost the advantage so quickly, only that she had. Her chin angled. "You seem determined to lose that hand, Murdock."

He gave her an easy smile, patted Delilah's neck, then turned toward his own horse. "I'll see you soon, Jillian."

She waited, seething, until he'd swung into the saddle. Delilah sidestepped skittishly until the horses were nearly nose to nose. "Stay on your own side," Jillian ordered, then pressed in her heels. The straining mare lunged forward.

Samson tossed his head and pranced as they both watched Jillian race off on Delilah. "Not this time," Aaron murmured to himself, soothing his horse. "But soon." He gave a quick laugh, then pointed his horse in the opposite direction. "Damn soon."

Jillian could get rid of a lot of anger and frustration with the speed and the wind. She rode as the mare wanted—fast. Perhaps Delilah needed to outrace her blood, as well, Jillian thought wryly. Both male animals had been compelling. If the stallion had belonged to anyone but a Murdock, she would've found a way to have Delilah bred with him—no matter what the stud fee. If she had any hope of increasing and improving Utopia's line of horses, the bulk of the burden rested with her own mare. And there wasn't a stallion on her ranch that could compare with Murdock's Samson.

It was a pity Aaron Murdock hadn't been the smooth, fastidious, boring businessman she'd envisioned him. That type would never have made her blood heat. A woman in her position couldn't afford to acknowledge that kind of attraction, especially with a rival. It would put her at an immediate disadvantage when she needed every edge she could get.

So much depended on the next six months if she was going to have the chance to expand. Oh, the ranch could go on, making its cozy little profit, but she wanted more. The fire of her grandfather's ambition hadn't dimmed so much with age as it had been transferred to her. With her youth and energy, and with that fickle lady called luck, she could turn Utopia into the empire her ancestors had dreamed about.

She had the land and the knowledge. She had the skill and the determination. Already, Jillian had poured the cash portion of her inheritance back into the ranch. She'd put a down payment on the small plane her grandfather had been too stubborn to buy. With a plane, the ranch could be patrolled in hours, stray cattle spotted, broken fences reported. Though she still believed in the necessity of a skilled puncher and cow pony, Jillian understood the beauty of mixing new techniques with the old.

Pickups and Jeeps roamed the range as well as horses. CBs could be used to communicate over long distances, while the lariat was still carried by every hand—in the saddle or behind the wheel. The cattle would be driven to feed lots when necessary and the calves herded into the corral for branding, though the iron would be heated by a butane torch rather than an open fire. Times had changed, but the spirit and the code remained.

Above all, the rancher, like any other country person, depended on two things: the sky and the earth. Because the first was always fickle and the second often unyielding, the rancher had no choice but to rely, ultimately, on himself. That was Jillian's philosophy.

With that in mind, she changed directions without changing her pace. She'd ride along the Murdock boundary and check the fences after all.

She trotted along an open pasture while broad-rumped, white-faced Herefords barely glanced up from their grazing. The spring grass was growing thick and full. Hearing the rumble of an engine, she stopped. In almost the same manner as her mount, Jillian scented the air. Gasoline. It was a shame to spoil the scent of grass and cattle with it. Philosophically she turned Delilah in the direction of the sound and rode.

It was easy to spot the battered pickup in the rolling terrain. Jillian lifted her hand in half salute and rode toward it. Her mood had lifted again, though her jeans were still damp and her boots soggy. She considered Gil Haley one of the few dyed-in-the-wool cowboys left on her ranch or any other. A hundred years before, he'd have been happy riding the range with his saddle, bedroll and plug of tobacco. If he had the chance, she mused, he'd be just as happy that way today.

"Gil." Jillian stopped Delilah by the driver's window and grinned at him.

"You disappeared this morning." His greeting was brusque in a voice that sounded perpetually peppery. He didn't expect an explanation, nor would she have given one.

Jillian nodded to the two men with him, another breed of cowhand, distinguished by their heavy work shoes. Gil might give in to the pickup because he could patrol fifty thousand acres quicker and more thoroughly than on horseback, but he'd never give up his boots. "Any problem?"

"Dumb cow tangled in the wire a ways back." He shifted his tobacco plug while looking up at her with his perpetual squint. "Got her out before she did any damage. Looks like we've got to clear out some of that damn tumbleweed again. Knocked down some line."

Jillian accepted this with a nod. "Anyone check the fence along the west section today?"

There was no change in the squint as he eyed her. "Nope."

"I'll see to it now, then." Jillian hesitated. If there was anyone who knew the gossip, it would be Gil. "I happened to run into Aaron Murdock about an hour ago," she put in casually. "I thought he was in Billings."

"Nope."

Jillian gave him a mild look. "I realize that, Gil. What's he doing around here?"

"Got himself a ranch."

Gamely Jillian hung on to her temper. "I realize that, too. He's also got himself an oil field—or his father does."

"Kid sister married herself an oil man," Gil told her. "The old man did some shifting around and got the boy back where he wants him."

"You mean…" Jillian narrowed her eyes. "Aaron Murdock's staying on the Double M?"

"Managing it," Gil stated, then spit expertly. "Guess things've simmered down after the blowup a few years back. Murdock's getting on, you know, close on to seventy or more. Maybe he wants to sit back and relax now."

"Managing it," Jillian muttered. So she was going to be plagued with a Murdock after all. At least she and the old man had managed to stay out of each other's way. Aaron had already invaded what she considered her private haven—even if he did own half of it. "How long's he been back?"

Gil took his time answering, tugging absently at the grizzled gray mustache that hung over his lip—a habit Jillian usually found amusing. "Couple weeks."

And she'd already plowed into him. Well, she'd had five years of peace, Jillian reminded herself. In country with this much space, she should be able to avoid one man without too much trouble. There were other questions she wanted to ask, but they'd wait until she and Gil were alone.

"I'll check the fence," she said briefly, then turned the mare and rode west.

Gil watched her with a twinkle. He might squint, but his eyesight was sharp enough to have noticed her damp clothes. And the fire in her eyes. Ran into Aaron Murdock, did she? With a wheeze and a chuckle, he started the pickup. It gave a man something to speculate on.

"Keep your eyes front, son," he grumbled to the young hand who was craning his neck to get a last look of Jillian as she galloped over the pasture.

Chapter Two

The day began before sunrise. There was stock to be fed, eggs to be gathered, cows to be milked. Even with machines, capable hands were needed. Jillian had grown so accustomed to helping with the early morning chores, it never occurred to her to stop now that she was the owner. Ranch life was a routine that varied only in the number of animals to be tended and the weather in which you tended them.

It was pleasantly cool when Jillian made the trip from the ranch house to the stables, but she'd crossed the same ground when the air had been so hot and thick it seemed to stick to her skin, or when the snow had been past her boot tops. There was only a faint lessening in the dark, a hint of color in the eastern sky, but the ranch yard already held signs of life. She caught the scent of grilled meat and coffee as the ranch cook started breakfast.

Men and women went about their chores quietly, with an occasional oath, or a quick laugh. Because all of them had just been through a Montana winter, this sweet spring morning was prized. Spring gave way to summer heat, and summer drought too quickly.

Jillian crossed the concrete passageway and opened Delilah's stall. As always, she would tend her first before going on to the other horses, then the dairy cows. A few of the men were there before her, measuring out grain, filling troughs. There was the click of boot heels on concrete, the jingle of spurs.

Some of them owned their own horses, but the bulk of them used Utopia's line. All of them owned their own saddles. Her grandfather's hard-and-fast rule.

The stables smelled comfortably of horses and hay and sweet grain. By the time the stock had been fed and led out to the corrals, it was nearly light. Automatically, Jillian headed for the vast white barn where cows waited to be milked.

"Jillian."

She stopped, waiting for Joe Carlson, her herdsman, to cross the ranch yard. He didn't walk like a cowboy, or dress like one, simply because he wasn't one. He had a smooth, even gait that suited his rather cocky good looks. The early sun teased out the gold in his curling hair. He rode a Jeep rather than a horse and preferred a dry wine to beer, but he knew cattle. Jillian needed him if she was to make a real success out of what was now just dabbling in the purebred industry. She'd hired him six months before over her grandfather's grumbles, and didn't regret it.

"Morning, Joe."

"Jillian." He shook his head when he reached her, then pushed back the powder-gray hat he kept meticulously clean. "When are you going to stop working a fifteen-hour day?"

She laughed and started toward the dairy barn again, matching her longer, looser stride with his. "In August, when I have to start working an eighteen-hour day."

"Jillian." He put a hand on her shoulder, stopping her at the entrance of the barn. His hand was neat and well shaped, tanned but not callused. For some reason it reminded her of a stronger hand, a harder one. She frowned at the horizon. "You know it's not necessary for you to tie yourself down to every aspect of this ranch. You've got enough hands working for you. If you'd hire a manager…"

It was an old routine and Jillian answered it in the usual way. "I am the manager," she said simply. "I don't consider the ranch a toy or a tax break, Joe. Before I hire someone to take over for me, I'll sell out."

"You work too damn hard."

"You worry too much," she countered, but smiled. "I appreciate it. How's the bull?"

Joe's teeth flashed, straight, even, and white. "Mean as ever, but he's bred with every cow we've let within ten feet of him. He's a beauty."

"I hope so," Jillian murmured, remembering just what the purebred Hereford bull had cost her. Still, if he was everything Joe had claimed, he was her start in improving the quality of Utopia's beef.

"Just wait till the calves start dropping," Joe advised, giving her shoulder a quick squeeze. "You want to come take a look at him?"

"Mmmm, maybe later." She took a step inside the barn, then shot a look over her shoulder. "I'd like to see that bull take the blue ribbon over the Murdock entry in July." She grinned, quick and insolent. "Damned if I wouldn't."

By the time the stock had been fed and Jillian had bolted down her own breakfast, it was full light. The long hours and demands should have kept her mind occupied. They always had. Between her concerns over feed and wages and fence, there shouldn't have been room for thoughts of Aaron Murdock. But there was. Jillian decided that once she had the answers to her questions she'd be able to put him out of her mind. So she'd better see about getting them. She hailed Gil before he could climb into his pickup.

"I'm going with you today," she told him as she hopped into the passenger's seat.

He shrugged and spit tobacco out the window. "Suit yourself."

Jillian grinned at the greeting and pushed her hat back on her head. A few heavy red curls dipped over her brow. "Why is it you've never gotten married, Gil? You're such a charmer."

Beneath his grizzled mustache his lips quivered. "Always was a smart aleck." He started the engine and aimed his squint at her. "What about you? You might be skinny, but you ain't ugly."

She propped a booted foot on his dash. "I'd rather run my own life," she said easily. "Men want to tell you what to do and how to do it."

"Woman ain't got no business out here on her own," Gil said stubbornly as he drove out of the ranch yard.

"And men do?" Jillian countered, lazily examining the toe of her boot.

"Men's different."

"Better?"

He shifted, knowing he was already getting out of his depth. "Different," he said again and clamped his lips.

Jillian laughed and settled back. "You old coot," she said fondly. "Tell me about this blowup at the Murdocks'."

"Had a few of them. They're a hardheaded bunch."

"So I've heard. The one that happened before Aaron Murdock went to Billings."

"Kid had lots of ideas when he come back from college." He snorted at education in the way of a man who considered the best learning came from doing. "Maybe some of them were right enough," he conceded. "Always was smart, and knew how to sit a horse."

"Isn't that why he went to college?" Jillian probed. "To get ideas?"

Gil grunted. "Seems the old man felt the boy was taking over too quick. Rumor is the boy agreed to work for his father for three years, then he was supposed to take over. Manage the place like."

Gil stopped at a gate and Jillian climbed out to open it, waiting until he'd driven through before closing and locking it behind her. Another dry day, she thought with a glance at the sky. They'd need some rain soon. A pheasant shot out of the field to her right and wheeled with a flash of color into the sky. She could smell sweet clover.

"So?" she said when she hopped into the truck again.

"So when the three years was up, the old man balked. Wouldn't give the boy the authority they'd agreed on. Well, they got tempers, those Murdocks." He grinned, showing off his dentures. "The boy up and quit, said he'd start his own spread."

"That's what I'd've done," Jillian muttered. "Murdock had no right to go back on his word."

"Maybe not. But he talked the boy into going to Billings 'cause there was some trouble there with the books and such. Nobody could much figure why he did it, unless the old man made it worth his while."

Jillian sneered. Money, she thought derisively. If Aaron had had any guts, he'd've thumbed his nose at his father and started his own place. Probably couldn't handle the idea of starting from the ground up. But she remembered his face, the hard, strong feel of his hand. Something, she thought, puzzled, just didn't fit.

"What do you think of him, Gil—personally?"

"Who?"

"Aaron Murdock," she snapped.

"Can't say much," Gil began slowly, rubbing a hand over his face to conceal another grin. "Was a bright kid and full of sass, like one or two others I've known." He gave a hoot when Jillian narrowed her eyes at him. "Wasn't afraid of work neither. By the time he'd grown whiskers, he had the ladies sighing over him, too." Gil put a hand to his heart and gave an exaggerated sigh of his own. Jillian punched him enthusiastically in the arm.

"I'm not interested in his love life, Gil," she began and then immediately changed gears. "He's never married?"

"Guess he figured a woman might want to tell him what to do and how to do it," Gil returned blandly.

Jillian started to swear at him, then laughed instead. "You're a clever old devil, Gil Haley. Look here!" She put a hand on his arm. "We've got calves."

They got out to walk the pasture together, taking a head count and enjoying one of the first true pleasures of spring: new life.

"These'd be from the new bull." Jillian watched a calf nurse frantically while its mother half dozed in the sun.

"Yep." Gil's squint narrowed further while he

skimmed over the grazing herd and the new offspring. "I reckon Joe knows what he's about," he murmured and rubbed his chin. "How many younguns you count?"

"Ten and looks like twenty more cows nearly ready to drop." She frowned over the numbers a moment. "Wasn't there—" Jillian broke off as a new sound came over the bored mooing and rustling. "Over there," she said even as Gil started forward.

They found him collapsed and frightened beside his dying mother. A day old, no more than two, Jillian estimated as she gathered up the calf, crooning to him. The cow lay bleeding, barely breathing. The birth had gone wrong. Jillian didn't need Gil to tell her that. The cow had survived the breech, then had crawled off to die.

If the plane had been up…Jillian thought grimly as Gil walked silently back to the pickup. If the plane had been up, someone would've spotted her from the air, and… She shook her head and nuzzled the calf. This was the price of it, she reminded herself. You couldn't mourn over every cow or horse you lost in the course of a year. But when she saw Gil returning with his rifle, she gave him a look of helpless grief. Then she turned and walked away.

One shudder rippled through her at the sound of the shot, then she forced herself to push the weakness away. Still carrying the calf, she went back to Gil.

"Going to have to call for some men on the CB," he told her. "It's going to take more than you and me to load her up." He cupped the calf's head in his hand and studied him. "Hope this one's got some fight in him or he ain't going to make it."

"He'll make it," Jillian said simply. "I'm going to see to it." She went back to the truck, murmuring to soothe the newborn in her arms.

By nine o'clock that evening she was exhausted. Antelope had raced through a hay field and damaged half an acre's crop. One of her men fractured his arm when his horse was spooked by a snake. They'd found three breaks in the wire along the Murdock boundary and some of her cows had strayed. It had taken the better part of the day to round them up again and repair the fence.

Every spare minute Jillian had been able to scrape together had been dedicated to the orphaned calf. She'd given him a warm, dry stall in the cattle barn and had taken charge of his feeding herself. She ended her day there, with one low light burning and the scent and sound of animals around her.

"Here, now." She sat cross-legged on the fresh hay and stroked the calf's small white face. "You're feeling better." He let out a high, shaky sound that made her laugh. "Yes, Baby, I'm your momma now."

To her relief he took the nipple easily. Twice before, she'd had to force feed him. This time, she had to take a firm hold on the bottle to prevent him from tugging it right out of her hand. He's catching on, she thought, stroking him as he sucked. It's a tough life, but the only one we've got.

"Pretty Baby," she murmured, then laughed when he wobbled and sat down hard, back legs spread, without releasing the nipple. "Go ahead and be greedy." Jillian tilted the bottle higher. "You're entitled." His eyes clung to hers as he pulled in his feed. "In a few months you'll be out in the pasture with the rest of them, eating grass and raising hell. I've got a feeling about you, Baby," she said thoughtfully as she scratched his ears. "You might just be a real success with the ladies."

When he started to suck air, Jillian pulled the nipple away. The calf immediately began to nibble at her jeans. "Idiot, you're not a goat." Jillian gave him a gentle shove so that he rolled over and lay, content to have her stroke him.

"Making a pet out of him?"

She whipped her head around quickly and stared up at Aaron Murdock. While he watched, the laughter died out of her eyes. "What are you doing here?"

"One of your favorite questions," he commented as he stepped inside the stall. "Nice-looking calf." He crouched beside her.

Sandalwood and leather. Jillian caught just a whiff of it on him and automatically shifted away. She wanted no scent to creep up and remind her of him when he was gone. "Did you take a wrong turn, Murdock?" she asked dryly. "This is my ranch."

Slowly, he turned his head until their eyes met. Aaron wasn't certain just how long he'd stood watching her—he hadn't intended to watch at all. Maybe it had been the way she'd laughed, that low, smoky sound that had a way of rippling along a man's skin. Maybe it had been the way her hair had glistened—firelike in the low light. Or maybe it had just been that softness he'd seen in her eyes when she'd murmured to the calf. There'd been something about that look that had had tiny aches rushing to the surface. A man needed a woman to look at him like that—first thing in the morning, last thing at night.

There was no softness in her eyes now, but a challenge, a defiance. That stirred something in him, as well, something he recognized with more ease. Desire was so simple to label. He smiled.

"I didn't take a wrong turn, Jillian. I wanted to talk to you."

She wouldn't allow herself the luxury of shifting away from him again, or him the pleasure of knowing how badly she wanted to. She sat where she was and tilted her chin. "About what?"

His gaze skimmed over her face. He was beginning to wish he hadn't stayed in Billings quite so long. "Horse breeding—for a start."

Excitement flickered into her eyes and gave her away even though she schooled her voice to casual disinterest. "Horse breeding?"

"Your Delilah." Casually he wound her hair around his finger. What kind of secret female trick did she use to make it so soft? he wondered. "My Samson. I'm too romantic to let a coincidence like that pass."

"Romantic, my foot." Jillian brushed his hand aside only to find her fingers caught in his.

"You'd be surprised," Aaron said softly. So softly only a well-tuned ear would have heard the steel in it. "I also know a—" his gaze skimmed insolently over her face again "—prime filly when I see one." He laughed when her eyes flashed at him. "Are you always so ready to wrestle, Jillian?"

"I'm always ready to talk business, Murdock," she countered. *Don't be too anxious.* Jillian remembered her grandfather's schooling well. *Always play your cards close to your chest.* "I might be interested in breeding Delilah with your stallion, but I'll need another look at him first."

"Fair enough. Come by tomorrow—nine."

She wanted to jump at it. Five years in Montana and she'd never seen the Murdock spread. And that stallion… Still, she'd been taught too well. "If I can manage it. Middle of the morning's a busy time." Then she was laughing because the calf, weary of being ignored, was butting against her knee. "Spoiled already." Obligingly she tickled his belly.

"Acts more like a puppy than a cow," Aaron stated, but reached over to scratch the calf's ears. It surprised her how gentle his fingers could be. "How'd he lose his mother?"

"Birthing went wrong." She grinned when the calf licked the back of Aaron's hand. "He likes you. Too young to know better."

Amused, Aaron lifted a brow. "Like I said, it's a matter of touching the right way." He slid one lean hand over the calf's head and massaged its neck. "There's one technique for soothing babies, another for breaking horses and another for gentling a woman."

"Gentling a woman?" Jillian sent him an arch look that held humor rather than annoyance. "That's a remarkable phrase."

"An apt one, in certain cases."

She watched as the calf, satisfied, his belly full, curled up on the hay to sleep. "A typical male animal," Jillian remarked, still smiling, "Apparently, you're another."

There wasn't any heat in the comment, but an acceptance. "Could be," he agreed, "though I wouldn't say you were typical."

Unconsciously relaxed, Jillian studied him. "I don't *think* you meant that as a compliment."

"No, it was an observation. You'd spit a compliment back in my face."

Delighted, Jillian threw back her head and laughed. "Whatever else you are, Murdock, you're not stupid." Still chuckling, she leaned back against the wall of the stall, bringing up one knee and circling it with her hands.

At the moment she didn't want to question why she was pleased to have his company.

"I have a first name." A trick of the angle had the light slanting over her eyes, highlighting them and casting her face in shadow. He felt the stir again. "Ever thought of using it?"

"Not really." But that was a lie, she realized. She already thought of him as Aaron. The real trouble was that she thought of him at all. Yet she smiled again, too comfortable to make an issue of it. "Baby's asleep," she murmured.

Aaron glanced over, grinning. Would she still call him Baby when he was a bull weighing several hundred pounds? Probably. "It's been a long day."

"Mmmm." She stretched her arms to the ceiling, feeling her muscles loosen. The exhaustion she dragged into the barn with her had become a rather pleasant fatigue. "They're never long enough. If I had just ten hours more in a week, I'd catch up."

With what? he wondered. Herself? "Ever heard of overachievement, Jillian?"

"Ambition," she corrected. Her eyes met his again and held. "I'm not the one who's willing to settle for what's handed to her."

Temper surged into him so quickly he clenched at the hay under him. It was clear she was referring to his father's ranch and his own position there. His expression remained completely passive as he battled back the need to strike out where he was struck. "Each of us does what he has to do," Aaron said mildly and let the hay sift through his hands.

It annoyed her that he didn't defend himself. She wanted him to give her his excuses, his reasons. It shouldn't matter, Jillian reminded herself. He shouldn't matter. He didn't, she assured herself with something perilously close to panic. Of course he didn't. Rising, she dusted off her jeans.

"I've got paperwork to see to before I turn in."

He rose, too, more slowly, so that it was too late when she realized she was backed into the corner of the stall. "Not even going to offer me a cup of coffee, Jillian?"

There was a band of tension at the back of her neck, a thudding at her ribs. She recognized the temper in his eyes, and though she wondered that she hadn't noticed it before, it wasn't his temper that worried her. It was her own shaky pulse. "No," she said evenly. "I'm not."

He hooked his thumbs through his belt loops and studied her lazily. "You've got a problem with manners."

Her chin came up. "Manners don't concern me."

"No?" He smiled then, in a way that made her brace herself. "Then we'll drop them."

In a move too quick for her to evade, he gathered her shirtfront in one hand and yanked her against him. The first shock came from the feel of that long, hard body against hers. "Damn you, Murdock—" The second shock came when his mouth closed over hers.

Oh, no... It was that sweet, weak thought that drifted through her mind even as she fought back like a tiger. Oh, no. He shouldn't feel so good, taste so wonderful. She shouldn't want it to go on and on and on.

Jillian shoved against him and found herself caught closer so that she couldn't shove again. She squirmed and only succeeded in driving herself mad at the feel of her body rubbing against his. Stop it! her mind shouted as the fire began to flicker inside her. She couldn't— wouldn't—let it happen. She knew how to outwit desire.

For five years she'd done so with hardly an effort. But now…now something was sprinting inside her too fast, twisting and turning so that she couldn't grab on and stop it from getting further and further out of her reach.

Her blood began to swim, her hands began to clutch. And her mouth began to answer.

He'd expected her temper. Because his own had peaked, he'd wanted it. He'd known she'd be furious, that she'd fight against him for outmaneuvering her and taking something without her permission. His anger demanded that she fight, just as his desire demanded that he take.

He'd expected her mouth to be soft. Why else would he have wanted to taste it so badly that he'd spent two days thinking of little else? He'd known her body would be firm with only hints of the subtle dips and curves of woman. It fit unerringly to his as though it had been fashioned to do so. She strained away from him, shifting, making his skin tingle at the friction her movements caused.

Then, abruptly, her arms were clasped around him. Her lips parted, not in surrender but with an urgency that rocked him. If her passion had been simmering, she'd concealed it well. It seemed to explode in one blinding white flash of heat that came from nowhere. Shaken, Aaron drew back, trying to judge his own reaction, fighting to keep his own needs in perspective.

Jillian stared up at him, her breath coming in jerks. Her hair streamed behind her back, catching the light while her eyes glinted in the dark. Her mind was reeling and she shook her head as if to clear it. Just as she began to draw her first coherent thought, he swore and crushed his mouth to hers again.

There was no hint of struggle this time, nor any hint of surrender. Passion for passion she met him, matching his need with hers, degree by degree. Sandalwood and leather. Now she drew it in, absorbed the aroma as she absorbed the hard, relentless texture of his lips. She let her tongue toy with his while she drank up all those hot, heady male tastes. There was something unapologetically primitive in the way he held her, kissed her. Jillian reveled in it. If she was to take a man, she neither needed nor wanted any polish or gloss that clouded or chipped away so easily.

She let her body take control. How long had she yearned for this? To have someone hold her, spin her away so that she couldn't think, couldn't worry? There were no responsibilities here, and the only demands were of the flesh. Here, with a warm, moist mouth on hers, with a hard body against her, she was finally and ultimately only a woman. Selfishly a woman. She'd forgotten just how glorious it could feel, or perhaps she'd never fully known the sensation before.

What was she doing to him? Aaron tried to pull himself back and found his hands were trapped in the thick softness of her hair. He tried to think and found his senses swimming with the scent of her. And the taste… A low sound started in his throat as he ravaged her mouth. How could he have known she'd taste like this? Seductive, pungent, alluring. Her flavor held all the lushness her body lacked, and the combination was devastating. He wondered how he'd ever lived without it. With that thought came the knowledge that he was getting in much too deep much too fast.

Aaron drew away carefully because the hands on her shoulders weren't as steady as he'd have liked.

Jillian started to sway and caught herself. Good God, what was she doing? What had she done? As the breath rushed swiftly and unevenly through her lips, she stared up at him. Those dark, wicked looks and clever mouth… She'd forgotten. She'd forgotten who she was, and who he was. Forgotten everything but that heady feeling of freedom and heat. He'd use that against her, she thought grimly. If she let him. But something had happened when—

Don't think now! she ordered herself. *Just get him out of here before you make a complete fool of yourself.* Very carefully, Jillian brushed Aaron's hands from her shoulders. Tilting her chin, she prayed her voice would be steady.

"Well, Murdock, you've had your fun. Now clear out."

Fun? he thought, staring at her. Whatever had happened it didn't have anything to do with fun. The room was tilting a bit, like it had when he'd downed his first six-pack of beer a hundred years before. That hadn't been much fun either, but it'd been a hell of an experience. And he'd paid for it the next day. He supposed he'd pay for this one, as well.

He wouldn't apologize, he told himself as he forced himself to relax. Damned if he would, but he would back off while he still could. Casually he bent down to pick up the hat that had fallen off when her fingers had combed through his hair. He took his time putting it on.

"You're right, Jillian," he said mildly—when he could. "A man would have a hard time resisting a woman like you." He grinned at her and tipped his hat. "But I'll do my best."

"See that you do, Murdock!" she called out after him, then hugged herself because she'd begun to tremble.

Even after his footsteps died away, she waited five full minutes before leaving the barn. When Jillian stepped outside, the ranch yard was dark and quiet. She thought she could just hear the murmur of a television or radio from the bunkhouse. There were a few lights farther down the road where her grandfather had built quarters for the married hands. She stopped and listened, but couldn't hear the engine of whatever vehicle Aaron had used to drive from his ranch to hers.

Long gone, she thought, and turned on her heel to stride to the house. It was a two-story stone-and-wood structure. All native Montana material. The rambling building had been constructed on the site of the original homestead. Her grandfather had been fond of bragging that he'd been born in a house that would have fit into the kitchen of this one. Jillian entered by the front door, which was still never locked.

She'd always loved the space, and the clever use of wood and tile and stone that made up the living area. You could roast one of Utopia's steers in the fireplace. Her grandmother's ivory lace curtains still hung at the windows. Jillian often wished she'd known her. All she knew was that she'd been an Irishwoman with dainty looks and a strong back. Jillian had inherited her coloring and, from her grandfather's accounting, her temper. And perhaps, Jillian thought wryly as she climbed the stairs, her back.

God, she wished she had a woman to talk to. Halfway up the stairs she paused and pressed her fingers to her temple. Where did that come from? she wondered. As far back as she could remember, she'd never sought out the company of women. So few of them were interested in the same things she was. And, when there was no niggling sexual problem to overcome, she found men easier to deal with.

But now, with the house so empty around her, with her blood still churning, she wished for a woman who might understand the war going on inside her. Her mother? With a quiet laugh, Jillian pushed open the door to her bedroom. If she called her mother and said she was burning up with desire and had no place to put it, the gentle doctor's wife would blush crimson and stammer out a recommendation for a good book on the subject.

No, as fond as she was of her mother, she wasn't a woman who would understand—well, cravings, Jillian admitted, stripping out of her work shirt. If she was going to be honest, that's what she'd felt in Aaron's arms. Perhaps it was all she was capable of feeling. Frowning, she dropped her jeans into a heap on top of her work shirt and walked naked to the bath.

She should probably be grateful she'd felt that. With a jerk of the wrist, she turned the hot water on full, then added a trickle of cold. She'd felt nothing at all for any man in years. Five years, Jillian admitted and dumped in bath salts with a lavish hand. With an expert twist and a couple of pins, she secured her hair to the top of her head.

It was a good thing she remembered Kevin and that very brief, very unhappy affair. Did one night in bed equal an affair? she wondered ruefully, then lowered herself into the steaming water. Whatever you called it, it had been a fiasco. That's what she had to remember. She'd been so young. Jillian could almost—almost— think of it with amusement now.

The young, dewy-eyed virgin, the smooth, charming intern with eyes as clear as a lake. He hadn't talked her into bed, hadn't pressured her. No, Jillian had to admit that she'd wanted to go with him. And he'd been gentle and sweet with her. It had simply been that the words *I love you* had meant two different things to each of them. To Jillian, they'd been a pledge. To him, they'd been a phrase.

She'd learned the hard way that making love didn't equal love or commitment or marriage. He'd laughed at her, perhaps not unkindly, when she'd naively talked of their future together. He hadn't wanted a wife, or even a partner, but a companion willing to share his bed from time to time. His casualness had devastated her.

She'd been willing to mold herself into whatever he'd wanted—a tidy, socially wise doctor's wife like her mother; a clever, dedicated housewife; an organized marriage partner who could juggle career and family. It had taken her months before she'd realized that she'd made a fool of herself over him, taking every compliment or sweet word literally, because that's what she'd wanted to hear. It had taken more time and several thousand miles of distance before she'd been able to admit that he'd done her a favor.

Not only had he saved her from trying to force her personality into a mold that would never have fit, but he'd given her a solid view of the male species. They weren't to be trusted on a personal level. Once you gave them your love, the power to hurt you, you were lost, ready to do anything to please them even at the loss of self.

When she was young, she'd tried to please her father that way and had failed because she was too like her grandfather. The only man she'd ever loved who'd accepted her for what she was had been Clay Baron. And he was gone.

Jillian lay back, closed her eyes and let the hot water

steam away her fatigue. Aaron Murdock wasn't looking for a partner and neither was she. What had happened between them in the barn was a mistake that wouldn't be repeated. He might be looking for a lover, but she wasn't.

Jillian Baron was on her own, and that's the way she liked it.

Chapter Three

He wondered if she would come. Aaron drove back from a line camp on a road that had once been fit only for horses or mules. It wasn't in much better shape now. The Jeep bucked along much like a bad-tempered bronc might, dipping into ruts, bounding over rocks. He rather liked it. Just as he'd enjoyed the early morning visit with five of his men at the line camp. If he could spare the time, he would appreciate a few days at one of the camps in unabashedly male company. Hard, sweaty work during the day, a few beers and a poker game at night. Riding herd far enough from the ranch so that you could forget there was civilization anywhere. Yes, he'd enjoy that, but...

He appreciated the conservative, traditional ways of his father—particularly when they were mixed with his own experimental ideas. The men would still rope and flank cattle in the open pasture, but two tractors dragging a cable would clear off more brush in a day than axmen could in a month. And a plane…

With a wry smile Aaron remembered how he'd fought six years before for the plane his father had considered a foolish luxury. He'd ended up paying for it himself and flying it himself. His father had never admitted that the plane had become indispensable. That didn't matter to Aaron, as long as it was used. He had no desire to push the cowboy out of existence, just to make him sweat a little less.

Downshifting for the decline, he let the Jeep bump its way down the hill. The differences with his father that had come to a head five years before had eased, but not vanished. Aaron knew he'd have to fight for every change, every improvement, every deviation. And he'd win. Paul Murdock might be stubborn, but he wasn't stupid. And he was sick. In six months…

Aaron rammed the Jeep back into Fourth. He didn't like to dwell on the battle his father was losing. A battle Aaron could do nothing about. Helplessness was something Aaron wasn't accustomed to. He was too much like his father. Perhaps that's why they spent most of their time arguing.

He pushed his father and mortality out of his mind and thought of Jillian. There was life, and youth, and vitality.

Would she come? Grinning, Aaron sped past a pasture covered with mesquite grass. Damn right she would. She'd come if for no other reason than to prove to him that she couldn't be intimidated. She'd throw her chin up and give him one of those cool go-to-hell looks. No wonder he wanted her so badly it caused an ache in the pit of his belly. The ache had burned like fire when he'd kissed her.

There hadn't been a female who'd made him come so close to stammering since Emma Lou Swanson had initiated him into life's pleasures in the hayloft. It was one thing for a teenager to lose the power of speech and reason with soft arms around him, and quite another for it to happen to a grown man who'd made a study of the delights and frustrations of women. Aaron couldn't quite account for it, but he knew he was going to have to have more. Soon.

She was a typical Baron, he decided. Hotheaded, stubborn, opinionated. Aaron grinned again. He figured the main reason the Barons and Murdocks had never gotten on was that they'd been too much alike. She wasn't going to have an easy time taking over the ranch, but he didn't doubt she'd do it. He didn't doubt he was going to enjoy watching her. Almost as much as he was going to enjoy bedding her.

Whistling between his teeth, Aaron braked in front of the ranch house. Over near the cattle barn a dog was barking halfheartedly. Someone was playing a radio by the feed lot—a slow, twangy country lament. There were asters popping up in the flower bed and not a weed in sight. As he climbed out of the Jeep he heard the porch door open and glanced over. His mother walked out, lips curved, eyes weary.

She was so beautiful—he'd never gotten used to it. Very small, very slender, Karen Murdock walked with the gliding step of a runway model. She was twenty-two years younger than her husband, and neither the cold winters nor the bright sun of Montana had dimmed the luster of her skin. His sister had those looks, Aaron mused, the classic blond beauty that went on and on with the years. Karen wore slimming slacks, a rose-colored blouse, with her hair loosely coiled at the neck. She could've walked into the Beverly Wilshire without changing a stitch. If the need had arisen, she could've saddled up a horse and ridden out to string wire.

"Everything all right?" she asked him, holding out a hand.

"Fine. They've rounded up the strays we were losing through the south fence." Studying her face, Aaron took her hand. "You look tired."

"No." She squeezed his fingers as much for support as reassurance. "Your father didn't sleep well last night. You didn't come by to see him."

"That wouldn't've made him sleep any better."

"Arguing with you is about all the entertainment he has these days."

Aaron grinned because she wanted him to. "I'll come in later and tell him about the five hundred acres of mesquite I want to clear."

Karen laughed and put her hands on her son's shoulders. With her standing on the porch and him on the ground, their eyes were level. "You're good for him, Aaron. No, don't raise your brow at me," she told him mildly.

"When I saw him yesterday morning, he told me to go to the devil."

"Exactly." Her fingers kneaded absently at his shoulders. "I tend to pamper him, even though I shouldn't. He needs you around to make him angry enough to live a bit longer. He knows you're right—that you've been right all along. He's proud of you."

"You don't have to explain him to me." The steel had crept into his voice before he could prevent it. "I know him well enough."

"Almost well enough," Karen murmured, laying her cheek against Aaron's.

When Jillian drove into the ranch yard, she saw Aaron with his arms around a slim, elegant blonde. The surge of jealousy stunned, then infuriated her. He was a man after all, she reminded herself, gripping the steering wheel tightly for a moment. It was so easy for a man to enjoy quick passion in a horse stall one evening, then a sweet embrace in the sunshine the next day. True emotion never entered into it. Why should it? she thought, setting her teeth. She braked sharply beside Aaron's Jeep.

He turned, and while she had the disadvantage of the sun in her eyes, she met his amused look with ice. Not for a moment would she give him the satisfaction of knowing she'd spent a restless, dream-disturbed night. Jillian stepped out of her aging compact and managed not to slam the door.

"Murdock," she said curtly.

"Good morning, Jillian." He gave her a bland smile with something sharper hovering in his eyes.

She walked to him, since he didn't seem inclined to drop the blonde's hand and come to her. "I've come to see your stud."

"We talked about manners last night, didn't we?" His grin only widened when she glared at him. "I don't think you two have met."

"No, indeed." Karen came down the porch steps, amused by the gleam in her son's eye, and the fire in the woman's. "You must be Jillian Baron. I'm Karen Murdock, Aaron's mother."

As her mouth fell open Jillian turned to look at Mrs. Murdock. Soft, elegant, beautiful. "Mother?" she repeated before she could stop herself.

Karen laughed, and rested a hand on Aaron's shoulder. "I think I've just been given a wonderful compliment."

He grinned down at her. "Or I have."

Laughing again, she turned back to Jillian. Karen filed away her quick assessment. "I'll leave you two to go about your business. Please, stop in for coffee before you go if you've time, Jillian. I have so little opportunity these days to talk with another woman."

"Yes, ah—thank you." With her brows drawn together, Jillian watched her go back through the porch door.

"I don't think you're often at a loss for words," Aaron commented.

"No." With a little shake of her head she looked up at him. "Your mother's beautiful."

"Surprised?"

"No. That is, I'd heard she was lovely, but..." Jillian shrugged and wished he'd stop looking down at her with that infernal smile on his face. "You don't look a thing like her."

Aaron swung his arm around her shoulders as they turned away from the house. "You're trying to charm me again, Jillian."

She had to bite down on her lip to keep the chuckle back. "I've better uses for my time." Though the weight felt good, she plucked his arm away.

"You smell of jasmine," he said lazily. "Did you wear it for me?"

Rather than dignify the question with an answer, Jillian stopped, tilted her chin and gave him one long icy look that only wavered when he began to laugh. With a careless flick he knocked the hat from her head, pulled her against him and gave her a hard, thorough kiss. She felt her legs dissolve from the knees down.

Though he released her before she'd even thought to demand it, Jillian gathered her wits quickly enough. "What the hell do you think—"

"Sorry." His eyes were laughing, but he held his hands up, palms out in a gesture of peace. "Lost my head. Something comes over me when you look at me as though you'd like to cut me into small pieces. *Very* small pieces," he added as he took the hat from where it hung at her back and placed it back on her head.

"Next time I won't just look," she said precisely, wheeling away toward the corral.

Aaron fell into step beside her. "How's the calf?"

"He's doing well. Vet's coming by to check him over this afternoon, but he took the bottle again this morning."

"Was he sired by that new bull of yours?" When Jillian sent him a sharp look, Aaron smiled blandly. "Word gets around. As it happens, you snatched him up from under my nose. I was making arrangements to go to England to check him out for myself when I heard you'd bought him."

"Really?" It was news—and news she couldn't help but be pleased to hear.

"Thought that might make your day," Aaron said mildly.

"Nasty of me," Jillian admitted as they came to the corral fence. Resting a foot on the lower rail, she smiled at him. "I'm not a nice person, Murdock."

He gave her an odd look and nodded. "Then we'll deal well enough together. What's the nickname your hands have dubbed that bull?"

Her smile warmed so that the dimple flickered. He was going to have to find out what it felt like to put his lips just there. "The Terror's the cleanest in polite company."

He chuckled. "I don't think that was the one I heard. How many calves so far?"

"Fifty. It's early yet."

"Mmm. Are you using artificial insemination?"

Her eyes narrowed. "Why?"

"Just curious. We are in the same business, Jillian."

"That's not something I'll forget," she said evenly.

Annoyance tightened his mouth. "Which doesn't mean we have to be opponents."

"Doesn't it?" Jillian shifted her hat lower on her forehead. "I came to look at your stud, Murdock."

He stood watching her a moment, long enough, directly enough, to make Jillian want to squirm. "So you did," Aaron said quietly. Plucking a halter from the fence post, he swung lithely over the corral fence.

Rude, Jillian condemned herself. It was one thing to be cautious, even unfriendly, but another to be pointedly rude. It wasn't like her. Frowning, Jillian leaned on the fence and rested her chin in her open hand. Yet she'd been rude to Aaron almost continually since their first encounter. Her frown cleared as she watched him approach the stallion.

Both males were strong and well built, and each was inclined to want his own way. At the moment the stallion wasn't in the mood for the halter. He pranced away from Aaron to lap disinterestedly at his water trough. Aaron murmured something that had Samson shaking his head and trotting off again.

"You devil," she heard Aaron say, but there was a laugh in his voice. Aaron crossed to him again, and again the stallion danced off in the opposite direction.

Laughing, Jillian climbed the fence and sat on the top rung. "Round 'em up, cowboy," she drawled.

Aaron flashed her a grin, then shrugged as though he'd given up and turned his back on the stallion. By the time he'd crossed the center of the corral, Samson had come up behind him to nudge his head into Aaron's back.

"Now you wanna make up," he murmured, turning to ruffle the horse's mane before he slipped on the halter. "After you've made me look like a greenhorn in front of the lady."

Greenhorn, hell, Jillian thought, watching the way he handled the skittish stallion. If he cared about impressing anyone, he'd have made the difficult look difficult instead of making it look easy. With a sigh, she felt her respect for him go up another notch.

Automatically she reached out to stroke the stallion's neck as Aaron led him to her. He had a coat like silk, and eyes that were wary but not mean. "Aaron…" She glanced down in time to see his brow lift at her voluntary use of his name. "I'm sorry," she said simply.

Something flickered in his eyes, but they were so dark it was difficult to read it. "All right," he said just as simply and held out a hand. She took it and hopped down.

"He's beautiful." Jillian ran her hands along Samson's wide chest and sleek flank. "Have you bred him before?"

"Twice in Billings," he said, watching her.

"How long have you had him?" She went to Samson's head, then passed under him to the other side.

"Since he was a foal. It took me five days to catch his father." Jillian looked up and caught the light in his eyes. "There must've been a hundred and fifty mustangs in his herd. He was a cagey devil, damn near killed me the first time I got a rope around him. Then he busted down the stall and nearly got away again. You should've seen him, blood spurting out of his leg, fire in his eyes. It took six of us to control him when we bred him to the mare."

"What did you do with him?" Jillian swallowed, thinking how easy it would be to breed the wild stallion again and again, then geld him. Break his spirit.

Aaron's eyes met hers over Samson's withers. "I let him go. Some things you don't fence."

She smiled. Before she realized it, she reached over Samson for Aaron's hand. "I'm glad."

With his eyes on hers, Aaron stroked a thumb over her knuckles. The palm of his hand was rough, the back of hers smooth. "You're an interesting woman, Jillian, with a few rather appealing soft spots."

Disturbed, she tried to slip her hand from his. "Very few."

"Which is why they're appealing. You were beautiful last night, sitting in the hay, crooning to the calf, with the light in your hair."

She knew about clever words. Why were these making her pulse jerky? "I'm not beautiful," she said flatly. "I don't want to be."

He tilted his head when he realized she was perfectly serious. "Well, we can't have everything we want, can we?"

"Don't start again, Murdock," she ordered, sharply enough that the stallion moved restlessly under their joined hands.

"Start what?"

"You know, I wondered why I always end up being rude to you," she began. "I realize it's simply because you don't understand anything else. Let go of my hand."

His eyes narrowed at her tone. "No." Tightening his hold, he gave the stallion a quick pat that sent him trotting off, leaving nothing between himself and Jillian. "I wondered why I always end up wanting to toss you over my knee—or my shoulder," he added thoughtfully. "Must be for the same reason."

"Your reasons don't interest me, Murdock."

His lips curved slowly, but his eyes held something entirely different from humor. "Now, I might've believed that, Jillian, if it hadn't been for last night." He took a step closer. "Maybe I kissed you first, but, lady, you kissed me right back. I had a whole long night to think about that. And about just what I was going to do about it."

Maybe it was because he'd spoken the truth when she didn't care to hear it. Maybe it had something to do with the wicked gleam in his eyes or the insolence of his smile. It might have been a combination of all three that loosened Jillian's temper. Before she had a chance to think about it, or Aaron a chance to react, she'd drawn back her fist and plunged it hard into his stomach.

"That's what *I* intend to do about it!" she declared as he grunted. She had only a fleeting glimpse of the astonishment on his face before she spun on her heel and strode away. She didn't get far.

Jillian's breath was knocked out of her as he brought her down in a tackle. She found herself flat on her back, pinned under him with a face filled with fury rather than astonishment looming over hers. It only took her a second to fight back, and little more to realize she was outmatched.

"You hellion," Aaron grunted as he held her down. "You've been asking for a thrashing since the first time I laid eyes on you."

"It'll take a better man than you, Murdock." She nearly succeeded in bringing her knee up and scoring a very important point. Instead he shifted until her position was only more vulnerable. Heat that had nothing to do with temper surged into her stomach.

"By God, you tempt me to prove you wrong." She squirmed again and stirred something dangerous in him. "Woman, if you want to fight dirty, you've come to the right place." He closed his mouth over hers before she could swear at him. At the instant of contact he felt the pulse in her wrist bound under his hands. Then he felt nothing but the hot give of her mouth.

If she was still struggling beneath him, he wasn't aware of it. Aaron felt himself sinking, and sinking much deeper than he'd expected. The sun was warm on his back, she was soft under him, yet he felt only that moist, silky texture that was her lips. He thought he could make do with that sensation alone for the rest of his life. It scared him to death.

Pulling himself back, he stared down at her. She'd stolen the breath from him much more successfully this time than she had with the quick jab to the gut. "I ought to beat you," he said softly.

Somehow in her prone position she managed to thrust her chin out. "I'd prefer it." It wasn't the first lie she'd told, but it might have been the biggest.

She told herself a woman didn't want to be kissed by a man who tossed her on the ground. Yet her conscience played back that she'd deserved that at the least. She wasn't a fragile doll and didn't want to be treated like one. But she shouldn't want him to kiss her again…want it so badly she could already taste it. "Will you get off me?" she said between her teeth. "You're not as skinny as you look."

"It's safer talking to you this way."

"I don't want to talk to you."

The gleam shot back in his eyes. "Then we won't talk."

Before Jillian could protest, or Aaron could do what he'd intended, Samson lowered his head between their faces.

"Get your own filly," Aaron muttered, shoving him aside.

"He's got a smoother technique than you," Jillian began, then choked on a laugh as the horse bent down again. "Oh, for God's sake, Aaron, let me up. This is ridiculous."

Instead of obliging he looked back down at her. Her eyes were bright with laughter now, her dimple flashing. Her hair spread like fire in the dust. "I'm beginning to like it. You don't do that enough."

She blew the hair out of her eyes. "What?"

"Smile at me."

She laughed again and he felt the arms under his hands relax. "Why should I?"

"Because I like it."

She tried to give a long-winded sigh, but it ended on a chuckle. "If I apologize for hitting you, will you let me up?"

"Don't spoil it—besides, you won't catch me off guard again."

No, she didn't imagine she would. "Well, in any case you deserved it—and you paid me back. Now get up, Murdock. This ground's hard."

"Is it? You're not." He lifted a brow as he shifted into a more comfortable position. He wondered if her legs would look as nice as they felt. "Anyway, we still have to discuss that remark about my technique."

"The best I can say about it," Jillian began as Aaron

pushed absently at Samson's head again, "is that it needs some polishing. If you'll excuse me, I really have to get back. Some of us work for a living."

"Polishing," he murmured, ignoring the rest. "You'd like something a little—smoother." His voice dropped intimately as he brushed his lips over her cheek, light as a whisper. He heard the quick, involuntary sound she made as he moved lazily toward her mouth.

"Don't." Her voice trembled on the word so that he looked down at her again. Vulnerability. It was in her eyes. That, and a touch of panic. He hadn't expected to see either.

"An Achilles' heel," he murmured, moved, aroused. "You've given me an advantage, Jillian." Lifting a hand, he traced her mouth with a fingertip and felt it tremble. "It's only fair to warn you that I'll use it."

"Your only advantage at the moment is your weight."

He grinned, but before he could speak a shadow fell over them.

"Boy, what're you doing with that little lady on the ground?"

Jillian turned her head and saw an old man with sharp, well-defined features and dark eyes. Though he was pale and had an air of fragility, she saw the resemblance. Astonished, she stared at him. Could this bent old man who leaned heavily on a cane, who was so painfully thin, be the much feared and respected Paul Murdock? His eyes, dark and intense as Aaron's, skimmed over her. The hand on the cane had the faintest of tremors.

Aaron looked up at his father and grinned. "I'm not sure yet," he said easily. "It's a choice between beating her or making love."

Murdock gave a wheezing laugh and curled one

hand around the rail of the fence. "It's a stupid man who wouldn't know which choice to make, but you'll do neither here. Let the filly up so I can have a look at her."

Aaron obliged, taking Jillian by the arm and hauling her unceremoniously to her feet. She slanted him a killing glare before she looked back at his father. What nasty twist of fate had decided that she would meet Paul J. Murdock for the first time with corral dust clinging to her and her body still warm from his son's? she wondered as she silently cursed Aaron. Then she tossed back her hair and lifted her chin.

Murdock's face remained calm and unexpressive. "So, you're Clay Baron's granddaughter."

She met his steady hawklike gaze levelly. "Yes, I am."

"You look like your grandmother."

Her chin lifted a fraction higher. "So I've been told."

"She was a fire-eater." A ghost of a smile touched his eyes. "Hasn't been a Baron on my land since she marched over here to pay her respects to Karen after the wedding. If some young buck had tried to wrestle with her, she'd have blackened his eye."

Aaron leaned on the fence, running a hand over his stomach. "She hit me first," he drawled, grinning at Jillian. "Hard."

Jillian slipped her hat from her back and meticulously began to dust it off and straighten it. "Better tighten up those muscles, Murdock," she suggested as she set the hat back on her head. "I can hit a lot harder." She glanced over as Paul Murdock began to laugh.

"I always thought I should've thrashed him a sight more. What's your name, girl?"

She eyed him uncertainly. "Jillian."

"You're a pretty thing," he said with a nod. "And it

doesn't appear you lack for sense. My wife would be glad for some company."

For a minute she could only stare at him. This was the fierce Murdock—her grandfather's archrival—inviting her into his home? "Thank you, Mr. Murdock."

"Come in for coffee, then," he said briskly, then shot a look at Aaron. "You and I have some business to clear up."

Jillian felt something pass between the two men that wasn't entirely pleasant before Murdock turned to walk back toward the house. "You'll come in," Aaron said as he unlatched the gate. It wasn't an invitation but a statement. Curious, Jillian let it pass.

"For a little while. I've got to get back."

They walked through the gate together and relatched it. Though they moved slowly, they caught up with Murdock as he reached the porch steps. Seeing his struggle to negotiate them with the cane, Jillian automatically started to reach out for his arm. Aaron grabbed her wrist. He shook his head, then waited until his father had painstakingly gained the porch.

"Karen!" It might have been a bellow if it hadn't been so breathless. "You've got company." Murdock swung open the front door and gestured Jillian in.

It was more palatial than Utopia's main building, but had the same Western feel that had first charmed a little girl from Chicago. All the wood was highly polished— the floor, the beams in the ceilings, the woodwork—all satiny oak. But here was something Utopia lacked. That subtle woman's touch.

There were fresh flowers arranged in a pottery bowl, and softer colors. Though Jillian's grandfather had kept the ivory lace curtains at the windows, his ranch house had reverted to a man's dwelling over the years. Until she walked into the Murdock home and felt Karen's presence, Jillian hadn't realized it.

There was a huge Indian rug spread over the floor in the living area and glossy brass urns beside the fireplace that held tall dried flowers. A seat was fashioned into a bow window and piled with hand-worked pillows. The room had a sense of order and welcome.

"Aren't either of you men going to offer Jillian a chair?" Karen asked mildly as she wheeled in a coffee cart.

"She seems to be Aaron's filly," Murdock commented as he lowered himself into a wing-backed chair and hooked his cane over the arm.

Jillian's automatic retort was stifled as Aaron nudged her onto the sofa. Gritting her teeth, she turned to Karen. "You have a lovely home, Mrs. Murdock."

Karen didn't attempt to disguise her amusement. "Thank you. I believe I saw you at the rodeo last year," she continued as she began to pour coffee. "I remember thinking you looked like Maggie—your grandmother. Do you plan to compete again this year?"

"Yes." Jillian accepted the cup, declining cream or sugar. "Even though my foreman squawked quite a bit when I beat his time in the calf roping."

Aaron reached over to toy with her hair. "That tempts me to enter myself."

"It'd be a pretty sorry day when a son of mine couldn't rope a calf quicker than a female," Murdock muttered.

Aaron sent him a bland look. "That would depend on the female."

"You might be out of practice," Jillian said coolly as she sipped her coffee. "After five years behind a desk."

As soon as she'd said it, Jillian felt the tension between father and son, a bit more strained, a bit more unpleasant than she'd felt once before.

"I suppose things like that are in the blood," Karen said smoothly. "You've taken to ranch life, but you were raised back east, weren't you?"

"Chicago," Jillian admitted, wondering what she'd stirred up. "I never fit in." It was out before she realized it. A frown flickered briefly in her eyes before she controlled it. "I suppose ranching just skipped a generation in my family," she said easily.

"You have a brother, don't you?" Karen stirred the slightest bit of cream into her own coffee.

"Yes, he's a doctor. He and my father share a practice now."

"I remember the boy—your father," Murdock told her, then chugged down half a cup of coffee. "Quiet, serious fellow who never said three words if two would do."

Jillian had to smile. "You remember him well."

"Easy to understand why Baron left the ranch to you instead." Murdock held out his cup for more coffee, but Jillian noticed that Karen only filled it halfway. "Guess you can't do much better than Gil Haley for running things."

Her dimple flickered. It was, she supposed, a compliment of sorts. "Gil's the best foreman I could ask for," Jillian said mildly. "But I run Utopia."

Murdock's brows drew together. "Women don't run ranches, girl."

Her chin angled. "This one does."

"Nothing but trouble when you start having cowboys in skirts," he said with a snort.

"I don't wear them when I'm hazing cattle."

He set down his cup and leaned forward. "Whatever I felt about your grandfather, it wouldn't sit well with me to see what he worked for blown away because of some female."

"Paul," Karen began, but Jillian was already rolling.

"Clay wasn't so narrow-minded," Jillian shot back. "If a person was capable, it didn't matter what sex they were. I run Utopia, and before I'm done you'll be watching your back door." She rose, unconsciously regal. "I've got work to do. Thank you for the coffee, Mrs. Murdock." She shot a look at Aaron, who was still lounging back on the sofa. "We still have to discuss your stud."

"What's this?" Murdock demanded, banging his cane.

"I'm breeding Samson to one of Jillian's mares," Aaron said easily.

Color surged into Murdock's pale face. "A Murdock doesn't do business with a Baron."

Aaron unfolded himself slowly and stood. "I do business as I please," Jillian heard him say as she started for the door. She was already at her car when Aaron caught up with her.

"What's your fee?" she said between her teeth.

He leaned against the car. If he was angry, she couldn't see it. "You spark easily, Jillian. I'm usually the only one who can put my father in a rage these days."

"Your father," she said precisely, "is a bigot."

With his thumbs hooked idly in his pockets, Aaron studied the house. "Yeah. But he knows his cows."

She let out a long breath because she wanted to chuckle. "About the stud fee, Murdock."

"Come to dinner tonight, we'll talk about it."

"I haven't time for socializing," she said flatly.

"You've been around long enough to know the advantages of a business dinner."

She frowned at the house. An evening with the Murdocks? No, she didn't think she could get through one without throwing something. "Look, Aaron, I'd like to breed Delilah with Samson—if the terms are right. I'm not interested in anything more to do with you or your family."

"Why?"

"There's been bad blood between the Barons and Murdocks for almost a century."

He gave her a lazy look under lowered lids. "Now who's a bigot?"

Bull's-eye, she thought and sighed. Putting her hands on her hips, she tried to bring her temper to order. Murdock was an old man, and from the looks of him, a sick one. He was also, though she'd choke rather than admit it, a great deal like her grandfather. She'd be a pretty poor individual if she couldn't drum up some understanding. "All right, I'll come to dinner." She turned back to him. "But I won't be responsible if it ends up with a lot of shouting."

"I think we might avoid that. I'll pick you up at seven."

"I know the way," she countered and started to push him aside to open her door. His hand curled over her forearm.

"I'll pick you up, Jillian." The steel was back, in his eyes, his voice.

She shrugged. "Suit yourself."

He cupped the back of her head and kissed her before she could prevent it. "I intend to," he told her easily, then left her to walk back into the house.

Chapter Four

Jillian was still smarting when she returned to Utopia. Murdock's comments, and Aaron's arrogance, had set her back up. She wasn't the sort of woman who made a habit of calming down gracefully. She told herself the only reason she was going back to the Double M to deal with the Murdocks again was because she was interested in a breeding contract. She wanted to believe it.

Dust flew out from her wheels as she drove up the hard-packed road to the ranch yard. It was nearly deserted now at mid-morning, with most of the men out on the range, others busy in the outbuildings. But even an audience wouldn't have prevented her from springing out of her car and slamming the door with a vicious swing. She'd never been a woman who believed in letting her temper simmer if it could boil.

The sound of the door slam echoed like a pistol shot.

Fleetingly she thought of the paperwork waiting for her in the office, then brushed it aside. She couldn't deal with ledgers and numbers at the moment. She needed something physical to drain off the anger before she tackled the dry practicality of checks and balances. Spinning on her heel, she headed for the stables. There'd be stalls to muck out and tack to clean.

"Anybody in particular you'd like to mow down?"

With her eyes still sparkling with anger, Jillian whipped her head around. Joe Carlson walked toward her, his neat hat shading his eyes, a faint, friendly smile on his lips.

"Murdocks."

He nodded after the short explosion of the word. "Figured it was something along those lines. Couldn't come to an agreement on the stud fee?"

"We haven't started negotiating yet." Her jaw clenched. "I'm going back this evening."

Joe scanned her face, wondering that a woman who played poker so craftily should be so utterly readable when riled. "Oh?" he said simply and earned a glare.

"That's right." She bit off each word. "If Murdock didn't have such a damn beautiful horse, I'd tell him to go to the devil and to take his father with him."

This time Joe grinned. "You met Paul Murdock, then."

"He gave me his opinion on cowboys in skirts." Her teeth shut with an audible click.

"Really?"

The dry tone was irresistible. Jillian grinned back at him. "Yes, really." Then she sighed, remembering how difficult it had been for Paul Murdock to climb the four steps to his own porch. "Oh, hell," she murmured, cooling off as quickly as she'd flared. "I shouldn't have let him get under my skin. He's an old man and—"

She broke off, stopping herself before she added *ill*. For some indefinable reason she found it necessary to allow Murdock whatever illusions he had left. Instead she shrugged and glanced toward the corral. "I suppose I'm just used to the way Clay was. If you could ride and drive cattle, he didn't care if you were male or female."

Joe gave her one sharp glance. It wasn't what she'd started to say, but he'd get nothing out of her by probing. One thing he'd learned in the past six months was that Jillian Baron was a woman who did things her way. If a man got too close, one freezing look reminded him how much distance was expected.

"Maybe you'd like to take another look at the bull now, if you've got a few minutes."

"Hmm?" Abstracted, she looked back at him.

"The bull," Joe repeated.

"Oh, yeah." Hooking her thumbs in her pockets, she began to walk with him. "Gil told you about the calves we counted yesterday?"

"Took a look in the south section today. You've got some more."

"How many?"

"Oh, thirty or so. In another week all the calves should be dropped."

"You know, when we were checking the pasture yesterday, I thought the numbers were a little light." Frowning, she went over the numbers in her head again. "I'm going to need someone to go out there and see that some of the bred cows haven't strayed."

"I'll take care of it. How's the orphan?"

With a grin Jillian glanced back toward the cattle barn.

"He's going to be fine." Attachments were a mistake, she knew. But it was already too late between her and Baby. "I'd swear he's grown since yesterday."

"And here's Poppa," Joe announced as they came to the bull's paddock.

After angling the hat farther over her eyes, Jillian leaned on the fence. Beautiful, she thought. Absolutely beautiful.

The bull eyed them balefully and snorted air. He didn't have the bulk or girth of an Angus but was built, Jillian thought, like a sleek tank. His red hide glistened as he stood in the full sun. She didn't see boredom in his expression as she'd seen in so many of the steers or cows, but arrogance. His horns curved around the wide white face and gave him a sense of dangerous royalty. It occurred to her that the little orphan she had sheltered in the cattle barn would look essentially the same in a year's time. The bull snorted again and pawed the ground as if daring them to come inside and try their luck.

"His personality's grim at best," Joe commented.

"I don't need him to be polite," Jillian murmured. "I just need him to produce."

"Well, you don't have any problem there." His gaze skimmed over the bull. "From the looks of the calves in this first batch, he's already done a good job for us. Since we're using artificial insemination now, he should be able to service every Hereford cow on the ranch this spring. Your shorthorn bull's a fine piece of beef, Jillian, but he doesn't come up to this one."

"No." Smiling, she rested her elbows on the rail. "As a matter of fact, I found out today that Aaron Murdock was interested in our, ah, Casanova. I can't help but pat myself on the back when I remember how I sent off to

England for him on a hunch. Damned expensive hunch," she added, thinking of the hefty dent in the books. "Aaron told me today that he was planning on going over to England to take a look at the bull himself when he learned we'd bought him."

"That was a year ago," Joe commented with a frown. "He was still in Billings."

Jillian shrugged. "I guess he was keeping his finger in the pie. In any case, we've got him." She pushed away from the rail. "I meant what I said about the fair in July, Joe. I can't say I cared much about competition and ribbons before. This year I want to win."

Joe brought his attention from the bull and studied her. "Personal?"

"Yeah." She gave him a grim smile. "You could say it's personal. In the meantime, I'm counting on this guy to give me the best line of beef cattle in Montana. I need a good price in Miles City if I'm going to keep the books in the black. And next year when some of his calves are ready…" She trailed off with a last look at the bull. "Well, we'll just take it a bit at a time. Get back to me on those numbers, Joe. I want to take a look at Baby before I go into the office."

"I'll take care of it," he said again and watched her walk away.

By five Jillian had brought the books up to date and was, if not elated with the figures, at least satisfied. True, the expenses had taken a sharp increase over the past year, but by roundup time, she anticipated a tidy profit from the Livestock Auction Saleyard in Miles City. The expenses had been a gamble, but a necessary one. The plane would be in use within the week and the bull had already proved himself.

Tipping back in her grandfather's worn leather chair, she studied the ceiling. If she could find the time, she'd like to learn how to fly the plane herself. As owner she felt it imperative that she have at least a working knowledge of every aspect of the ranch. In a pinch she could shoe a horse or stitch up a rent hide. She'd learned to operate a hay baler and a bulldozer during a summer visit when she'd still been a teenager—the same year she'd wielded her first and last knife to turn a calf into a steer.

When and if she could afford the luxury, she thought, she'd hire someone to take over the books. Grimacing, she closed the ledger. She had more energy left after ten hours on horseback than she did after four behind a desk.

For now it couldn't be helped. She could justify adding another puncher to the payroll, but not a paper pusher. Next year... She laughed at herself and rested her feet on the desk.

Trouble was, she was counting too heavily on next year and too many things could happen. A drought could mean the loss of crops, a blizzard the loss of cattle. And that was just nature. If feed prices continued to rise, she was going to have to seriously consider selling off a larger portion of the calves as baby beef. Then there was the repair bill for the Jeep, the vet bill, the food bill for the hands. The bill for fuel that would rise once the plane was in use. Yes, she was going to need top dollar in Miles City and a blue ribbon or two wouldn't hurt.

In the meantime she was going to keep an eye on her spring calves. And Aaron Murdock. With a half smile, Jillian thought of him. He was an arrogant son of a bitch, she mused with something very close to admi-

ration, and sharp as they came. It was a pity she didn't
trust him enough to discuss ranch business with him
and kick around ideas. She'd missed that luxury since
her grandfather died. The men were friendly enough,
but you didn't talk about your business with a hand who
might be working for someone else next year. And Gil
was…Gil was Gil, she thought with a grin. He was fond
of her, even respected her abilities, though he wouldn't
come out and say so. But he was too steeped in his own
ways to talk about ideas and changes. So that left—no
one, Jillian admitted.

There had been times in Chicago when she could have
screamed for privacy, for solitude. Now there were times
she ached just to have someone to share an hour's conversation with. With a shake of her head she rose. She
was getting foolish. She had dozens of people to talk to.
All she had to do was go down to the barn or the stables.
Wherever this sudden discontent had come from it would
fade again quickly enough. She didn't have time for it.

Her boots clicked lightly on the floor as she walked
through the house and up the stairs. From outside she
could hear the ring of the triangle, those quick three notes
that ran faster and faster until it was one high sound. Her
hands would be sitting down to their meal. She'd better
get ready for her own.

Jillian toyed with the idea of just slipping into clean
jeans and a shirt. The deliberate casualness of such an
outfit would be pointedly rude. She was still annoyed
enough at both Aaron and his father to do it, but she
thought of Karen Murdock. With a sigh, Jillian rejected
the idea and hunted through her closet.

It was a matter of her own choice that she had few
dresses. They were relegated to one side of her closet,

and she rooted them out on the occasions when she entertained other ranchers or businessmen. She stuck with simple styles, having found it to her advantage not to call her femininity to attention. Standing in a brief teddy, she skimmed over her options.

The oversized white cotton shirt wasn't precisely masculine in cut, but it was still casual. Matched with a full white wrap skirt with yards of sash, it made an outfit she thought not only suitable but understated. She made a small concession with a touch of makeup, hesitated over jewelry, then, shrugging, clipped small swirls of gold at her ears. Her mother, Jillian thought, would have badgered her to do something more sophisticated with her hair. Instead she ran a brush through it and left it down. She didn't need elegant styles to discuss breeding contracts.

When she heard the sound of a car drive up outside, she stopped herself from going to the window to peer out. Deliberately she took her time going back downstairs.

Aaron wasn't wearing a hat. Without it Jillian realized he still looked like what he was—a rugged outdoorsman with touches of the aristocracy. He didn't need the uniform to show it.

Looking at him, she wondered how he had found the patience to sit in Billings behind a desk. Trim black slacks and a thin black sweater fit him as truly as his work clothes, yet they seemed to accent the wickedness of his dark looks. She felt an involuntary stir and met his eyes coolly.

"You're prompt," she commented and let the door swing shut behind her. It might not be wise to be alone with him any longer than necessary.

"So are you." He let his gaze move over her slowly, appreciating the simplicity of her outfit—the way the sash accented her small waist and narrow hips, the way the unrelieved white made her skin glow and her hair spark like fire. "And beautiful," he added, taking her hand. "Whether you like it or not."

Because her pulse reacted immediately, Jillian knew she had to tread carefully. "You keep risking that hand of yours, Murdock." When she tried to slip hers from it, he merely tightened his fingers.

"One thing I've learned is that nothing's worth having if you don't have trouble getting it." Very deliberately he brought her hand to his lips, watching her steadily.

It wasn't a gesture she expected from him. Perhaps that was why she did nothing but stare at him as the sun dipped lower in the sky. She should've jerked her hand away—she wanted to spread her fingers so that she could touch that high curve of cheekbone, that lean line of jaw. She did nothing—until he smiled.

"Maybe I should warn you," Jillian said evenly, "that the next time I hit you, I'm going to aim a bit lower."

He grinned, then kissed her hand again before he released it. "I believe it."

Because she couldn't stop her own smile, she gave up. "Are you going to feed me, Murdock, or not?" Without waiting for an answer, she walked down the steps in front of him.

His car was more in tune with the oil man she'd first envisioned. A low, sleek Maserati. She admired anything well built and fast and settled into her seat with a little sigh. "Nice toy," she commented with a hint of the smile still playing around her mouth.

"I like it," Aaron said easily when he started the engine. It roared into life, then settled down to a purr. "A man doesn't always like to take a woman out in a Jeep or pickup."

"This isn't a date," she reminded him but skimmed her fingers over the smooth leather of the upholstery.

"I admire your practical streak—most of the time."

Jillian turned in her seat to watch the way he handled the car. As well as he handles a horse, she decided. As well as she was certain he handled a woman. The smile curved her lips again. He was going to discover that she wasn't a woman who took to being handled. She settled back to enjoy the ride.

"How does your father feel about me coming to dinner?" she asked idly. Those last slanting rays of the sun were tipping the grass with gold. She heard a cow moo lazily.

"How should he feel about it?" Aaron countered.

"He was amiable enough when I was simply Clay Baron's granddaughter," Jillian pointed out. "But once he found out I was *the* Baron, so to speak, he changed his tune. You're fraternizing with the enemy, aren't you?"

Aaron took his eyes off the road long enough to meet her amused look with one of his own. "So to speak. Aren't you?"

"I suppose I prefer to look at it as making a mutually advantageous bargain. Aaron…" She hesitated, picking her way carefully over what she knew was none of her business. "Your father's very ill, isn't he?"

She could see his expression draw inward, though it barely changed at all. "Yes."

"I'm sorry." Jillian turned to look out the side window. "It's hard," she murmured, thinking of her grandfather. "It's so hard for them."

"He's dying," Aaron said flatly.

"Oh, but—"

"He's dying," he repeated. "Five years ago they told him he had a year, two at most. He outfoxed them. But now…" His fingers contracted briefly on the wheel, then relaxed again. "He might make it to the first snow, but he won't make it to the last."

He sounded so matter-of-fact. Perhaps she'd imagined that quick tension in his fingers. "There hasn't even been a rumor of his illness."

"No, we intend to keep it that way."

She frowned at his profile. "Then why did you tell me?"

"Because you understand about pride and you don't play games."

Jillian studied him another moment, then turned away. No soft words or whispered compliments could have moved her more than that brisk, emotionless statement. "It must be difficult for your mother."

"She's tougher than she looks."

"Yes." Jillian smiled again. "She'd have to be to put up with him."

They drove under the high-arched *Double M* at the entrance to the ranch. The day was hovering at dusk when the light grew lazy and the air soft. Cattle stood slack-hipped in the pasture to the right. She saw a mother licking patiently to clean her baby's hide while other calves were busy at their evening feeding. In another few months they'd be heifers and steers, the maternal bond forgotten, but for now they were just babies with awkward legs and demanding stomachs.

"I like this time of day," she murmured, half to herself. "When work's over and it isn't time to think about tomorrow yet."

He glanced down at her hand that lay relaxed against the seat. Competent, unpampered, with narrow bones and slender fingers. "Did you ever consider that you work too hard?"

Jillian turned and met his gaze calmly. "No."

"I didn't think you did."

"Cowboys in skirts again, Murdock?"

"No." But he'd made a few discreet inquiries. Jillian Baron had a reputation for working a twelve-hour day— on a horse, in a pickup, on her feet. If she wasn't riding fence or hazing cattle, she was feeding her stock, overseeing repairs or poring over the books. "What do you do to relax?" he asked abruptly. Her blank look gave him the answer before she did.

"I don't have a lot of time for that right now. When I do there are books or the toy Clay bought a couple years ago."

"Toy?"

"Videotape machine," she said with a grin. "He loved the movies."

"Solitary entertainments," Aaron mused.

"It's a solitary way of life," Jillian countered, then glanced over curiously when he stopped in front of a simple white frame house. "What's this?"

"It's where I live," Aaron told her easily before he stepped from the car.

She sat where she was, frowning at the house. She'd taken it for granted that he lived in the sprawling main house another quarter mile or so up the road. Just as she'd taken it for granted that they were having dinner there, with his parents. Jillian turned her head as he opened her door and sent him an uncompromising look. "What are you up to, Murdock?"

"Dinner." Taking her hand, he pulled her from the car. "Isn't that what we'd agreed on?"

"I was under the impression we were having it up there." She gestured in the general direction of the ranch house.

Aaron followed the movement of her hand. When he turned back to her, his mouth was solemn, his eyes amused. "Wrong impression."

"You didn't do anything to correct it."

"Or to promote it," he countered. "My parents don't have anything to do with what's between us, Jillian."

"Nothing is."

Now his lips smiled, as well. "There's a matter of the horses—yours and mine." When she continued to frown, he stepped closer, his body just brushing hers. "Afraid to be alone with me, Jillian?"

Her chin came up. "You overestimate yourself, Murdock."

He saw from the look in her eyes that she wouldn't back down no matter what he did. The temptation was too great. Lowering his head, he nipped at her bottom lip. "Maybe," he said softly. "Maybe not. We can always ride on up to the main house if you're—nervous."

Her heart had already risen to the base of her throat to pound. But she knew what it was to deal with a stray wildcat. "You don't worry me," she said mildly, then turned to walk to the house.

Oh, yes, I do, Aaron thought, and admired her all the more because she was determined to face him down. He decided, as he moved to open the front door, that it promised to be an interesting evening.

She couldn't fault his taste. Jillian glanced around his living quarters, wondering just how much she could learn about him from his choice of furnishings. Apparently, he had his mother's flair for style and color, though there were no subtle feminine touches here. Buffs and creams were offset by a stunning wall hanging slashed with vivid blues and greens. He favored antiques and clean lines. Though the room was small, there was no sense of clutter. Curious, she wandered to a curved mahogany shelf and studied his collection of pewter.

The mustang at full gallop caught her attention, though all the animals in the miniature menagerie were finely crafted. For a moment she wished he wasn't a man who appreciated what appealed to her quite so much. Then, remembering the stand she had to take, she turned around. "This is very nice. Though it is a bit simple for a man who grew up the way you did."

His brow lifted. "I'll take the compliment. How do you like your steak?"

Jillian dipped her hands in the wide pockets of her skirt. "Medium rare."

"Keep me company while I fix them." He curled a hand around her arm and moved through the house with her.

"So, I get Murdock beef prepared by a Murdock." She shot him a look. "I suppose I should be complimented."

"We might consider it a peace offering."

"We might," Jillian said cautiously, then smiled. "Providing you know how to cook. I haven't eaten since breakfast."

"Why not?"

He gave her such a disapproving look that she laughed. "I got bogged down in paperwork. I can't work up much of an appetite sitting at a desk. Well, well," she added, glancing around his kitchen. Its simplicity suited the house, with its hardwood floor and plain counters. There wasn't a crumb out of place. "You're a tidy one, aren't you?"

"I lived in the bunkhouse for a while." Aaron uncorked a bottle of wine that stood on the counter next to two glasses. "It either corrupts or reforms you."

"Why the bunkhouse when—" She cut herself off, annoyed that she'd begun to pry again.

"My father and I deal together better when there's some distance." He poured wine into both glasses. "You'd have heard by now that we don't always agree."

"I heard you'd had a falling-out a few years ago, before you went to Billings."

"And you wondered why I—buckled under instead of telling him to go to hell and starting my own place."

Jillian accepted the wine he handed her. "All right, yes, I wondered. It's none of my business."

He looked into his glass a moment, as if studying the dark red color of the wine. "No." Aaron glanced back up and sipped. "It's not."

Without another word he turned to take two hefty steaks out of the refrigerator. Jillian sipped her wine and remained quiet, watching him as he began preparation of the meal with the deft, economical moves that were characteristic of him. Five years ago they'd given his father a year, perhaps two, to live. Aaron had told her that without even a hint of emotion in his voice. And he'd gone to Billings five years before.

To wait his father out? she wondered and winced at the thought. No, she couldn't believe that of him—a man cool and calculating enough to wait for his father to die? Even if his feelings for his father didn't run deep, it was too cold, too heartless. With a shudder, Jillian took a deep swallow of her wine, then set it down. She wouldn't believe it of him.

"Anything I can do?"

Aaron glanced over his shoulder to see her calmly watching him. He knew what direction her thoughts had taken—the logical direction. Now he saw she'd decided in his favor. He told himself he didn't give a damn one way or the other. It wasn't just astonishing to find out he did, it was enervating. He could feel the emotion stir, and drain him. To give himself a moment to settle, he slipped the steaks under the broiler and turned it on.

"Yeah, there's something you can do." Crossing to her, Aaron framed her face in his hands, seeing her eyes widen in surprise just before his mouth closed over hers. He meant to keep it hard and brief. A gesture—a gesture only to rid him of whatever emotion had suddenly sprung up in him. But as his lips moved over hers the emotion swelled, threatening to take over as the kiss lingered.

She stiffened, and lifted her hands to his chest in automatic defense. Aaron found he didn't want the struggle that usually appealed to him, but the softness he knew she'd give to very few. "Jillian, don't." His fingers tangled in her hair. His voice had roughened with feelings—mysterious, unnamed—he didn't pause to question. "Don't fight me—just this once."

Something in his voice, that quiet hint of need, had her hands relaxing against him before the thought to do so had registered. So she yielded, and in yielding brought herself a moment of sweet, mindless pleasure.

His mouth gentled on hers even as he took her deeper. Her hands crept up to his shoulders, her head tilted back so that he might take what he needed and bring her more of that soft, soft delight she hadn't been aware existed. With a sigh that came from discovery, she gave.

He hadn't known he was capable of tenderness. There'd never been a woman who'd drawn it from him before. He hadn't been aware that desire could ever be calm and easy. Yet while the need built inside him, he felt a quiet wave of contentment. Aaron basked in it until it made him light-headed. Shaken, he eased her away, studying her face like a man who had seen something he didn't quite understand. And wasn't sure he wanted to.

Jillian took a step back, regaining her balance by placing her palm down on the scrubbed wooden table. She found sweetness in the last place she expected to. There was nothing she was more determined to fight. "I came here for dinner," she began, eyeing him just as warily as he was eyeing her. "And to talk business. Don't do that again."

"You've got a point," he murmured before he turned back to the stove to tend the steaks. "Drink your wine, Jillian. We'll both be safer."

She did as he suggested only because she wanted something to calm her nerves. "I'll set the table," she offered.

"Dishes're up there." Aaron pointed to a cabinet without looking up. The steaks sizzled when he flipped them. "There's salad in the refrigerator."

They finished up the cooking and preparation in silence, with only the sound of sizzling meat and frying potatoes. Jillian finished off her first glass of wine and looked at the food with real enthusiasm.

"Either you know what you're doing, or I'm starved."

"Both." Aaron passed her some ranch dressing. "Eat. When you're skinny you can't afford to miss meals."

Unoffended, she shrugged. "Metabolism," she told him as she speared into the salad. "It doesn't matter how much I eat, nothing sticks."

"Some people call it nervous energy."

She glanced up as he tilted more wine into her glass. "I call it metabolism. I'm never nervous."

"Not often, in any case," he acknowledged. "Why did you leave Chicago?" Aaron asked before she could formulate a response.

"I didn't belong there."

"You could have, if you'd chosen to."

Jillian gave him a long neutral look, then nodded. "I didn't choose to, then. I felt at home here the first summer I visited."

"What about your family?"

She laughed. "They didn't."

"I mean, how do they feel about you living here, running Utopia?"

"How should they feel?" Jillian countered. She frowned into her wine a moment, then shrugged again. "I suppose you could say my father feels about Chicago the way I feel about Montana. It's where he belongs. You'd think he'd been born and raised there. And of course, my mother was, so... We just never worked out as a family."

"How?"

Jillian dashed some salt on her steak and cut into it. "I hated my piano lessons," she said simply.

"As easy as that?"

"As basic as that. Marc—my brother—he just melded right in. I suppose it helped that he developed an interest in medicine early, and he loves opera. My mother's quite a fan," she said with a smile. "Anyway, I still cringe a bit when I have to use a needle on a cow, and I've never been able to appreciate *La Traviata*."

"Is that what it takes to suit as a family?" Aaron wondered.

"It was important in mine. When I came here the first time, things started to change. Clay understood me. He yelled and swore instead of lecturing."

Aaron grinned, offering her more steak fries. "You like being yelled at?"

"Patient lecturing is the worst form of punishment."

"I guess I've never had to deal with it. We had a wood shed." He liked the way she laughed, low, appreciative. "Why didn't you come out to stay sooner?"

She moved her shoulders restlessly as she continued to eat. "I was in college. Both my parents thought a degree was vital, and I felt it was important to try to please them in that if nothing else. Then I got involved with—" She stopped herself, stunned that she'd almost told him of her relationship with that long-ago intern. Meticulously she cut a piece of steak. "It just didn't work out," she concluded, "so I came out here."

The someone who touched her wrong, Aaron decided. The astonishment in her eyes had been brief, her cover-up swift and smooth, but not smooth enough. He wouldn't probe there, not on a spot that was obviously tender. But he wondered who it had been who had touched her, and hurt her while she'd still been too young to build defenses.

"I think my mother was right," he commented. "Some things are just in the blood. You belong here."

There was something in the tone that made her look up carefully. She wasn't certain at that moment whether he referred to the ranch or to himself. His eyes reminded her just how ruthless he could be when he wanted something. "I belong at Utopia," she said precisely. "And I intend to stay. Your father said something today, too," she reminded him. "That a Murdock doesn't do business with a Baron."

"My father doesn't run my life, personally or professionally."

"Are you going to breed your stallion with Delilah to spite him?"

"I don't waste time with spite." It was said very simply, with that undercurrent of steel that made her think if he wanted revenge, he'd choose a very direct route. "I want the mare—" his dark eyes met hers and held "—for reasons of my own."

"Which are?"

Lifting his wine, he drank. "My own."

Jillian opened her mouth to speak, then shut it again. His reasons didn't matter. Business was business. "All right, what fee are you asking?"

Aaron took his time, calmly watching her face. "You seem to be finished."

Distracted, Jillian looked down to see that she'd eaten every bite on her plate. "Apparently," she said with a half laugh. "Well, I almost hate to admit it, Murdock, but it was good—almost as good as Utopia beef."

He answered her grin as he rose to clear off the table. "Why don't we take the wine in the other room, unless you'd like some coffee."

"No." She got up to help him stack the dishes. "I drank a full pot when I was fooling with the damn books."

"Don't care for paperwork?" Aaron picked up the half-full bottle of wine as they walked out of the kitchen.

"Putting it mildly," she murmured. "But someone has to do it."

"You could get a bookkeeper."

"The thought's crossed my mind. Maybe next year," she said with a move of her shoulders. "I've gotten used to keeping my finger on the pulse, let's say."

"Rumor is you rope a steer with the best of them."

Jillian sat on the couch, the full white skirt billowing around her. "Rumor's fact, Murdock," she said with a cocky smile. "Anytime you want to put some money on it, we'll go head to head."

He sat down beside her and toyed with the end of her sash. "I'll keep that in mind. But I have to admit, it isn't a hardship to look at you in a skirt."

Over the rim of her glass she watched him. "We were talking stud fees. What'd you have in mind for Samson?"

Idly he twisted a lock of her hair around his finger. "The first foal."

Chapter Five

For a moment there was complete silence in the room as they measured each other. She'd thought she had him pegged. It infuriated her to realize he was still a step ahead of her. "The first—" Jillian set down her glass of wine with a snap. "You're out of your mind."

"I'm not interested in cash. Two guaranteed breedings. I take the first foal, colt or filly. You take the second. I like the looks of your mare."

"You expect me to breed Delilah, cover all the expenses while she's carrying a foal, lose the use of her for three to four months, deal with the vet fees, then turn the result over to you?"

Relaxed, Aaron leaned back. He'd almost forgotten how good it was to haggle. "You'd have the second for nothing. I'd be willing to negotiate on the expenses."

"A flat fee," Jillian said, rising. "We're not talking about dogs, where you can take the pick of the litter."

"I don't need cash," Aaron repeated, lounging back on the couch. "I want a foal, take it or leave it."

Oh, she'd like to leave it. She'd like to have tossed it back in his face. Simmering, she stalked over to the window and stared out. It surprised her that she didn't. Until that moment Jillian hadn't realized just how much she wanted to breed those two horses. Another hunch, she thought, remembering the bull. She could feel that something special would come out of it. Clay had often told her she had a feel. More than once she'd singled out an animal for no other reason than a feeling. Now she had to weigh that with the absurdity of Aaron's suggestion.

She stared hard out of the window into the full night, full dark. Behind her, Aaron remained silent, waiting, watching her with a faint smile. He wondered if she knew just how lovely she was when she was annoyed. It was tempting to keep her that way.

"I get the first foal," she said suddenly. "You get the second. It's my mare who's taking the risk in pregnancy, who won't be any use for working when she's at term and nursing. I'm the one bearing the brunt of the expense."

Aaron considered a moment. She was playing it precisely as he'd have done himself if the situation was reversed. He found it pleased him. "We breed her back as soon as she's weaned the foal."

"Agreed. You pay half the vet bills—on both foalings."

His brows raised. Whatever she knew about cattle, she wasn't a fool when it came to horse trading. "Half," he agreed. "We breed them as soon as she comes in season."

With a nod, Jillian offered her hand on it. "Do you want to draw up the papers or shall I?"

Standing, Aaron took her hand. "I'm not particular. A handshake's binding enough for me."

"Agreed," she said again. "But it never hurts to have words written down."

He grinned, skimming his thumb over her knuckles. "Don't you trust me, Jillian?"

"Not an inch," she said easily, then laughed because he seemed more pleased than offended. "No, not an inch. And you'd be disappointed if I did."

"You have a way of cutting through to the heart of things. It's a pity I've been away for five years." He inclined his head. "But I have a feeling we'll be making up for lost time."

"I haven't lost any time," Jillian countered. "Now that we've concluded our business successfully, Murdock, I have a long day tomorrow."

He tightened his fingers on hers before she could turn away. "Not all our business."

"All I came for." Her voice was cool, even when he stepped closer. "I don't want to make a habit out of hitting you."

"You won't connect this time." He took her other hand and held both lightly, though not so lightly she could draw away. "I'm going to have you, Jillian."

She didn't try to pull her hands away. She didn't back up. Her eyes stayed level with his and her voice just as matter-of-fact. "The hell you are."

"And when I do," he went on as if she hadn't spoken, "it's not going to be something either one of us is going to forget. You stirred something in me—" he yanked her closer so that the unrelieved white of her skirt flowed against the stark black of his slacks "—from the first minute I saw you. It hasn't settled yet."

"Your problem." She angled her chin, but her voice was breathless. "You don't interest me, Murdock."

"Tell me that again," he challenged, "in just a minute."

He brought his mouth down on hers, harder, rougher than he'd intended. His emotions seemed to have no middle ground with her. It was either all soft tenderness or raw passion. Her arms strained against his hold, her body jerked as if to reject him. Then he felt it—the instant she became as consumed as he. In seconds his arms were around her, and hers around him.

It felt just as she'd wanted it to. Heady, overpowering. She could forget everything but that delicious churning within her own body. The rich flavor of wine that lingered on his tongue would make her drunk, but it didn't matter. Her head could whirl and spin, but she could only be grateful for the giddiness. With unapologetic passion, she met his demand with demand.

When his mouth left hers, she would have protested, but the sound became a moan as his lips raced down her throat. Instinctively she tilted her head back to give him more freedom, and the sharp scent of soap drifted over her, laced with a hint of sandalwood. Then his mouth was at her ear, his teeth tugging and nipping before he whispered something she didn't understand. The words didn't matter, the sound alone made her tremble. With a murmur of desperation, she dragged his lips back to hers.

Jillian was demanding he take more. Aaron could feel the strain of her body against his and knew she was aching to be touched. But his hands were still tangled in her hair as they tumbled onto the couch. Then his hands were everywhere, and he couldn't touch enough fast enough. Her body was so slender under all those yards of thin white cotton. So responsive. Her breast was almost lost under the span of his hand, yet it was so firm. And her heartbeat pounded like thunder beneath it.

His legs tangled with hers before he slipped between them. When she sank into the cushions, he nearly lost himself in the simple give of her body. His mouth ravaged hers—he couldn't prevent it, she didn't protest. She only answered and demanded until he was half mad again. Her scent, part subtle, part sultry, enveloped him so that he knew he'd be able to smell her when she was miles from him. He could hear her breath rush from between her lips into his mouth, where it whispered warm and sweet and promising.

Her body was responding of its own accord while her mind raced off in a dozen directions. His weight, that hard, firm press of his body, felt so good, so natural against hers. Those rough, ruthless kisses gave her everything she needed long before she knew she needed. He threatened her with words of passion that were only whispered madness in a world of color without form.

His cheek grazed hers as his lips raced over her face. No one had ever wanted her like this. But more, she'd never wanted this wildly. Her only taste of lovemaking had been so mild, so quiet. Nothing had prepared her for a violence of need that came from within herself. She wanted to fly with it. Too much.

His hand skimmed up her leg, seeking, and everything that was inside her built to a fever pitch. If it exploded, she'd be lost. Pieces of herself might scatter so that she'd never be strong enough to stand on her own again.

In a panic, she began to struggle while part of her fought to yield. And to take.

"No." Moaning, she pushed against him.

"Jillian, for God's sake." Her name came out in a gasp as he felt himself drowning.

"No!" With the strength of fear, she managed to shove

him aside and scramble up. Before either of them could think, she was dashing outside, running away from something that followed much too closely. Aaron was cursing steadily when he caught her.

"What the hell's wrong with you?" he demanded as he whipped her back around.

"Let me go! I won't be pawed that way."

"Pawed?" He didn't even hear her gasp as his fingers tightened. "Damn you," he said under his breath. "You were doing some pawing of your own, if that's what you want to call it."

"Just let me go," she said unsteadily. "I told you I don't like to be touched."

"Oh, you like to be touched," he grated, then caught the glint of fear in her eyes. There was pride there, as well, a kind of terrorized pride laced with passion. It reminded him sharply of the eyes of a stallion he'd once tied in a stall. Then he realized his fingers were digging into the flesh of very slender arms.

No, he wasn't a gentle man, but she was the first and only woman who'd caused him to lose control to the point where he'd mark her skin. Carefully he loosened his hold without releasing her. Even as his fingers relaxed, he knew he could drag her back inside and have her willing to give herself to him within moments. But some things you didn't fence.

"Jillian." His voice was still rough, only slightly calmer. "You can postpone what's going to happen between us, but you can't stop it." She opened her mouth, but he shook his head in warning. "No, you'd be much better off not to say anything just now. I want you, and at the moment it's a damned uncomfortable feeling. I'm going to take you home while I've got myself convinced

I play by the rules. It wouldn't take me long to remember I've never followed any."

He pulled open the passenger door, then strode around to the driver's seat without another word. They drove away in a silence that remained thick for miles. Because her body was still throbbing, Jillian sat very straight. She cursed Aaron, then when she began to calm, she cursed herself. She'd wanted him, and every time he touched her, her initial restraint vanished within moments.

The hands in her lap balled into fists. There was a name for a woman who was willing and eager one moment and hurling accusations the next. It wasn't pleasant. She'd never played that kind of game and had nothing but disdain for anyone who did.

He had a right to be furious, Jillian admitted, but then, so did she. He was the one who'd come barging into her life, stirring things up she wanted left alone. She didn't want to feel all those hungers, all those aches that raged through her when he held her.

She couldn't give in to them. Once she did, she'd start depending. If that happened, she'd start chipping away at her own self-reliance until he had more of who and what she was than she did. It had happened before and the need had been nothing like this. She'd gotten a hint, during that strangely gentle kiss in his kitchen, just how easily she could lose herself to him. And yet… Yet when it was all said and done, Jillian was forced to admit, she'd acted like an idiot. The one thing she detested more than anything else was finding herself in the wrong.

A deer bounded over the fence to the left, pausing in the road, as it was trapped in the headlights. Even as Aaron braked, it was sprinting off, slender legs lifting as it took the next fence and disappeared into the darkness. The sight warmed Jillian as it always did. With a soft laugh, she turned back to see the smile in Aaron's eyes. The flood of emotion swamped her.

"I'm sorry." The words came quickly, before she realized she would say them. "I overreacted."

He gave her a long look. He'd wanted to stay angry. Somehow it was easier—now it was impossible. "Maybe we both did. We have a tendency to spark something off each other."

She couldn't deny that, but neither did she want to think about it too carefully just then. "Since we're going to have to deal with each other from time to time, maybe we should come to some kind of understanding."

A smile began to tug at his mouth. "That sounds reasonable. What kind of understanding did you have in mind?"

"We're business associates," she said very dryly because of the amusement in his question.

"Uh-huh." Aaron rested his arm on the back of the seat as he began to enjoy himself.

"Do you practice being an idiot, Murdock, or does it come naturally?"

"Oh, no, no insults, Jillian. We're coming to an understanding."

Jillian fought against a grin and lost. "You have a strange sense of humor."

"A keen sense of the ridiculous," he countered. "So we're business associates. You forgot neighbors."

"And neighbors," she agreed with a nod. "Colleagues, if you want to belabor a point."

"Belabor it," Aaron suggested. "But can I ask you a question?"

"Yes." She drew out the word cautiously.

"What *is* the point?"

"Damn it, Aaron," she said with a laugh. "I'm trying to put things in order so I don't end up apologizing again. I hate apologizing."

"I like the way you do it, very simple and sincere right before you lose your temper again."

"I'm not going to lose my temper again."

"I'll give you five to one."

"Damn it, Aaron." Her laugh rippled, low and smooth. "If I took that bet, you'd go out of your way to make me mad."

"You see, we understand each other already. But you were telling me your point." He pulled into the darkened ranch yard. The light from Jillian's front porch spilled into the car and cast his face in shadows.

"We could have a successful business association *if* we both put a lot of effort into it."

"Agreed." He turned and in the small confines of the car was already touching her. Just the skim of his fingers over her shoulder, the brush of leg against leg.

"We'll continue to be neighbors because neither of us is moving. As long as we remember those things, we should be able to deal with each other without too much fighting."

"You forgot something."

"Did I?"

"You've said what we are to each other, not what we're going to be." He watched her eyes narrow.

"Which is?"

"Lovers." He ran his finger casually down the side of her neck. "I still mean to have you."

Jillian let out a long breath and worked on keeping

her temper in check. "It's obvious you can't carry on a reasonable conversation."

"A lot of things are obvious." He put his hand over hers as she reached for the handle. With their faces close, he let his gaze linger on her mouth just long enough for the ache to spread. "I'm not a patient man," Aaron murmured. "But there are some things I can wait for."

"You'll have a long wait."

"Maybe longer than I'd like," he agreed. "But shorter than you think." His hand was still over hers as he pressed down the handle to release the door. "Sleep well, Jillian."

She swung out of the car, then gave him a smoldering look. "Don't cross the line until you're invited, Murdock." Slamming the door, she sprinted up the steps, cursing the low, easy laughter that followed her.

In the days that followed, Jillian tried not to think about Aaron. When she couldn't stop him from creeping into her mind, she did her best to think of him with scorn. Occasionally she was successful enough to dismiss him as a spoiled, willful man who was used to getting what he wanted by demanding it. If she were successful, she could forget that he made her laugh, made her want.

Her days were long and full and demanding enough that she had little time to dwell on him or her feelings. But though the nights were growing shorter, she swore against the hours she spent alone and unoccupied. It was then she remembered exactly how it felt to be held against him. It was then she remembered how his eyes could laugh while the rest of his face remained serious and solemn. And how firm and strong his mouth could be against hers.

She began to rise earlier, to work later. She exhausted

herself on the range or in the outbuildings until she could tumble boneless into bed. But still there were dreams.

Jillian was out in the pasture as soon as it was light. The sky was still tipped with the colors of sunrise so that gold and rose tinted the hazy blue. Like most of her men, she wore a light work jacket and chaps as they began the job of rounding up the first hundred calves and cows for corral branding. This part of the job would be slow and easy. It was too common to run twenty-five pounds off a cow with a lot of racing and roping. A good deal of the work could be done on foot, the rest with experienced horses or four wheels. If they hazed the mothers along gently, the babies would follow.

Jillian turned Delilah, keeping her at a walk as she urged a cow and calf away from a group of heifers. She looked forward to a long hard morning and the satisfaction of a job well done. When she saw Joe slowly prodding cows along on foot, she tipped her hat to him.

"I always thought branding was a kind of stag party," he commented as he came alongside of her.

Looking down, she laughed. "Not on Utopia." She looked around as punchers nudged cows along with soft calls and footwork. "When we brand again in a couple of days, the plane should be in. God knows it'll be easier to spot the strays."

"You've been working too hard. No, don't give me that look," he insisted. "You know you have. What's up?"

Aaron sneaked past her defenses, but now she just shook her head. "Nothing. It's a busy time of year. We'll be haying soon, first crop should come in right after the spring branding. Then there's the rodeo." She glanced down again as Delilah shifted under her. "I'm counting on those blue ribbons, Joe."

"You've been working from first light to last for a week," he pointed out. "You're entitled to a couple days off."

"The boss is the last one entitled to a couple days off." Satisfied that her cows had joined the slowly moving group headed for the pasture, she wheeled Delilah around. She spotted a calf racing west, spooked by the number of men, horses and trucks. Sending Delilah into an easy lope, Jillian went after him.

Her first amusement at the frantic pace the dogie was setting faded as she saw he was heading directly for the wire. With a soft oath, she nudged more speed out of her mare and reached for her rope. With an expert movement of arm and wrist, she swung it over her head, then shot it out to loop over the maverick's neck. Jillian pulled him up a foot from the wire where he cried and struggled until his mother caught up.

"Dumb cow," she muttered as she dismounted to release him. "Fat lot of good you'd've done yourself if you'd tangled in that." She cast a glance at the sharp points of wire before she slipped the rope from around his head. The mother eyed her with annoyance as she began to recoil the rope. "Yeah, you're welcome," Jillian told her with a grin. Glancing over, she saw Gil crossing to her on foot. "Still think you can beat my time in July?" she demanded.

"You put too much fancy work on the spin."

Though his words were said in his usual rough-and-ready style, something in his eyes alerted her. "What is it?"

"Something you oughta see down here a ways."

Without a word, she gathered Delilah's reins in her hand and began to walk beside him. There was no use asking, so she didn't bother. Part of her mind still registered the sights and sounds around her—the irritated mooing, the high sound of puzzled calves, the ponderous majestic movements of their mothers, the swish of men and animals through grass. They'd start branding by mid-morning.

"Look here."

Jillian saw the small section of broken fence and swore. "Damn it, we just took care of this line a week ago. I rode this section myself." Jillian scowled into the opposite pasture wondering how many of her cattle had strayed. That would account for the fact that though the numbers reported to her were right, her eye had told her differently that morning. "I'll need a few hands to round up the strays."

"Yeah." Reaching over, he caught a strand of wire in his fingers. "Take a look."

Distracted, she glanced down. Almost immediately, Jillian stiffened and took the wire in her own fingers. The break was much too sharp, much too clean. "It's been cut," she said quietly, then looked up and over into the next pasture. Murdock land.

She expected to feel rage and was stunned when she felt hurt instead. Was he capable? Jillian thought he could be ruthless, even lawless if it suited him. But to deliberately cut wire… Could he have found his own way to pay her back for their personal differences and professional enmity? She let the wire fall.

"Send three of the men over to check for strays," she said flatly. "I'd like you to see to this wire yourself." She met Gil's eyes coolly and on level. "And keep it to yourself."

He squinted at her, then spit. "You're the boss."

"If I'm not back by the time the cattle are ready in the corral, get started. We don't have any time to waste getting brands on the calves."

"Maybe we waited a few days too long already."

Jillian swung into the saddle. "We'll see about that." She led Delilah carefully through the break in the wire, then dug in her heels.

It didn't take her long to come across her first group of men. Delilah pulled up at the Jeep and Jillian stared down her nose. "Where's Murdock?" she demanded. "Aaron Murdock."

The man tipped his hat, recognizing an outraged female when he saw one. "In the north section, ma'am, rounding up calves."

"There's a break in the fence," she said briefly. "Some of my men are coming over to look for strays. You might want to do the same."

"Yes, ma'am." But he said it to her back as she galloped away.

The Murdock crew worked essentially the same way her own did. She saw them fanned out, moving slowly, steadily, with the cows plodding along in front of them. A few were farther afield, outflanking the mavericks and driving them back to the herd.

Jillian saw him well out to the right, twisting and turning Samson around a reluctant calf. Ignoring the curious glances of his men, Jillian picked her way through them. She heard them laugh, then shout something short and rude at the calf before he saw her.

The brim of his hat shaded his face from the early morning sun. She couldn't see his expression, only that he watched her come toward him. Delilah pricked up her ears as she scented the stallion and sidestepped skittishly.

Aaron waited until they were side by side. "Jillian." Because he could already see that something was wrong, he didn't bother with any more words.

"I want to talk to you, Murdock."

"So talk." He nudged the calf, but Jillian reached over to grip his saddle horn. His eyes flicked down to rest on her restraining hand.

"Alone."

His expression remained placid—but she still couldn't see his eyes. Signaling to one of his men to take charge of the maverick, Aaron turned his horse and walked farther north. "You'll have to keep it short, I haven't got time to socialize right now."

"This isn't a social call," she bit off, controlling Delilah as the mare eyed the stallion cautiously.

"So I gathered. What's the problem?"

When she was certain they were out of earshot, Jillian pulled up her mount. "There's a break in the west boundary line."

He looked over her head to watch his men. "You want one of my hands to fix it?"

"I want to know who cut it."

His eyes came back to hers quickly. She could see only that they were dark. The single sign of his mood was the sudden nervous shift of his stallion. Aaron controlled him without taking his eyes off Jillian. "Cut it?"

"That's right." Her voice was even now, with rage bubbling just beneath. "Gil found it, and I saw it myself."

Very slowly he tipped back his hat. For the first time she saw his face unshadowed. She'd seen that expression once before—when it had loomed over her as he pinned her to the ground in Samson's corral. "What are you accusing me of?"

"I'm telling you what I know." Her eyes caught the slant of the morning sun and glittered with it. "You can take it from there."

In what seemed to be a very calm, very deliberate motion, he reached over and gathered the front of her jacket in his hand. "I don't cut fence."

She didn't jerk away from him and her gaze remained steady. A single stray breeze stirred the flame-colored curls that flowed from her hat. "Maybe you don't, but you've got a lot of men working your place. Three of my men are in your pasture now, rounding up my strays. I'm missing some cows."

"I'll send some men to check your herd for any of mine."

"I already suggested that to one of your hands in the border pasture."

He nodded, but his eyes remained very intense and very angry. "A wire can be cut from either side, Jillian."

Dumbfounded, she stared at him. Rage boiled out as she knocked his hand away from her jacket. "That's ridiculous. I wouldn't be telling you about the damn wire if I'd cut it."

Aaron watched her settle her moody mare before he gave her a grim smile. "You have a lot of men working your place," he repeated.

As she continued to stare her angry color drained. Hurt and anger hadn't allowed her to think through the logic of it. Some of her men she'd known and trusted for years. Others—they came and they went, earning a stake, then drifting to another ranch, another county. You rarely knew their names, only their faces. But it was her count that was short, she reminded herself.

"You missing any cattle?" she demanded.

"I'll let you know."

"I'll be doing a thorough count in the west section." She turned away to stare at the rising sun. It could've been one of her men just as easily as it could've been one of his. And she was responsible for everyone who was on Utopia's payroll. She had to face that. "I've no use for your beef, Aaron," she said quietly.

"Any more than I do for yours."

"It wouldn't be the first time." When she looked back at him, her chin stayed up. "The Murdocks made a habit out of cutting Baron wire."

"You want to go back eighty years?" he demanded. "There's two sides to a story, Jillian, just like there's two sides to a line. You and I weren't even alive then, what the hell difference does it make to us?"

"I don't know, but it happened—it could happen again. Clay may be gone, but your father still has some bad feelings."

Temper sprang back into his eyes. "Maybe he dragged himself out here and cut the wire so he could cause you trouble."

"I'm not a fool," she retorted.

"No?" Furious, he wheeled his horse so that they were face-to-face. "You do a damn good imitation. I'll check the west line myself and get back to you."

Before she could throw any of her fury back at him, he galloped away. Teeth gritted, Jillian headed south, back to Utopia.

Chapter Six

By the time Jillian galloped into the ranch yard the cattle were already penned. A glance at the sun told her it was only shortly after eight. Cows and calves were milling and mooing in the largest board pen and the workmen had already begun to separate them. No easy task. Listening to the sounds of men and cattle, Jillian dismounted and unsaddled her mare. There wasn't time to brood over the cut wire when branding was under way.

Some of the men remained on horseback, keeping the cows moving as they worked to chase the frantic mothers into a wire pen while the calves were herded into another board corral. The air was already peppered with curses that were more imaginative than profane.

With blows and shouts, a cow and her calf were driven out of the big corral. Men on foot were strung out in a line too tight to allow the cow to follow as the calf slipped through. Relying mostly on arm waving, shrieks, and whistles, the men propelled the cow into the wire pen. Then the process repeated itself. She watched Gil spinning his wiry little body and cheering with an energy that promised to see him through the day despite his years. With a half laugh, Jillian settled her hat firmly on her head and went to join them, lariat in hand.

Calves streaked like terriers back into the cow pen. Dust flew. Cows bullied their way through the line for a reunion with their offspring. Men ran them back with shouts, brute force, or ropes. Men might be outnumbered and outweighed, but the cattle were no match for western ingenuity.

Gil singled a calf out in the cow pen, roped it, and dragged it to him, cursing all the way. With a swat on the flank, he sent it into the calf corral, then squinted at Jillian.

"Fence repaired?" she asked briefly.

"Yep."

"I'll see to the rest myself." She paused, then swung her lariat. "I'm going to want to talk to you later, Gil."

He removed his hat, swiped the sweat off his brow with the arm of his dusty shirt, then perched it on his head again. "When you're ready." He glanced around as Jillian pulled in a calf. "Just about done—time to gang up on 'em."

So saying, he joined the line of men who closed in on the unruly cows to drive the last of them into their proper place. Inside the smaller corral calves bawled and crowded together.

"It isn't pleasant," Jillian muttered to them. "But it'll be quick."

The gate creaked as it was swung across to hold them

in. The rest wasn't a business she cared for, though she never would've admitted it to anyone but herself. Knife and needle and iron were used with precision, with a rhythm that started off uneven, then gained fluidity and speed. Calves came through the chute one at a time, dreaming of liberation, only to be hoisted onto the calf table.

She watched the next calf roll his big eyes in astonishment as the table tilted, leaving him helpless on his side, as high as a man's waist. Then he was dealt with as any calf is at a roundup.

It was hot, dirty work. There was a smell of sweat, blood, smoking hide and medicine. Throughout the steady action reminiscences could be heard—stories no one would believe and everyone tried to top. Cows surged in the wire pen; their babies squealed at the bite of needle or knife. The language grew as steamy as the air in the pen.

It wasn't Jillian's first branding, and yet each one— for all the sweat and blood—made her remember why she was here instead of on one of the wide busy streets back east. It was hard work, but honest. It took a special brand of person to do it. The cattle milling and calling in the corral were hers. Just as the land was. She relieved a man at the table and began her turn at the vaccinations.

The sun rose higher, heading toward afternoon before the last calf was released. When it was done, the men were hungry, the calves exhausted and bawling pitifully for their mothers.

Hot and hungry herself, Jillian sat on a handy crate and wiped the grime from her face. Her shirt stuck to her with patches of wet cutting through the dirt. That was only the first hundred, she thought as she arched her back. They wouldn't finish with the spring brandings until the end of that week or into the next. She waited until nearly all the men had made their way toward the cookhouse before she signaled to Gil. He plucked two beers out of a cooler and went to join her.

"Thanks." Jillian twisted off the cap, then let the cold, yeasty taste wash away some of the dust. "Murdock's going to check the rest of the line himself," she began without preamble. "Tell me straight—" she held the bottle to her brow a moment, enjoying the chill "—is he the kind of man who'd play this sort of game?"

"What do you think?" he countered.

What could she think? Jillian asked herself. No matter how hard she tried, her feelings kept getting in the way. Feelings she'd yet to understand because she didn't dare. "I'm asking you."

"Kid's got class," Gil said briefly. "Now, the old man…" He grinned a bit, then squinted into the sun. "Well, he might've done something of the sort years back, just for devilment. Give your grandpaw something to swear about. But the kid—don't strike me like his devilment runs that way. Another thing…" He spit tobacco and shifted his weight. "I did a head count in the pasture this morning. Might be a few off, seeing as they were spread out and scattered during roundup."

Jillian took another swig from the bottle, then set it aside. "But?"

"Looked to me like we were light an easy hundred."

"A hundred?" she repeated in a whisper of shock. "That many cattle aren't going to stray through a break in the fence, not on their own."

"Boys got back midway through the branding. Only rounded up a dozen on Murdock land."

"I see." She let out a long breath. "Then it doesn't look like the wire was cut for mischief, does it?"

"Nope."

"I want an accurate head count in the morning, down to the last calf. Start with the west pasture." She looked down at her hands. They were filthy. Her fingers ached. It was as innate in her to work for what was hers as it was to fight for it. "Gil, the chances are pretty good that someone on the Murdock payroll's rustling our cattle, maybe for the Double M, but more likely for themselves."

He tugged on his ear. "Maybe."

"Or, it's one of our own."

He met her eyes calmly. He'd wondered if that would occur to her. "Just as likely," he said simply. "Murdock might find his numbers light, too."

"I want that head count by sundown tomorrow." She rose to face him. "Pick men you're sure of, no one that's been here less than a season. Men who know how to keep their thoughts to themselves."

He nodded, understanding the need for discretion. Rustling wasn't any less deadly a foe than it had been a century before. "You gonna work with Murdock on this?"

"If I have to." She remembered the fury on his face—something she recognized as angry pride. She had plenty of that herself. The sigh came before she could prevent it and spoke of weariness. "Go get something to eat."

"You coming?"

"No." She walked back to Delilah and hefted the saddle. Mechanically she began to hook cinches and tighten them. In the corral the cattle were beginning to calm.

When she'd finished, Gil tapped her on the shoulder. Turning her head, she saw him hold out a thick biscuit crammed with meat.

"You eat this, damn it," he said gruffly. "You're going to blow away in a high wind if you keep it up."

Accepting the biscuit, she took a huge bite. "You mangy old dog," she muttered with her mouth full. Then, because no one was around to see and razz him, she kissed both his cheeks. Though it pleased him, he cursed her for it and made her laugh as she vaulted into the saddle.

Jillian trotted the mare out of the ranch yard, then, turning toward solitude, rode her hard.

To satisfy her own curiosity, she headed for the west pasture first. Riding slowly now, she checked the repaired fence, then began to count the cattle still grazing. It didn't take long for her to conclude that Gil's estimate had been very close to the mark. A hundred head. Closing her eyes, she tried to think calmly.

The winter had only cost her twenty—that was something every rancher had to deal with. But it hadn't been nature who'd taken these cows from her. She had to find out who, and quickly, before the losses continued. Jillian glanced over the boundary line. On both sides cattle grazed placidly, at peace now that man had left them to their own pursuits. As far as she could see there was nothing but rolling grass and the cattle growing sleek on it. A hundred head, she thought again. Enough to put a small but appreciable dent in her herd—and her profit. She wasn't going to sit still for it.

Grimly she sent Delilah into a gallop. She couldn't afford the luxury of panicking. She'd have to take it step by step, ascertaining a firm and accurate account of her losses before she went to the authorities. But for now she was tired, dirty and discouraged. The best thing to do was to take care of that before she went back to the ranch.

It had been only a week since she'd last ridden out to the pond, but even in that short time the aspen and cottonwood were greener. She could see hints of bitterroot and of the wild roses that were lovely and so destructive when they sprang up in the pastures. The sun was beginning its gradual decline westward. Jillian judged it to be somewhere between one and two. She'd give herself an hour here to recharge before she went back to begin the painstaking job of checking and rechecking the number of cattle in her books, and their locations. Dismounting, she tethered her mare to a branch of an aspen and let her graze.

Carelessly Jillian tossed her hat aside, then sat on a rock to pull off her boots. As her jeans and shirt followed she listened to the sound of a warbler singing importantly of spring and sunshine. Black-eyed Susans were springing up at the edge of the grass.

The water was deliciously cool. When she lowered herself into it, she could forget about the aches in her muscles, the faint, dull pain in her lower back, and the sense of despair that had followed her out of the west pasture. As owner and boss of Utopia, she'd deal with what needed to be dealt with. For now, she needed to be only Jillian. It was spring, the sun was warm. If the breeze was right, she could smell the young roses. Dipping her head back, she let the water flow over her face and hair.

Aaron didn't ask himself how he'd known she'd be there. He didn't ask himself why knowing it, he'd come. Both he and the stallion remained still as he watched her. She didn't splash around but simply drifted quietly so that the water made soft lapping sounds that didn't disturb the birdsong. He thought he could see the fatigue drain from her. It was the first time he'd seen her completely relaxed without the light of adventure or temper or even laughter in her eyes. This was something she did for herself, and though he knew he intruded, he stayed where he was.

Her skin was milky pale where the sun hadn't touched it. Beneath the rippling water, he could see the slender curves of her body. Her hair clung to her head and shoulders and burned like fire. So did the need that started low in his stomach and spread through his blood.

Did she know how exquisite she was with that long, limber body and creamy skin? Did she know how seductive she looked with that mass of chestnut hair sleek around a face that held both delicacy and strength? No, he thought as she sank beneath the surface, she wouldn't know—wouldn't allow herself to know. Perhaps it was time he showed her. With the slightest of signals, he walked Samson to a tree on his side of the boundary.

Jillian surfaced and found herself looking directly up into Aaron's eyes. Her first shock gave way to annoyance and annoyance to outrage when she remembered her disadvantage. Aaron saw all three emotions. His lips twitched.

"What're you doing here?" she demanded. She knew she could do nothing about modesty and didn't attempt to. Instead she relied on bravado.

"How's the water?" Aaron asked easily. Another woman, he mused, would've made some frantic and useless attempt to conceal herself. Not Jillian. She just tossed up her chin.

"It's cold. Now, why don't you go back to wherever you came from so I can finish what I'm doing."

"It was a long, dusty morning." He sat on a rock near the edge of the pool and smiled companionably. Like Jillian's, his clothes and skin were streaked with grime and sweat. The signs of hard work and effort suited him. Aaron tilted back his hat. "Looks inviting."

"I was here first," she said between her teeth. "If you had any sense of decency, you'd go away."

"Yep." He bent over and pulled off his boots.

Jillian watched first one then the other hit the grass. "What the hell do you think you're doing?"

"Thought I'd take a dip." He gave her an engaging grin as he tossed his hat aside.

"Think again."

He rose, and his brow lifted slowly as he unbuttoned his shirt. "I'm on my own land," he pointed out. He tossed the shirt aside so that Jillian had an unwanted and fascinating view of a hard, lean torso with brown skin stretched tight over the rib cage and a dark vee of hair that trailed down to the low-slung waist of his jeans.

"Damn you, Murdock," she muttered, and judged the distance to her own clothes. Too far to be any use.

"Relax," he suggested, enjoying himself. "We can pretend there's wire strung clean down the middle." With this he unhooked his belt.

His eyes stayed on hers. Jillian's first instinct to look away was overruled by the amusement she saw there. Coolly she watched him strip. If she had to swallow, she did it quietly.

Damn, did he have to be so beautiful? she asked herself and kept well to her own side as he slid into the water. The ripples his body made spread out to tease her own skin. Shivering, she sank a little deeper.

"You're really getting a kick out of this, aren't you?"

Aaron gave a long sigh as the water rinsed away dust and cooled his blood. "Have to admit I am. View from in here's no different from the one I had out there," he reminded her easily. "And I'd already given some thought to what you'd look like without your clothes. Most redheads have freckles."

"I'm just lucky, I guess." Her dimple flickered briefly. At least they were on equal ground again. "You're built like most cowboys," she told him in a drawl. "Lots of leg, no hips." She let her arms float lazily. "I've seen better," she lied. Laughing, she tilted her head and let her legs come up, unable to resist the urge to tease him.

He had only to reach out to grab her ankle and drag her to him. Aaron rubbed his itchy palm on his thigh and relaxed. "You make a habit of skinny-dipping up here?"

"No one comes here." Tossing the hair out of her eyes, she shot him a look. "Or no one did. If you're going to start using the pond regularly, we'll have to work out some kind of schedule."

"I don't mind the company." He drifted closer so that his body brushed the imaginary line.

"Keep to your own side, Murdock," she warned softly, but smiled. "Trespassers still get shot these days." To show her lack of concern, she closed her eyes and floated. "I like to come here on Sunday afternoons, when the men are in the ranch yard, pitching horseshoes and swapping lies."

Aaron studied her face. No, he'd never seen her this relaxed. He wondered if she realized just how little space she gave herself. "Don't you like to swap lies?"

"Men tend to remember I'm a woman on Sunday afternoons. Having me around puts a censor on the—ah, kind of lies."

"They only remember on Sunday afternoons?"

"It's easy to forget the way a person's built when you're out on the range or shoveling out stalls."

He let his eyes skim down the length of her, covered by only a few inches of water. "You say so," he murmured.

"And they need time to complain." With another laugh, she let her legs sink. "About the food, the pay, the work. Hard to do all that when the boss is there." She spun her hand just under the surface and sent the water waving all the way to the edge. He thought it was the first purely frivolous gesture he'd ever seen her make. "Your men complain, Murdock?"

"You should've heard them when my sister decided to fix up the bunkhouse six or seven years back." The memory made him grin. "Seems she thought the place needed some pretty paint and curtains—gingham curtains, baby-blue paint."

"Oh, my God." Jillian tried to imagine what her crew's reaction would be if they were faced with gingham. Throwing back her head, she laughed until her sides ached. "What did they do?"

"They refused to wash anything, sweep anything, or throw anything away. In two weeks' time the place looked like the county dump—smelled like it, too."

"Why'd your father let her do it?" Jillian asked, wiping her eyes.

"She looks like my mother," Aaron said simply.

Nodding, she sighed from the effort of laughing. "But they got rid of the curtains."

"I—let's say they disappeared one night," he amended.

Jillian gave him a swift appraising look. "You took them down and burned them."

"If I haven't admitted that in seven years, I'm not going to admit it now. It took damned near a week to get that place cleared out," he remembered. She was smiling at him in such an easy, friendly way it took all his willpower not to reach over and pull her to his side. "Did you do the orphan today?"

"Earmarked, vaccinated and branded," Jillian returned, trailing her hands through the water again.

"Is that all?"

She grinned, knowing his meaning. "In a couple of years Baby's going to be giving his poppa some competition." She shrugged, so that her body shifted and the water lapped close at the curve of her breast. The less she seemed concerned about her body, the more he became fascinated by it. "I have a feeling about him," she continued. "No use making a steer out of a potential breeder." A cloud of worry came into her eyes. "I rode the west fence before I came up here. I didn't see any more breaks."

"There weren't any more." He'd known they had to discuss it, but it annoyed him to have the few moments of simple camaraderie interrupted. He couldn't remember sharing that sort of simplicity with a woman before. "My men rounded up six cows that had strayed to your side. Seemed like you had about twice that many on mine."

She hesitated a moment, worrying her bottom lip. "Then your count balances?"

He heard the tension in her voice and narrowed his eyes. "Seems to. Why?"

She kept her eyes level and expressionless. "I'm a good hundred head short."

"Hundred?" He'd grabbed her arm before he realized it. "A hundred head? Are you sure?"

"As sure as I can be until we count again and go over the books. But we're short, I'm sure of that."

He stared at her as his thoughts ran along the same path hers had. That many cows didn't stray on their own. "I'll do a count of my own herd in the morning, but I can tell you, I'd know if I had that much extra cattle in my pasture."

"I'm sure you would. I don't think that's where they are."

Aaron reached up to touch her cheek. "I'd like to help you—if you need some extra hands. We can take the plane up. Maybe they wandered in the other direction."

She felt something soften inside her that shouldn't have. A simple offer of help when she needed it—and his hand was gentle on her face. "I appreciate it," Jillian began unsteadily. "But I don't think the cattle wandered any more than you do."

"No." He combed the hair away from her face. "I'll go with you to the sheriff."

Unused to unselfish support, she stared at him. Neither was aware that they were both drifting to the line, and each other. "No—I…it isn't necessary, I can deal with it."

"You don't have to deal with it alone." How was it he'd never noticed how fragile she was? he wondered. Her eyes were so young, so vulnerable. The curve of her cheek was so delicate. He ran his thumb over it and felt her tremble. Somehow his hand was at her lower back, bringing her closer. "Jillian…" But he didn't have the words, only the needs. His mouth came to hers gently.

Her hands ran up his back, skimming up wet, cool skin. Her lips parted softly under his. The tip of his tongue ran lazily around the inside of her mouth, stopping to tease hers. Jillian relaxed against him, content for the long, moist kiss to go on and on. She couldn't remember ever feeling so pliant, so much in tune with another's movements and wishes. His lips grew warmer and heated hers. Against her own, she could feel his heartbeat—quick and steady. His mouth left hers only long enough to change the angle before he began to slowly deepen the kiss.

It happened so gradually she had no defense. It was an emptiness that started in her stomach like a hunger, then spread until it was an ache to be loved. Her body yearned for it. Her heart began to tell her he was the one she could share herself with, not without risk, not without pain, but with something she'd almost forgotten to ask for: hope.

But when her mind started to cloud, she struggled to clear it. It wasn't sharing, she told herself even as his lips slanted over hers to persuade her. It was giving, and if she gave she could lose. Only a fool would forget the boundary line that stood between them.

She pulled out of his hold and stared at him. Was she mad? Making love to a Murdock when her fence had been cut and a hundred of her cows were missing? Was she so weak that a gentle touch, a tender kiss, made her forget her responsibilities and obligations?

"I told you to stay on your own side," she said unsteadily. "I meant it." Turning away, she cut through the water and scrambled up the bank.

Breathing fast, Aaron watched her. She'd been so soft, so giving in his arms. He'd never wanted a woman more—never felt just that way. It came like a blow that she was the first who'd really mattered, and the first to throw his own emotion back in his face. Grimly he swam back to his own side.

"You're one tough lady, aren't you?"

Jillian heard the water lap as he pulled himself from it. Without bothering to shake it out, she dragged on her dusty shirt. "That's right. God knows why I was fool enough to think I could trust you." Why did she want so badly to weep when she never wept? she wondered and buttoned her shirt with shaky fingers. "All that talk about helping me, just so you could get what you wanted." Keeping her back to him, she pulled up her brief panties.

Aaron's hands paused on the snap of his jeans. Rage and frustration tumbled through him so quickly he didn't think he'd be able to control it. "Be careful, Jillian."

She whirled around, eyes brilliant, breasts heaving. "Don't you tell me what to do. You've been clear right from the beginning about what you wanted."

Muscles tense, he laid a hand on the saddle of his stallion. "That's right."

The calm answer only filled her with more fury. "I might've respected your honesty if it wasn't for the fact that I've got a cut fence and missing cattle. Things like that didn't happen when you were in Billings waiting for your father to—" She cut herself off, appalled at what she'd been about to say. Whatever apology she might have made was swallowed at the murderous look he sent her.

"Waiting for him to what?" Aaron said softly—too softly.

The ripple of fear made her lift her chin. "That's for you to answer."

He knew he didn't dare go near her. If he did she might not come out whole. His fingers tightened on the rope that hung on his saddle. "Then you'd better keep your thoughts to yourself."

She'd have given half her spread to have been able to take those hateful, spiteful words back. But they'd been said. "And you keep your hands to yourself," she said evenly. "I want you to stay away from me and mine. I don't need soft words, Murdock. I don't want them from you or anyone. You're a damn sight easier to take without the pretense." She stalked away to grab at her jeans.

He acted swiftly. He didn't think. His mind was still reeling from her words—words that had stung because he'd never felt or shown that kind of tenderness to another woman. What had flowed through him in the pond had been much more than a physical need and complex enough to allow him to be hurt for the first time by a woman.

Jillian gave out a gasp of astonishment as the circle of rope slipped around her, snapping snugly just about her waist and pinning her arms above the elbows. Whirling on her heel, she grabbed at the line. "What the hell do you think you're doing?"

With a jerk, Aaron brought her stumbling forward. "What I should've done a week ago." His eyes were nearly black with fury as she fell helplessly against him. "You won't get any more soft words out of me."

She struggled impotently against the rope, but her eyes were defiant and fearless. "You're going to pay for this, Murdock."

He didn't doubt it, but at that moment he didn't give a damn. Gathering her wet hair in one hand, he dragged her closer. "By God," he muttered. "I think it'll be worth it. You make a man ache, Jillian, in the middle of the night when he should have some peace. One minute you're so damn soft, and the next you're snarling. Since you can't make up your mind, I'll do it for you."

His mouth came down on hers so that she could taste enraged desire. She fought against it even as it found some answering chord in her. His chest was still naked, still wet, so that her shirt soaked up the moisture. The air rippled against her bare legs as he scooped them out from under her. With her mouth still imprisoned by his, she found herself lying on the sun-warmed grass beneath him. Her fury didn't leave room for panic.

She squirmed under him, kicking and straining against the rope, cursing him when he released her mouth to savage her neck. But an oath ended on a moan when his mouth came back to hers. He nipped into her full bottom lip as if to draw out passion. Her movements beneath him altered in tone from protest to demand, but neither of them noticed. Jillian only knew her body was on fire, and that this time she'd submit to it no matter what the cost.

He was drowning in her. He'd forgotten about the rope, forgotten his anger and his hurt. All he knew was that she was warm and slender beneath him and that her mouth was enough to drive a man over the line of reason. Nothing about her was calm. Her lips were avid and seeking; her fingers dug into his waist. He could feel the thunder of her heart race to match his. When she caught his lip between her teeth and drew it into her mouth, he groaned and let her have her way.

Jillian flew with the sensations. The grass rubbed against her legs as she shifted them to allow him more intimacy. His hair smelled of the water that ran from it onto her skin. She tasted it, and the light flavor of salt and flesh when she pressed her lips to his throat. Her name shivered in a desperate whisper against her ear. No soft words. There was nothing soft, nothing gentle about what they brought to each other now. This was a raw, primitive passion that she understood even as it was tapped for the first time. She felt his fingers skim down her shirt, releasing buttons so that he could find her. But it was his mouth not his hand that closed over the taut peak, hot and greedy. The need erupted and shattered her.

Lips, teeth and tongue were busy on her flesh as she

lay dazed from the first swift, unexpected crest. While she fought to catch her breath, Aaron tugged on her shirt to remove it, cursing when it remained tight at her waist. In an urgent move his hand swept down. His fingers touched rope. He froze, his breath heaving in his lungs.

Good God, what was he doing? Squeezing his eyes tight, he fought for reason. His face was nuzzled in the slender valley between her breasts so that he could feel as well as hear the frantic beat of her heart.

He was about to force himself on a helpless woman. No matter what the provocation, there could be no absolution for what he was on the edge of doing. Cursing himself, Aaron tugged on the rope, then yanked it over her head. After he'd tossed it aside, he looked down at her.

Her mouth was swollen from his. Her eyes were nearly closed and so clouded he couldn't read them. She lay so still he could feel each separate tremor from her body. He wanted her badly enough to beg. "You can make me pay now," he said softly and rolled from her onto his back.

She didn't move, but looked up into the calm blue sky while needs churned inside her. The warbler was still singing, the roses still blooming.

Yes, she could make him pay—she'd recognized the look of self-disgust in his eyes. She had only to get up and walk away to do it. She'd never considered herself a fool. Deliberately she rolled over on top of him. Aaron automatically put his hands on her arms to steady her. Their eyes met so that desire stared into desire.

"You'll pay—if you don't finish what you've started." Diving her hands into his hair, she brought her mouth down on his.

Her shirt fluttered open so that her naked skin slid over his. Jillian felt his groan of pleasure every bit as clearly as she heard it. Then it was all speed and fire, so fast, so hot, there wasn't time for thought. Tasting, feeling was enough as they raced over each other in a frenzy of demand. Her shirt fell away just before she pulled at the snap of his jeans.

She tugged them down, then lost herself in the long lean line of his hips. Her fingers found a narrow raised scar that ran six inches down the bone. She felt a ripple of pain as if her own skin had been rent. Then he was struggling out of his jeans and the feel of him, hot and ready against her, drove everything else out of her mind. But when she reached for him, he shifted so she was beneath him again.

"Aaron..." What she would have demanded ended in a helpless moan as he slid a finger under the elastic riding high on her thigh. With a clever, thorough touch of fingertips he brought her to a racking climax.

She was pulsing all over, inside and out. No longer was she aware that she clung to him, her hands bringing him as much torturous pleasure as his brought her. She only knew that her need built and was met time and time again while he held off that last, that ultimate fulfillment. With eyes dazed with passion, she watched his mouth come toward hers again. Their lips met—he plunged into her, swallowing her gasps.

For a long time she lay spent. The sky overhead was still calm. With her hands on Aaron's shoulders, she could feel each labored breath. There seemed to be no peace for them even in the aftermath of passion. Was this the way it was supposed to be? she wondered. She'd known nothing like this before. Needs that hurt and remained unsettled even after they'd been satisfied. She still wanted him—that moment when her body was hot and trembling from their merging.

After all the years she'd been so careful to distance herself from any chance of an involvement, she found herself needing a man she hardly knew. A man she'd been schooled to distrust. Yet she did trust him…that's what frightened her most of all. She had no reason to—no logical reason. He'd made her forget her ambitions, her work, her responsibilities, and reminded her that beneath it all, she was first a woman. More, he'd made her glory in it.

Aaron raised his head slowly, for the first time in his memory unsure of himself. She'd gotten to a place inside him no one had ever touched. He realized he didn't want her to walk away and leave it empty again—and that he'd never be able to hold her unless she was willing. "Jillian…" He brushed her damp, tangled hair from her cheek. "This was supposed to be easy. Why isn't it?"

"I don't know." She held onto the weakness another moment, bringing his cheek down to hers so that she could draw in his scent and remember. "I need to think."

"About what?"

She closed her eyes a moment and shook her head. "I don't know. Let me go now, Aaron."

His fingers tightened in her hair. "For how long?"

"I don't know that either. I need some time."

It would be easy to keep her—for the moment. He had only to lower his mouth to hers again. He remembered the wild mustang—the hell he'd gone through to catch it, the hell he'd gone through to set it free. Saying nothing, he released her.

They dressed in silence—both of them too battered by feelings they'd never tried to put into words. When Jillian reached for her hat, Aaron took her arm.

"If I told you this meant something to me, more than I'd expected, maybe more than I'd wanted, would you believe me?"

Jillian moistened her lips. "I do now. I have to be sure I do tomorrow."

Aaron picked up his own hat and shaded his face with it. "I'll wait—but I won't wait long." Lifting a hand, he cupped her chin. "If you don't come to me, I'll come after you."

She ignored the little thrill of excitement that rushed up her spine. "If I don't come to you, you won't be able to come after me." Turning away, she untied her mare and vaulted into the saddle. Aaron slipped his hand under the bridle and gave her one long look.

"Don't bet on it," he said quietly. He walked back over the boundary line to his own mount.

Chapter Seven

If you don't come to me, I'll come after you.

They weren't words Jillian would forget. She hadn't
yet decided what to do about them—any more than she'd
decided what to do about what had happened between
her and Aaron. There'd been more than passion in that
fiery afternoon at the pond, more than pleasure, however intense. Perhaps she could have faced the passion
and the pleasure, but it was the something more that kept
her awake at nights.

If she went to him, what would she be going to? A man
she'd yet to scratch the surface of—an affair that promised to have more hills and valleys than she knew how
to negotiate. The risk—she was beginning to understand
the risk too well. If she relaxed her hands on the reins
this time, she'd tumble into love before she could regain
control. That was difficult for her to admit, and impossible for her to understand.

She'd always believed that people fell in love because they wanted to, because they were looking for, or were ready for, romance. Certainly she'd been ready for it once before, open for all those soft feelings and heightened emotions. Yet now, when she believed she was on the border of love again, she was neither ready for it, nor was she experiencing any soft feelings. Aaron Murdock didn't ask for them—and in not asking, he demanded so much more.

If she went to him...could she balance her responsibilities, her ambitions, with the needs he drew out of her? When she was in his arms she didn't think of the ranch, or her position there that she had to struggle every day to maintain.

If she fell in love with him...could she deal with the imbalance of feelings between them and cope when the time came for him to go his own way? She never doubted he would. Other than Clay, there'd never been a man who'd remained constant to her.

Indecision tore at her, as it would in a woman accustomed to following her own route in her own way.

And while her personal life was in turmoil, her professional one fared no better. Five hundred of her cattle were missing. There was no longer any doubt that her herd had been systematically and successfully rustled.

Jillian hung up the phone, rubbing at the headache that drummed behind her temples.

"Well?" Hat in lap, Joe Carlson sat on the other side of her desk.

"They can't deliver the plane until the end of the week." Grimly she set her jaw as she looked over at him. "It hardly matters now. Unless they're fools, they've got the cattle well away by this time. Probably transported them over the border into Wyoming."

He studied the brim of his neat Stetson. "Maybe not, that would make it federal."

"It's what I'd do," she murmured. "You can't hide five hundred head of prime beef." Rising, she dragged her hands through her hair. *Five hundred.* The words continued to flash in her mind—a sign of failure, impotence, vulnerability. "Well, the sheriff's doing what he can, but they've got the jump on us, Joe. There's nothing I can do." On a sound of frustration, she balled her fists. "I hate being helpless."

"Jillian…" Joe ran the brim of his hat through his hands, frowning down at it another moment. During his silence she could hear the old clock on her grandfather's desk tick the time away. "I wouldn't feel right if I didn't bring it up," he said at length and looked back at her. "It wouldn't be too difficult to hide five hundred head if they were scattered through a few thousand."

Her eyes chilled. "Why don't you speak plainly, Joe?"

He rose. After more than six months on Utopia, he still looked more businessman than outdoorsman. And she understood it was the businessman who spoke now. "Jillian, you can't just ignore the fact that the west boundary line was cut. That pasture leads directly onto Murdock land."

"I know where it leads," she said coolly. "Just as I know I need more than a cut line to accuse anyone, particularly the Murdocks, of rustling."

Joe opened his mouth to speak again, met her uncompromising look, then shut it. "Okay."

The simplicity of his answer only fanned her temper. And her doubts. "Aaron told me he was going to take a thorough head count. He'd know if there were fifty extra head on his spread, much less five hundred."

It was her tone much more than her words that told him where the land lay now. "I know."

Jillian stared at him. His eyes were steady and compassionate. "Damn it, he doesn't need to steal cattle from me."

"Jillian, you lose five hundred head now and your profit dwindles down to nothing. Lose that much again, half that much again, and…you might have to start thinking about selling off some of your pasture. There're other reasons than the price per head for rustling."

She spun around, shutting her eyes tight. She'd thought of that—and hated herself for it. "He would've asked me if he wanted to buy my land."

"Maybe, but your answer would've been no. Rumor is he was going to start his own place a few years back. He didn't—but that doesn't mean he's content to make do with what his father has."

She couldn't contradict him, not on anything he'd said. But she couldn't live with it either. "Leave the investigating to the sheriff, Joe. That's his job."

He drew very straight and very stiff at the clipped tone of her voice. "All right. I guess I better get back to mine."

On a wave of frustration and guilt, she turned before he reached the door. "Joe—I'm sorry. I know you're only thinking about Utopia."

"I'm thinking about you, too."

"I appreciate it, I really do." She picked up her worn leather work glove from the desk and ran it through her hands. "I have to handle this my own way, and I need a little more time to decide just what that is."

"Okay." He put his hat on and lowered the brim with

his finger. "Just so you know you've got support if you need it."

"I won't forget it."

When he'd gone, Jillian stopped in the center of the office. God, she wanted so badly to panic. Just to throw up her hands and tell whoever'd listen that she couldn't deal with it. There had to be someone else, somewhere, who could take over and see her through until everything was back in order. But she wasn't allowed to panic, or to turn over her responsibilities even for a minute. The land was hers, and all that went with it.

Jillian picked up her hat and her other glove. There was work to be done. If they cleaned her out down to the last hundred head, there would still be work to be done, and a way to build things back up again. She had the land, and her grandfather's legacy of determination.

Even as she opened the front door to go out, she saw Karen Murdock drive up in front of the house. Surprised, Jillian hesitated, then went out on the porch to meet her.

"Hello, I hope you don't mind that I just dropped by."

"No, of course not." Jillian smiled, marveling for the second time at the soft, elegant looks of Aaron's mother. "It's nice to see you again, Mrs. Murdock."

"I've caught you at a bad time," she said, glancing down at the work gloves in Jillian's hand.

"No." Jillian stuck the gloves in her back pocket. "Would you like some coffee?"

"I'd love it."

Karen followed Jillian into the house, glancing around idly as they walked toward the kitchen. "Lord, it's been years since I've been in here. I used to visit your grandmother," she said with a rueful smile. "Of course your grandfather and Paul both knew, but we were all very careful not to mention it. How do you feel about old feuds, Jillian?"

There was a laugh in her voice that might have set Jillian's back up at one time. Now it simply nudged a smile from her. "Not precisely the same way I felt a few weeks ago."

"I'm glad to hear it." Karen took a seat at the kitchen table while Jillian began to brew a fresh pot of coffee. "I realize Paul said some things the other day that were bound to rub you the wrong way. I have to confess he does some of it on purpose. Your reaction was the high point of his day."

Jillian smiled a little as she looked over her shoulder. "Maybe he's more like Clay than I'd imagined."

"They were out of the same mold. There aren't many of them," she murmured. "Jillian—we've heard about your missing cattle. I can't tell you how badly I feel. I realize the words *if there's anything I can do* sound empty, but I mean them."

Turning back to the coffeepot, Jillian managed to shrug. She wasn't sure she could deal easily with sympathy right then. "It's a risk we all take. The sheriff's doing what he can."

"A risk we all take," Karen agreed. "When it happens to one of us, all of us feel it." She hesitated a moment, knowing the ground was delicate. "Jillian, Aaron mentioned the cut line to me, though he's kept it from his father."

"I'm not worried about the cut line," Jillian told her quietly. "I know Aaron didn't have any part in it—I'm not a fool."

No, Karen thought, studying the clean-lined profile. *A fool you're not.* "He's very concerned about you."

"He needn't be." She swung open a cupboard door for cups. "It's my problem, I have to deal with it."

Karen watched calmly as Jillian poured. "No support accepted?"

With a sigh, Jillian turned around. "I don't mean to be rude, Mrs. Murdock. Running a ranch is a difficult, chancy business. When you're a woman you double those stakes." Bringing the coffee to the table, she sat across from her. "I have to be twice as good as a man would be in my place because this is still a man's world. I can't afford to cave in."

"I understand that." Karen sipped and glanced around the room. "There's no one here you have to prove anything to."

Jillian looked up from her own cup and saw the compassion, and the unique bond one woman can have with another. As she did, the tight band of control loosened. "I'm so scared," she whispered. "Most of the time I don't dare admit it to myself because there's so much riding on this year. I've taken a lot of gambles—if they pay off… Five hundred head." She let out a long breath as the numbers pounded in her mind. "It won't put me under, I can't let it put me under, but it's going to take a long time to recover."

Reaching out, Karen covered her hand with her own. "They could be found."

"You know the chances of that now." For a moment she sat still, accepting the comfort of the touch before she put her hand back on her cup. "Whichever way it goes, I'm still boss at Utopia. I have a responsibility to make what was passed on to me work. Clay trusted me with what was his. I'm going to make it work."

Karen gave her a long, thorough look very much like one of her son's. "For Clay or for yourself?"

"For both of us," Jillian told her. "I owe him for the land, and for what he taught me."

"You can put too much of yourself into this land," Karen said abruptly. "Paul would swear I'd taken leave of my senses if he heard me say so, but it's true. Aaron—" She smiled, indulgent, proud. "He's a great deal like his father, but he doesn't have Paul's rigidity. Perhaps he hasn't needed it. You can't let the land swallow you, Jillian."

"It's all I have."

"You don't mean that. Oh, you think you do," she murmured when Jillian said nothing. "But if you lost every acre of this land tomorrow, you'd make something else. You've the guts for it. I recognize it in you just as I've always seen it in Aaron."

"He had other options." Agitated, Jillian rose to pour coffee she no longer wanted.

"You're thinking of the oil." For a moment Karen said nothing as she weighed the pros and cons of what she was going to say. "He did that for me—and for his father," she said at length. "I hope I don't ever have to ask anything like that of him again."

Jillian came back to the table but didn't sit. "I don't understand."

"Paul was wrong. He's a good man and his mistakes have always been made with the same force and vigor as he does everything." A smile flickered on her lips, but her eyes were serious. "He'd promised something to Aaron, something that had been understood since Aaron was a boy. The Double M would be his, if he'd earned it. By God, he did," she whispered. "I think you understand what I mean."

"Yes." Jillian looked down at her cup, then set it down. "Yes, I do."

"When Aaron came back from college, Paul wasn't ready to let go. That's when Aaron agreed to work it his father's way for three years. He was to take over as manager after that—with full authority."

"I've heard," Jillian began, then changed her tack. "It can't be easy for a man to give up what he's worked for, even to his own son."

"It was time for Paul to give," Karen told her, but she held her head high. "Perhaps he would have if…" She gestured with her hands as though she were slowing herself down. "When he refused to stick to the bargain, Aaron was furious. They had a terrible argument—the kind that's inevitable between two strong, self-willed men. Aaron was determined to go down to Wyoming, buy some land for himself, and start from scratch. As much as he loved the ranch, I think it was something he'd been itching to do in any case."

"But he didn't."

"No." Karen's eyes were very clear. "Because I asked him not to. The doctors had just diagnosed Paul as terminal. They'd given him two years at the outside. He was infuriated that age had caught up with him, that his body was betraying him. He's a very proud man, Jillian. He'd beaten everything he'd ever gone up against."

She remembered the hawklike gaze and trembling hands. "I'm sorry."

"He didn't want anyone to know, not even Aaron. I can count the times I've gone against Paul on one hand." She glanced down at her own palms. Something in her expression told Jillian very clearly that if the woman had acquiesced over the years, it had been because of strength and not weakness. "I knew if Aaron went away like that, Paul would stop fighting for whatever time he had left. And then Aaron, once he knew, would never be able to live with it. So I told him." She let out a long sigh and turned her hands over. "I asked him to give up what he wanted. He went to Billings, and though I'm sure he's always thought he did it for me, I know he did it for his father. I don't imagine the doctors would agree, but Aaron gave his father five years."

Jillian turned away as her throat began to ache. "I've said some horrible things to him."

"You wouldn't be the first, I'm sure. Aaron knew what it would look like. He's never given a damn what people think of him. What most people think," she corrected softly.

"I can't apologize," Jillian said as she fought to control herself. "He'd be furious if I told him I knew."

"You know him well."

"I don't," Jillian returned with sudden passion. "I don't know him, I don't understand him, and—" She cut herself off, amazed that she was about to bare her soul to Aaron's mother.

"I'm his mother," Karen said, interpreting the look. "But I'm still a woman. And one who understands very well what it is to have feelings for a man that promise to lead to difficulties." This time she didn't weigh her words but spoke freely. "I was barely twenty when I met Paul, he was past forty. His friends thought he was mad and that I wanted his money." She laughed, then sat back with a little sigh. "I can promise you, I didn't see the humor in it thirty years ago. I'm not here to offer advice on whatever's between you and Aaron, but to offer support if you'll take it."

Jillian looked at her—the enduring beauty, the strength that showed in her eyes, the kindness. "I'm not sure I know how."

Rising, Karen placed her hands on Jillian's shoulders. So young, she thought wistfully. So dead set. "Do you know how to accept friendship?"

Jillian smiled and touched Karen's hands, still resting on her shoulders. "Yes."

"That'll do. You're busy," she said briskly, giving Jillian a quick squeeze before she released her. "But if you need a woman, as we sometimes do, call me."

"I will. Thank you."

Karen shook her head. "No, it's not all unselfish. I've lived over thirty years in this man's world." Briefly she touched Jillian's cheek. "I miss my daughter."

Aaron stood on the porch and watched the moon rise. The night was so still he heard the whisk of a hawk's wings over his head before it dove after its night prey. In one hand he held a can of iced beer that he sipped occasionally, though he wasn't registering the taste. It was one of those warm spring nights when you could taste the scent of the flowers and smell the hint of summer, which was creeping closer.

He'd be damned if he'd wait much longer.

It had been a week since he'd touched her. Every night after the long, dusty day was over, he found himself aching to have her with him, to fill that emptiness inside him he'd become so suddenly aware of. It was difficult enough to have discovered he didn't want Jillian in the

same way he'd wanted any other woman, but to have discovered his own vulnerabilities…

She could hurt him—had hurt him. That was a first,
Aaron thought grimly and lifted his beer. He hadn't yet
worked out how to prevent it from happening again. But
that didn't stop him from wanting her.

She didn't trust him. Though he'd once agreed that
he didn't want her to, Aaron had learned that was a lie.
He wanted her to give him her trust—to believe in him
enough to share her problems with him. She must be
going through hell now, he thought as his fingers tightened on the can. But she wouldn't come to him, wouldn't
let him help. Maybe it was about time he did something
about that—whether she liked it or not.

Abruptly impatient, angry, he started toward the steps.
The sound of an approaching car reached him before the
headlights did. Glancing toward the sound, he watched
the twin beams cut through the darkness. His initial disinterest became a tension he felt in his shoulder and stomach muscles.

Aaron set the half-empty beer on the porch rail as Jillian pulled up in front of his house. Whatever his needs
were, he still had enough sense of self-preservation to
prevent himself from just rushing down the stairs and
grabbing her. He waited.

She'd been so sure her nerves would calm during the
drive over. It was difficult for her, as a woman who simply didn't permit herself to be nervous, to deal with a
jumpy stomach and dry throat. Not once since his mother
had left her that morning had Aaron been out of her
thoughts. Yet Jillian had gone through an agony of doubt
before she'd made the final decision to come. In com-

ing, she was giving him something she'd never intended to—a portion of her private self.

With the moon at her back she stood by her car a moment, looking up at him. Perhaps because her legs weren't as strong as they should've been, she kept her chin high as she walked up the porch steps.

"This is a mistake," she told him.

Aaron remained where he was, one shoulder leaning against the rail post. "Is it?"

"It's going to complicate things at a time when my life's complicated enough."

His stomach had twisted into a mass of knots that were only tugging tighter as he looked at her. She was pale, but there wasn't a hint of a tremor in her voice. "You took your sweet time coming here," he said mildly, but he folded his fingers into his palm to keep from touching her.

"I wouldn't have come at all if I could've stopped myself."

"That so?" It was more of an admission than he'd expected. The first muscles began to relax. "Well, since you're here, why don't you come a little closer?"

He wasn't going to make it easy for her, Jillian realized. And she'd have detested herself if she'd let him. With her eyes on his, she stepped forward until their bodies brushed. "Is this close enough?"

His eyes skimmed her face, then he smiled. "No."

Jillian hooked her hands behind his head and pressed her lips to his. "Now?"

"Closer." He allowed himself to touch her—one hand at the small of her back rode slowly up to grip her hair. His eyes glittered in the moonlight, touched with triumph, amusement, and passion. "A damn sight closer, Jillian."

Her eyes stayed open as she fit her body more intimately to his. She felt the answering response of his muscles against her own, the echoing thud of his heart. "If we get much closer out here on the porch," she murmured with her mouth a whisper from his, "we're going to be illegal."

"Yeah." He traced her bottom lip, moistening it, and felt her little jerk of breath on his tongue. "I'll post bond if you're worried."

Her lips throbbed from the expert flick of his tongue. "Shut up, Murdock," she muttered and crushed her mouth to his. Jillian let all the passions, all the emotions that had been chasing her around for days, have their way. Even as they sprang out of her, they consumed her. Mindlessly she pressed against him so that he was caught between her body and the post.

The thrill of pleasure was so intense it almost sliced through his skin. Aaron's arm came around her so that he could cup the back of her head and keep that wildly aggressive mouth on his own. Then, swiftly, his arm scooped under her knees and lifted her off her feet.

"Aaron—" Her protest was smothered by another ruthless kiss before he walked across the porch to the door. Though she admired the way he could swing the screen open, and slam the heavy door with his arms full, she laughed. "Aaron, put me down. I can walk."

"Don't see how when I'm carrying you," he pointed out as he started up the narrow steps to the second floor.

"Is this the sort of thing you do to express male dominance?"

She was rewarded with a narrow-eyed glare and smiled sweetly.

"No," Aaron said in mild tones. "This is the sort of thing I do to express romance. Now, when I want to express male dominance..." As he drew near the top of the steps he shifted her quickly so that she hung over his shoulder.

After the initial shock Jillian had to acknowledge a hit. "Had that one coming," she admitted, blowing the hair out of her face. "I think my point was that I wasn't looking for romance or dominance."

Aaron's brow lifted as he walked into the bedroom. The words had been light enough, but he'd caught the sincerity of tone. Slowly he drew her down so that before her feet had touched the floor every angle of her body had rubbed against his. Weakened by the maneuver, she stared up at him with eyes already stormy with desire. "Don't you like romance, Jillian?"

"That's not what I'm asking for," she managed, reaching for him.

He grabbed her wrists, holding her off. "That's too bad, then." Very lightly he nipped at her ear. "You'll just have to put up with it. Do you reckon straight passion's safer?"

"As anything could be with you." She caught her breath as his tongue traced down the side of her throat.

Aaron laughed, then began lazily, determinedly, to seduce her with his mouth alone. "This right here," he murmured, nibbling at a point just above her collar. "So soft, so delicate. A man could almost forget there're places like this on you until he finds them for himself. You throw up that damn-the-devil chin and it's tempting to give it one good clip, but then—" he tilted his head to a new angle and his lips skimmed along her skin "—right under it's just like silk."

He tugged with his teeth at the cord of her neck and felt her arms go boneless. That's what he wanted, he thought with rising excitement. To have her melting and pliant and out of control, if only for a few minutes. Hot blood and fire were rewards in themselves, but this time, perhaps only this time, he wanted the satisfaction of knowing he could make her as weak as she could make him.

He slanted his mouth over hers, teasing her tongue with the tip of his until her breath was short and shallow. Her pulse pounded into his palms. He was going to take his time undressing her, he thought. A long, leisurely time that would drive them both crazy.

Without hurry Aaron backed her toward the bed, then eased her down until she sat on the edge. In the moonlight he could see that her eyes had already misted with need, her skin softly flushed with it. Watching her, he ran a long finger down her throat to the first button on her shirt. His eyes remained steady as he undid it, then the second—then the third. He stopped there to move his hands down her, lightly over her breasts, the nipped waist, and narrow hips to the long, slender thighs. She was very still but for the quiver of her flesh.

Turning, he tucked her leg between his and began pulling off her boot. The first hit the floor, but when he took the other and tugged, Jillian gave him some assistance with a well-placed foot.

Surprised, he glanced back to see her shoot him a cocky smile. She recovered quickly, he thought. It would be all the more exciting to turn her to putty again. "You might do the same for me," Aaron suggested, then dropped on the bed, leaned back on his elbows, and held out a booted foot.

Jillian rose to oblige him and straddled his leg. This— the wicked grin, the reckless eyes—she knew how to deal with. It might light a fire in her, but it didn't bring on that uncontrollable softness. When she'd finally made her decision to come, she'd made it to come on equal terms, with no quiet promises or tender phrases that meant no more than the breath it took to make them. She'd told herself she wouldn't fall in love with him as long as she listened to her body and blocked off her heart.

The minute his second boot hit the floor, Aaron grabbed her around the waist and swung her back so that she fell onto the bed, laughing. "You're a tough guy, Murdock." Jillian hooked her arms around his neck and grinned up at him. "Always tossing women around."

"Bad habit of mine." Lowering his head, he nibbled idly at her lips, resisting her attempt to deepen the kiss. "I like your mouth," he murmured. "It's another of those soft, surprising places." Gently he sucked on her lower lip until he felt the hands at his neck grow lax.

The mists were closing in again and she forgot the ways and means to hold them off. This wasn't what she wanted…was it? Yet it seemed to be everything she wanted. Her mind was floating, out of her body, so that she could almost see herself lying languorous and pliant under Aaron. She could see the tension and anxieties of the past days drain out of her own face until it was soft and relaxed under the lazy touch of his mouth and tongue. She could feel her heartbeat drop to a light pace that wasn't quite steady but not yet frantic. Perhaps this was what it felt like to be pampered, to be prized. She wasn't sure, but knew she couldn't bear to lose the sensation. Her sigh came slowly with the release of doubts.

When he bent to whisper something foolish in her ear, she could smell his evening shower on him. His face was rough with the stubble of a long day, but she rubbed her cheek against it, enjoying the scrape. Then his lips grazed across the skin that was alive and tingling until they found their way back to hers.

She felt the brush of strong, clever fingers as they trailed down to release the last buttons of her shirt. Then they skimmed over her rib cage, lightly, effortlessly drawing her deeper into the realm of sensation. He barely touched her. The kisses remained soft, his hands gentle. All coherent thought spun away.

"My shirt's in the way," he murmured against her ear. "I want to feel you against me."

She lifted her hands, and though her fingers didn't fumble, she couldn't make them move quickly. It seemed like hours before she felt the press of his flesh against hers. With a sigh, she slid her hands up to his shoulders and back until she'd drawn the shirt away. The ridge of muscle was so hard. As she rubbed her palms over him, Jillian realized she'd only had flashes of impressions the first time they'd made love. Everything had been so fast and wild she hadn't been able to appreciate just how well he was formed.

Tight sinew, taut flesh. Aaron was a man used to using his back and his hands to do a day's work. She didn't stop to reason why that in itself was a pleasure to her. Then she could reason nothing because his mouth had begun to roam.

He hadn't known he could gain such complete satisfaction in thinking of another's pleasure. He wanted her—wanted her quick and fast and furious, and yet it was a heady feeling to know he had the power to make her weak with a touch.

The underside of her breast was so soft…and he lingered. The skin above the waistband of her jeans was white and smooth…and his hand was content to move just there. He felt her first trembles; they rippled under his lips and hands until his senses swam. Denim strained against denim until he pulled the jeans down over her hips to find her.

Jillian wasn't certain when the languor had become hunger. She arched against him, demanding, but he continued to move without haste. She couldn't understand his fascination with her body when she'd always considered it too straight, too slim and practical. Yet now he seemed anxious to touch, to taste every inch. And the murmurs that reached her whispered approval. His hand cupped her knee so that his fingers trailed over the sensitive back. Years of riding, walking, working, had made her legs strong, and very susceptible.

When his teeth scraped down her thigh, she cried out, stunned to be catapulted to the taut edge of the first peak. But he didn't allow her to go over. Not yet. His warm breath teased her, then the light play of his tongue. She felt the threat of explosion building, growing in power and depth. Yet somehow he knew the instant before it shattered her, and retreated. Again and again he took her to the verge and brought her back until she was weak and desperate.

Jillian shifted beneath Aaron, willing him to take anything, all that he wanted—not even aware that he'd removed the last barrier of clothing until he was once more lying full length on her. She felt each warm, unsteady breath on her face just before his lips raced over it.

"This time…" Aaron pulled air into his lungs so that he could speak. "This time you tell me—you tell me that you want me."

"Yes." She locked herself around him, shuddering with need. "Yes, I want you. Now."

Something flashed in his eyes. "Not just now," he said roughly and drove into her.

Jillian slid over the first edge and was blinded. But there was more, so much more.

Chapter Eight

It was the scent of her hair that slowly brought him back to reason. His face was buried in it. The fragrance reminded him of the wildflowers his mother would sometimes gather and place in a little porcelain vase on a window ledge. It was tangled in his hands, and so soft against his skin he knew he'd be content to stay just as he was through the night.

She lay still beneath him, her breathing so quiet and even she might have been asleep. But when he turned his head to press his lips to her neck, her arms tightened around him. Lifting his head, he looked down at her.

Her eyes were nearly closed, heavy. He'd seen the shadows beneath them when she'd first walked toward him on the porch. With a small frown, Aaron traced his thumb over them. "You haven't been sleeping well."

Surprised by the statement, and his tone, she lifted

her brows. After where they'd just gone together, she might've expected him to say something foolish or arousing. Instead his brows had drawn together and his tone was disapproving. She wasn't sure why it made her want to laugh, but it did.

"I'm fine," she said with a smile.

"No." He cut her off and cupped her chin in his hand. "You're not."

She stared up, realizing how easy it would be to just pour out her thoughts and feelings. The worries, the fears, the problems that seemed to build up faster than she could cope with them—how reassuring it would be to say it all out loud, to him.

She'd done too much of that with his mother, but somehow Jillian could justify that. It was one thing to confess fears and doubts to another woman, and another to give a man an insight on your weaknesses. At dawn they'd both be ranchers again, with a boundary line between them that had stood for nearly a century.

"Aaron, I didn't come here to—"

"I know why you came," he interrupted. His voice was much milder than his eyes. "Because you couldn't stay away. I understand that. Now you're just going to have to accept what comes with it."

It was difficult to drum up a great deal of dignity when she was naked and warm beneath him, but she came close to succeeding. "Which is?"

The annoyance in his eyes lightened to amusement. "I like the way you say that—just like my third grade teacher."

Her lips quivered. "It's one of the few things I managed to pick up from my mother. But you haven't answered the question, Murdock."

"I'm crazy about you," he said suddenly and the mouth that had curved into a smile fell open. She wasn't ready to hear that one, Aaron mused. He wasn't sure he was ready for the consequences of it himself, and decided to play it light. "Of course, I've always been partial to nasty-tempered females. I mean to help you, Jillian." His eyes were abruptly sober. "If I have to climb over your back to do it."

"There isn't anything you can do even if I wanted you to."

He didn't comment immediately but shifted, pulling the pillows up against the headboard, then leaning back before he drew her against him. Jillian didn't stiffen as much as go still. There was something quietly possessive about the move, and irresistibly sweet. Before she could stop it, she'd relaxed against him.

Aaron felt the hesitation but didn't comment. When you went after trust, you did it slowly. "Tell me what's been done."

"Aaron, I don't want to bring you into this."

"I am in it, if for no other reason than that cut line."

She could accept that, and let her eyes close. "We did a full head count and came up five hundred short. As a precaution, we branded what calves were left right away. I estimate we lost fifty or sixty of them. The sheriff's been out."

"What'd he find?"

She moved her shoulders. "Can't tell where they took them out. If they'd cut any more wire, they'd fixed it. Very neat and tidy," she murmured, knowing something died inside her each time she thought of it. "It seems as though they didn't take them all at once, but skimmed a few head here and there."

"Seems odd they left the one line down."

"Maybe they didn't have time to fix it."

"Or maybe they wanted to throw your attention my way until they'd finished."

"Maybe." She turned her face into his shoulder—only slightly, only for an instant—but for Jillian it was a large step toward sharing. "Aaron, I didn't mean the things I said about you and your father."

"Forget it."

She tilted her head back and looked at him. "I can't."

He kissed her roughly. "Try harder," he suggested. "I heard you were getting a plane."

"Yes." She dropped her head on his shoulder and tried to order her thoughts. "It doesn't look like it's going to be ready until next week."

"Then we'll go up in mine tomorrow."

"But why—"

"Nothing against the sheriff," he said easily. "But you know your land better."

Jillian pressed her lips together. "Aaron, I don't want to be obligated to you. I don't know how to explain it, but—"

"Then don't." Taking hold of her hair, he jerked it until her face came up to his. "You're going to find I'm not the kind who'll always give a damn about what you want. You can fight me, sometimes you might even win. But you won't stop me."

Her eyes kindled. "Why do you gear me up for a fight when I'm trying to be grateful?"

In one swift move he shifted so that they lay crosswise across the bed. "Maybe I like you better that way. You're a hell of a lot more dangerous when you soften up."

She threw up her chin. "That's not something that's going to happen very often around you."

"Good," he said and crushed his mouth onto hers. "You'll stay with me tonight."

"I'm not—" Then he silenced her with a savage kiss that left no room for thought, much less words.

"Tonight," he said with a laugh that held more challenge than humor, "you stay with me."

And he took her in a fury that whispered of desperation.

The birds woke her. There was a short stretch of time during the summer when the sun rose early enough that the birds were up before her. With a sigh, Jillian snuggled into the pillow. She could always fool her system into thinking she'd been lazy when she woke to daylight and birdsong.

Groggily she went over the day's workload. She'd have to check Baby before she went in to the horses. He liked to have his bottle right off. With one luxurious stretch, she rolled over, then stared blankly around the room. Aaron's room. He'd won that battle.

Lying back for a moment, she thought about the night with a mixture of pleasure and discomfort. He'd said once before that it wasn't as easy as it should've been. But could he have any idea what it had done to her to lie beside him through the night? She'd never known the simple pleasure of sleeping with someone else, sharing warmth and quiet and darkness. What had made her believe that she could have an affair and remain practical about it?

But she wasn't in love with him. Jillian reached over to touch the side of the bed where he'd slept. She still had too much sense to let that happen. Her fingers dug into the sheet as she closed her eyes. Oh, God, she hoped she did.

The birdcalls distracted her so that she looked over at the window. The sun poured through. But it wasn't summer, Jillian remembered abruptly. What was she still doing in bed when the sun was up? Furious with herself, she sat up just as the door opened. Aaron walked in, carrying a mug of coffee.

"Too bad," he commented as he crossed to her. "I was looking forward to waking you up."

"I've got to get back," she said, tossing her hair from her eyes. "I should've been up hours ago."

Aaron held her in place effortlessly with a hand on her shoulder. "What you should do is sleep till noon," he corrected as he studied her face. "But you look better."

"I've got a ranch to run."

"And there isn't a ranch in the country that can't do without one person for one day." He sat down beside her and pushed the cup into her hand. "Drink your coffee."

She might've been annoyed by his peremptory order, but the scent of coffee was more persuasive. "What time is it?" she asked between sips.

"A bit after nine."

"Nine!" Her eyes grew comically wide. "Good God, I've got to get back."

Again Aaron held her in bed without effort. "You've got to drink your coffee," he corrected. "Then you've got to have some breakfast."

After a quick, abortive struggle, Jillian shot him an exasperated look. "Will you stop treating me as though I were eight years old?"

He glanced down to where she held the sheet absently at her breasts. "It's tempting," he agreed.

"Eyes front, Murdock," she ordered when her mouth twitched. "Look, I appreciate the service," Jillian continued, gesturing with her cup, "but I can't sit around until midday."

"When's the last time you had eight hours' sleep?" He watched the annoyance flicker into her eyes as she lifted the coffee again, sipping rather than answering. "You'd have had more than that last night if you hadn't—distracted me."

She lifted her brows. "Is that what I did?"

"Several times, as I recall." Something in her expression, a question, a hint of doubt, made him study her a bit more carefully. Was it possible a woman like her would need reassurance after the night they'd spent together? What a strange mixture of tough and vulnerable she was. Aaron bent over and brushed his lips over her brow, knowing what would happen if he allowed himself just one taste of her mouth. "Apparently, you don't have to try very hard," he murmured. His lips trailed down to her temple before he could prevent them. "If you'd like to take advantage of me…"

Jillian let out an unsteady breath. "I think—I'd better have pity on you this morning, Murdock."

"Well…" He hooked a finger under the sheet and began to draw it down. "Can't say I've ever cared much for pity."

"Aaron." Jillian tightened her hold on the sheet. "It's nine o'clock in the morning."

"Probably a bit past that by now."

When he started to lean closer, she lifted the mug and held it against his chest. "I've got stock to check and fences to ride," she reminded him. "And so do you."

He had a woman to protect, he thought, surprising

himself. But he had enough sense not to mention it to the woman. "Sometimes," he began, then gave her a friendly kiss, "you're just no fun, Jillian."

Laughing, she drained the coffee. "Why don't you get out of here so I can have a shower and get dressed?"

"See what I mean." But he rose. "I'll fix your breakfast," he told her, then continued before she could say it wasn't necessary. "And neither of us is riding fence today. We're going up in the plane."

"Aaron, you don't have to take the time away from your own ranch to do this."

He hooked his hands in his pockets and studied her for so long her brows drew together. "For a sharp woman, you can be amazingly slow. If it's easier for you, just remember that rustling is every rancher's business."

She could see he was annoyed; she could hear it in the sudden coolness of tone. "I don't understand you."

"No." He inclined his head in a gesture that might've been resignation or acceptance. "I can see that." He started for the door, and Jillian watched him, baffled.

"I..." What the devil did she want to say? "I have to drive over and let Gil know what I'm doing."

"I sent a man over earlier." Aaron paused at the door and turned back to her. "He knows you're with me."

"He knows—you sent—" She broke off, her fingers tightening on the handle of the mug. "You sent a man over to tell him I was here, this morning?"

"That's right."

She dragged a hand through her hair and sunlight shimmered gold at the ends. "Do you realize what that looks like?"

His eyes became very cool and remote. "It looks like

what it is. Sorry, I didn't realize you wanted an assignation."

"Aaron—" But he was already closing the door behind him. Jillian brought the mug back in a full swing and barely prevented herself from following through. With a sound of disgust, she set it down and pulled herself from bed. That had been clumsy of her, she berated herself. How was he to understand that it wasn't shame, but insecurity? Perhaps it was better if he didn't understand.

Aaron could cheerfully have strangled her. In the kitchen, he slapped a slice of ham into the skillet. His own fault, he thought as it began to sizzle. Damn it, it was his own fault. He'd had no business letting things get beyond what they were meant to. If he stretched things, he could say that she had a wary sort of affection for him. It was unlikely it would ever go beyond that. If his feelings had, he had only himself to blame, and himself to deal with.

Since when did he want fences around him? Aaron thought savagely as he plunged a kitchen fork into the grilling meat. Since when did he want more from a woman, any woman, than companionship, intelligence, and a warm bed? Maybe his feelings had slipped a bit past that, but he wasn't out of control yet.

Pouring coffee, he drank it hot and black. He'd been around too long to lose his head over a firebrand who didn't want anything more than a practical, uncomplicated affair. After all, he hadn't been looking for any more than that himself. He'd just let himself get caught up because of the problems she was facing, and the unwavering manner with which she faced them.

The coffee calmed him. Reassured, he pulled a carton of eggs out of the refrigerator. He'd help her as much as he could over the rustling, take her to bed as often as possible, and that would be that.

When she came into the room, he glanced over casually. Her hair was still wet, her face naked and glowing with health and a good night's sleep.

Oh, God, he was in love with her. And what the hell was he going to do?

The easy comment she'd been about to make about the smell of food vanished. Why was he staring at her as if he'd never seen her before? Uncharacteristically self-conscious, she shifted her weight. He looked as though someone had just knocked the wind from him. "Is something wrong?"

"What?"

His answer was so dazed she smiled. What in the world had he been thinking about when she'd interrupted him? she wondered. "I said, is something wrong? You look like you've just taken a quick fall from a tall horse."

He cursed himself and turned away. "Nothing. How do you want your eggs?"

"Over easy, thanks." She took a step toward him, then hesitated. It wasn't a simple matter for her to make an outward show of affection. She'd met with too many lukewarm receptions in her life. Drawing up her courage, she crossed the room and touched his shoulder. He stiffened. She withdrew. "Aaron…" How calm her voice was, she mused. But then, she'd grown very adept very early at concealing hurt. "I'm not very good at accepting support."

"I've noticed." He cracked an egg and let it slide into the pan.

She blinked because her eyes had filled. Stupid! she railed at herself. Never put your weaknesses on display.

Swallowing pride came hard to her, but there were times it was necessary. "What I'd like to say is that I appreciate what you're doing. I appreciate it very much."

Emotions were clawing him. He smacked another egg on the side of the pan. "Don't mention it."

She backed away. *What else did you expect?* she asked herself. *You've never been the kind of person who inspires tender feelings. You don't want to be.* "Fine," she said carelessly. "I won't." Moving to the coffeepot, she filled her mug again. "Aren't you eating?"

"I ate before." Aaron flipped the eggs, then reached for a plate.

She eyed his back with dislike. "I realize I'm keeping you from a lot of pressing matters. Why don't you just send me up with one of your men?"

"I said I'd take you." He piled her plate with food, then dropped it unceremoniously on the table.

Chin lifted, Jillian took her seat. "Suit yourself, Murdock."

He turned to see her hack a slice from the ham. "I always do." On impulse he grabbed the back of her head and covered her mouth in a long, ruthlessly thorough kiss that left them both simmering with anger and need.

When it was done, Jillian put all her concentration into keeping her hands steady. "A man should be more cautious," she said mildly as she cut another slice, "when a woman's holding a knife."

With a short laugh, he dropped into the chair across from her. "Caution doesn't seem to be something I hold on to well around you." Sipping his coffee, Aaron watched her as she worked her way systematically through the meal. Maybe it was too late to realize that intimacy between them had been a mistake, but if he could keep their relationship on its old footing otherwise, he might get his feelings back in line.

"You know, you should've bought a plane for Utopia years ago," he commented, perfectly aware that it would annoy her.

Her gaze lifted from her plate, slow and deliberate. "Is that so?"

"Only an idiot argues with progress."

Jillian tapped her fork against her empty plate. "What a fascinating statement," she said sweetly. "Do you have any other suggestions on how I might improve the running of Utopia?"

"As a matter of fact—" Aaron drained his coffee "—I could come up with several."

"Really." She set down the fork before she stabbed him with it. "Would you like me to tell you what you can do with each and every one of them?"

"Maybe later." He rose. "Let's get going. The day's half gone already."

Grinding her teeth, Jillian followed him out the back door. She thought it was a pity she'd wasted even a moment on gratitude.

The small two-seater plane gave her a bad moment. She eyed the propellers while Aaron checked the gauges before takeoff. She trusted things with four legs or four wheels. There, she felt, you had some control—a control she'd be relinquishing the moment Aaron took the plane off the ground. With a show of indifference, she hooked her seat belt while he started the engine.

"Ever been up in one of these?" he asked idly. He slipped on sunglasses before he started down the narrow paved runway.

"Of course I went up in the one I bought." She didn't

mention the jitters that one ride had given her. As much as she hated to agree with him, a plane was a necessary part of ranch life in the late twentieth century.

The engine roared and the ground tilted away. She'd just have to get used to it, she reminded herself, since she was going to learn to fly herself. She let her hands lie loosely on her knees and ignored the rolling pitch of her stomach.

"Are you the only one who flies this?" *This tuna can with propellers,* she thought dismally.

"No, two of our men are licensed pilots. It isn't smart to have only one person who can handle a specific job."

She nodded. "Yes. I've had a man on the payroll for over a month who can fly, but I'm going to have to get a license myself."

He glanced over. "I could teach you." Aaron noticed that her fingers were moving back and forth rhythmically over her knees. Nerves, he realized with some surprise. She hid them very well. "These little jobs're small," he said idly. "But the beauty is maneuverability. You can set them down in a pasture if you have to and hardly disturb the cattle."

"They're very small," Jillian muttered.

"Look down," he suggested. "It's very big."

She did so because she wouldn't, for a moment, have let him know how badly she wanted to be safe on the ground. Oddly her stomach stopped jumping when she did. Her fingers relaxed.

The landscape rolled under them, green and fresh, with strips of brown and amber so neat and tidy they seemed laid out with a ruler. She saw the stream that ran through her property and his, winding blue. Cattle were clumps of black and brown and red. Two young foals frol-

icked in a pasture while adult horses sunned themselves
and grazed. She saw men riding below. Now and again
one would take off his hat and wave it in a salute. Aaron
dipped his wings in answer. Laughing, Jillian looked farther, to the plains and isolated mountains.

"It's fabulous. God, sometimes I look at it and I can't
believe it belongs to me."

"I know." He skimmed the border line and banked
the plane over her land. "You can't get tired of looking
at it, smelling it."

She rested her head against the window. He loves it as
much as I do, she thought. Those five years in Billings
must have eaten at him. Every time she thought of it, of
the five years he'd given up, her admiration for him grew.

"Don't laugh," she told him and watched him glance
over curiously. No, he wouldn't laugh, she realized.
"When I was little—the first time I came out—I got a
box and dug up a couple handfuls of pasture to take home
with me. It didn't stay sweet for long, but it didn't matter."

Good God, sometimes she was so totally disarming it
took his breath away. "How long did you keep it?"

"Until my mother found it and threw it away."

He had to bite back an angry remark on insensitiv-
ity and ignorance. "She didn't understand you," Aaron
said instead.

"No, of course not." She gave a quick laugh at the
idea. Who could've expected her to? "Look, that's Gil's
truck." The idea of waving down to him distracted her so
that she missed Aaron's smoldering look. He'd had some
rocky times with his own father, some painful times, but
he'd always been understood.

"Tell me about your family."

Jillian turned her head to look at him, not quite trusting the fact that she couldn't see his eyes through his tinted sunglasses. "No, not now." She looked back out the window. "I wish I knew what I was looking for," she murmured.

So do I, he thought grimly and banked down his frustration. It wasn't going to work, he decided. He wasn't going to be able to talk himself out of needing her, all of her, any time soon. "Maybe you'll know when you see it. Could you figure if they took more cattle from any specific section?"

"It seems the north section was the hardest hit. I can't figure out how it got by me. Five hundred head, right under my nose."

"You wouldn't be the first," he reminded her. "Or the last. If you were going to drive cattle out of your north section, where would you go with them?"

"If they weren't mine," she said dryly, "I suppose I'd load them up and get them over the border."

"Maybe." He wondered if his own idea would be any harder for her to take. "Packaged beef's a lot easier to transport than it is on the hoof."

Slowly she turned back to him. She'd thought of it herself—more than once. But every time she'd pushed it aside. The last fragile hope of recovering what was hers would be lost. "I know that." Her voice was calm, her eyes steady. "If that's what was done, there's still the matter of catching who did it. They're not going to get away with it."

Aaron grinned in pure admiration. "Okay. Then let's think about it from this angle a minute. You've got the cattle—the cows are worth a lot more than the calves at this point, so maybe you're going to ship them off to greener pastures for a while. Unless we're dealing with a bunch of idiots, they're not going to slaughter a registered cow for the few hundred the calf would bring."

"A bunch of idiots couldn't have rustled my cattle," she said precisely.

"No." He nodded in simple agreement. "The steers, now…it might be a smart choice to pick out a quiet spot and butcher them. The meat would bring in some quick cash while you worked out the deal for the rest." He made a slight adjustment in course and headed north.

"If you were smarter still, you'd have already set up a deal for the cows and the yearlings," Jillian pointed out. "That accounts for nearly half of what I lost. If I were using a trailer, and slipping them out a few head at a time, I'd make use of one of the canyons in the mountains."

"Yeah. Thought we'd take a look."

Her euphoria was gone, though the landscape below was a rambling map of color and texture. The ground grew more uneven, with the asphalt two-lane road cutting through the twists and angles. The barren clump of mountain wasn't majestic like its brothers farther west, but sat alone, inhabited by coyotes and wildcats who preferred to keep man at a distance.

Aaron took the plane higher and circled. Jillian looked down at jagged peaks and flat-bottomed canyons. Yes, if she had butchering in mind, no place made better sense. Then she saw the vultures, and her heart sank down to her stomach.

"I'm going to set her down," Aaron said simply.

Jillian said nothing but began to check off her options if they found what she thought they would. There were a few economies she could and would have to make before winter, even after the livestock auction at the end of the summer. The old Jeep would simply have to be repaired again instead of being replaced. There were two foals she could sell and keep her books in the black. Checks and balances, she thought as the plane bumped on the ground. Nothing personal.

Aaron shut off the engine. "Why don't you wait here while I take a look?"

"My cattle," she said simply and climbed out of the plane.

The ground was hard and dusty from the lack of rain. She could smell its faintly metallic odor, so unlike the scent of grass and animals that permeated her own land. With no trees for shade, the sun beat down hard and bright. She heard the flap of a vulture's wings as one circled in and settled on a ridge.

It wasn't difficult going over the low rocky ground through the break in the mountain. No problem at all for a four-wheel drive, she thought and angled the brim of her hat to compensate for the glare of sunlight.

The canyon wasn't large and was cupped between three walls of rock, worn gray with some stubborn sage clinging here and there. Their boots made echoing hollow sounds. From somewhere, surprisingly, she heard a faint tinkling of water. The spring must be small, she mused, or she'd smell it. All she smelled here was…

She stopped and let out a long breath. "Oh, God."

Aaron recognized the odor, sickeningly hot and sweet, even as she did. "Jillian—"

She shook her head. There was no longer room for comfort or hope. "Damn. I wonder how many."

They walked on and saw, behind a rock, the bones a coyote had dug up and picked clean.

Aaron swore in a low soft stream that was all the more pungent in its control. "There's a shovel in the plane," he began. "We can see what's here, or go back for the sheriff."

"It's my business." Jillian wiped her damp hands on her jeans. "I'd rather know now."

He knew better than to suggest she wait at the plane again. In her place, he'd have done precisely what she was ready to do. Without another word, he left her alone.

When she heard his footsteps die away, she squeezed her eyes tight, doubled her hands into fists. She wanted to scream out the useless, impotent rage. What was hers had been stolen, slaughtered, and sold. There could be no restitution now, no bringing back this part of what she'd worked for. Slowly, painfully, she brought herself under tight control. No restitution, but she'd have justice. Sometimes it was just a cleaner word for revenge.

When Aaron returned with the shovel, he saw the anger glittering in her eyes. He preferred it to that brief glimpse of despair he'd seen. "Let's just make sure. After we know, we go into town for the sheriff."

She agreed with a nod. If they found one hide, it would be one too many. The shovel bit into the ground with a thud.

Aaron didn't have to dig long. He glanced up at Jillian to see her face perfectly composed, then uncovered the first stack of hides. Though the stench was vile, she crouched down and made out the *U* of her brand.

"Well, this should be proof enough," she murmured and stayed where she was because she wanted to drop her head to her knees and weep. "How many—"

"Let the sheriff deal with it," Aaron bit off, as infuriated by their find as he would have been if the hide had borne his own brand. With an oath, he scraped the shovel across the loosened dirt and dislodged something.

Jillian reached down and picked it up. The glove was filthy, but the leather was quality—the kind any cowhand would need for working with the wire. A bubble of excitement rose in her. "One of them must've lost it when they were burying these." She sprang to her feet, holding the glove in both hands. "Oh, they're going to pay for it," she said savagely. "This is one mistake they're going to pay for. Most of my hands score their initials on the inside." Ignoring the grime, she turned the bottom of the glove over and found them.

Aaron watched her color drain as she stared at the inside flap of the glove. Her fingers whitened against the leather before she lifted her eyes to his. Without a word, she handed it to him. Watching her, he took the soiled leather in his hand, then glanced down. There were initials inside. His own.

His face was expressionless when he looked back at her. "Well," he said coolly, "it looks like we're back to square one, doesn't it?" He passed the glove back to her. "You'll need this for the sheriff."

She sent him a look of smoldering anger that cut straight through him. "Do you think I'm stupid enough to believe you had anything to do with this?" Spinning around, she stalked away before he had a chance to understand, much less react. Then he stood where he was for another instant as it struck him, forcibly.

He caught her before she had clambered over the last rocks leading out of the canyon. His hands weren't gentle as he whirled her around, his breath wasn't steady.

"Maybe I do." She jerked away only to have him grab her again. "Maybe I want you to tell me why you don't."

"I might believe a lot of things of you, I might not like everything I believe. But not this." Her voice broke and she fought to even it. "Integrity—integrity isn't something that has to be polite. You wouldn't cut my lines and you wouldn't butcher my cattle."

Her words alone would've shaken him, but he saw her eyes were swimming with tears. What he knew about comforting a woman could be said in one sentence: get out of the way. Aaron held on to her and lifted a hand to her cheek. "Jillian…"

"No! For God's sake don't be kind now." She tried to turn away, only to find herself held close, her face buried against his shoulder. His body was like a solid wall of support and understanding. If she leaned against it now, what would she do when he removed it? "Aaron, don't do this." But her hands clutched at him as he held on.

"I've got to do something," he murmured, stroking her hair. "Lean on me for a minute. It won't hurt you."

But it did. She'd always found tears a painful experience. There was no stopping them, so she wept with the passion they both understood while he held her near the barren mountain under the strong light of the sun.

Chapter Nine

Jillian didn't have time to grieve over her losses. Over two hundred hides had been unearthed from the canyon floor, all bearing the Utopia brand. She'd had interviews with the sheriff, talked to the Cattlemen's Association and dealt with the visits and calls from neighboring ranchers. After her single bout of weeping, her despair had iced over to a frigid rage she found much more useful. It carried her through each day, pushing her to work just that much harder, helping her not to break down when she was faced with sympathetic words.

For two weeks she knew there was little talk of anything else, on her ranch or for miles around. There hadn't been a rustling of this size in thirty years. It became easier for her when the talk began to die down, though it became equally more difficult to go on believing that the investigation would yield fruit. She had accepted the loss of her cattle because she had no choice, but she couldn't accept the total victory of the thieves.

They were clever—she had to admit it. They'd pulled off a rustling as smooth as anything the old-timers in the area claimed to remember. The cut wire, Aaron's glove; deliberate and subtle "mistakes" that were designed to turn her attention toward Murdock land. Perhaps the first of them had worked well enough to give the rustlers just enough extra time to cover their tracks. Jillian's only comfort was that she hadn't fallen for the second.

Aaron had given her no choice but to accept his support. She'd balked, particularly after recovering from her lapse in the canyon, but he'd proven to be every bit as obstinate as she. He'd taken her to the sheriff himself, stood by her with the Cattlemen's Association, and one evening had come by to drag her forty miles to a movie. Through it all he wasn't gentle with her, didn't pamper. For that more than anything else, Jillian felt she owed him. Kindness left her no defense and edged her back toward despair.

As the days passed, Jillian forced herself to take each one of them separately. She could fill the hours with dozens of tasks and worries and responsibilities. Then there wouldn't be time to mourn. For now, her first concern was the breeding of her mare with Aaron's stallion.

He'd brought two of his own men with him. With Gil and another of Jillian's hands, they would hold the restraining ropes on the stallion. Once he caught the scent of Jillian's mare in heat, he'd be as wild as his father had been, and as dangerous.

When Jillian brought Delilah into the paddock, she cast a look at the stallion surrounded by men. A gorgeous creature, she thought, wholly male—not quite tamed. Her gaze flicked over to Aaron, who stood at the horse's head.

His dark hair sprang from under his hat to curl carelessly over his neck and ears. His body was erect and lean. One might look at him and think he was perfectly relaxed. But Jillian saw more—the coiled tension beneath, the power that was always there and came out unexpectedly. Eyes nearly as dark as his hair were half hidden by the brim of his hat as he both soothed and controlled his stallion.

No mount could've suited him more. Her lover, she realized with the peculiar little jolt that always accompanied the thought. Would her nerves ever stop skidding along whenever she remembered what it was like to be with him—or imagined what it would be like to be with him again? He'd opened up so many places inside of her. When she was alone, it came close to frightening her; when she saw him, her feelings had nothing to do with fear.

Maybe it was the thick, heavy air that threatened rain or the half-nervous, half-impatient quiverings of her mare, but Jillian's heart was already pounding. The horses caught each other's scent.

Samson plunged and began to fight against the ropes. With his head thrown back, his mane flowing, he called the mare. One of the men cursed in reflex. Jillian tightened her grip on Delilah's bridle as the mare began to struggle—against the restraint or against the inevitable, Jillian would never be sure. She soothed her with words that weren't even heard. Samson gave a long, passionate whinny that was answered. Delilah reared, nearly ripping the bridle from Jillian's hand. Watching the struggle and flying hooves, Aaron felt his heart leap into his throat.

"Help her hold the mare," he ordered.

"No." Jillian fought for new purchase and got it. "She doesn't trust anyone but me. Let's get it done." A long line of sweat held her shirt to her back.

The stallion was wild, plunging and straining, his coat glossy with sweat, his eyes fierce. With five men surrounding him, he reared back, hanging poised and magnificent for a heartbeat before he mounted the mare.

The horses were beyond any thought, any fear, any respect for the humans now. Instinct drove them, primitive and consuming. Jillian forgot her aching arms and the rivulets of sweat that poured down her sides. Her feet were planted, her leg muscles taut as she pitted all her strength toward keeping the mare from bolting or rearing and injuring herself.

She was caught up in the fire and desperation of the horses, and the elemental beauty. The air was ripe with the scent of sweat and animal passion. She couldn't breathe but that she drew it in. Since she'd been a child she'd seen animals breed, helped with the matings whenever necessary, but now, for the first time, she understood the consuming force that drove them. The need of a woman for a man could be equally unrestrained, equally primitive.

Then it began to rain, slowly, heavily, coolly over her skin. With her face lifted to the mare's, Jillian let it flow over her cheeks. Another of the men swore as the ropes grew wet and slippery.

When her eyes met Aaron's, she found her heart was still in her throat, the beat as lurching and uneven as the mare's would be. She felt the flash of need that was both shocking and basic. He saw and recognized. As the rain poured over him, he smiled. Her thigh muscles went lax so quickly she had to fight to strengthen them again and maintain her control of the mare. But she didn't look away. Excitement was nearly painful, knowledge enervating. As if his hands were on her, she felt the need pulse from him.

Gradually a softer feeling drifted in. There was a strange sensation of being safe even though the safety was circled with dangers. This time she didn't question it or fight against it. They were helping to create new life. Now there was a bond between them.

The horses' sides were heaving when they drew them apart. The rain continued to sluice down. She heard Gil give a cackle of laughter over something one of the men said under his breath. Jillian forgot them, giving her full attention to the mare. Soothing and murmuring, she walked her back into the stables.

The light was dim, the air heavy with the scent of dry hay and oiled leather. After removing the bridle, Jillian began to groom the mare with long slow strokes until the quivering stopped.

"There now, love." Jillian nuzzled her face into Delilah's neck. "There's not much any of us can do about their bodies."

"Is that how you look at it?"

Jillian turned her head to see Aaron standing at the entrance to the stall. He was drenched and apparently unconcerned about it. She saw his eyes make a short but very thorough scan of her face—a habit he'd developed since their discovery in the canyon. She knew he looked for signs of strain and somewhere along the line had stopped resenting it.

"I'm not a horse," she returned easily and patted Delilah's neck.

Aaron came into the stall and ran his hands over the mare himself. She was dry and still. "She all right?"

"Mmmm. We were right not to field breed them," she added. "Both of them are spirited enough to have done damage." Laughing, she turned to him. "The foal's going to be a champion. I can feel it. There was something special out there just now, something important." On impulse, she threw her arms around Aaron's neck and kissed him ardently.

Surprise held him very still. His hands came to her waist more in instinct than response. It was the first time she'd given him any spontaneous show of affection or offered him any part of herself without reluctance. The ache of need wove through him, throbbing with what he now understood was connected to passion but not exclusive of it.

She was still smiling when she drew away, but he wasn't. Before the puzzlement over what was in his eyes had fully registered with her, Aaron drew her back against him and just held on. Jillian found the unexpected sweetness disconcerting and wonderful.

"Hadn't you better see to Samson?" she murmured.

"My men have already taken him back."

She rubbed her cheek against his wet shirt. They'd steal some time, she thought. An hour, a moment—just some time. "I'll fix you some coffee."

"Yeah." He slipped an arm around her shoulders as they went back into the rain. "Heard anything from the sheriff?"

"Nothing new."

They crossed the ranch yard together, both too accustomed to the elements to heed the rain as anything but necessary.

"It's got the whole county in an uproar."

"I know." They paused at the kitchen door to rid themselves of muddy boots. Jillian ran a careless hand through her hair and scattered rain. "It might do more good than anything else. Every rancher I know or've heard of in this part of Montana's got his eyes open. And any number over the border, from what I'm told. I'm toying with offering a reward."

"Not a bad idea." Aaron sat down at the table and stretched out long legs as Jillian brewed coffee. The rain was a constant soothing sound against the roof and windows. He found an odd comfort there in the gloomy light, in the warm kitchen. It might be like this if it were their ranch they were in rather than hers, or his. It might be like this if he could ever make her a permanent part of his life.

It took only a second for the thoughts to go through his head, and another for him to be jolted by them. Marriage. He was thinking marriage. He sat for a moment while the idea settled over him, not uncomfortably but inevitably. *I'll be damned,* he thought and nearly laughed before he brought himself back to what she'd been saying.

"Let me do it," he said briskly. She turned, words of refusal on the tip of her tongue. "Wait," Aaron ordered. "Hear me out. My father got wind of the cut wire." He watched her subside before she turned away for mugs. "Obviously it didn't set well with him. These old stories between the Murdocks and Barons don't need much fanning to come to life again. Some people are going to think, even if they don't say, that he's eating your beef."

Jillian poured the coffee, then turned with a mug in each hand. "I don't think it."

"I know." He gave her an odd look, holding out a hand. She placed a mug in it, but Aaron set it down on the table and lightly took her fingers. "That means a great deal to me." Because she didn't know how to respond to that tone, she didn't respond at all but only continued to look down at him. "Jillian, this has set him back some. A few years ago the idea of people thinking he'd done something unethical or illegal would probably have pleased him. He's not as strong as he was. Your grandfather was a rival, but he was also a contemporary, someone he understood, even respected. It would help if he could do something. I don't like to ask for favors any more than you like to accept them."

She looked down at their joined hands, both tanned, both lean and strong, yet hers was so easily swallowed up by his. "You love him very much."

"Yes." It was said very simply, in the same emotionless tone he'd used to tell her his father was dying. This time Jillian understood him better.

"I'd appreciate it if you'd stake the reward."

He laced his fingers with hers. "Good."

"Want some more coffee?"

"No." That wicked light of humor shot into his eyes. "But I was thinking I should help you out of those wet clothes."

With a laugh, Jillian sat down. "You know I'm still planning on beating out the Double M on July Fourth."

"I was hoping you were planning on it," Aaron returned easily. "But about doing it…"

"You a gambling man, Murdock?"

He lifted his brow. "It's been said."

"I've got fifty that says my Hereford bull will take the blue ribbon over anything you have to put against him."

Aaron contemplated the dregs of his coffee as if considering. If everything he'd heard about Jillian's bull was true, he was tolerably sure he was throwing money away. "Fifty," he agreed and smiled. "And another fifty that says I beat your time in the calf roping."

"My pleasure." Jillian held out a hand to seal it.

"Are you competing in anything else?"

"I don't think so." She stretched her back, thinking what a luxury it was to sit stone still in the middle of the afternoon. "The barrel racing doesn't much interest me and I know better than to try bronc riding."

"Know better?"

"Two reasons. First the men would do a lot of muttering and complaining if I did. And second—" she grinned and shrugged "—I'd probably break my neck."

It occurred to him that she wouldn't have admitted the second to him even a week before. Laughing, he leaned over and kissed her. But the friendly kiss stirred something, and cupping the back of her neck, he kissed her again, lingeringly. "It's your mouth," he murmured while his fingertips toyed with her skin. "Once I get started on it, I can't find a single reason to stop."

Her breath fluttered unevenly through her lips, through his. "It's the middle of the day."

He smiled, then teased her tongue with the tip of his. "Yeah. Are you going to take me to bed?"

The eyes that were nearly closed opened again. In them he saw desire and confusion, a combination he found very much to his liking. "I have to check the—" His teeth nipped persuasively into her bottom lip.

"The what?" he whispered as her words ended on a little shiver.

"The, uh…" His lips were skimming over hers in something much more provocative than a kiss. The lazy caress of his tongue kept them moist. His fingers were very light on the back of her neck. Their knees were brushing. Somehow she could already feel the press of his body against hers and the issuing warmth the pressure always brought. "I can't think," she murmured.

It was what he wanted. Or he wanted her to think of him and only him. For himself, he needed to know that she put him first this time, or at least her need for him. Over her ranch, her men, her cattle, her ambitions. If he could draw her feelings out to match his once, he might be able to do so again and again until she was as rashly in love with him as he was with her. "Why do you have to?" he asked and, rising, drew her to her feet. "You can feel."

Yes, with her arms around him and her head cradled against his chest, she could feel. Emotions nudging at her, urging her to acknowledge them—needs, pressing and searingly urgent, demanding that she fulfill them. They were all connected to him, the hungers, the tiny fears, the wishes. She couldn't deny them all. Perhaps, just this once, she didn't need to.

"I want to make love with you." She sighed with the words and nuzzled closer. "I can't seem to stop wanting to."

He tilted her head back so that he could see her face, then, half smiling, skimmed his thumb over her jaw. "In the middle of the day?"

She tossed the hair out of her eyes and settled her linked hands comfortably behind his neck. "I'm going to have you now, Murdock. Right now."

He glanced at the tidy kitchen table and his grin was wicked. "Right now?"

"Your mind takes some unusual turns," she commented. "I think I can give you time enough to get upstairs." Releasing him, she walked over and flicked off the coffeepot. "If you hurry." Even as he grinned, she crossed back to him. Putting her hands on his shoulders, she leaped up, locking her legs around his waist, her arms around his neck. "You know where the stairs are?"

"I can find them."

She pressed her lips to his throat. "Top of the stairs, second door on the right," she told him as she began to please herself with his taste.

As Aaron wound through the house Jillian wondered what he would think or say if he knew she'd never done anything quite like this before. She'd come to realize that the man from her youth hadn't been a lover, but an incident. It took more than one night to make a lover. She'd feel much too foolish telling Aaron he was the first—much too inadequate. How could she tell him that the first rush of passion had loosened the locks she'd put on parts of herself? How could she trust her own feelings when they were so muddled and new?

She rested her head on his shoulder a moment and closed her eyes. For once in her life she was going to enjoy without worrying about the consequences. Shifting, she leaned back so that she could smile at him. "You're out of shape, Murdock. One flight of stairs and your heart's pounding."

"So's yours," he pointed out. "And you had a ride up."

"Must be the rain," she said loftily.

"Your clothes're still damp." He moved into the room she'd directed him to and glanced around briefly.

It was consistent with her style—understated femininity, practicality. It was a room without frills or pastels, but he'd have known it for a woman's. It had none of the feminine disorder of his sister's old room at the ranch, nor the subtle elegance of his mother's. Like the woman he still held, Aaron found the room unique.

Plain walls, plain floors, easy colors, no clutter. No, Jillian wasn't a woman to clutter her life. She wouldn't give herself the time. Perhaps it was the few indulgences she'd allowed herself that gave him the most insight.

A stoneware vase with fluted edges held pussy willow—soft brown nubs that wouldn't quite be considered a flower. There was a small carved box on her dresser he was certain would play some soft tune when the top was lifted. She might lift it sometimes when she was alone, or lonely. On the wall was a watercolor with all the bleeding passion of sunset. How carefully, how painstakingly, he thought, she'd controlled whatever romanticism she was prone to. How surprised she'd be to know that because she did, it only shouted out louder.

Recognizing his survey, Jillian cocked her head. "There's not a lot to see in here."

"You'd be surprised," he murmured.

The enigmatic answer made her glance around herself. "I don't spend a lot of time in here," she began, realizing it was rather sparse even compared to his room in the white frame house.

"You misunderstood me." Aaron let his hands run up her sides as she slid down. "I'd've known this was your room. It even smells like you."

She laughed, pleased without knowing why. "Are you being poetic?"

"Maybe."

Lifting a hand, she toyed with the top button of his shirt. "Want me to help you out of those wet clothes?"

"Absolutely."

She began to oblige him, then shot him an amused

look as she slid the shirt over his shoulders. "If you expect me to seduce you, you're going to be disappointed."

His stomach muscles were already knotted with need. "I am?"

"I don't know any tricks." Before he could comment, she launched herself at him, overbalancing him so that they tumbled back onto the bed. "No wiles," she continued. "No subtlety."

"You're a pushy lady, all right." He could feel the heat of her body through her damp shirt.

"I like the way you look, Murdock." She trailed her fingers through his thick dark hair as she studied his face. "It used to annoy the hell out of me, but now it's kind of nice."

"The way I look?"

"That I like the way you look. It's ruthless," she decided, skimming a finger down his jawline. "And when you smile it can be very charming—the kind of charm a smart woman recognizes as highly dangerous."

He grinned, cupping her hips in his hands. "Did you?"

"I'm a smart woman." With a little laugh, she rubbed her nose against his. "I know a rattlesnake when I see one."

"But not enough to keep your distance."

"Apparently not—then I don't always look for a long, safe ride."

But a short, rocky one, he thought as her lips came down to his. He'd be happy to give her the wisps of danger and trouble, he decided, drawing her closer. But she was going to find out he intended it to last.

He started to shift her, but then her lips were racing over his face. Soft, light, but with a heat that seeped right into him. Her long, limber body seemed almost weightless over his, yet he could feel every line and curve. Moisture still clung to her hair and reminded him of the first time, when he'd dragged her to the ground, consumed with need and fury. Now he was helpless against her rapid assault on his senses. No, she had no wiles, nor he the patience for them.

He could hear the rain patter rhythmically against the window. He could smell it on her. When his lips brushed through her hair, he could taste it. It was almost as though they were alone in a quiet field, with the scent of wet grass and the rain slipping over their skin. The light was gray and indistinct; her mouth was vivid wherever it touched him.

She hadn't known it could be so exciting to weaken a man with herself. Feeling the strength drain from him made her almost light-headed with power. She'd met him on equal terms, and from time to time to her disadvantage, but never when she'd been so certain she could dominate. Her laugh was low and confident as it whispered along his skin, warm and sultry as it brushed over his lips.

He seemed content to lie still while she learned of him. She thought the air grew thicker. Perhaps that alone weighed him down and kept him from challenging her control. Her hands were eager, rushing here then there to linger over some small fascination: tight cords of muscle that ran down his upper arms to bunch and gather at her touch; smooth, taut skin that was surprisingly soft over his rib cage; the narrow, raised scar along his hipbone.

"Where'd you get this?" she murmured, outlining it with a fingertip.

"Brahma," he managed as she tugged his jeans down

infinitesimally lower. "Jillian—" But her lips drifted over his again and silenced him.

"A bull?"

"Rodeo, when I had more guts than brains."

She heard the sound of pleasure in his throat as her mouth journeyed down. His body was a treasure of delight to her. In the soft rainy light she could see it, brown and hard against the plain, serviceable bedspread. Rangy and loose limbed, it was made for riding well and long, toughened by physical work, burnished by the elements. Tiny jumping thrills coursed through her as she thought that it was hers to touch and taste, to look at as long as she liked.

She took a wandering route down him, feeling his skin heat and pulse as she stripped him. The room was filled with the sound of rain and quickening breathing. It was all she heard. The sweet scent of passion enveloped her—a fragrance mixed of the essence of both of them. Intimate. She could taste desire on his skin, a heady flavor that made her greedy when she felt the thud of his heart under her tongue. Even when her excitement grew until her blood was racing, she could have luxuriated in him for hours. The sharp urgency she'd once felt had mellowed into a glowing contentment. She pleasured him. It was more than she'd believed she could do for anyone.

There were flames in his stomach, spreading. God, she was like a drug and he was lost, half dreaming while his flesh was burning up. Her fingers were so cool as they tortured him, her mouth so hot. He'd never explored his own vulnerabilities; it had always been more important to work around them or ignore them altogether. Now he had no choice and he found the sensation incredible.

She aroused, teased and withdrew only to arouse

again. Her enervating, openmouthed kisses ranged over him while her hands stroked and explored lazily, finding point after sensitive point until he trembled. No woman had ever made him tremble. Even as this thought ran through his ravaged mind, she caused him to do so again. Then he knew she was driving him mad.

The wind kicked up, hurling rain against the window, then retreating with a distant howl. Something crazed sprang into him. Roughly he grabbed her, rolling over and pinning her, her arms above her head. His breathing was labored as he looked down.

Her chin was up, her hair spread out, her eyes glowing. There was no fear on her face, and nothing of submission. Though her own breathing came quickly, there was challenge in the look she gave him. A dare. He could take her, take her anyway he chose. And when he did so, he'd be taken, as well.

So be it, he thought with a muffled oath. His mouth devoured hers.

She matched his urgency, aroused simply by knowing she had taken him to the edge. He wanted her. Her. In some ways he knew her better than anyone ever had, and still he wanted her. She'd waited so long for that, not even knowing that she'd waited at all. She couldn't think of this, or what the effects might be when his long desperate kisses were rousing her, when she could see small, silvery explosions going on behind her closed lids.

She felt him tug at the buttons of her shirt, heard him swear. When she felt the material rip away she knew only that at last she could feel his flesh against hers. As it was meant to be. His hands wouldn't be still and drove her as she had driven him. He pulled clothes from her in a frenzy as his mouth greedily searched. Somewhere in her hazy brain she felt wonder that she could bring him to this just by being.

Their bodies pressed, their limbs entwined. Their mouths joined. He thought the mixing of their tastes the most intimate thing he'd ever known. Under him she arched, more a demand than an offer. He raised himself over her, wanting to see her, wanting her to see him when he made her his.

Her eyes were dark, misted with need. Need for him. He knew he had what he'd wanted: she thought of nothing and no one else. "I wanted you from the first minute," he murmured as he slipped inside her.

He saw the change in her face as he moved slowly, the flicker of pleasure, the softening that came just before delirium. Pushing back the rushing need in his blood, he drew out the sensations with a control so exquisite it burned in his muscles. Lowering his head, he nibbled at her lips.

She couldn't bear it. She couldn't stop it. When she thought she finally understood what passion was, he showed her there was more. Sensation after sensation slammed into her, leaving her weak and gasping. Even as the pressure built inside her, drumming under her skin and threatening to implode, she wanted it to go on. She could have wept from the joy of it, moaned from the ache. Unwittingly it was she who changed things simply by breathing his name as if she knew no other.

The instant his control snapped, she felt it. There was time only for a tingle of nervous excitement before he was catapulting her with him into a dark, frantic sky where it was all thunder and no air.

Chapter Ten

The lengthy, dusty drive into town and the soaring temperatures couldn't dull the spirit. It was the Fourth of July, and the long, raucous holiday had barely begun.

By early morning the fairgrounds were crowded—ranchers, punchers, wives and sweethearts, and those looking for a sweetheart to share the celebration with. Prized animals were on display to be discussed, bragged about and studied. Quilts and pies and preserves waited to be judged. As always, there was a pervasive air of expectancy.

Cowboys wore their best uniform—crisp shirts and pressed jeans, with the boots and hats that were saved and cherished for special occasions. Belt buckles gleamed. Children sported their finest, which promised to be dirt streaked and grass stained by the end of the long day.

For Jillian, it was the first carefree day in the season,

and one she was all the more determined to enjoy because of her recent problems. For twenty-four hours she was going to forget her worries, the numbers in her account books and the title of boss she worked day after day to earn. On this one sun-filled, heat-soaked day, she was going to simply enjoy the fact that she was part of a unique group of men and women who both lived and played off the land.

There was an excited babble of voices near the paddock and stable areas. The pungent aroma of animals permeated the air. From somewhere in the distance she could already hear fiddle music. There'd be more music after sundown, and dancing. Before then, there'd be games for young and old, the judgings, and enough food to feed the entire county twice over. She could smell the spicy aroma of an apple pie, still warm, as someone passed her with a laden basket. Her mouth watered.

First things first, she reminded herself as she wandered over to check out her bull's competition.

There were six entries altogether, all well muscled and fierce to look at. Horns gleamed, sharp and dangerous. Hides were sleek and well tended. Objectively Jillian studied each one, noting their high points and their weaknesses. There wasn't any doubt that her stiffest competitor would be the Double M's entry. He'd taken the blue ribbon three years running.

Not this year, she told him silently as her gaze skimmed over him. Pound for pound, he probably had her bull beat, but she thought hers had a bit more breadth in the shoulders. And there was no mistaking that her Hereford's coloring and markings were perfect, the shape of his head superior.

Time for you to move over and make room for new

blood, she told the reigning champion. Rather pleased with herself, she hooked her thumbs in her back pockets. First place and that little swatch of blue ribbon would go a long way to making up for everything that'd gone wrong in the past few weeks.

"Know a winner when you see one?"

Jillian turned at the thready voice that still held a hint of steel. Paul Murdock was dressed to perfection, but his hawklike face had little color under his Stetson. His cane was elegant and tipped with gold, but he leaned on it heavily. As they met hers, however, his eyes were very much alive and challenging.

"I know a winner when I see one," she agreed, then let her gaze skim over to her own bull.

He gave a snort of laughter and shifted his weight. "Been hearing a lot about your new boy." He studied the bull with a faint frown and couldn't prevent a twinge of envy. He, too, knew a winner when he saw one.

He felt the sun warm on his back and for a moment, for just a moment, wished desperately for his youth again. Years ate at strength. If he were fifty again and owned that bull... But he wasn't a man to sigh. "Got possibilities," he said shortly.

She recognized something of the envy and smiled. Nothing could've pleased her more. "Nothing wrong with second place," she said lightly.

Murdock glanced over sharply, pinned her eyes with his, then laughed when she didn't falter. "Damn, you're quite a woman, aren't you, Jillian Baron? The old man taught you well enough."

Her smile held more challenge than humor. "Well enough to run Utopia."

"Could be," he acknowledged. "Times change." There

wasn't any mistaking the resentment in the statement, but she understood it. Sympathized with it. "This rustling…" He glanced over to see her face, impassive and still. Murdock had a quick desire to sit across a poker table from her with a large, juicy pot in between. "It's a damn abomination," he said with a savagery that made him momentarily breathless. "There was a time a man'd have his neck stretched for stealing another man's beef."

"Hanging them won't get my cattle back," Jillian said calmly.

"Aaron told me about what you found in the canyon." Murdock stared at the well-muscled bulls. These were the life's blood of their ranches—the profit and the status. "A hard thing for you—for all of us," he added, shifting his eyes to hers again. "I want you to understand that your grandfather and I had our problems. He was a stubborn, stiff-necked bastard."

"Yes," Jillian agreed easily, so easily Murdock laughed. "You'd understand a man like that," she added.

Murdock stopped laughing to fix her with a glittering look. She returned it. "I understand a man like that," he acknowledged. "And I want you to know that if this had happened to him, I'd've been behind him, just as I'd've expected him to be behind me. Personal feelings don't come into it. We're ranchers."

It was said with a sting of pride that made her own chin lift. "I do know it."

"It'd be easy to say the cattle could've been driven over to my land."

"Easy to say," Jillian said with a nod. "If you knew me better, Mr. Murdock, you'd know I'm not a fool. If I believed you'd had my beef on your table, you'd already be paying for it."

His lips curved in a rock-hard, admiring smile. "Baron did well by you," he said after a moment. "Though I still think a woman needs a man beside her if she's going to run a ranch."

"Be careful, Mr. Murdock, I was just beginning to think I could tolerate you."

He laughed again, so obviously pleased that Jillian grinned. "Can't change an old dog, girl." His eyes narrowed fractionally as she'd seen his son's do. It occurred to her that in forty years Aaron would look like this—that honed-down strength that was just a little bit mean. It was the kind of strength you'd want behind you when there was trouble. "I've heard my boy's had his eye on you—can't say I fault his taste."

"Have you?" she returned mildly. "Do you believe everything you hear?"

"If he hasn't had his eye on you," Murdock countered, "he's not as smart as I give him credit for. Man needs a woman to settle him down."

"Really?" Jillian said very dryly.

"Don't get fired up, girl," Murdock ordered. "There'd've been a time when I'd have had his hide for looking twice at a Baron. Times change," he repeated with obvious reluctance. "Our land has run side by side for most of this century, whether we like it or not."

Jillian took a moment to brush off her sleeve. "I'm not looking to settle anyone, Mr. Murdock. And I'm not looking for a merger."

"Sometimes we wind up getting things we're not looking for." He smiled as she stared at him. "You take my Karen—never figured to hitch myself with a beauty who always made me feel like I should wipe my feet whether I'd been in the pastures or not."

Despite herself Jillian laughed, then surprised them both by hooking her arm through his as they began to walk. "I get the feeling you're trying to bury the hatchet." When he stiffened, she muffled a chuckle and continued. "Don't *you* get fired up," she said easily. "I'm willing to try a truce. Aaron and I have…we understand each other," she decided. "I like your wife, and I can just about tolerate you."

"You're your grandmother all over again," Murdock muttered.

"Thanks." As they walked Jillian noted the few speculative glances tossed their way. Baron and Murdock arm in arm; times had indeed changed. She wondered how Clay would feel and decided, in his grudging way, he would've approved. Especially if it caused talk.

When Aaron saw them walking slowly toward the arena area, he broke off the conversation he'd been having with a puncher. Jillian tossed back her hair, tilted her head slightly toward his father's and murmured something that made the old man hoot with laughter. If he hadn't already, Aaron would've fallen in love with her at that moment.

"Hey, isn't that Jillian Baron with your paw?"

"Hmmm? Yeah." Aaron didn't waste time glancing back at the puncher when he could look at Jillian.

"She sure is easy on the eyes," the puncher concluded a bit wistfully. "Heard you and her—" He broke off, chilled by the cool, neutral look Aaron aimed at him. The cowboy coughed into his hand. "Just meant people wonder about it, seeing as the Murdocks and Barons never had much dealings with each other."

"Do they?" Aaron relieved the cowboy by grinning be-

fore he walked off. Murdocks, the puncher thought with
a shake of his head. You could never be too sure of them.

"Life's full of surprises," Aaron commented as he
walked toward them. "No blood spilled?"

"Your father and I've reached a limited understanding." Jillian smiled at him, and though they touched in
no way, Murdock was now certain the rumors he'd heard
about Jillian and his son were true. Intimacy was something people often foolishly believed they could conceal,
and rarely did.

"Your mother's got me judging the mincemeat," Murdock grumbled. This time he didn't feel that twinge of
regret for what he'd lost, but an odd contentment at seeing his slice of immortality in his son. "We'll be in the
stands later to watch you." He gave Jillian an arch look.
"Both of you."

He walked off slowly. Jillian had to stuff her hands in
her pockets to keep from helping him. That, she knew,
would be met with cold annoyance. "He came over to the
pens," Jillian told Aaron when Murdock was out of earshot. "I think he did it on purpose so that he could talk
to me. He was very kind."

"Not many people see him as kind."

"Not many people had a grandfather like Clay Baron."
She turned to Aaron and smiled.

"How are you?" He couldn't have resisted the urge
to touch her if he'd wanted to. His fingertips skimmed
along her jaw.

"How do I look?"

"You don't like me to tell you you're beautiful."

She laughed, and the under-the-lashes look she sent
him was the first flirtatious move he'd ever seen from
her. "It's a holiday."

"Spend it with me?" He held out a hand, knowing if she put hers in it, in public, where there were curious eyes and tongues that appreciated a nice bit of gossip, it would be a commitment of sorts.

Her fingers laced with his. "I thought you'd never ask."

They spent the morning doing what couples had done at county fairs for decades. There was lemonade to be drunk, contests to be watched. It was easy to laugh when the sky was clear and the sun promised a dry, golden day.

Children raced by with balloons held by sticky fingers. Teenagers flirted with the nonchalance peculiar to their age. Old-timers chewed tobacco and out-lied each other. The air was touched with the scent of food and animals, and the starch in bandbox shirts had not yet wilted with sweat.

With Aaron's arm around her, Jillian crowded to the fence to watch the greased pig contest. The ground had been flooded and churned up so that the state of the mud was perfection. The pig was slick with lard and quick, so that he eluded the five men who lunged after him. The crowd called out suggestions and hooted with laughter. The pig squealed and shot, like a bullet, out of capturing arms. Men fell on their faces and swore good-naturedly.

Jillian shot him a look, then inclined her head toward the pen where the activity was still wild and loud. "Don't you like games, Murdock?"

"I like to make up my own." He swung her around. "Now, there's this real quiet hayloft I know of."

With a laugh, she eluded him. He'd never known her to be deliberately provocative and found himself not quite certain how to deal with it. The glitter in her eyes made him decide. In one smooth move, Aaron gathered her close and kissed her soundly. There was an approving whoop from a group of cowboys behind them. When Jillian managed to untangle herself, she glanced over to see two of her own men grinning at her.

"It's a holiday," Aaron reminded her when she let out a huff of breath.

She brought her head back slowly and took his measure. Oh, he was damn proud of himself, she decided. And two could play. Her smile had him wondering just what she had up her sleeve.

"You want fireworks?" she asked, then threw her arms around him and silenced him before he could agree or deny.

While his kiss had been firm yet still friendly, hers whispered of secrets only the two of them knew. Aaron never heard the second cheer go up, but he wouldn't have been surprised to feel the ground move.

"I missed you last night, Murdock," she whispered, then went from her toes to her flat feet so that their lips parted. She took a step back before she offered her hand, and the smile on those fascinating lips was cocky.

Carefully Aaron drew air into his lungs and released it. "You're going to finish that one later, Jillian."

She only laughed again. "I certainly hope so. Let's go see if Gil can win the pie-eating contest again this year."

He went wherever she wanted and felt foolishly, and appealingly, like a kid on his first date. It was the sudden carefree aura around her. Jillian had dropped everything, all worries and responsibilities, and had given herself a day for fun. Perhaps because she felt a slight twinge of guilt, like a kid playing hooky, the day was all the sweeter.

She would have sworn the sun had never been brighter, the sky so blue. In all of her life, she couldn't remember ever laughing so easily. A slice of cherry pie was ambrosia. If she could have concentrated the day down, section by section, she would have put it into a box where she could have taken out an hour at a time when she was alone and tired. Because she was too practical to believe that possible, Jillian chose to live each moment to the fullest.

By the time the rodeo officially opened, Jillian was nearly drunk on freedom. As the Fourth of July Queen and her court rode sedately around the arena, she still clutched her bull's blue ribbon in her hand. "That's fifty you owe me," she told Aaron with a grin.

He sat on the ground exchanging dress boots for worn, patched riding favorites. "Why don't we wait and see how the second bet comes out?"

"Okay." She perched on a barrel and listened to the crowd cheer from the stands. She was riding high and knew it. Her luck had turned—there wasn't a problem she could be hit with that she couldn't handle.

A lot of cowboys and potential competitors had already collected behind the chutes. Though it all seemed very casual—the lounging, the rigging bags set carelessly against the chain link fence—there was an air of suppressed excitement. There was the scent of tobacco from the little cans invariably carried in the right rear pocket of jeans, and mink oil on leather. Already she heard the jingle of spurs and harnesses as equipment was checked. The bareback riding was first. When she heard the announcement, Jillian rose and wandered to the fence to watch.

"I'm surprised you didn't give this one a try," Aaron commented.

She tilted her head so that it brushed his arm—one

of the rare signs of affection that made him weak. "Too much energy," she said with a laugh. "I'm dedicating the day to laziness. I noticed you were signed up for the bronc riding." Jillian nudged her hat back as she looked up at him. "Still more guts than brains?"

He grinned and shrugged. "Worried about me?"

Jillian gave a snort of laughter. "I've got some good liniment—it'll take the soreness out of the bruises you're going to get."

He ran a fingertip down her spine. "The idea tempts me to make sure I get a few. You know—" he turned her into his arms in a move both smooth and possessive "—it wouldn't take much for me to forget all about this little competition." Lowering his head, he nibbled at her lips, oblivious of whoever might be milling around them. "It's not such a long drive back to the ranch. Not a soul there. Pretty day like this—I start thinking about taking a swim."

"Do you?" She drew her head back so their eyes met.

"Mmmm. Water'd be cool, and quiet."

Chuckling, she pressed her lips to his. "After the calf roping," she said and drew away.

Jillian preferred the chutes to the stands. There she could listen to the men talk of other rodeos, other rides, while she checked over her own equipment. She watched a young girl in a stunning buckskin suit rev up her nerves before the barrel racing. An old hand worked rosin into the palm of a glove with tireless patience. The little breeze carried the scent of grilled meat from the concessions.

No, she thought, her family could never understand the appeal of this. The earthy smells, the earthy talk. They'd be just as much out of their element here as she'd always been at her mother's box at the opera. It was times like these, when she was accepted for simply being what she was, that she stopped remembering the little twinges of panic that had plagued her while she grew up. No, there was nothing lacking in her as she'd often thought. She was simply different.

She watched the bull riding, thrilling to the danger and daring as men pitted themselves against a ton of beef. There were spills and close calls and clowns who made the terrifying seem amusing. Half dreaming, she leaned on the fence as a riderless bull charged and snorted around the arena, poking bad temperedly at a clown in a barrel. The crowd was loud, but she could hear Aaron in an easy conversation with Gil from somewhere behind her. She caught snatches about the little sorrel mare Aaron had drawn in the bronc riding. A fire-eater. Out of the chute, then a lunge to the right. Liked to spin. Relaxed, Jillian thought she'd enjoy watching Aaron pit himself against the little fire-eater. After she'd won another fifty from him.

She thought the day had simply been set aside for her, warm and sunny and without demands. Perhaps she'd been this relaxed before, this happy, but it was difficult to remember when she'd shared the two sensations so clearly. She savored them.

Then everything happened so quickly she didn't have time to think, only to act.

She heard the childish laughter as she stretched her back muscles. She saw the quick flash of red zip through the fence and bounce on the dirt without fully registering it. But she saw the child skim through the rungs of the fence and into the arena. He was so close his jeans brushed hers as he scrambled through after his ball. Jillian was over the fence and running before his mother screamed. Part of her registered Aaron's voice, either furious or terrified, as he called her name.

Out of the corner of her eye Jillian saw the bull turn. His eyes, already wild from the ride, met hers, though she never paused. Her blood went cold.

She didn't hear the chaos as the crowd leaped to their feet or the mass confusion from behind the chutes as she sprinted after the boy. She did feel the ground tremble as the bull began its charge. There wasn't time to waste her breath on shouting. Running on instinct, she lunged, letting the momentum carry her forward. She went down hard, full length on the boy, and knocked the breath out of both of them. As the bull skimmed by them, she felt the hot rush of air.

Don't move, she told herself, mercilessly pinning the boy beneath her when he started to squirm. *Don't even breathe.* She could hear shouting, very close by now, but didn't dare move her head to look. She wasn't gored. Jillian swallowed on the thought. No, she'd know it if he'd caught her with his horns. And he hadn't trampled her. Yet.

Someone was cursing furiously. Jillian closed her eyes and wondered if she'd ever be able to stand up again. The boy was beginning to cry lustily. She tried to smother the sound with her body.

When hands came under her arms, she jolted and started to struggle. "You *idiot*!" Recognizing the voice, Jillian relaxed and allowed herself to be hauled to her feet. She might have swayed if she hadn't been held so tightly. "What kind of a stunt was that?" She stared up at Aaron's deathly white face while he shook her. "Are you hurt?" he demanded. "Are you hurt anywhere?"

"What?"

He shook her again because his hands were trembling. "Damn it, Jillian!"

Her head was spinning a bit like it had when she'd had that first plug of tobacco. It took her a moment to realize someone was gripping her hand. Bemused, she listened to the tearful gratitude of the mother while the boy wept loudly with his face buried in his father's shirt. The Simmons boy, she thought dazedly. The little Simmons boy, who played in the yard while his mother hung out the wash and his father worked on her own land.

"He's all right, Joleen," she managed, though her mouth didn't want to follow the order of her brain. "I might've put some bruises on him, though."

Aaron cut her off, barely suppressing the urge to suggest someone introduce the boy to a razor strap before he dragged Jillian away. She had a misty impression of a sea of faces and Aaron's simmering rage.

"...get you over to first aid."

"What?" she said again as his voice drifted in and out of her mind.

"I said I'm going to get you over to first aid." He bit off the words as he came to the fence.

"No, I'm fine." The light went gray for a moment and she shook her head.

"As soon as I'm sure of that, I'm going to strangle you."

She pulled her hand from his and straightened her shoulders. "I said I'm fine," she repeated. Then the ground tilted and rushed up at her.

The first thing she felt was the tickle of grass under her palm. Then there was a cool cloth, more wet than damp, on her face. Jillian moaned in annoyance as water trickled down to her collar. Opening her eyes, she saw a blur of light and shadow. She closed them again, then concentrated on focusing.

She saw Aaron first, grim and pale as he hitched her up to a half-sitting position and held a glass to her lips. Then Gil, shifting his weight from foot to foot while he ran his hat through his hands. "She ain't hurt none," he told Aaron in a voice raised to convince everyone, including himself. "Just had herself a spell, that's all. Women do."

"A lot you know," she muttered, then discovered what Aaron held to her lips wasn't a glass but a flask of neat brandy. It burned very effectively through the mists. "I didn't faint," Jillian said in disgust.

"You did a damn good imitation, then," Aaron snapped at her.

"Let the child breathe." Karen Murdock's calm, elegant voice had the magic effect of moving the crowd back. She slipped through and knelt at Jillian's side. Clucking her tongue, she took the dripping cloth from Jillian's brow and wrung it out. "Men'll always try to overcompensate. Well, Jillian, you caused quite a sensation."

Grimacing, Jillian sat up. "Did I?" She pressed her forehead to her knees a minute until she was certain the world wasn't going to do any more spinning. "I can't believe I fainted," she mumbled.

Aaron swore and took a healthy swig from the flask himself. "She almost gets herself killed and she's worried about what fainting's going to do to her image."

Jillian's head snapped up. "Look, Murdock—"

"I wouldn't push it if I were you," he warned and meticulously capped the flask. "If you can stand, I'll take you home."

"Of course I can stand," she retorted. "And I'm not going home."

"I'm sure you're fine," Karen began and shot her son a telling look. For a smart man, Karen mused, Aaron was showing a remarkable lack of sense. Then again, when love was around, sense customarily went out the window. "Trouble is, you're a seven-day wonder," she told Jillian with a brief glance at the gathering crowd. "You're going to be congratulated to death if you stay around here." She smiled as she saw her words sink in.

Grumbling, Jillian rose. "All right." The bruises were beginning to be felt. Rather than admit it, she brushed at the dust on her jeans. "There's no need for you to go," she told Aaron stiffly. "I'm perfectly capable of—"

His fingers were wrapped tight around her arm as he dragged her away. "I don't know what your problem is, Murdock," she said through her teeth. "But I don't have to take this."

"I'd keep a lid on it for a while if I were you." The crowd fell back as he strode through. If anyone considered speaking to Jillian, Aaron's challenging look changed their minds.

After wrenching open the door of his truck, Aaron gave her a none-too-gentle boost inside. Jillian pulled her hat from her back and, taking the brim in both hands, slammed it down on her head. Folding her arms, she prepared to endure the next hour's drive in absolute silence. As Aaron pulled out it occurred to her that she had missed not only the calf roping, but also her sacred right to gloat over her bull's victory at the evening barbecue. The injustice of it made her smolder.

And just what's he so worked up about? Jillian asked herself righteously. He hadn't scared himself blind, wrenched his knee, or humiliated himself by fainting in public. Gingerly she touched her elbow where she'd scraped most of the skin away. After all, if you wanted to be technical, she'd probably saved that kid's life. Jillian's chin angled as her arm began to ache with real enthusiasm. So why was he acting as though she'd committed some crime?

"One of these days you're going to put your chin out like that and someone's going to take you up on it."

Slowly she turned her head to glare at him. "You want to give it a shot, Murdock?"

"Don't tempt me." He punched on the gas until the speedometer hovered at seventy.

"Look, I don't know what your problem is," she said tightly. "But since you've got one, why don't you just spill it? I'm not in the mood for your nasty little comments."

He swung the truck over to the side of the road so abruptly she crashed into the door. By the time she'd recovered, he was out of his side and striding across the tough wild grass of a narrow field. Rubbing her sore arm, Jillian pushed out of the truck and went after him.

"What the hell is all this about?" Anger made her breathless as she caught at his shirtsleeve. "If you want to drive like a maniac, I'll hitch a ride back to the ranch."

"Just shut up." He jerked away from her. Distance, he told himself. He just needed some distance until he pulled himself together. He was still seeing those lowered horns sweeping past Jillian's tumbling body. His rope might've missed the mark, and then— He couldn't afford to think of any *and thens*. As it was, it had taken three well-placed ropes and several strong arms before they'd been able to drag the bull away from those two prone bodies. He'd nearly lost her. In one split second he'd nearly lost her.

"Don't you tell me to shut up." Spinning in front of him, Jillian gripped his shirtfront. Her hat tumbled down her back as she tossed her head and rage poured out of her. "I've had all I'm going to take from you. God knows why I've let you get away with this much, but no more. Now you can just hop back in your truck and head it in whatever direction you like. To hell would suit me just fine."

She whirled away, but before she could storm off she was spun back and crushed in his arms. Spitting mad, she struggled only to have his grip tighten. It wasn't until she stopped to marshal her forces that she realized he was trembling and that his breathing came fast and uneven. Emotion ruled him, yes, but it wasn't anger. Subsiding, she waited. Not certain what she was offering comfort for, she stroked his back. "Aaron?"

He shook his head and buried his face in her hair. It was the closest he could remember to just falling apart. It hadn't been distance he'd needed, he discovered, but this. To feel her warm and safe and solid in his arms.

"Oh, God, Jillian, do you know what you did to me?"

Baffled, she let her cheek rest against his drumming heart and continued to stroke his back. "I'm sorry," she offered, hoping it would be enough for whatever she'd done.

"It was so close. Inches—just inches more. I wasn't sure at first that he hadn't gotten you."

The bull, Jillian realized. It hadn't been anger, but fear. Something warm and sweet moved through her. "Don't," she murmured. "I wasn't hurt. It wasn't nearly as bad as it must've looked."

"The hell it wasn't." His hands came to her face and jerked it back. "I was only a few yards back when I got the first rope around him. He was more'n half crazy by then. Another couple of seconds and he'd've scooped you right up off that ground."

Jillian stared up at him and finally managed to swallow. "I—I didn't know."

He watched as the color her temper had given her fled from her cheeks. And I just had to tell you, he thought furiously. Taking both her hands, he brought them to his lips, burying his mouth in one palm, then the other. The gesture alone was enough to distract her. "It's done," Aaron said with more control. "I guess I overreacted. It's not easy to watch something like that." Because she needed it, he smiled at her. "I wouldn't have cared for it if you'd picked up any holes."

Relaxing a bit, she answered the smile. "Neither would I. As it is, I picked up a few bruises I'm not too fond of."

Still holding her hands, he bent over and kissed her with such exquisite gentleness that she felt the ground tilt for the second time. There was something different here, she realized dimly. Something... But she couldn't hold on to it.

Aaron drew away, knowing the time was coming when he'd have to tell her what he felt, whether she was ready to hear it or not. As he led her back to the truck he decided that since he was only going to bare his heart to one woman in his life, he was going to do it right.

"You're going to take a hot bath," he told her as he lifted her into the truck. "Then I'm going to fix you dinner."

Jillian settled back against the seat. "Maybe fainting isn't such a bad thing after all."

Chapter Eleven

By the time they drove into the ranch yard, Jillian had decided she'd probably enjoy a few hours of pampering. As far as she could remember, no one had ever fussed over her before. As a child, she'd been strong and healthy. Whenever she'd been ill, she'd been treated with competent practicality by her doctor father. She'd learned early that the fewer complaints you made the less likelihood there was for a hypodermic to come out of that little black bag. Clay had always treated bumps and blood as a routine part of the life. Wash up and get back to work.

Now she thought it might be a rather interesting experience to have someone murmur over her scrapes and bruises. Especially if he kissed her like he had on the side of the road...in that soft, gentle way that made the top of her head threaten to spin off.

Perhaps they wouldn't have the noise and lights and

music of the fairgrounds, but they could make their own fireworks, alone, on Utopia.

All the buildings were quiet, bunkhouse, barns, stables. Instead of the noise and action that would accompany any late afternoon, there was simple, absolute peace over acres of land. Whatever animals hadn't been taken to the fair had been left to graze for the day. It would be hours before anyone returned to Utopia.

"I don't think I've ever been here alone before," Jillian murmured when Aaron stopped the truck. She sat for a moment and absorbed the quiet and the stillness. It occurred to her that she could cup her hands and shout if she liked—no one would even hear the echo.

"It's funny, it even feels different. You always know there're people around." She stepped out of the truck, then listened to the echo of the slam. "Somebody in the bunkhouse or the cookhouse or one of the outbuildings. Some of the wives or children hanging out clothes or working in the gardens. You hardly think about it, but it's like a little town."

"Self-sufficient, independent." He took her hand, thinking that the words described her just as accurately as they described the ranch. They were two of the reasons he'd been drawn to her.

"It has to be, doesn't it? It's so easy to get cut off— one bad storm. Besides, it's what makes it all so special." Though she didn't understand the smile he sent her, she answered it. "I'm glad I've got so many married hands who've settled," she added. "It's harder to depend on the drifters." Jillian scanned the ranch yard, not quite understanding her own reluctance to go inside. It was as if she were missing something. With a shrug, she put it down to the oddity of being alone, but she caught herself searching the area again.

Aaron glanced down and saw the lowered-brow look of concentration. "Something wrong?"

"I don't know... It seems like there is." With another shrug, she turned to him. "I must be getting jumpy." Reaching up, she tipped back the brim of his hat. She liked the way it shadowed his face, accenting the angle of bone, adding just one more shade of darkness to his eyes. "You didn't mention anything about scrubbing my back when I took that hot bath, did you?"

"No, but I could probably be persuaded."

Agreeably she went into his arms. She thought she could catch just a trace of rosin on him, perhaps a hint of saddle soap. "Did I mention how sore I am?"

"No, you didn't."

"I don't like to complain..." She snuggled against him.

"But?" he prompted with a grin.

"Well, now that you mention it—there are one or two places that sting, just a bit."

"Want me to kiss them and make them better?"

She sighed as he nuzzled her ear. "If it wouldn't be too much trouble."

"I'm a humanitarian," he told her, then began to nudge her slowly toward the porch steps. It was then Jillian remembered. With a gasp, she broke out of his arms and raced across the yard. "Jillian—" Swearing, Aaron followed her.

Oh, God, how could she've missed it! Jillian raced to the paddock fence and leaned breathlessly against it. Empty. *Empty.* She balled her hands into fists as she looked at the bottle she'd left hanging at an angle in the shade. The trough of water glimmered in the sun. The few scoops of grain she'd left were barely touched.

"What's going on?"

"Baby," she muttered, tapping her hand rhythmically against the fence. "They've taken Baby." Her tone started out calm, then became more and more agitated. "They walked right into my backyard, right into my backyard, and stole from me."

"Maybe one of your hands put him back in the barn."

She only shook her head and continued to tap her hand on the fence. "The five hundred weren't enough," she murmured. "They had to come here and steal within a stone's throw of my house. I should've left Joe—he offered to stay. I should've stayed myself."

"Come on, we'll check the barn."

She looked at him, and her eyes were flat and dark. "He's not in the barn."

He'd rather have had her rage, weep, than look so— resigned. "Maybe not, but we'll be sure. Then we'll see if anything else was taken before we call the sheriff."

"The sheriff." Jillian laughed under her breath and stared blindly into the empty paddock. "The sheriff."

"Jillian—" Aaron slipped his arms around her, but she drew away immediately.

"No, I'm not going to fall apart this time." Her voice trembled slightly, but her eyes were clear. "They won't do that to me again."

It might be better if she did, Aaron thought. Her face was pale, but he knew that expression by now. There'd be no backing down. "You check the barn," he suggested. "I'll look in the stables."

Jillian followed the routine, though she knew it was hopeless. Baby's stall was empty. She watched the little motes of hay and dust as they floated in the slant of sunlight. Someone had taken her yearling. Someone. Her hands balled into fists. Somehow, some way, she was going to get a name. Spinning on her heel, she strode back out. Though she itched with impatience, she waited until Aaron crossed the yard to her. There wasn't any need for words. Together, they went into the house.

She's not going to take this one lying down, he decided, with as much admiration as concern. Yes, she was still pale, but her voice was strong and clear as she spoke to the sheriff's office. Resigned—yes, she was still resigned that it had been done. But she didn't consider it over.

He remembered the way she'd nuzzled the calf when it'd been newborn—the way her eyes had softened when she spoke of it. It was always a mistake to make a pet out of one of your stock, but there were times it happened. She was paying for it now.

Thoughtfully he began to brew coffee. Aaron considered it a foolish move for anyone to have stolen Utopia's prize yearling. For butchering? It hardly seemed worth the risk or effort. Yet what rancher in the area would buy a young Hereford so easily identified? Someone had gotten greedy, or stupid. Either way, it would make them easier to catch.

Jillian leaned against the kitchen wall and talked steadily into the phone. Aaron found himself wanting to shield, to protect. She took the coffee from him with a brief nod and continued talking. Shaking his head, he reminded himself he should know better by now. Protection wasn't something Jillian would take gracefully. He drank his own coffee, looking out of the kitchen window and wondering how a man dealt with loving a woman who had more grit than most men.

"He'll do what he can," she said as she hung up the phone with a snap. "I'm going to offer a separate reward for Baby." Jillian drank down half the coffee, hot and black. "Tomorrow I'll go see the Cattlemen's Association again. I want to put the pressure on, and put it on hard. People are going to realize this isn't going to stop at Utopia." She looked into her coffee, then grimly finished it off. "I kept telling myself it wasn't personal. Even when I saw the hides and bones in the canyon. Not this time. They got cocky, Aaron. It's always easier to catch arrogance."

There was relish in the tone of her voice, the kind of relish that made him smile as he turned to face her. "You're right."

"What're you grinning at?"

"I was thinking if the rustlers could see you now, they'd be shaking the dust of this county off their boots in a hurry."

Her lips curved. She hadn't thought it possible. "Thank you." She gestured with the cup, then set it back on the stove. "I seem to be saying that to you quite a bit these days."

"You don't have to say it at all. Hungry?"

"Hmmm." She put her hand on her stomach and thought about it. "I don't know."

"Go get yourself a bath, I'll rustle up something."

Walking to him, Jillian slipped her arms around his waist and rested her head on his chest. How was it he knew her so well? How did he understand that she needed a few moments alone to sort through her thoughts and feelings?

"Why are you so good to me?" she murmured.

With a half laugh, Aaron buried his face in her hair. "God knows. Go soak your bruises."

"Okay." But she gave in to the urge to hug him fiercely before she left the room.

She wished she knew a better way to express gratitude. As she climbed the stairs to the second floor, Jillian wished she were more clever with words. If she were, she'd be able to tell him how much it meant that he offered no more than she could comfortably take. His support today had been steady but unobtrusive. And he was giving her time alone without leaving her alone. Perhaps it had taken her quite some time to discover just how special a man he was, but she had discovered it. It wasn't something she'd forget.

As Jillian peeled off her clothes she found she was a bit more tender in places than she'd realized. Better, she decided, and turned the hot water on in the tub to let it steam. A few bruises were something solid to concentrate on. They were easier than the bruises she felt on the inside. It might have been foolish to feel as though she'd let her grandfather down, but she couldn't rid herself of the feeling. He'd given her something in trust and she hadn't protected it well enough. It would have soothed her if he'd been around to berate her for it.

Wincing a bit, she lowered herself into the water. The raw skin on her elbow objected and she ignored it. One of her own men? she thought with a grimace. It was too possible. Back up a truck to the paddock, load up the calf and go.

She'd start making a few discreet inquiries herself. Stealing the calf would've taken time. Maybe she could discover just who was away from the fair. Perhaps they'd

be confident enough to throw a little extra money around
if they thought they were safe and then… Then they'd
see, she thought as she relaxed in the water.

Poor Baby. No one would spend the time scratching
his ears or talking to him now. Sinking farther in the
water, she waited until her mind went blank.

It was nearly an hour before she came downstairs
again. She'd soaked the stiffness away and nearly all
the depression. Nothing practical could be done with depression. She caught the aroma of something spicy that
had her stomach juices churning.

Aaron's name was on the tip of her tongue as she
walked into the kitchen, but the room was empty. A pot
simmered on the stove with little hisses and puffs of
steam. It drew her, irresistibly. Jillian lifted the lid, closed
her eyes and breathed deep. Chili, thick and fragrant
enough to make the mouth water. She wouldn't have to
give it any thought if he asked if she was hungry now.

Picking up a spoon, she began to stir. Maybe just one
little taste…

"My mother used to smack my hand for that," Aaron
commented. Jillian dropped the lid with a clatter.

"Damn, Murdock! You scared me to—" Turning, she
saw the clutch of wildflowers in his hand.

Some men might've looked foolish holding small colorful blooms in a hand roughened by work and weather.
Other men might've seemed awkward. Aaron was neither. Something turned over in her chest when he smiled
at her.

She looked stunned—not that he minded. It wasn't
often you caught a woman like Jillian Baron off-balance.
As he watched, she put her hands behind her back and
gripped them together. He lifted a brow. If he'd known

he could make her nervous with a bunch of wildflowers, he'd have dug up a field of them long before this.

"Feel better?" he asked and slowly crossed to her.

She'd backed into the counter before she'd realized she made the defensive move. "Yes, thanks."

He gave her one of his long, serious looks while his eyes laughed. "Something wrong?"

"No. The chili smells great."

"Something I picked up at one of the line camps a few years back." Bending his head, he kissed the corners of her mouth. "Don't you want the flowers, Jillian?"

"Yes, I—" She found she was gripping her fingers together until they hurt. Annoyed with herself, she loosened them and took the flowers from his hand. "They're very pretty."

"It's what your hair smells like," he murmured and saw the cautious look she threw up at him. Tilting his head, he studied her. "Hasn't anyone ever given you flowers before?"

Not in years, she realized. Not since—florist boxes, ribbons and soft words. Realizing she was making a fool of herself, she shrugged. "Roses," she said carelessly. "Red roses."

Something in her tone warned him. He kept his touch very light as he wound her hair around his finger. It was the color of flame, the texture of silk. "Too tame," he said simply. "Much too tame."

Something flickered inside her—acknowledgment, caution, need. With a sigh, she looked down at the small bold flowers in her hand. "Once—a long time ago—I thought I could be, too."

He tugged on her hair until she looked up at him. "Is that what you wanted to be?"

"Then, I—" She broke off, but something in his eyes demanded an answer. "Yes, I would've tried."

"Were you in love with him?" He wasn't certain why he was hacking away at a wound—his and hers—but he couldn't stop.

"Aaron—"

"Were you?"

She let out a long breath. Mechanically she began to fill a water glass for the flowers. "I was very young. He was a great deal like my father—steady, quiet, dedicated. My father loved me because he had to, never because he wanted to. There's a tremendous difference." The sharp, clean scent of the wildflowers drifted up to her. "Maybe somewhere along the line I thought if I pleased him, I'd please my father. I don't know, I was foolish."

"That isn't an answer." He discovered jealousy tasted bitter even after it was swallowed.

"I guess I don't have one I'm sure of." She moved her shoulders and fluffed the flowers in the glass. "Shouldn't we eat?" She went very still when his hands came to her shoulders, but she didn't resist when he turned her around.

She had a moment's fear that he would say something gentle, something sweet, and undermine her completely. She saw something of it in his eyes, just as he saw the apprehension in hers. Aaron tugged her against him and brought his mouth down hard on hers.

She could understand the turbulence and let go. She could meet the desire, the violence of needs, without fear of stumbling past her own rules. Her arms went around him to hold him close. Her lips sought his hungrily. If through the relief came a stir of feeling, she could al-

most convince herself it was nothing more complex than
passion.

"Eat fast," Aaron told her. "I've been thinking about
making love with you for hours."

"Didn't we eat already?"

With a chuckle he nuzzled her neck. "No, you don't.
When I cook for a woman, she eats." He gave her a com-
panionable smack on the bottom as he drew away. "Get
the bowls."

Jillian handed him two and watched him scoop out
generous portions. "Smells fabulous. Want a beer?"

"Yeah."

Unearthing two from the refrigerator, she poured them
into glasses. "You know, if you ever get tired of ranching,
you could have a job in the cookhouse here at Utopia."

"Always a comfort to have something to fall back on."

"We've got a woman now," Jillian went on as she took
her seat. "The men call her Aunt Sally. She's got a way
with biscuits—" She broke off as she took the first bite.
Heat spread through her and woke up every cell in her
body. Swallowing, she met Aaron's grin. "You use a free
hand with the peppers."

"Separates the men from the boys." He took a generous forkful. "Too hot for you?"

Disdainfully she took a second bite. "There's nothing
you can dish out I can't take, Murdock."

Laughing, he continued to eat. Jillian decided the first
encounter had numbed her mouth right down to the vocal
cords. She ate with as much relish as he, cooling off occasionally with sips of cold beer.

"Those people in town don't know what they're missing," she commented as she scraped down to the bot-

tom of the bowl. "It isn't every day you get battery acid this tasty."

He glanced over as she ate the last forkful. "Want some more?"

"I want to live," she countered. "God, Aaron, a steady diet of that and you wouldn't have a stomach lining. It's fabulous."

"We had a Mexican foreman when I was a boy," Aaron told her. "Best damn cattleman I've ever known. I spent the best part of a summer with him up at the line camp. You should taste my flour tortillas."

The man was a constant surprise, Jillian decided as she rested her elbows on the table and cupped her chin in her hand. "What happened to him?"

"Saved his stake, went back to Mexico and started his own spread."

"The impossible dream," Jillian murmured.

"Too easy to lose a month's pay in a poker game."

She nodded, but her lips curved. "Do you play?"

"I've sat in on a hand or two. You?"

"Clay taught me. We'll have to arrange a game one of these days."

"Any time."

"I'm counting on a few poker skills to bring me out of this rustling business."

Aaron watched her rise to clear the table. "How?"

"People get careless when they think you're ready to fold. They made a mistake with the yearling, Aaron. I'm going to be able to find him—especially if nobody knows how hard I'm looking. I'm thinking about hiring an investigator. Whatever it costs, I'd rather pay it than have the stealing go on."

He sat for a moment, listening to her run water in the

sink—a homey, everyday sound. "How hard is all this hitting your books, Jillian?"

She cast a look over her shoulder, calm and cool. "I can still raise the bet."

He knew better than to offer her financial assistance. It irked him. Rising, he paced the kitchen until he'd come full circle behind her. "The Cattlemen's Association would back you."

"They'd have to know about it to do that. The less people who know, the more effective a private investigation would be."

"I want to help you."

Touched, she turned and took him into her arms. "You have helped me. I won't forget it."

"I have to hog-tie you before you'll let me do anything."

She laughed and lifted her face to his. "I'm not that bad."

"Worse," he countered. "If I offered you some men to help patrol your land…"

"Aaron—"

"See." He kissed her before she could finish the protest. "I could work for you myself until everything was straightened out."

"I couldn't let you—" Then his mouth was hard and bruising on hers again.

"I'm the one who has to watch you worry and struggle," he told her as his hands began to roam down. "Do you know what that does to me?"

She tried to concentrate on his words, but his mouth—his mouth was demanding all her attention. The hot, spicy kiss took her breath away, but she clung to him and fought for more. Each time he touched her it was only seconds until the needs took over completely. She'd never known anything so liberating, or so imprisoning. Jillian might have struggled against the latter if she'd known how. Instead she accepted the bars and locks even as she accepted the open sky and the wind. He was the only man who could tempt her to.

This was something he could do for her, Aaron knew. Make her forget, thrust her problems away from her, if only temporarily. Even so, he knew, if she had a choice, she would have kept some distance there, as well. She'd been hurt, and her trust wasn't completely his yet. The frustration of it made his mouth more ruthless, his hands more urgent. There was still only one way that she was his without question. He swept her up, then silenced her murmured protest.

Jillian was aware she was being carried. Some inner part of her rebelled against it. And yet... He wasn't taking her anywhere she wouldn't have gone willingly. Perhaps he needed this—romance he'd once called it. Romance frightened her, as the flowers had frightened her. It was so easy to lie in candlelight, so easy to deceive with fragrant blossoms and soft words. And she was no longer sure the defenses she'd once had were still there. Not with him.

"I want you." The words drifted from her to shimmer against his lips.

He would've taken her to bed. But it was too far. He would have given her the slow, easy loving a cherished woman deserves. But he was too hungry. With his mouth still fused to hers, he tumbled onto the couch with her and let the fire take them both.

She understood desperation. It was honest and real. There could be no doubting the frantic search of his mouth or the urgent pressure of his fingers against her skin. Desire had no shadows. She could feel it pulsing from him even as it pulsed from her. His curses as he tugged at her clothes made her laugh breathlessly. *She* made him clumsy. It was the greatest compliment she'd ever had.

He was relentless, spinning her beyond time and space the moment he could touch her flesh. She let herself go. Every touch, every frenzied caress, every deep, greedy kiss, took her further from the strict, practical world she'd formed for herself. Once she'd sought solitude and speed when she'd needed freedom. Now she needed only Aaron.

She felt his hair brush over her bare shoulder and savored even that simple contact. It brought a sweetness flowing into her while the burn of his mouth brought the fire. Only with him had she realized it was possible to have both. Only with him had she realized the great, yawning need in herself to have both. Her moan came as much from the revelation as from the passion.

Did she know how giving she was? How incredibly arousing? Aaron had to fight the need to take her quickly, ruthlessly, while they were both still half dressed. No woman had ever sapped his control the way she could. One look, one touch, and he was hers so completely— How could she not know?

Her body flowed, fluid as water, heady as wine, under his hands. Her lips had the punch of an electric current and the texture of silk. Could any woman remain unaware of such a deadly combination?

As if to catch his breath, he took his lips to her throat and burrowed there. He drew in the fragrance from her bath, some subtle woman's scent that lingered there, waiting to entice a lover. It was then he remembered the bruises. Aaron shook his head, trying to clear it.

"I'm hurting you."

"No." She drew him back, close. "No, you're not. You never do. I'm not fragile, Aaron."

"No?" He lifted his head so that he could see her face. There was the delicate line of bone she couldn't deny, the honey-touched skin that remained soft after hours in the sun. The frailty that came and went in her eyes at the right word, the right touch. "Sometimes you are," he murmured. "Let me show you."

"No—"

But even as she protested, his lips skimmed hers, so gentle, so reassuring. It did nothing to smother the fire, only banked it while he showed her what magic there could be with mouth to mouth. With his fingers he traced her face as though he might never see it with his eyes again—over the curve of cheekbone, down the slim line of jaw.

Patient, soft, murmuring, he seduced where no seduction was needed. Tender, thorough, easy, he let his lips show her what he hadn't yet spoken. The hand on his shoulder slid bonelessly down to his waist. He touched the tip of her tongue with his, then went deeper, slowly, in a soul-wrenching kiss that left them both limp. Then he began a careful worship of her body. She floated.

Was there any kind of pleasure he couldn't show her? Jillian wondered. Was this humming world just one more aspect to passion? She wanted desperately to give him something in return, yet her body was so heavy, weighed down with sensations. Sandalwood and leather—it would always bring him to her mind. The ridge of callus on his hand where the reins rubbed daily—nothing felt more perfect against her skin. He shifted so that she sank deeper into the cushions, and he with her.

She could taste him—and what she realized must be a wisp of herself on his lips. His cheek grazed hers, not quite smooth. She wanted to burrow against it. He whispered her name and generated a new layer of warmth.

Even when his hands began to roam, the excitement stayed hazy. She couldn't break through the mists, and no longer tried. Her skin was throbbing, but it went deeper, to the blood and bone. His mouth was light at her breast, his tongue clever enough to make her shudder, then settle, then shudder again.

He kept the pace easy, though she began to writhe under him. Time dripped away as he gave himself the pleasure of showing her each new delight. He knew afternoon was ending only by the way the light slanted over her face. The quiet was punctuated only with murmurs and sighs. He'd never felt more alone with her.

He took her slowly, savoring each moment, each movement, until there could be no more.

As she lay beneath him, Jillian watched the light shift toward dusk. It had been like a dream, she thought, like something you sigh over in the middle of the night when your wishes take control. Should it move her more than the fire and flash they usually brought each other? Somehow she knew what she'd just experienced had been more dangerous.

Aaron shifted, and though she made no objection to his weight, sat up, bringing her with him. "I like the way you stay soft and warm after I make love to you."

"It's never been just like that before," she murmured.

The words moved him; he couldn't stop it. "No." Tilting back her head, he kissed her again. "It will be again."

Perhaps because she wanted so badly to hold on, to stay, to depend, she drew away. "I'm never sure how to take you." Something warned her it was time to play it light. She was out of her depth—far, far out of her depth.

"In what way?"

She gave in to the urge to hold him again, just to feel the way his hand slid easily up and down her bare back. Reluctantly she slipped out of his arms and pulled on her shirt. "You're a lot of different people, Aaron Murdock. Every time I think I might get to know who you are, you're someone else."

"No, I'm not." Before she could button it, Aaron took her shirtfront and pulled her back to him. "Different moods don't make different people."

"Maybe not." She disconcerted him by kissing the back of his hand. "But I still can't get a handle on you."

"Is that what you want?"

"I'm a simple person."

He stared at her a moment as she continued to dress. "Are you joking?"

Because there was a laugh in his voice, she looked over, half serious, half embarrassed. "No, I am. I have to know where I stand, what my options are, what's expected of me. As long as I know I can do my job and take care of what's mine, I'm content."

He watched her thoughtfully as he pulled on his jeans. "Your job's what's vital in your life?"

"It's what I know," she countered. "I understand the land."

"And people?"

"I'm not really very good with people—a lot of people. Unless I understand them."

Aaron pulled his shirt on but left it open as he crossed to her. "And I'm one you don't understand?"

"Only sometimes," she murmured. "I guess I understand you best when I'm annoyed with you. Other times..." She was sinking even deeper and started to turn away.

"Other times," Aaron prompted, holding on to her arms.

"Other times I don't know. I never expected to get involved with you—this way."

He ran his thumbs over the pulses at the inside of her elbows. They weren't steady any longer. "This way, Jillian?"

"I didn't expect that we'd be lovers. I never expected—" Why was her heart pounding like this again, so soon? "To want you," she finished.

"Didn't you?" There was something about the way she looked at him—not quite sure of herself when he knew she was fighting to be—that made him reckless. "I wanted you from the first minute I saw you, riding hell for leather on that mare. There were other things I didn't expect. Finding those soft places, on you, in you."

"Aaron—"

He shook his head when she tried to stop him. "Thinking of you in the middle of the day, the middle of the night. Remembering just the way you say my name."

"Don't."

He felt her start to tremble before she tried to pull away. "Damn it, it's time you heard what I've been carrying around inside me. I love you, Jillian."

Panic came first, even when she began to build up the reserve. "No, you don't have to say that." Her voice was sharp and fast. "I don't expect to hear those kinds of things."

"What the hell are you talking about?" He shook her once in frustration, and a second time in anger. "I know what I have to say. I don't care if you expect to hear it or not, because you're going to."

She hung on to her temper because she knew it was emotion that brought on betrayal. If she hadn't had her pride, she would have told him just how much those words, that easily said empty phrase hurt her. "Aaron, I told you before I don't need the soft words. I don't even like them. Whatever's between us—"

"What is between us?" he demanded. He hadn't known he could be hurt, not like this. Not so he could all but feel the blood draining out of him where he stood. He'd just told a woman he loved her—the only woman, the first time. And she was answering him with ice. "You tell me what there is between us. Just this?" He swung a hand toward the couch, still rumpled from their bodies. "Is that it for you, Jillian?"

"I don't—" There was a tug-of-war going on inside of her, so fierce she was breathless from it. "It's all I thought you—" Frightened, she dragged both hands through her hair. Why was he doing this now, when she was just beginning to think she understood what he wanted from her, what she needed from him? "I don't know what you want. But I—I just can't give you any more than I already have. It's already more than I've ever given to anyone else."

His fingers loosened on her arms one by one, then dropped away. They were a match in many ways, and pride was one of them. Aaron watched her almost dispassionately as he buttoned his shirt. "You've let something freeze inside you, woman. If all you want's a warm body on a cold night, you shouldn't have much trouble. Personally, I like a little something more."

She watched him walk out of the door, heard the sound of his truck as it broke the silence. The sun was just slipping over the horizon.

Chapter Twelve

He worked until his muscles ached and he could think about little more than easing them. He probably drank too much. He rode the cattle, hours in the saddle, rounded strays and ate more dust than food. He spent the long, sweaty days of summer at the line camp, driving himself from sunup to sundown. Sometimes, only sometimes, he managed to push her out of his mind.

For three weeks Aaron was hell to be around. Or so his men mumbled whenever he was out of earshot. It was a woman, they told each other. Only a woman could drive a man to the edge, and then give him that gentle tap over. The Baron woman's name came up. Well, Murdocks and Barons had never mixed, so it was no wonder. No one'd expected much to come of that but hot tempers and bad feelings.

If Aaron heard the murmurs, he ignored them. He'd

come up to the camp to work—and he was going to do just that until she was out of his system. No woman was going to make him crawl. He'd told her he loved her, and she'd shoved his words, his emotions, right back in his face. Not interested.

Aaron dropped a new fence post into the ground as the sweat rolled freely down his back and sides. Maybe she was the first woman he'd ever loved—that didn't mean she'd be the last. He came down hard on the post with a sledgehammer, hissing with the effort.

He hadn't meant to tell her—not then, not that way. Somehow, the words had started rolling and he hadn't been able to stop them. Had she wanted them all tied up with a ribbon, neat and fancy? Cursing, he came down with the hammer again so that the post vibrated and the noise sang out. Maybe he had more finesse than he'd shown her, and maybe he could've used it. With someone else. Someone who didn't make his feelings come up and grab him by the throat.

Where in God's name had he ever come up with the idea that she had those soft parts, that sweet vulnerability under all that starch and fire? Must've been crazy, he told himself as he began running fresh wire. Jillian Baron was a cold, single-minded woman who cared more about her head count than any real emotion.

And he was almost sick with loving her.

He gripped the wire hard enough so that it bit through the leather of his glove and into his hand. He cursed again. He'd just have to get over it. He had his own land to tend.

Pausing, he looked out. It rolled, oceans of grass, high with summer, green and rippling. The sky was a merciless blue, and the sun beat down, strong and clean. It could be enough for a man—these thousands of acres. His cattle were fat and healthy, the yearlings growing strong. In a few weeks they'd round them up, drive them into Miles City. When those long days were over, the men would celebrate. It was their right to. And so would he, Aaron told himself grimly. So, by God, would he.

He'd have given half of what was his just to get her out of his mind for one day.

At dusk he washed off the day's sweat and dirt. He could smell the night's meal through the open windows of the cabin. Good red meat. Someone was playing a guitar and singing of lonely, lamented love. He found he wanted a beer more than he wanted his share of the steak. Because he knew a man couldn't work and not eat, he piled food on his plate and transferred it to his stomach. But he worked his way through one beer, then two, while the men made up their evening poker game. As they grew louder he took a six-pack and went out on the narrow wood porch.

The stars were just coming out. He heard a coyote call at the moon, then fall silent. The air was as still as it had been all day and barely cooler, but he could smell the sweet clover and wild roses. Resting his back against the porch rail, Aaron willed his mind to empty. But he thought of her...

Fully dressed and spitting mad, standing in the pond—crooning quietly to an orphaned calf—laughing up at him with her hair spread out over the earth of the corral—weeping in his arms over her butchered cattle. Soft one minute, prickly the next—no, she wasn't a temperate woman. But she was the only one he wanted. She was the only one he'd ever felt enough for to hurt over.

Aaron took a long swig from the bottle. He didn't care

much for emotional pain. The poets could have it. She didn't want him. Aaron swore and scowled into the dark. The hell she didn't—he wasn't a fool. Maybe her needs weren't the same as his, but she had them. For the first time in weeks he began to think calmly.

He hadn't played his hand well, he realized. It wasn't like him to fold so early—then again, he wasn't used to being soft-headed over a woman. Thoughtfully he tipped back his hat and looked at the stars. She was too set on having her own way, and it was time he gave her a run for her money.

No, he wasn't going back on his knees, Aaron thought with a grim smile. But he was going back. If he had to hobble and brand her, he was going to have Jillian Baron.

When the screen door opened he glanced around absently. His mood was more open to company.

"My luck's pretty poor."

Jennsen, Aaron thought, running through a quick mental outline of the man as he offered him a beer. A bit jittery, he mused. On his first season with the Double M, though he wasn't a greenhorn. He was a man who kept to himself and whose past was no more than could be seen in a worn saddle and patched boots.

Jennsen sat on the first step so that his lantern jaw was shadowed by the porch roof. Aaron thought he might be anywhere from thirty-five to fifty. There was age in his eyes—the kind that came from too many years of looking into the sun at another man's land.

"Cards aren't falling?" Aaron said conversationally while he watched Jennsen roll a cigarette. He didn't miss the fact that the fingers weren't quite steady.

"Haven't been for weeks." Jennsen gave a brief laugh as he struck a match. "Trouble is, I've never been much good at staying away from a gamble." He shot Aaron a sidelong look as he drank again. He'd been working his way up to this talk for days and nearly had enough beer in him to go through with it. "Your luck's pretty steady at the table."

"Comes and goes," Aaron said, deciding Jennsen was feeling his way along for an advance or a loan.

"Luck's a funny thing." Jennsen wiped his mouth with the back of his hand. "Had some bad luck over at the Baron place lately. Losing that cattle," he continued when Aaron glanced over at him. "Somebody made a pretty profit off that beef."

He caught the trace of bitterness. Casually he twisted the top from another bottle and handed it over. "It's easy to make a profit when you don't pay for the beef. Whoever skimmed from the Baron place did a smooth job of it."

"Yeah." Jennsen drew in strong tobacco. He'd heard the rumors about something going on between Aaron Murdock and the Baron woman, but there didn't seem to be anything to it. Most of the talk was about the bad blood between the two families. It'd been going on for years, and it seemed as though it would go on for years more. At the moment he needed badly to believe it. "Guess it doesn't much matter on this side of the fence how much cattle slips away from the Baron spread."

Aaron stretched out his legs and crossed them at the ankles. The lowered brim of his hat shadowed his eyes. "People have to look out for themselves," he said lazily.

Jennsen moistened his lips and prodded a bit further. "I've heard stories about your grandpaw helping himself to Baron beef."

Aaron's eyes narrowed to slits, but he checked his temper. "Stories," he agreed. "No proof."

Jennsen took another long swallow of beer. "I heard that somebody waltzed right onto Baron land and loaded up a prize yearling, sired by that fancy bull."

"Did a tidy job of it." Aaron kept his voice expressionless. Jennsen was testing the waters all right, but he wasn't looking for a loan. "It'd be a shame if they took it for baby beef," he added. "The yearling has the look of his sire—a real moneymaker. 'Course, in a few months he'd stand out like a sore thumb on a small spread. Hate to see a good bloodline wasted."

"Man hears things," Jennsen mumbled, accepting the fresh beer Aaron handed him. "You were interested in the Baron bull."

Aaron took a swig from his bottle, tipped back his hat, and grinned agreeably. "I'm always interested in good stock. Know where I can get my hands on some?"

Jennsen searched his face and swallowed. "Maybe."

Jillian slowed down as she passed the white frame house. Empty. Of course it was empty, she told herself. Even if he'd come back, he wouldn't be home in the middle of the morning. She shouldn't be here on Murdock land when she had her hands full of her own work. She couldn't stay away. If he didn't come back soon, she was going to make a fool of herself and go up to the line camp and…

And what? she asked herself. Half the time she didn't know what she wanted to do, how she felt, what she thought. The one thing she was certain of was that she'd never spent three more miserable weeks in her life. It was perilously close to grief.

Something had died in her when he'd left—something she hadn't acknowledged had been alive. She'd convinced herself that she wouldn't fall in love with him. It would be impossible to count the times she'd told herself it wouldn't happen—even after it already had. Why hadn't she recognized it?

Jillian supposed it wasn't always easy to recognize something you'd never experienced before. Especially when it had no explanation. A woman so accustomed to getting and going her own way had no business falling for a man who was equally obstinate and independent.

Falling in love. Jillian thought it an apt phrase. When it happened you just lost your foothold and plunged.

Maybe he'd meant it, she thought. Maybe they had been more than words to him. If he loved her back, didn't it mean she had someone to hold on to while she was falling? She let out a long breath as she pulled up in front of the ranch house. If he'd meant it, why wasn't he here? Mistake, she told herself with forced calm. It was always a mistake to depend too much. People pulled back or just went away. But if she could only see him again…

"Going to just sit there in that Jeep all morning?"

With a jerk, Jillian turned to watch Paul Murdock take a few slow, measured steps out onto the porch. She got out of the Jeep, wondering which of the excuses she'd made up before she'd set out would work the best.

"Sit," Murdock ordered before she could come to a decision. "Karen's fixing up a pitcher of tea."

"Thank you." Feeling awkward, she sat on the edge of the porch swing and searched for something to say.

"He hasn't come down from the camp yet," Murdock told her bluntly as he lowered himself into a rocker. "Don't frazzle your brain, girl," he ordered with an impatient brush of his hand. "I may be old, but I can see what's going on under my nose. What'd the two of you spat about?"

"Paul." Karen carried a tray laden with glasses and an iced pitcher. "Jillian's entitled to her privacy."

"Privacy!" he snorted while Karen arranged the tray on a table. "She's dangling after my son."

"Dangling!" Jillian was on her feet in a flash. "I don't dangle after anything or anyone. If I want something, I get it."

He laughed, rocking back and forth and wheezing with the effort as she glared down at him. "I like you, girl, damn if I don't. Got a fetching face, doesn't she, Karen?"

"Lovely." With a smile, Karen offered Jillian a glass of tea.

"Thank you." Stiffly she took her seat again. "I just stopped by to let Aaron know that the mare's doing well. The vet was by yesterday to check her out."

"That the best you could do?" Murdock demanded.

"Paul." Karen sat on the arm of the rocker and laid a hand on his arm.

"If I want manure, all I have to do is walk my own pasture," he grumbled, then pointed his cane at Jillian. "You going to tell me you don't want my boy?"

"Mr. Murdock," Jillian began with icy dignity, "Aaron and I have a business arrangement."

"When a man's dying he doesn't like to waste time," Murdock said with a scowl. "Now, you want to look me in the eye and tell me straight you've got no feelings for that son of mine, fine. We'll talk about the weather a bit."

Jillian opened her mouth, then closed it again with a helpless shake of her head. "When's he coming back?" she whispered. "It's been three weeks."

"He'll come back when he stops being as thick-headed as you are," Murdock told her curtly.

"I don't know what to do." After the words had tumbled out, she sat in amazement. She'd never in her life said that out loud to anyone.

"What do you want?" Karen asked her.

Jillian looked over and studied them—the old man and his beautiful wife. Karen's hand was over his on top of the cane. Their shoulders brushed. A few scattered times in her life she'd seen that kind of perfect intimacy that came from deep abiding love. It was easy to recognize, enviable. And a little scary. It came as a shock to discover she wanted that for herself. One man, one lifetime. But if that was ultimately what love equaled for her, she understood it had to be a shared dream.

"I'm still finding out," she murmured.

"That Jeep." Murdock nodded toward it. "You wouldn't have any trouble getting up to the line camp in a four-wheel drive."

Jillian smiled and set her glass aside. "I can't do it that way. It wouldn't work for me if I didn't meet him on equal terms."

"Stubborn young fool," Murdock grumbled.

"Yes." Jillian smiled again as she rose. "If he wants me, that's what he's going to get." The sound of an engine had her glancing over. When she recognized Gil's truck, she frowned and started down the steps.

"Ma'am." He tipped his hat to Karen but didn't even open the door of the truck. "Mr. Murdock. Got a problem," he said briefly, shifting his eyes to Jillian.

"What is it?"

"Sheriff called. Seems your yearling's been identified on a spread 'bout hundred and fifty miles south of here. Wants you to go down and take a look for yourself."

Jillian gripped the bottom of the open window. "Where?"

"Old Larraby spread. I'll take you now."

"Leave your Jeep here," Murdock told her, getting to his feet. "One of my men'll take it back to your place."

"Thanks." Quickly she dashed around to the other side of the truck. "Let's go," she ordered the moment the door shut beside her. "How, Gil?" she demanded as they drove out of the ranch yard. "Who identified him?"

Gil spit out the window and felt rather pleased with himself. "Aaron Murdock."

"Aaron—"

Gil was a bit more pleased when Jillian's mouth fell open. "Yep." When he came to the fork in the road, he headed south at a steady, mile-eating clip.

"But how? Aaron's been up at his line camp for weeks, and—"

"Maybe you'd like to settle down so I can tell you, or maybe you wouldn't."

Seething with impatience, Jillian subsided. "Tell me."

"Seems one of the Murdock men had a hand in the rustling, fellow named Jennsen. Well, he wasn't too happy with his cut and gambled away most of it anyhow. Decided if they could slice off five hundred and get away with it, he'd take one more for himself."

"Baby," Jillian muttered and crossed her arms over her chest.

"Yep. Had himself a tiger by the tail there. Knew the makings of a prize bull when he saw it and took it over to Larraby. Used to work there before Larraby fell on hard times. Anyhow, he started to get nervous once the man who headed up the rustling got wind of who took the little bull, figured he better get it off his hands. Last night he tried to sell him to Aaron Murdock."

"I see." That was one more she owed him, Jillian thought with a scowl. It was hard to meet a man toe to toe when you were piling up debts. "If it is Baby, and this Jennsen was involved, we'll get the rest of them."

"We'll see if it's Baby," Gil said, then eased a cautious look at her. "The sheriff's already rounding up the rest of them. Picked up Joe Carlson a couple hours ago."

"Joe?" Stunned, she turned completely around in her seat to stare at Gil. "Joe Carlson?"

"Seems he bought himself a little place over in Wyoming. From the sound of it, he's already got a couple hundred head of your cattle grazing there."

"Joe." Shifting, Jillian stared straight ahead. So much for trust, she thought. So much for her expert reading of character. Clay hadn't wanted to hire him—she'd insisted. One of her first major independent decisions on Utopia had been her first major mistake.

"Guess he fooled me, too," Gil muttered after a moment. "Knew his cattle front and back." He spit again and set his teeth. "Shoulda known better than to trust a man with soft hands and a clean hat."

"I hired him," Jillian muttered.

"I worked with him," Gil tossed back. "Side by side. And if you don't think that sticks in my craw, then you ain't too smart. Bamboozled me," he grumbled. *"Me!"*

It was his insulted pride that made her laugh. Jillian propped her feet up on the dash. What was done was over, she told herself. She was going to get a good chunk of her cattle back and see justice done. And at roundup time her books would shift back into the black. Maybe they'd have that new Jeep after all. "Did you get the full story from the sheriff?"

"Aaron Murdock," Gil told her. "He came by right before I set out after you."

"He came by the ranch?" she asked with a casualness that wouldn't have fooled anyone.

"Stopped by so I'd have the details."

"Did he—ah—say anything else?"

"Just that he had a lot of things to see to. Busy man."

"Oh." Jillian turned her head and stared out the window. Gil took a chance and grinned hugely.

She waited until it was nearly dark. It was impossible to bank down the hope that he'd come by or call, if only to see that everything had gone well. She worked out a dozen opening speeches and revised them. She paced. When she knew that she'd scream if she spent another minute within four walls, Jillian went out to the stables and saddled her mare.

"Men," she grumbled as she pulled the cinch. "If this is all part of the game, I'm not interested."

Ready for a run, Delilah sniffed the air the moment Jillian led her outside. When Jillian swung into the saddle, the mare danced and strained against the bit. Within moments they'd left the lights of the ranch yard behind.

The ride would clear her head, she told herself. Anyone would be a bit crazed after a day like this one. Getting Baby back had eased the sting of betrayal she'd felt after learning Joe Carlson had stolen from her. Methodically stolen, she thought, while offering advice and sympathy. He'd certainly been clever, she mused, subtly, systematically turning her attention toward the Murdocks while he was slipping her own cattle through her own fences. Until she found a new herdsman, she'd have to add his duties to her own.

It would do her good, she decided, keep her mind off things. Aaron. If he'd wanted to see her, he'd known where to find her. Apparently, she'd done them both a favor by pushing him away weeks before. If she hadn't, they'd have found themselves in a very painful situation. As it was, they were each just going their own way— exactly as she'd known they would from the beginning. Perhaps she'd had a few moments of weakness, like the one that morning on the Double M, but they wouldn't last. In the next few weeks she'd be too busy to worry about Aaron Murdock and some foolish dreams.

Jillan told herself she hadn't deliberately ridden to the pond, but had simply let Delilah go her own way. In any case, it was still a spot she'd choose for solitude, no matter what memories lingered there.

The moon was full and white, the brush silvered with it. She told herself she wasn't unhappy, just tired after a long day of traveling, dealing with the sheriff, answering questions. She couldn't be unhappy when she finally had what was hers back. When the weariness passed, she'd celebrate. She could have wept, and hated herself.

When she saw the moon reflected on the water, she slowed Delilah to an easy lope. There wasn't a sound but the steady hoofbeats of her own mount. She heard the stallion even as her mare scented him. With her own heart pounding, Jillian controlled the now skittish Delilah and brought her to a halt. Aaron stepped out of the shadow of a cottonwood and said nothing at all.

He'd known she'd come—sooner or later. He could've gone to her, or waited for her to come to him. Somehow he'd known they had to meet here on land that belonged to them both.

It was better to face it all now and be done with it, Jillian told herself, then found her hands were wet with nerves as she dismounted. Nothing could've stiffened her spine more effectively. In thrumming silence she tethered her mare. When she turned, she found Aaron had moved behind her, as silently as the wildcat she'd once compared him to. She stood very straight, kept her tone very impassive.

"So, you came back."

His eyes were lazy and amused as he scanned her face. "Did you think I wouldn't?"

Her chin came up as he'd known it would. "I didn't think about it at all."

"No?" He smiled then—it should have warned her. "Did you think about this?" He dragged her to him, one hand at her waist, one at the back of her head, and devoured the mouth he'd starved for. He expected her to struggle—perhaps he would've relished it just then—but she met the demands of his mouth with the strength and verve he remembered.

When he tore his mouth from hers, she clung, burying her face in his shoulder. He still wanted her—the thought pounded inside her head. She hadn't lost him, not yet. "Hold me," she murmured. "Please, just for a minute."

How could she do this to him? Aaron wondered. How could she shift his mood from crazed to tender in the space of seconds? Maybe he'd never figure out quite how to handle her, but he didn't intend to stop learning.

When she felt her nerves come back, she drew away. "I want to thank you for what you did. The sheriff told me that you got the evidence from Jennsen, and—"

"I don't want to talk about the cattle, Jillian."

"No." Linking her hands together, she turned away. No, it was time they put that aside and dealt with what was really important. What was vital. "I've thought about what happened—about what you said the last time we saw each other." Where were all those speeches she'd planned? They'd all been so calm, so lucid. She twisted her fingers until they hurt, then separated them. "Aaron, I meant it when I said that I don't expect to be told those things. Some women do."

"I wasn't saying them to some women."

"It's so easy to say," she told him in a vibrating whisper. "So easy."

"Not for me."

She turned slowly, warily, as if she expected him to make a move she wasn't prepared for. He looked so calm, she thought. And yet the way the moonlight hit his eyes… "It's hard," she murmured.

"What is?"

"Loving you."

He could have gone to her then, right then, and pulled her to him until there was no more talk, no more thought. But her chin was up and her eyes were swimming. "Maybe it's supposed to be. I'm not offering you an easy road."

"No one's ever loved me back the way I wanted." Swallowing, she stepped away. "No one but Clay, and he never told me. He never had to."

"I'm not Clay, or your father. And there's no one who's ever going to love you the way I do." He took a step toward her, and though she didn't back up, he thought he could see every muscle brace. "What are you afraid of?"

"I'm not afraid!"

He came closer. "Like hell."

"That you'll stop." It wrenched out of her as she gripped her hands behind her back. Once started, the words rushed out quickly and ran together. "That you'll decide you never really loved me anyway. And I'll have let myself want and start depending and needing you. I've spent most of my life working on not depending on anyone, not for anything."

"I'm not anyone," he said quietly.

Her breath came shuddering out. "Since you've been gone I haven't cared about anything except you coming back."

He ran his hands up her arms. "Now that I am?"

"I couldn't bear it if you didn't stay. And though I think I could stand the hurt, I just can't stand being afraid." She put her hands to his chest when he started to draw her to him.

"Jillian, do you think you can tell me things I've been waiting to hear and have me keep my hands off you? Don't you know there's risk on both sides? Dependence on both sides?"

"Maybe." She made herself breathe evenly until she got it all out. "But people aren't always looking for the same things."

"Such as?"

This time she moistened her lips. "Are you going to marry me?" The surprise in his eyes made her muscles stiffen again.

"You asking?"

She dragged herself out of his hold, cursing herself for being a fool and him for laughing at her. "Go to hell," she told him as she started for her horse.

He caught her around the waist, lifting her off the

ground as she kicked out. "Damn, you've got a short fuse," he muttered and ended by pinning her to the ground. "I have a feeling I'm going to spend the best part of my life wrestling with you." Showing an amazing amount of patience, he waited until she'd run out of curses and had subsided, panting. "I'd planned to put the question to you a bit differently," he began. "As in, will you. But as I see it, that's a waste of time." As she stared up at him, he smiled. "God, you're beautiful. Don't argue," he warned as she opened her mouth. "I'm going to tell you that whenever I please so you might as well start swallowing it now."

"You were laughing at me," she began, but he cut her off.

"At both of us." Lowering his head, he kissed her, gently at first, then with building passion. "Now..." Cautiously he let her wrists go until he was certain she wasn't going to take a swing at him. "I'll give you a week to get things organized at your ranch."

"A week—"

"Shut up," he suggested. "A week, then we're both taking the next week off to get married."

Jillian lay very still and soaked it in. It was pure joy. "It doesn't take a week to get married."

"The way I do it does. When we get back—"

"Get back from where?"

"From any place where we can be alone," he told her. "We're going to start making some plans."

She reached for his cheek. "So far I like them. Aaron, say it again, while I'm looking at you."

"I love you, Jillian. A good bit of the time I like you, as well, though I can't say I mind fighting with you."

"I guess you really mean it." She closed her eyes a moment. When she opened them again, they were laughing. "It's hard to take a Murdock at his word, but I'm going to gamble."

"What about a Baron?"

"A Baron's word's gold," she said, angling her chin. "I love you, Aaron. I'm going to make you a frustrating wife and a hell of a partner." She grinned as his lips pressed against hers. "What about those plans?"

"You've got a ranch, I've got a ranch," he pointed out as he kissed her palm. "I don't much care whether we run them separately or together, but there's a matter of living. Your house, my house—that's not going to work for either of us. So we'll build our house, and that's where we're going to raise our children."

Our. She decided it was the most exciting word in the English language. She was going to use it a dozen times every day for the rest of her life. "Where?"

He glanced over her head, skimming the pool, the solitude. "Right on the damn boundary line."

With a laugh, Jillian circled his neck. "What boundary line?"

* * * * *

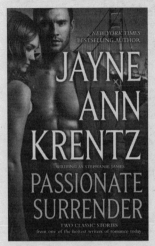

REQUEST YOUR FREE BOOKS!

2 FREE NOVELS
FROM THE ROMANCE COLLECTION
PLUS 2 FREE GIFTS!

YES! Please send me 2 FREE novels from the Romance Collection and my 2 FREE gifts (gifts are worth about $10). After receiving them, if I don't wish to receive any more books, I can return the shipping statement marked "cancel." If I don't cancel, I will receive 4 brand-new novels every month and be billed just $6.24 per book in the U.S. or $6.74 per book in Canada. That's a savings of at least 22% off the cover price. It's quite a bargain! Shipping and handling is just 50¢ per book in the U.S. and 75¢ per book in Canada.* I understand that accepting the 2 free books and gifts places me under no obligation to buy anything. I can always return a shipment and cancel at any time. Even if I never buy another book, the two free books and gifts are mine to keep forever.

194/394 MDN F4XY

Name _____ (PLEASE PRINT)

Address _____ Apt. #

City _____ State/Prov. _____ Zip/Postal Code

Signature (if under 18, a parent or guardian must sign)

Mail to the Harlequin® Reader Service:
IN U.S.A.: P.O. Box 1867, Buffalo, NY 14240-1867
IN CANADA: P.O. Box 609, Fort Erie, Ontario L2A 5X3

Want to try two free books from another line?
Call 1-800-873-8635 or visit www.ReaderService.com.

* Terms and prices subject to change without notice. Prices do not include applicable taxes. Sales tax applicable in N.Y. Canadian residents will be charged applicable taxes. Offer not valid in Quebec. This offer is limited to one order per household. Not valid for current subscribers to the Romance Collection or the Romance/Suspense Collection. All orders subject to credit approval. Credit or debit balances in a customer's account(s) may be offset by any other outstanding balance owed by or to the customer. Please allow 4 to 6 weeks for delivery. Offer available while quantities last.

Your Privacy—The Harlequin® Reader Service is committed to protecting your privacy. Our Privacy Policy is available online at www.ReaderService.com or upon request from the Harlequin Reader Service.

We make a portion of our mailing list available to reputable third parties that offer products we believe may interest you. If you prefer that we not exchange your name with third parties, or if you wish to clarify or modify your communication preferences, please visit us at www.ReaderService.com/consumerchoice or write to us at Harlequin Reader Service Preference Service, P.O. Box 9062, Buffalo, NY 14269. Include your complete name and address.

ROM13R

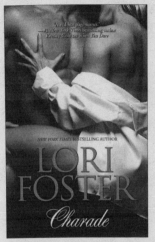

NORA ROBERTS

		U.S.		CAN.
28594	O'HURLEY'S RETURN	___ $7.99 U.S.	___ $9.99	CAN.
28590	SWEET RAINS	___ $7.99 U.S.	___ $9.99	CAN.
28588	NIGHT TALES:			
	NIGHT SHIELD & NIGHT MOVES	___ $7.99 U.S.	___ $9.99	CAN.
28587	NIGHT TALES:			
	NIGHTSHADE & NIGHT SMOKE	___ $7.99 U.S.	___ $9.99	CAN.
28586	NIGHT TALES:			
	NIGHT SHIFT & NIGHT SHADOW	___ $7.99 U.S.	___ $9.99	CAN.
28578	THE LAW OF LOVE	___ $7.99 U.S.	___ $8.99	CAN.
28182	SOMETHING NEW	___ $7.99 U.S.	___ $8.99	CAN.
28181	PLAY IT AGAIN	___ $7.99 U.S.	___ $8.99	CAN.
28180	A CHANGE OF PLANS	___ $7.99 U.S.	___ $8.99	CAN.
28172	WHISPERED PROMISES	___ $7.99 U.S.	___ $8.99	CAN.
28171	FOREVER	___ $7.99 U.S.	___ $9.99	CAN.
28170	REFLECTIONS & DREAMS	___ $7.99 U.S.	___ $8.99	CAN.
28168	CHANGE OF HEART	___ $7.99 U.S.	___ $9.99	CAN.
28167	CHARMED & ENCHANTED	___ $7.99 U.S.	___ $9.99	CAN.
28166	PLAYING FOR KEEPS	___ $7.99 U.S.	___ $8.99	CAN.
28165	CAPTIVATED & ENTRANCED	___ $7.99 U.S.	___ $9.99	CAN.
28162	A DAY AWAY	___ $7.99 U.S.	___ $9.99	CAN.
28161	MYSTERIOUS	___ $7.99 U.S.	___ $9.99	CAN.
28160	THE MacGREGOR GROOMS	___ $7.99 U.S.	___ $9.99	CAN.
28159	THE MacGREGOR BRIDES	___ $7.99 U.S.	___ $9.99	CAN.
28158	ROBERT & CYBIL	___ $7.99 U.S.	___ $9.99	CAN.
28156	DANIEL & IAN	___ $7.99 U.S.	___ $9.99	CAN.
28154	GABRIELLA & ALEXANDER	___ $7.99 U.S.	___ $9.99	CAN.
28150	IRISH HEARTS	___ $7.99 U.S.	___ $9.99	CAN.
28133	THE MacGREGORS: SERENA & CAINE	___ $7.99 U.S.	___ $9.99	CAN.

(limited quantities available)

TOTAL AMOUNT	$	_____
POSTAGE & HANDLING	$	_____
($1.00 FOR 1 BOOK, 50¢ for each additional)		
APPLICABLE TAXES*	$	_____
TOTAL PAYABLE	$	_____

(check or money order—please do not send cash)

To order, complete this form and send it, along with a check or money order for the total above, payable to Harlequin Books, to: **In the U.S.:** 3010 Walden Avenue, P.O. Box 9077, Buffalo, NY 14269-9077; **In Canada:** P.O. Box 636, Fort Erie, Ontario, L2A 5X3.

Name: _____

Address: _____ City: _____

State/Prov.: _____ Zip/Postal Code: _____

Account Number (if applicable): _____

075 CSAS

*New York residents remit applicable sales taxes.
*Canadian residents remit applicable GST and provincial taxes.

Silhouette®

Where love comes alive™

Visit Silhouette Books at www.Harlequin.com

PSNR1014BL